**Here's w
Kathleen Ba**

"Fans of Janet Evanovich will be glad to see that you don't always have to go to the burgh for mirthful murder and mayhem."
- Booklist

"Filled with dumb-blonde jokes, nonstop action and rapid-fire banter, this is a perfect read for chick-lit fans who enjoy a dash of mystery."
- Publishers Weekly

"Fun and lighthearted with an interesting mystery, a light touch of romance and some fascinating characters."
- RT Book Reviews

"Throw in two parts Nancy Drew, one part Lucille Ball, add a dash of Stephanie Plum, shake it all up and you've got a one-of-a-kind amateur sleuth with a penchant for junk food and hot-pink snakeskin cowgirl boots. A word to the wise: if you're prone to laughing out loud when reading funny books, try not to read Calamity Jayne when you're sandwiched between two sleeping passengers on an airplane…sometimes we learn these things the hard way."
- Chick Lit Cafe

"Bacus provides lots of small-town fun with this lovable, fair-haired klutz and lively story, liberally salted with dumb-blonde jokes."
- Booklist *starred review*

BOOKS BY KATHLEEN BACUS

Calamity Jayne Mysteries:

Calamity Jayne

Calamity Jayne and Fowl Play at the Fair

Calamity Jayne and the Haunted Homecoming

Calamity Jayne and the Campus Caper

Calamity Jayne in the Wild, Wild West

Calamity Jayne and the Hijinks on the High Seas

Calamity Jayne and the Trouble with Tandems

Six Geese A 'Slaying (a holiday short story)

Other Works:

Fiancé at Her Fingertips

Trading Spaces

CALAMITY JAYNE AND THE TROUBLE WITH TANDEMS

a Calamity Jayne mystery

Kathleen Bacus

CALAMITY JAYNE AND THE TROUBLE WITH TANDEMS
Copyright © 2014 by Kathleen Cecil Bacus

Published by Gemma Halliday Publishing
All Rights Reserved. Except for use in any review, the reproduction or utilization of this work in whole or in part in any form by any electronic, mechanical, or other means, now known or hereafter invented, including xerography, photocopying and recording, or in any information storage and retrieval system is forbidden without the written permission of the publisher, Gemma Halliday.

This is a work of fiction. Names, characters, places, and incidents are either the product of the author's imagination or are used fictitiously, and any resemblance to actual persons, living or dead, business establishments, or events or locales is entirely coincidental.

CALAMITY JAYNE AND THE TROUBLE WITH TANDEMS

CHAPTER ONE

Two blondes are riding along on a tandem when suddenly the blonde in front slams on the brakes, gets off, and starts letting air out of the tires.

"Hey! What are you doing that for?" the blonde on the back yells.

"My seat's too high, and it's hurting my butt," the first blonde replies. "I want to lower it a bit."

The blonde on the back has had enough. She jumps off, loosens her own seat, and spins it around to face the other direction.

Now it's the first blonde's turn to wonder what's going on.

"What are you doing?" she asks her friend.

"Look," says the blonde rider in the back, "if you're going to do stupid stuff like that, I'm going home!"

* * *

Buyer's remorse.

That's what it was. A case of buyer's remorse. Okay, so I wasn't exactly a *buyer* and the remorse part had nothing to do with the quality of the…er…transaction. In fact, the delivery of the, um, *goods* left no room for complaint. No room at all. On the contrary. The entire experience was one of pure…*satisfaction.*

Which, of course, was the very reason panic set in. With a vengeance.

And me? I did what I do best.

I booked. No. Not as in visiting the local library. I amscrayed. Vamoosed. Took a powder. Boogied. Got the hell outta Dodge.

Okay. So I ran like a little girl. Sue me.

In case you haven't caught on yet, I'm not talking about a consumer retail exchange that falls under the auspices of a consumer fraud agency even though the words "let the buyer beware" and "too good to be true" have a certain prophetic ring to them.

No. I'm talking about *it*: the S word.

You know. The one that rhymes with "vex". Or...*hex*.

Yeah. *That* word.

And *it* was incredible. Moonlight and roses. Shooting stars and fireworks. Bombs bursting in air. In fact, *it* threatened to become as addictive as Cadbury Crème eggs at Easter (Okay, and beyond the wabbit holiday, if you buy extra and freeze them.) And *it* scared the hell-o out of me. Hence, my own slightly modified version of a Julia Roberts flick.

Tressa Jayne Turner. *Runaway cowgirl bride*.

Except—despite hearing wedding bells in my head that almost turned into death *knells, (so* another story) I didn't actually make it anywhere near the altar.

And, of course, I'm no Julia Roberts. Sigh.

I know. I know. I've lost you, right?

What else is new?

"How much longer do you think Stan's gonna pay you to sit there and mope, Miz Rodeo Queen Runner-up?" A hand on the back of my ergonomically-approved office chair spun me around. "You've been OD-ing on angst ever since you got back from the honeymoon cruise. What gives?"

I had to look up, up, up, to meet the way too perceptive scrutiny of Shelby Lynn Sawyer, recent high school graduate and last year's underdog homecoming queen and part-time intern/reporter for my employer, the *Grandville Gazette*. I feel a certain sisterhood with Shelby Lynn. Much like yours truly, Shelby's had a history of nickname nightmares. A carrot-topped Paula Bunyan-type who can stand eye-to-eye with the high school varsity squad's center, Shelby got tagged "Sasquatch," compliments of the mean girl factions at Grandville High. I figure *Calamity Jayne* is tame in comparison.

Last fall Shelby Lynn and I became involved in a very high-profile investigative journalistic coup relating to a reclusive mystery author. Okay, so Shelby actually blackmailed me into including her in the scoop of the century. (I'd use the term "strong-armed" here, but my, er, statuesque associate can get a wee testy when it comes to those kinds of characterizations.)

Our professional collaboration had led to more than a few Abbott and Costello contretemps, a bit of female bonding, and, as my own moniker implies, the odd moments of abject terror and mortal danger. Shelby Lynn recently filled in for me at the *Gazette* while I took a long overdue vacation to see my grandmother tie the knot. If anyone can fill my shoes, it's Shelby Lynn and her size twelve wides. (Oops! Sorry. Couldn't resist!)

Following the Arizona nuptials, the wedding party set sail aboard the cruise ship *Epiphany,* which promised fun in the sun, splendid and bountiful cuisine, and to-die-for sunsets.

What this novice sailor got was a yo-ho-ho and a bottle of V-8 served with restricted portions of low-fat fare, a shipboard mystery, a near burial at sea, and my very own shiver-me-timbers epiphany concerning a certain swashbuckling ranger-type. That ranger—and our eventual *Love Boat,* this-has-been-coming-for-a-long-time, consummation on the final night of the cruise was what had me channeling Debbie Downer at present.

"You haven't said much about the happy honeymoon cruise," Shelby observed.

"More like haunted honeymoon cruise," I muttered. "Minus one sexy Captain Jack Sparrow ghostie. Unfortunately."

"So…exactly what happened?" Shelby Lynn pressed. "Or are you still experiencing selective amnesia?" This, a reference to my shipboard, soap-opera-inspired stint as a fake amnesiac hatched in the haze of post-concussive desperation—a Bermuda-triangle brainchild designed to save me bootie from unknown danger on the high seas.

"Funny," I mumbled, and recited a condensed version of my very own odyssey at sea.

"Let me get this straight," Shelby said, holding up a hand to tick off each item on fingers Shaquille O'Neal would die for. "You were on the cruise. Rick Townsend, the guy you've had this loath/lust/love relationship with since grade school was on this cruise. And Manny DeMarco, your buff, brawny, bad-boy bogus beau ends up on the same cruise."

"You're forgetting Manny's marriage-obsessed Aunt Mo with a history of cardiac episodes and the single-minded determination of a Navy SEAL when it comes to her mission in life."

"Mission?" Shelby raised an eyebrow.

"Mo's Matrimony Mission," I elaborated. "She's determined to get her beloved nephew wedded and with a Manny Jr. on the way."

"Holy *S.S. Minnow*!" Shelby exclaimed. "The *Titanic's* got nothing on you."

I winced. "'Twas indeed an ill wind that clipped me sails and left me foundered on the jagged rocks of destiny aboard ye *S.S. Epiphany*. Arrgh!"

It was Shelby's turn to wince.

"Ugh. I heard all about your penchant for 'pirate prattle,' as Joe Townsend put it. He said that made him more bilious than the combined effects of the lo-cal cruise cuisine and the rocking of the ship."

"Alas, one of the few perks the cruise afforded," I lamented, adding a woe-is-me sigh.

"So where *do* you stand? With the men in your life, that is?"

I grimaced. *Limboland*. Where all commitment phobes love to hang out and procrastinate. That's where.

I'd taken a Bigfoot-sized (oops!) leap of faith when, on the final night of the cruise, I'd signed on as Ranger Rick Townsend's cabin mate. And that *enlistment* was…unforgettable. Wine and roses. Soft candlelight and breath-stealing caresses. Wooing words and seductive kisses.

My own white flag moment*: surrender.*

The next morning reality hit me like an anchor upside the head, and I'd found myself hip-wader deep in "where do we go from here?" doubts and misgivings.

You know the ones, ladies.

Like, *"Oh, God. Now he'll see my body in the unforgiving light of day and turn away in disgust."*

Or the oldie, yet often apt, *"Smart moove, Bessie, ol' gal. You go ahead. You give that milk away for free."*

And, my personal favorite, *"Is this love or lust?"*

"I'm no longer a faux fiancé," I finally mumbled a response.

"Oh. I see. Should I offer congratulations or condolences?"

"Manny and I have an…understanding." I bit my lip, remembering the look on Manny's face when I delivered that news.

"Is that why you're down in the dumps? You're no longer Manny DeMarco's on-again-off-again bride-to-be?" Shelby asked.

"I was never really engaged to Manny, you know, Shelby. It was a ruse. A scam. My kind and caring attempt to grant a dying wish to a sweet, sentimental woman."

"Sweet? Sentimental? Mo Dishman?" Shelby scratched her head. "Didn't you shinny off to Arizona when sweet, sentimental Mo was hot on your trail to finalize wedding plans?"

My cheeks stung with the warmth of a blush.

"You make it sound like a posse was on my tail," I said, annoyed at her characterization of purely coincidental plans to leave the state.

"Well, Manny's Aunt Mo sure tracked you down, didn't she? All the way to the Caribbean. That's one highly-motivated individual."

Motivated and…scary.

"Face it, Calamity Jayne," Shelby continued. "You're destined to be an outlaw. Or did you let someone else lasso you on your little getaway?"

My face grew hotter.

"Where did you hear that?"

"A skinny little guy with bird legs so white they could blind you."

Great. Grandville's resident *Ye Olde Town Crier*, Joe Townsend was already out trumpeting all the news that wasn't news and sure as heck wasn't anyone's business.

I shook my head.

"Senility. Such a sad thing," I said.

"Then you didn't play 'find the bootie' with Rick Townsend?"

"I'm more interested in whether she can play 'find the story,'" editor-in-chief and publisher of the *Grandville Gazette*, Stan Rodgers, barked from behind me.

I whirled around in my chair, surprised to find myself in the rather unique position of being grateful for Stan's growling interruption.

"Hey. Show a little respect," I said. "Remember, I'm your ace cub reporter. Newshound extraordinaire. The sultan of scoops. A—"

"A pain in the ass," Stan interjected. Then, for some reason, he looked like he wanted to laugh.

I bristled. "Nice. What other journalist has brought you the plethora of sensational stories I have in the short time I've been employed here?" I asked. "So, forgive me if I'm feeling a tad bit unappreciated here."

I did have an impressive résumé. From a murder no one even believed happened, to a carnival caper turned deadly and a campus crime spree where failure was not an option, I'd delivered.

Stan stuck the cigar his wife had forbidden him to light in the side of his mouth. "Unappreciated! Are you forgetting the top of the line office furniture and the high tech upgrades you're enjoying as a result of my generosity?"

"Top of the line?" I snorted. "You got this desk and chair at a hotel auction. And correct me if I'm wrong, but the laptop, while admittedly a step up from the dino desktop I had before, was your son's hand-me-down. By the way, I won't tell a soul about the, uh, er, questionable websites little Stan Jr. visited," I said with an exaggerated wink. "That's strictly between us."

For a second, the Stan Rodgers I knew returned. His brows lowered to form a dark, furry vee above his nose. He peered at me over the top of his half-glasses and looked like he was fixing to bite clean through his cee-gar.

I waited for the gasket to blow.

Stan's customary, "Tell me, Turner. How much does it cost to keep a horse again?" broke-girl reminder.

Curiously—very curiously—Stan's thunder brows cleared, and the side of his mouth—the side without the cigar hanging out—lifted in just the suggestion of a smile.

I suddenly felt very uneasy.

"Oh, my. I see I've interrupted a discussion of, shall we say, a personal nature," Stan said, removing his glasses and sticking them in his shirt pocket. "I apologize. Please. Shelby Lynn. Feel free to continue your minute dissection of our newshound's rather complicated love life. And once you ladies have probed and analyzed it to your mutual satisfaction, would it be possible, Ms. Turner, for you to spare me a brief moment to discuss a special assignment I have in mind for you?" He removed his cigar and performed an abbreviated bow. "Ladies."

I watched him walk away.

"Did you see that?" I asked Shelby.

"See what?"

"That...that spring in his step."

"Spring? In Stan's step? Are you nuts?"

"Something's wrong," I said, my gaze narrowing in on a spot in the middle of my boss's retreating back. "I sense a disturbance in the force."

Shelby frowned. "Huh?"

"Stan's up to something," I translated.

"How can you tell?" she asked.

"He almost smiled," I said.

He'd just taken a seat behind his massive desk when I rapped on his door and stuck my head inside his office.

"So...this special assignment—"

"—has Tressa Jayne Turner's name written all over it," Stan finished. "Come in! Sit down! Although, come to think of it, you'll be doing a healthy—or maybe unhealthy—amount of sitting in the not-too-distant future, so maybe you'd better stand."

I leaned over Stan, the palms of my hands flat on the top of his desk.

"What does that mean?" I asked, my uneasiness going up, up, up.

"A little joke," Stan said.

Joke? Stan No-Nonsense Rodgers? The guy who watched *1000 Ways to Die* for comedic entertainment? My stomach began to ache. Visions of Bridget Jones's Brazilian-sized butt sliding down a fireman's pole played in my head.

"You've heard of the renowned annual bike ride across Iowa. Right?"

I frowned. "You mean TribRide? Sure. I've heard of it."

Ten thousand obsessed bikers pedaling their way across the state in the summer heat and humidity? Heard of it? For the last five years I'd been nagged by Ranger Rick Townsend—serious bike enthusiast and eager participant in the hot, grueling trek from border to border—to sign on to the great event. And each year I respectfully—but emphatically—declined.

You come up with a horse ride across Iowa? Dude. I'm so there.

"I'd like you to cover the bike ride."

I felt the tension leave my body.

Sweet! Talk about your piece-o-cake assignments. This year the annual bike ride made its way through the central part of the state. Grandville and its closest neighboring hamlet, New Holland, would be the riders' mid-trek overnight hosts. The streets and campgrounds would be full of bikers, beer, and bands. Plus a smorgasbord of food to tempt all palates.

I nodded. "Cover TribRide? Sure. Absolutely. You can count on me. I'll hang with the bikers. Wrangle some interesting human interest stuff. Snap some photos. It'll be fun."

"Good," Stan stuck his unlit cigar in an unused ashtray. "That's exactly what I had in mind. Real in-depth stuff. We've all heard stories about what goes on during that week. The food. The booze—"

"The naked slide," I inserted.

Stan winced. "We want the whole TribRide experience. From start to finish," Stan said.

I blinked. Start to...gulp...finish?

"You want me to cover the entire bike ride?" I asked.

Stan nodded. "We felt it would be entertaining for our readers to have an opportunity to get up close and personal with the annual event from an insider's perspective. Along with the traditional print coverage, we'll have an ongoing social media presence. Facebook. Tweets. You get the picture."

I'm pretty sure my eyeballs got half-dollar huge here. I'd gotten short shrift on my cruise perks and amenities. The idea of a weeklong *part-ee* with downtime spent poolside at a nice hotel with cable and complimentary breakfast was most appealing. I flashed a big grin in Stan's direction.

"I think that's a fabulous idea, Boss," I said. "A real slice of Americana and all that. Of course, I'll need a phone upgrade. With a 4G network, of course. Nothing fancy."

"You never fail to surprise me, Turner," Stan said, easing back in his gi-normous desk chair. "Frankly, I expected to have to spend a ridiculous amount of time bickering, threatening, and arm-twisting to get you to agree."

I frowned. "Seriously? Why is that? I'm a team player. I'm more than willing to inconvenience myself by hitting the road for a week or so. No sweat."

Stan's shoulders went up and down in quick succession. He put a hand up to cover his mouth to cover a cough.

"Good. It's settled then."

"So, I get the phone?"

Again that ghost of a smile. "Of course. Your sponsors will provide everything you need. Phone. Tablet. Backpack. Tent...spandex."

It took me a while to process Stan's TribRide list.

"Tent?" My voice raised several octaves. "Spandex?" I squeaked.

"Would you rather run the risk of a wedgie?"

"Wedgie?" I seemed to have lost the ability to string a series of words together. Not, I might add, a run-of-the-mill occurrence with me.

"That's right. It would be pure hell if you had to deal with a wedgie going all that distance in all that heat," Stan said.

"I think I'm missing something here," I admitted.

"How do you mean, Turner?"

"I thought I was going to cover TribRide."

"You are."

"But...a tent? And," I swallowed. Way loud. "Spandex?"

"Well, you have to have some place to sleep. And spandex is a biker's best friend. Or so I hear."

I dropped into a chair.

"Biker?" I managed.

"Don't worry, Turner. I didn't really expect you to pedal all the way across the state on your own, you know."

I sat back in my chair, blessed relief washing over me.

"Thank God," I sighed.

"No. Thank the *New Holland News*," Stan said. I sat back up, resisting a sudden urge to pull my trousers away from my butt crack.

"Um…what?"

"This is a collaborative effort," Stan said. "We're partnering with the *New Holland News*."

I blinked. "Hold on. You're calling a truce with our closest competitor—a newspaper you refer to as 'that red-headed stepchild rag'?"

Stan shrugged. "Let's call it a temporary cessation of hostilities."

"So what does our rival to the east have to do with our covering TribRide?" I asked, instinctively knowing I wasn't going to like Stan's answer.

"You'll be covering the bike ride as a participant joined by a reporter from the *New Holland News*," Stan announced.

I jumped to my feet.

"Wait a minute! What!"

"You'll be traveling in tandem, Turner," Stan said, sitting back in his chair.

"Tandem?" I managed.

He nodded. "I told you I wouldn't expect you to pedal all that way on your own. No, no. You'll be tooling across Iowa on a bicycle built for two with the fellow reporter you fondly refer to as 'the missing link.'"

I gasped and took a step backwards.

The missing link! Try unscrupulous hack and the bane of my journalistic existence: Drew 'The Shrew' Van Vleet! The answer to the *Family Feud* question, "name something you wouldn't want to find in your basement when investigating a terrible smell."

I dropped back into my chair, my sphincters already beginning to pucker.

Holy spokes and spandex! Talk about trouble in tandem.

Make that trouble in Tandemonium…and where, I was pretty sure, the ultimate wedgie was bound to be the least of my worries.

CHAPTER TWO

"Now look here, Stan. I'm a serious journalist!" I found myself parroting a certain buxom Brit's similar assertion and winced.

"And TribRide is serious news for a lot of readers, Turner," Stan said.

I felt the noose tightening. Or rather the spandex encroaching.

"I'm not sure I'm the best person for this assignment, Boss," I said. "Maybe Shelby—"

"Shelby Lynn on a tandem? Get real, Turner. We'd spend a fortune in tire tubes. Besides, Shelby's gonna have her hands full here," Stan said.

"I'm not sure—"

"We never did discuss that raise of yours, did we, Turner?" Stan leaned back in his chair and propped his feet up on his desk. I shook my head. The sly old dog knew the location of my Achilles' heel: The State Savings Bank at First and Main. Yep. *My* bank.

"Raise? You're giving me a raise?"

"I like to reward the employees who give that little extra effort to pursue the news—wherever it takes them."

"And *on* whatever takes them, right, Stan?" I added. "How interesting that your uncharacteristic generosity happens to coincide with an assignment only Lance Armstrong could love."

"Sorry, Turner," Stan replied, looking anything but. "Lance can't make the bike ride this year. Still, that doesn't mean the event will be without a celebrity."

"Celebrity?"

"That's right."

"Let me guess," I said, thinking Stan's idea of a celeb was probably not on the 'A List' of pop culture. "The cast of *Swamp*

People are joining TribRide. Oo! Look at the goose bumps on my arms. I'm all a quiver."

"Well, I wouldn't expect your heart to go all pitter-patter over a dame, Turner," Stan remarked.

"Dame? The celeb is a woman?"

"Disappointed? Considering your 'Bermuda Love Triangle' I'd have thought you had more male attention than you can handle at the moment."

"Yeah. I'm a regular siren, Stan," I said. "So who's this big name whose yellow brick bike path leads to the Heartland?" I asked.

"Keelie Keller," Stan announced with a big grin.

I blinked. "Keelie Keller? Reality TV princess slash playgirl Keelie Keller?"

"Is there any other?"

"You follow Keelie Keller?" I asked—dumfounded that Stan even knew who the flighty, flirty diva wannabe was.

"You forget. I've got two teenagers at home, Turner."

I frowned.

"Why on earth would Keelie Keller want to spend a week in the middle of summer tooling across Iowa? What's in it for her?" *Besides a high profile wedgie, that is.*

"What every celebrity wants, Turner. Publicity," Stan said. "I guess she's bringing her cast mates with her."

"You mean Tiara Fordham and Langley Carlisle the Third?" Tiara was Keelie's BFF. She'd played second banana to Keelie's wannabe teen sleuth on a popular cable series. Langley? Keelie's somewhat androgynous go-to-guy pal whose Daddy was a highly sought-after motion picture director.

Stan made a face. "What the hell happened to nice, plain names like Mary, Wilma, Sue, Betty, and Dorothy?"

It was my turn to make a face. "Ugh. Sounds like the Flintstones Meet the Wiz. And who would watch a reality TV show that headlined with a Wilma?"

"Freds," Stan said, freaking me out for the second time with what could pass for levity.

"This is so not gonna work, Stan. You know my history with Drew Van Vleet. That episode last fall with Elizabeth Courtney Howard—"

"So Van Vleet's a slimeball." Stan shot me a knowing look. "You aren't still holding a grudge because of that senior center Halloween dance photo spread, are you—'Witchiepoo'?" Stan asked. "The tango wasn't it? With Joe Townsend? Not exactly Pulitzer Prize stuff, but entertaining nonetheless."

"I'm glad my humiliation provided you with so much amusement," I huffed.

"Ah, give it a rest, would you, Turner? Besides, it's a done deal. No one is asking you to be best biker buds with Van Vleet. You don't even have to talk to him if you don't want to. Hell. You probably won't have breath to spare for chit-chat anyway."

"I want it on the record that I think this is a very bad idea," I said.

"Duly noted," Stan said. "Anything else?"

"The guy can't be trusted," I warned Stan. "I don't plan to take my eyes off Drew the Shrew for a minute."

Stan chuckled. He grabbed a handful of chocolate candies from his Hawkeyes dish. "Looks like you'll be bringing up the rear on that bicycle built for two then," he observed and tossed the color-coated candy into his mouth. "Happy bike trails, Ace Cub Reporter!"

Oh, the pain.

* * *

"You? And Drew Van Vleet? On a bicycle built for two?"

My Aunt Reggie and my sister, Taylor, stood behind the counter of Uncle Frank and Aunt Reggie's Dairee Freeze and stared down at me as I drowned my sorrows in a double fudge cookie dough and caramel ice cream concoction.

"It sounds even worse when you say it," I said, spooning a heaping, sure-to-cause-brain-freeze helping of the cold confection into my mouth.

Taylor's lips tightened into a worried slash. "And you agreed?"

I helped myself to another spoonful of Mr. Freezee.

"What else can I do? Stan the Sadistic Puppet Man is dangling the carrot of a raise over my head. 'I got no strings to hold me down.'" I warbled, holding my arms up to perform a spastic Pinocchio move that only increased the anxiety levels radiating from clearly concerned relatives.

"But you? On a bicycle? In summer's heat? Hundreds of miles. Up and down hills. Steam rising from the pavement. Pedaling. Pedaling. How long has it been since you've ridden a bicycle?"

I shrugged. I'd spent most of my life on the back of a majestic, four-legged animal, not a two-wheeled metal contraption.

"It'll come back to me," I said. "You know what they say. 'It's as easy as riding a bicycle.'"

"*They* don't know *you*," Taylor pointed out.

"At least you'll have Taylor here and Frankie to look out for you," Aunt Reggie said.

I frowned.

"What are you talking about?" I asked.

"Your Uncle Frank couldn't resist the lure of an uninterrupted stream of hot, hungry bike riders looking for cold comfort so Frank Jr. and Taylor are taking the mobile ice cream trailer on TribRide," Aunt Reggie explained.

My Uncle Frank is on the, er, frugal side. He substituted generic chocolate sandwich cookies for the real deal in his Mr. Freezees until he got complaints. Okay. So I accidentally outted him. It's not as if cookie connoisseurs can't tell the difference.

"I thought Frankie was taking summer classes," I said. Earlier this year my cousin, Frankie, ("Frankfurter" to those who know and love him) had ambitious plans to enter the state police academy. Unfortunately, Frankie is—how to put this nicely—a bit of a…wimp. A wimp with severe allergy and sinus issues and enough hypochondria to keep the local doc in yearly country club memberships.

When it became clear Frankie couldn't pass the physical strength and agility tests, (so not a pretty sight) he decided it might be cool to become a criminal analyst or one of those CSI techs. To make things even more interesting, Frankie's main squeeze, Dixie 'The Destructor' Daggett, had caught Frankie's crime-fighter bug. And, amazingly, she had whizzed through each phase of the application process with relative ease.

I'm somewhat dubious. Personally, it's hard for me to

picture roll-out-the-barrel Daggett as a lean-mean crime-fighter. Okay. The 'mean' part, maybe.

Dixie and I have...issues. She thinks I'm a flake and I think she's scary. But since she's fated to become a member of the family, I'm trying to adopt an attitude of...er...inevitability if not acceptance. (I can see the wedding video now: *The Bride of Frankie starring Frankie the Frankfurter as the mad-in-love groom and featuring Dixie "Cankles" Daggett as his gruesome mate.*)

Talk about your monster matinees. You bring the beverages. I'll supply the popcorn and candy.

"Frankie is taking mostly online courses this term," Aunt Reggie told me.

I looked at Taylor and raised a questioning eyebrow. My sister's driving abilities didn't extend to maneuvering a large vehicle pulling a trailer—a skill I'd practiced and perfected over years of hauling horse trailers hither and thither.

"Maybe we could work out a deal," I proposed. "I could drive the pickup and you could—"

"Dixie's driving the rig." Taylor cut me off like the hook at a vintage comedy club.

Nice.

"Dixie of Dixie's Demolition Derby, Inc.? Good luck with that."

"Good luck with your itty-bitty bicycle seat," Taylor volleyed.

I blinked.

Taylor had changed since her abrupt decision to take a break from books and higher education. She's become more vocal. More testy. More like...me.

"I understand that nice Trooper Dawkins who has been so helpful to Frankie and Dixie will also be riding," Aunt Reggie said. I noticed the sudden lifting of her eyebrows at roughly the same time a sudden flush reddened Taylor's cheeks.

"P.D. Dawkins is going on TribRide?"

Aunt Reggie nodded. "He'll be on duty. He's riding one of the state patrol bikes."

I'd met Patrick Dawkins, P.D. for short, last August at the Iowa State Fair, and we hit it off right from the start. He likes me just the way I am (wow, what a concept!) And me? I'm a sucker for a good-looking guy in uniform.

P.D.'s fondness for farm life from summers spent on his uncle's farm, his natural affinity for animals, and his patient tolerance for eccentric seniors in their dotage, cemented the connection. At one time it wouldn't have taken much encouragement from me for Trooper Dawkins to pursue a relationship on a more...intimate level.

But old habits die hard. A decade of courting danger with a certain ranger via feuding worthy of the Hatfields and McCoys, interspersed with episodes of lust, angst, and heartburn, had left me dazed and confused about what I wanted and needed in a mate. (Shocker, right?)

"You hear that, Taylor?" I said. "Trooper Dawkins is going on TribRide. Why, it'll be just like old home week!"

I totally deserved the look Taylor gave me—one of those eyes-narrowed-to-tiny-slits numbers I suspect she reserves just for me.

I'd only recently discovered that Taylor had a serious case of the *hots* for the hunky brown shirt, Dawkins. However, rather than horn in on her older sister's supposed territory, Taylor had piously hidden her attachment to the peace officer until she realized my affections were fixed, er, elsewhere.

I suppose I should mention here that Taylor is considered the sensitive, caring sister.

What's that? Oh. You figured that out, huh?

"So, when are you and your biking buddy planning to get together for some pedaling practice?" Taylor asked.

"Pedaling practice?" I wrinkled my nose.

"You do know there's more to riding a tandem bicycle than getting on the bike and pushing the pedals, Tressa," Taylor reminded me. "You have to get a rhythm going, achieve and maintain your balance, get in sync with your partner."

"In sync? Isn't that the name of a has-been boyband?" I said with a snort.

"Would you get serious?" Taylor said. "Every year a biker is injured or even killed on the ride. Inexperience can be deadly."

Wasn't she just little Mary Sunshine?

"And there's the equipment you'll require," *Mary* continued.

Hello. Again with the spandex?

"Doesn't Rick Townsend usually ride?" Aunt Reggie offered. "I bet he'll know exactly what you'll need."

This time it was *my* cheeks that did a burn-baby-burn number.

"I doubt he'll be all that eager to help," I said, tucking into my ice cream again. When you deliberately avoided someone you'd been, well, intimate with, that person probably wouldn't be in the mood to offer you bicycle safety lessons.

Aunt Reggie frowned. "Have you two been going at it again?"

I almost choked on my ice cream.

"Tressa?" Taylor pounded me on the back. "Are you okay?"

"Okay? Of course. I'm fine. Just fine. Tip-top. Dandy. In the pink. Mahvelous."

Babbling for all I was worth.

"You two aren't feuding again, are you?" Aunt Reggie persisted.

"Feuding?" I suddenly realized Aunt Reggie's "going at it" reference was about our history of pistols at twenty paces rather than my recent surrender at sea. "Oh, no. No. We're past all that, Aunt Reggie."

And then some.

"So why wouldn't he be eager to help?" Taylor the human I-smell-something-fishy detector zoned in on my earlier flustered bluster like my gammy does on the dessert table at church potlucks.

Okay. Me, too.

"No reason other than he's probably über busy," I said. "'Tis the boating season, after all."

"Well, I'm sure we'd all rest easier if you found someone with experience to mentor you, Tressa," Aunt Reggie said.

"Maybe Lance Armstrong's looking for a daunting, new challenge," Taylor suggested with a wink at Aunt Reggie.

"Thank you both for your concern, but I've managed to survive bucking horses, killer geese, broken down fair rides, and runaway farm implements and lived to tell the tale. I think I can tame a tandem."

Taylor shrugged. "If you say so."

Aunt Reggie reached out and patted my hand. "Of course, you can, Tressa. Why, you're a regular little engine that could!"

I stared into my Freezee.

I think I can. I think I can.

I think I'm...screwed.

I shoved my ice cream aside, grabbed my keys, and left the Freeze. I needed to clear my head, approach this latest challenge in a responsible manner.

The time had come for a woman-to-woman talk with myself. One of those inner dialogues that can be so helpful and cathartic. Mine went something like this:

Cheerleader Tressa: You can do this!

Debbie Downer Tressa: You *have* to do this.

Cheerleader Tressa: Think of the sense of accomplishment!

Debbie Downer Tressa: Think of the hemorrhoids.

Cheerleader Tressa: Be a team player!

Debbie Downer Tressa: Girl, you've never played well with others.

Cheerleader Tressa: You'll meet new people!

Debbie Downer Tressa: You'll be riding with a guy whose knuckles will drag on the pavement.

Cheerleader Tressa: It's only a week.

Debbie Downer Tressa: It's a whole friggin' week!

Cheerleader Tressa: It's a matter of pride.

Debbie Downer Tressa: It's a matter of your bottom line.

I sighed and Googled the number for the *New Holland News*.

"Hello. Drew Van Vleet. Tressa Turner here. We need to talk."

"Well, well, well, if it isn't Witchiepoo, Grandville's very own tango queen. Hey, Witchie Woman. Dipped any old men lately?"

Wham! Bam!

What was that, you ask? That was the sound of Debbie Downer Tressa bitch-slapping Cheerleader Tressa.

Rah.

CHAPTER THREE

'Stanley, Stanley, here is my answer true.
I can't cycle, or I'll get black and blue.
It won't be a pleasant ending, With all my bones a' mending,
'Cuz I'll get pitched and land in the ditch,
on a bicycle built for two.'

That little ditty—my personalized version—played in my head like an annoying sing-along song from a Broadway musical you can't stop humming. (Last week I couldn't get the 'he had it coming' song from *Chicago* out of my head.)

I'd made arrangements to meet Drew Van Vleet on the courthouse grounds at four P.M. sharp. Neutral territory. Plus, I didn't want to drive the eight miles to New Holland on my dime.

I spotted Van Vleet near the big cedar bandstand that's a magnet for graffiti. I've lost track of how many paint jobs the structure has had over the years.

"You're late," Van Vleet barked.

"Saw-ree. I didn't know I was on a time clock. I'll try to be more punctual in future," I said.

"See that you do, Witchiepoo."

"So, Drew, how are things in New Holland? Break into any residences lately? Violate anyone's privacy?" I inquired, a reference to Drew Van Vleet's abrasive, intrusive, borderline-criminal style of journalism. "That turned out so well for you the last time."

"Whoa. Idle back on the passive aggressive hostility, would you? Surely you can't still have that warty nose out of joint over my little Halloween spread," he said.

Van Vleet's Halloween devilry had unleashed a not-sonostalgic blast from the past—and kick-started a reputation I'd struggled to distance myself from.

Hmm. Warty nose out of joint? Let's just say if I possessed the powers of witchcraft, Mr. Van Vleet would be resting on a lily pad on a quaint little farm pond somewhere going "Ribb-it, Ribb-it" and trying to catch flies with his gi-normous tongue. *Thhwop*!

"Drew. Please. How could I be so petty? You know, especially considering how humiliating it must have been for you to be scooped so thoroughly by the competition, and with me getting all those accolades—" I hesitated for effect. "Well, I figure, under the circumstances and all, it would be mean-spirited of me to, well, hold a grudge."

Van Vleet's jaw tightened. I could almost hear the grinding of his teeth. Sometimes I wonder how many guys I've known had to seek dental reconstruction due to chronic and long-term teeth grinding.

"That's awfully big of you," Van Vleet said.

I shrugged. "What can I say? I'm a sensitive, caring kind of gal—as well as a consummate professional."

"Oh, God, I need to sit down." Van Vleet said, dropping onto a nearby park bench. "I take it you've heard about this fiasco they're sending us on."

"What? You couldn't tell by my cheery disposition?"

"Hey, blondie. I don't like the idea any better than you. But after you screwed me over on that Courtney-Howard story, I've got to go along to get along. So if that means I have to bike across Iowa with a ditzy blonde Barbara WaWa wannabe who stumbles onto stiffs on a semi-regular basis, I say, bring it on."

"Bring it on?" I made a sourpuss face. *Bring it on*? Drew Van Vleet made it sound like he was about to embark on some super-sensitive, ultra-perilous undertaking. "Uh, dude, we're not parachuting into a secret compound in Pakistan in the middle of the night or participating in a high-risk, overseas mission imbedded with a deployed military unit. It's a bike ride across Iowa. Hardly what you could classify as hazardous duty."

"That remains to be seen…Calamity," he said with one of those smirks you itch to obliterate with a well-placed jab. Or two. "You've got a history that would make a mercenary think twice about signing on."

I crossed my arms. "Why, Drew. It sounds like you have reservations. Maybe you should reconsider taking this assignment."

Van Vleet shook his head. "No way, Toots. I've got to redeem myself with my employer. Thanks to you, I have the credibility of..." He paused for a second. "Well...you!" He finished with a what-can-I-say lift of shoulders.

His insult landed a glancing blow to my ego. Fortunately for Van Vleet, my recent string of journalistic coups had made me less sensitive on the subject of past job performances.

"At least your boss was scoop-savvy enough to organize your little ride along with me. It seems the fact that I have a nose for news hasn't gone unnoticed by the publisher of the *New Holland News*," I said.

Van Vleet made a noisy—and insultingly prolonged—raspberry sound.

"Nose for news? Right. I hate to burst your self-delusional bubble, but it wasn't *my* boss who planned this road trip from hell. It was yours."

I blinked.

"What? Wait a minute. What are you talking about?"

"It was Stan Rodgers' idea. He approached my boss with an olive branch—along with, I understand, a bit of a wager."

I frowned. "Wager?"

"On who will land the best story of the week," he said. The *News* or the *Gazette*. I understand there's also a little side bet on who craps out first. I've got to tell you, Turner. So far, those odds are way in my favor."

Odds? Wagers? Bets! Olive branch my soon-to-be sore ass.

"Of all the slimy, underhanded, unethical—"

"So, how much experience have you had on a tandem?" Van Vleet cut me off in mid-tirade.

My expression must've betrayed my inexperience.

"You have ridden a tandem before, right?" he added.

I tried to wipe my face clear of emotion—unsuccessfully, apparently, as Van Vleet's forehead suddenly had enough deep furrows to plant a respectable crop.

"You've ridden a *bicycle* before," Van Vleet asked.

I snorted. "Of course I've ridden a bicycle."

His eyes narrowed to slits. "*Oo*kay. When was the last time you were on a bicycle?" he pressed.

"I live in the country. Gravel roads. Washboard surfaces. Not exactly your ideal bike trails." I responded. I chewed my lip. How long *had* it been since I rode a bike? Let's see. It had to be when we lived in town before we moved to the country. I was around seven then. I grimaced. Good God. I hadn't ridden a bicycle in…seventeen years!

My non-existent poker face betrayed me. Again.

"Oh, God. How long has it been, Turner?"

I looked down at my hands. "I think I was about…uh…seven-years-old the last time I rode a bike," I mumbled.

"Seven-years-old! You haven't been on a bicycle since you were seven! Holy shit!" Van Vleet exclaimed.

"Okay. So, what part of 'I live in the country' did you miss? Forgive me if I prefer a four-legged horse to a two-wheeled velocipede," I said.

"Hell. We'd better get together ASAP to practice," Van Vleet said. "I don't want to look like an idiot in front of Keelie Keller and company."

I sat up in my chair. "Keelie Keller? Reality star bimbo of the moment? Uh, Drew, sorry to burst your bubble, scoop, but like ten thousand plus people ride in TribRide. How do you figure you're gonna get close enough to Keelie Keller and entourage for her to notice you and your dubious tandem talent?"

"Leave that to me, Blondie. First things first. Practice makes perfect. We won't have a prayer out there if you aren't up to the task. Meet me below the dam on the spillway side at 7 sharp tomorrow morning. They have a decent bike path there. Lots of hills to challenge us."

"Hills?" I gulped. "I think we'd better start out with something a little more…beginner-friendly," I suggested. "You know. Fewer turns. Less of a grade."

Van Vleet looked at me and shook his head.

"Have it your way. Shady Rest Cemetery. Seven A.M."

"Shady Rest…Cemetery?" I swallowed.

"Little traffic. Even fewer witnesses." He grinned. "Dress

appropriately. And come prepared for a very long workout."

"But it's gonna be like a hundred degrees tomorrow!" I could detect a nasally whine in my voice.

"Geez, Turner. It's starting to sound like you're the one who should bow out gracefully. Or should I say, gratefully?" Van Vleet observed, an amused look spreading across his face. "I get it. You're not up to the task. No shame in backing out. No shame at all."

Great. Just what I needed. A game of chicken on a tandem.

"I'll be there. With pedal pushers on," I said, with a lift of one brow.

"Oh, and one more thing, Blondie," Van Vleet added as I turned to leave.

"Yes?"

"No boots allowed."

I supposed that went for spurs, too.

CHAPTER FOUR

A cemetery was no place to experiment with tandem cycling, (Okay, so I didn't want to tempt fate.) and I had arranged to meet Drew Van Vleet at the county park instead. The park has a nice, wide paved road that winds its way around a modest-sized pond. The baseball and softball fields are located at the top of a long hill. Since Craig was a star pitcher on the high school team, and I was an okay softball third baseman, we'd spent a lot of time at the park. Plus they have all kinds of cool playground equipment, a couple of covered bridges, and a totally cool pioneer village that includes a little white church, a little red schoolhouse, a stagecoach inn, and a used-to-be train station.

Rather than watch Craig save the day—or I guess in his case, the game—I'd spend my time nosing around the historic village, seeing how high I could go on the swings, or pestering the temperamental geese that inhabited the park. Hold on. Don't go PETA-cidal on me here, folks. The goose-baiting was strictly payback from being psychologically scarred as a child from the renegade band of felonious fowl who found extraordinary delight in chasing me around the park and pecking at my backside. They gave as good as they got. Honest.

Thankfully, it was a weekday. The campgrounds wouldn't be quite so busy, and the ball fields wouldn't start seeing ball players until later in the day.

He'd get our transportation to the park, Van Vleet said. I wasn't sure how he planned to accomplish this. I chewed my lip. Could a person ride a tandem alone? Possible, I supposed. Advisable? Uh, not so much.

I had my answer almost immediately when a black pickup swung into the gravel lot where I was parked and working my way through a sausage, egg, and cheese breakfast sandwich paired with a Diet Coke. A pickup pulled alongside me. When I spotted the bright red tandem in the truck bed, my breakfast quickly lost its appeal.

"Well, well, well. What do you know? She actually showed," Van Vleet said from the cab, yanking his sunglasses off, his eyes narrow slits of amusement. "I'd have taken bets you wouldn't be here, Turner. I have to hand it to you. Your capacity for self-abasement is impressive."

Translation: I was a glutton for punishment.

Seriously? Like I haven't heard that before.

"What took you so long?" I asked. "For a minute there I was ready to send out a posse to hunt you down, pilgrim."

"Yeah, right," Van Vleet said, shaking his head. "Calamity Jayne and the Grandville Geriatric gang in hot pursuit." He put a hand to his forehead and closed his eyes. "The visuals that brings to mind."

I watched Van Vleet pull the endgate down and haul himself up into the back of his truck. He maneuvered the elongated bike towards the tailgate.

"A little assistance, if you don't mind," he said, and I stuffed the last of my breakfast in my mouth before moving to the back of the truck.

"Uh, who picked the color?" I asked, and helped lower the heavier than expected fire truck red bike to the ground. "Red really doesn't do much for me."

"Beats me." Van Vleet jumped down from the bed of the truck. "They probably borrowed the bike. This isn't what you'd call a heavily financed operation, in case you thought otherwise."

"But does it have to be red?" The bike I'd performed the triple double on had been red, too. Not exactly an encouraging omen.

"Who cares what color it is? I'm more concerned with how well it rides."

Oh. Yeah. There was that.

"Has the bike been checked out?" I asked. "You know. By a certified bike shop? Someone who knows what they're doing?"

He shrugged. "Guess we'll soon find out, won't we?"

Nice.

"You did bring a bike helmet."

"Of course." Actually, I'd lifted Taylor's helmet from a shelf in the folks' garage. I figured. Why spend money I didn't have for something she wouldn't miss and I'd likely never want to lay eyes on ever again?

I wrinkled my nose and picked the black helmet up and set it on my head. Leave it to Taylor to pick a boring color. I could hear it now: *What's black and white and red all over? Tressa Turner on TribRide.*

I fumbled with the straps, having difficulty getting the blasted thing fastened.

"Uh, Einstein. You have your helmet on backwards," Van Vleet pointed out.

I rotated the helmet, cinched the straps, and leveled an annoyed look at my pedaling partner.

"So, what makes you such an expert? You don't seem like the bike type to me."

Van Vleet fiddled with the bicycle.

"I ride," he said.

Was I imagining it—or had he lost a bit of his swagger?

He fastened his own bike helmet on his head—a shiny silver number—took hold of the bike's handlebars and swung a leg over the bike, settling his bike-shorts-clad fanny on the front seat of the bike.

"Climb on, Calamity." Van Vleet nodded towards the seat behind him. "Let's see what you can do."

I frowned. "Hold on. Who says you get the front seat?"

"My guardian angel. That's who. You haven't ridden a bicycle since you were in grade school. No way am I going to trust the driver's seat to someone who has the nickname you do—and the history to justify it."

"I see. So you get the view of the wide-open road and I get what? The view of your wide, open posterior all the way across the state? No way."

"Oh, for heaven's sake. As soon as I'm convinced I won't end up as someone's hood ornament, we'll talk about taking turns. Until then, get used to the back seat, backside view. Now would you get on the damned bike?"

I was about to protest more but realized he was probably right. I wasn't ready to take the helm yet. I'd need some time in the saddle. But once I was up to speed? Well, this little cowgirl wasn't about to take a back seat to anyone.

I grabbed the handlebars behind Van Vleet's seat and started to swing a leg over the bicycle's bar when the bike wobbled precariously to one side.

"Whoa! Hold your horses, Calamity! A little finesse, if you please!" Van Vleet scolded. "This is a bike, not a steed. You don't gallop up and throw yourself on a tandem like some half-assed ramrod or we'll tip over!" He repositioned the bike and planted a foot on either side of the bicycle to balance it. "Position yourself thus," he instructed.

"Thus?" I made a face. "*Thus*?"

"Just do it!" Van Vleet barked.

"Okay! Okay! I'll position myself *thus*." I assumed the position. "There. Happy?" I said to the rigid back in front of me.

Van Vleet turned in his seat.

"Do I look happy?"

"Did you spend any time at all researching the technique of riding tandem?" he asked. "You know. In between screwing up obits and dispensing candy sprinkles on soft serve?"

"I didn't think it was compulsory to Google riding a bicycle," I responded.

Van Vleet shook his head. "I thought as much. Okay. Lesson one. Definition of terms."

Terms?

"Term One: Captain. The captain is the front seat rider and the bike boss, the rider in control, if you will. The captain controls breaking, steering, and shifting gears." He jabbed a thumb into his chest. "That's me. I am the captain."

I blinked. Was this guy for real? I struck a salute pose.

"Aye, aye, Captain! Permission to speak, sir!"

Van Vleet did one of those eye roll numbers. "Do I have a choice?"

"Sir! No, sir!"

"Oh, for God's sake. What is it?"

"Why do you get to be the bike boss again?"

"Uh, firstly because I actually know what I'm doing and secondly because I don't want to die. Now, may I please proceed?"

I sighed. "If you must."

"Term Number Two: Stroker."

"Stroker?" I frowned, already prepared to be insulted.

Van Vleet nodded. "Stroker. Also known as the motor. You, Miss Motormouth, are the stroker."

"I'm the motor. Me?"

"Technically, you're the stroker."

"And technically you are…an ass," I said.

"Would you get serious?"

I stared at him. "I've just been assigned *stroker* duties and you want *me* to get serious. Dude. That's whacked."

"Turner—"

"Do we have to use the term *stroker*? That just sounds…wrong."

"Oh, for God's sake, call yourself whatever the hell you want," Van Vleet snapped.

"Xena, Biker Princess," I proclaimed.

"Funny. The point is you provide the propulsion."

I looked at him.

"You expect *me* to provide the pedal power for both of us?"

His glance shifted to the area of my body that falls between the pelvis and the knees. "You don't really want me to answer that question, do you?"

"Listen. These thighs were sculpted from years of horse hugging, roping, riding, and rodeo-ing, buddy. That doesn't mean they are pedal-power approved," I said. What can I say? I have cowgirl thighs.

"No matter. Those thunder thighs will have to do, and you'll have to get used to second seat spinning," Van Vleet told me. "Now, for the correct mounting procedure."

"Mounting procedure? First, 'stroking' and now 'mounting.' You aren't getting fresh, are you, Van Vleet?" I snorted.

"In your dreams, TT."

"TT? Oh. As in Tressa Turner."

"No. As in thunder thighs."

I let the dig go. Never fear. I'd have a week to come up with appropriate names for my pedaling partner. As well as for my employer…

"Now," Van Vleet went on. "I've got the brake engaged so

the bike won't roll. The stroker positions the pedal in the lowest position to use as a step. Go ahead and do it."

I complied.

"Now mount the bicycle. Try to center your balance as much as possible. Okay. Now, clip your feet and tie off the straps."

I fumbled a bit, but managed to do as he instructed.

"Next you're going to rotate the pedals to a good starting position for me," Van Vleet said. "Okay. A little more. There. That should do. Right. We should be ready to go. Remember. We've got to get the bike going quickly so we don't tip over. And it's important that we match our cadence. You do know what that means, right?"

"Oh, shucks, Cap'n. All us strokers know what cadence is," I guffawed.

"Since you're the weakest link, you determine how fast or slow the cadence is," Van Vleet went on. "I'll take my cue from you."

"How do you figure I'm the weakest link?" I objected. "I could turn out to be a tandem rock star."

"Prove it, Witchiepoo," Van Vleet said.

"Let's roll," I said with more confidence than I felt

"Okay. I'm going to push off. Ready. And go!"

The tandem shot forward.

"Pedal! Set the cadence!" Van Vleet yelled.

I bent over the handlebars, trying to remember to maintain a centered balance, stepping into the raised pedal with one foot, then the other.

"Faster! Faster!" Van Vleet yelled, and I kicked it up a notch.

"Too slow! Too slow!" Van Vleet's hollered warning came as my right foot somehow managed to come loose from the tie securing it to the pedal. I tried to recover my foothold, and leaned slightly to my left.

"Pedal! Pedal!" Van Vleet yelled.

"I'm trying! I'm trying!" I yelled back.

Every time I thought I'd gained a foothold, the speed of the pedals changed and my foot flailed in mid-air.

"Try harder! I can't do it alone! You're like dead weight

back there!"

I felt my balanced center begin to wobble. My one remaining anchor flew off the pedal and both legs shot out in opposite directions.

Look Ma! No feet!

The bicycle began to tip.

"Timber!" I screamed and squeezed my eyes shut to block out the sight of the roadside ditch looming closer and closer.

My prayer during that split-second descent? *Dear Lord, protect the teeth. Amen.*

* * *

Four hours later I had a new appreciation for individuals so committed to the pursuit of health and fitness that they balanced themselves on a seat no bigger than a generous slice of pie and traversed the highways and byways by virtue of leg power—and willpower—alone.

My backside felt like someone had used a hot poker on it. Okay. In it.

That wasn't all.

My thighs hurt. My calves hurt. Even my feet hurt, my toes cramping and curling up like talons clutching prey from being strapped to the damned pedals for so long. I limped to a picnic table and dropped onto the seat, gasping as my buttocks hit the hard wood.

"You don't look so good," Van Vleet observed. "Maybe you better bow out. There's no shame in throwing in the towel. Really. I can do the bike ride solo. Swap this bike out for a one seat number."

I rubbed a thigh muscle. "You'd like that, wouldn't you, Drew? I quit. You win whatever idiotic wager is going on, and secure bragging rights into infinity and beyond." I shook my head. "Not a chance. I'm in it 'til the bitter end. Back aches, blisters, bad attitudes, and all."

I may be many things—but, a quitter? Not in my DNA, dude.

Van Vleet secured the bicycle in his truck bed and shut the endgate. "See you at six."

"Six?"

"Our next practice. And this time? Wear bike shorts. We can't keep stopping so you can pull your panties out of your butt crack."

I winced.

I'm gonna need a bigger bike seat.

CHAPTER FIVE

"Water! I need water!"

I dropped into a booth at Hazel's Hometown Café, garnering a startled look from the other patrons and a "what now?" look from chief cook and bottle washer, Donita Smith. Technically, "Hazel" has been retired for over a decade, but her family continues to run the iconic eatery. At any given time, farmers, retirees, business folk, and busybodies congregate to enjoy a heapin' helping of hometown cooking guaranteed to have you letting out your belt a notch or wishing you'd donned stretchy pants for the occasion.

Donnie set a glass of ice water on the table in front of me. I picked it up, drained it.

"A pitcher! I need a pitcher!" I placed the cold plastic to my forehead. "STAT!" I bellowed when Donnie didn't move quickly enough. I received a "what did I do to deserve this?" look before she headed back to the counter. By the time she returned with a pitcher of water, I'd chewed half the ice and was ready to dump the other half down the front of my shirt.

Donita filled my glass. I drained it. She poured me another. I downed it.

"Thank you, thank you, thank you! You're a Godsend, Donnie!" I managed between swallows.

"I don't know whether to call you Tressa or 'camel.' You filling up for a trek across the Sahara?" Donnie asked.

I wished. A caravan across burning sands would probably be more bearable.

"What on earth has you so hot and bothered?" Donnie asked. "Don't tell me you're on the trail of another dead guy."

"Maybe the dead guy is on her tail for once. Aren't zombies all the rage these days?" Joltin' Joe Townsend slid into the booth across from me. He picked up a menu. "What are you having?"

"Lunch now, apparently," I said. "On my brand spanking new grandpappy."

"Let me guess. You want the hot beef sandwich, right?" Donnie guessed before I could order.

"She'll have the diet plate," Joe co-opted my fare choice. "She's in training. *I'll* have the hot beef. Extra gravy."

Donnie raised an eyebrow. "One diet. One hot beef coming up."

"And another pitcher of water, please," I added.

"Donnie's right. A camel's got nothing on you," Joe observed, watching me gulp another glass of water. "Tandem troubles?"

I wiped the water from my chin and shrugged. "I'm getting the hang of it," I said. "I'll be up to speed in no time."

"That bad, huh?" Joe shook his head.

I made a face. "How'd you guess?"

"The skinned elbow and the rock-encrusted trim on your shirt tipped me off. That not-so-subtle look of quiet desperation on your sweaty, dirt-streaked face cinched it."

"Wow. Look at you. Going all *Criminal Minds* on me. Should Aaron Hotchner at the BAU be worried?" I asked.

"It doesn't take a profiler to figure out you've got tandem trouble, Missy," Joe pointed out. "Which brings me to Rick."

Uh-oh. Here it came. Danger! Danger! Senior snoop on the scent!

"How do you make the leap from my sucking at tandem bike-riding to your grandson?"

"Rick's a top notch bike rider. He can train you. Help you keep your spokes steady."

I made a face. It would take more than the acumen of a certain ranger to see yours truly "looking neat and oh-so-sweet on a bicycle built for two".

"I'll keep that in mind," I said, not ready to talk about Rick Townsend with anyone, especially Joe Townsend. The wily old coot had an uncanny ability to weasel admissions from me I never intended to blurt.

"Still mum on what transpired between the grandson and you on the final day of the cruise, huh? You know I'm gonna find out eventually, Toots, so you might as well save us both a lot of time and grief and just spill it now."

"This is so…inappropriate. Do I interrogate you on your love life?"

"What do you want to know, blondie? Frequency? Technique? Duration?"

I put my hands on my ears. "Stop! Stop, before I spew!"

The geriatric Joe Friday sat back in his seat and observed me with an appraising look.

"'Fess up, sister," he said. "How many times?"

I blinked.

He couldn't be asking…

"How many spills did you really take?"

I let out a relieved breath.

"Just the one," I said.

"Please. Don't try to play a player," Joe said.

I couldn't help but snigger. Joe was such a legend in his own mind.

"I happen to know," Joe went on, "that you were observed getting up close and personal with the pavement on at least four separate occasions at the County Park this morning."

"Are you stalking me, old man?" I asked.

"Of course not. Your grandmother informed me."

I raised an eyebrow.

"Oh, really. And how did she happen by that information?"

"Hannah had a hair appointment at the Kut 'n' Kurl," Joe said, as if that explained everything.

"Her hairdresser outted me?"

Joe shook his head back and forth. "No! It was the gal who did her nails."

"Her manicurist?"

Joe nodded.

"She's Drew Van Vleet's cousin."

"Van Vleet told his cousin about our practice session?"

"Didn't have to. A picture speaks a thousand words."

I frowned. "You've so lost me."

"Van Vleet texted pictures to his cousin."

"Texted?"

"And there was this blog. And Facebook. Oh, and

"Yeah. Usually from the mouths of attention whores who don't give a flip about the impact they're having on young, impressionable minds."

Debbie Daggett does the soapbox. I only hoped the soap box wouldn't buckle under the weight.

"You're one to talk about manipulating people, Whitver," Vinny was saying. "What the hell do you think you've been doing to Keelie with your little prankster friend here?" Vinny asked.

"Hello! Read my lips: I am not responsible for any of the malicious pranks targeting Keelie. Maybe you'd do better to spend your time checking out your own back yard," I suggested.

"What the hell do you mean by that?" Vinny barked.

"You can't deny Keelie's reality TV ratings are getting a shot in the arm from all the drama," I said. "And ratings bumps benefit everyone involved with the show: producers, advertisers, cast members, their agents…"

"I resent your implication!"

"Welcome to the club," I responded.

"Vinny, you're spoiling our séance!" Keelie hooked an arm through Manny's and Frankie's arms. "Nothing's going to happen to me when I have all these big strong men here to protect me."

"I think I'm gonna be sick," Dixie muttered.

"Come on, everybody! Let's finish our potty breaks, make nice, and go back in and see if we can raise a little hell!" Keelie pumped a fist in the air. "Murder House! Murder House! Murder House!"

Tiara joined her pal in the ghoulish chant.

"You will join us as we repair to the haunted Ax Murder House for another go-round at a ghostie, won't you, Vinny, ol' boy?" Langley asked, putting a hand out to the owly agent.

"Hell, no! I'm going to sit out here, have a smoke, and thank God I'm too old and too smart to piss away what time I have left on this earth trying to contact the damned boogeyman."

Langley raised an eyebrow and an "I tried" shoulder.

"As you say, Vinny," he said. "Miss Turner?"

He lifted his elbow, inviting me to take his arm.

I found myself accepting.

What can I say? I'm a sucker for a guy with good manners

and an accent.

Langley tucked my arm into his and patted my hand.

"You mustn't take Vinny too seriously," Langley said. "His bark is worse than his bite."

Somehow I doubted that. Vinny came off like a feisty pit bull with a bone to pick.

With me.

By the time we returned to the parlor, Keelie and Tiara had lost interest in the boogeyman board. Instead, they began to dance around the parlor to a pretty awful rendition of *Monster Mash*.

"Sorry, love," Langley said, and gently let go of my arm. "Sounds like the duet could do with a soprano." He gave me a wave and went to join his BFFs. Soon Tiara had grabbed Frankie and pulled him into the chorus line.

I grabbed my sleeping bag and claimed the wall nearest the front door. You know. Just in case.

"I hope you're happy," Dixie said, dropping to the floor beside me.

"What? Frankie's finally coming out of his shell. That's a good thing."

"Shells exist for a reason. It's called protection," Dixie pointed out.

A second later, Langley threw an arm around Patrick and pulled the reluctant trooper into the sing-along.

"I hope you're happy." Taylor dropped to the floor on my other side.

"What? Patrick's showing he can be a good sport. Gotta love that in a guy."

"Oh? And being a good sport includes being groped by someone you just met?" Taylor asked.

"What do you mean, groped? I can see both of Langley's hands."

"Not Langley, you idiot. Keelie," Taylor hissed.

I blinked. She was right. Keelie was definitely putting the moves on Patrick, who was now the yummy, meaty filling between two slices of bread.

He looked like Mr. Spock did when his human half was showing.

I crossed my arms. "And you would know this...how?"

"I have my own history, Turner."

"You seriously want me to pose for pictures with my hair looking like this?" I tugged at what was left of my ponytail. I have hair issues. My head of hair takes the term "windblown" to a whole new level. I go through a jug of gel each month trying to tame my wild mustang of a mane. Mostly, my "do" comes out the victor.

"What's wrong with your hair? Looks the same as it always does," Stan observed.

Great. Now Stan was channeling Vidal Sassoon.

"I have a professional reputation to think about," I said. "I can't be photographed looking like a blonde bozo."

Stan started to chuckle. "Blonde bozo. That's a good one. I'll have to remember that one."

"Forget the scary hair. You'll be wearing a bicycle helmet so nobody will see it anyway," Shelby Lynn pointed out.

I shrugged. Shelby Lynn had a point. The bike helmet would hide a multitude of hair sins.

"So. Where's Van Vleet anyway? I bet he got more notice so he could do some pre-pic primping," I said.

"He mentioned something about picking up T-shirts," Shelby Lynn said.

"T-shirts?" I turned to Stan. "What did you do? Sell advertising space for the shirts on our backs?"

Stan slapped his forehead. "Damn. Why didn't I think of that?"

"Greetings, fellow earthlings!"

Van Vleet crossed the courthouse lawn and headed in our direction.

"Holy shit. Would you look at that?" Stan said under his breath. "Talk about your friggin' twinkies. I almost feel sorry for you, Turner."

I could only stare. Drew Van Vleet wore what looked suspiciously like a *Star Trek* shirt.

"Captain Kirk, I presume," I greeted Van Vleet. "Nice, uh, top."

"Glad you approve, Turner."

I sensed yet another disturbance in the force. I know. Wrong outer space show. But you get the point.

"I hope you're not suggesting that I—"

"I love it!" I felt a ham-fisted slap on my back. "It's perfect!" Stan gushed.

"You've got to be kidding," I said.

"What? You don't like *Star Trek*?" Van Vleet said.

"I don't like looking like a lame-oh in front of thousands of people."

"But we'll stand out from the crowd," Van Vleet insisted.

"Exactly my point. I prefer to ride below the radar."

Stan chuckled. "This coming from the person who finds bodies in car trunks and on boats, chases dunk tank clowns on the midway at state fairs, and nabs a campus crime spree perp with a zombie movie voice-over. Nice try, Turner, but no cigar." He stuck his own cigar in his mouth.

"I have an image to uphold," I tried again.

"Image? As what? Crime beat's Betty Boop?" Van Vleet sneered.

"At least I know a crime when I see one."

"Not too hard when the crime involves you."

"Your reporting should be a crime."

"Now, now children. Let's not quarrel," Stan put a hand on Van Vleet's shoulder. "After all, you're stuck with each other for an entire week. You'll need to pull together as a team. Cooperate. Play nice."

Stan Rodgers preaching on the benefits of working well with others almost made me forget the fashion disaster about to befall me.

Almost.

"But the shirt, Stan! The shirt!"

"Will be a big hit with the TribRide participants and followers."

"I didn't think this assignment required your wardrobe approval," I said.

"Nonetheless, I approve," Stan grinned. "I most definitely approve."

I shook my head. "Where's my friggin' T-shirt?" I asked.

Van Vleet tossed a plastic bag at me. I fished inside and pulled out the top. I held it up to my chest.

"Red! A *red* shirt! I'm wearing a red shirt? Hell, no!"

"What's the matter, Turner?" Stan asked.

"What's the matter? What's the matter? Have you watched an episode of *Star Trek*? Are you aware that the life expectancy of a *Star Trek* red shirt is roughly the same as that of the drone ant!"

"What are you talking about, Tressa?" Shelby Lynn said.

"I'm talking about the expendables. *Star Trek expendables*. Come on. Everyone knows when a red shirt transports down to an unknown planet, he isn't gonna beam back up alive—if he beams back up at all. No. Hell, no." I thrust the offending garment at Van Vleet. "*You* can wear the red shirt."

"I can't," Van Vleet said. "Remember, I'm the captain. The captain wears gold. Not red."

"What the hell, Turner? Who gives a flying rip what color you wear?" Stan bellowed. "Let's get this little photo shoot wrapped up so I can get back inside my air-conditioned office. It's hotter than the devil's underpants."

"The devil wears underpants?" I said.

"Turner!"

"Okay, okay. I'll put the red shirt on for now. But I expect to take my turn at the helm wearing the gold shirt. Just so you know."

Stan shook his head. "Everyone's a prima donna."

I pulled the red shirt on over my head and yanked it down over my tank top. I set the bike helmet on my head (this time correctly) and stomped to the bicycle. I started to get on the front seat.

Van Vleet motioned to the rear seat. "Stroker, remember?"

I mumbled words that would have had me drummed out of *Star Fleet* and lowered my butt to the back seat. Shelby Lynn's digital camera immortalized the moment.

I raised my eyes to the heavens.

Scotty! Anyone! For God's sake, beam me up!

CHAPTER SIX

"Oh. Ow. Ew. Ahhh."

I repositioned the bag of frozen peas cushioning my tender bottom, hitched the temperature up a notch on the heating pad resting against my back, and prayed I wouldn't somehow electrocute myself.

I eased back against the sofa and flipped my laptop open, pulling up the web browser. The laptop was a hand-me-down from my bookkeeper/CPA mother. When she upgraded her home office equipment, I became the grateful beneficiary of her old lappy toppy.

Okay. So I also pirate her Internet service. Don't judge. You were probably a struggling young professional once yourself.

I keystroked Keelie Keller and hit enter.

Keelie's claim to fame was dubious at best. Her parents didn't own a large hotel chain. Her daddy wasn't a high-powered attorney or financier. She didn't hold a royal title and wasn't heir to one. Her sleuth series ending and acting roles drying up, Keelie's career seemed to be circling the drain until she started a highly publicized, on-again-off-again romance with rising country-pop heartthrob, Jax Whitver. That notoriety helped her nab a spot on a matchmaking reality TV show. She hadn't received a proposal of marriage, but her performance on the show got her an offer for her own reality gig. Since then, her popularity had skyrocketed. She boasted an army of social media followers, a handpicked, fame-obsessed clique, and a legion of paparazzi on her trail.

Keelie and her BFF, Tiara Fordham, had partnered up again for the reality TV gig and enjoyed frequent—and highly publicized—nights on the club circuit, partying along with third musketeer, Langley Carlisle III.

Langley, or "Lang" as his BFFs called him—a pale, wiry, flamboyant blonde with strawberry highlights—was perfectly cast as sounding board, therapist, and—mediator/referee for two gal pals who often found themselves at odds over boys, booze, and big bucks.

Between Keelie's "It's all about me" airs, Tiara's "Poor little me" boo hoos, and Lang's "You can talk to me" assurances, the threesome made a colorful trio—which translated into an impressive ratings leader.

I shrugged. What did I care about the Tinsel Town Trio? The likelihood that I'd ever be within a TribRide mile of the threesome was roughly the same as me completing the rigorous course without one hint of a hemorrhoid.

Yes. That's right. Slim to none.

The doorbell dinged. I set my computer on the coffee table, inched my fanny off the front of the sofa, and pushed myself to my feet. I sucked in a painful breath and attempted to straighten my stiff back, gave up, and shuffled to the door, acquiring a whole new empathy for my slightly stoop-backed gammy.

I pulled the door open.

"This better be good," I mumbled.

Rick Townsend stood on my porch, fist raised, apparently ready to rap on my door.

"I've been told I'm good," Townsend said, with a lift of one eyebrow. "Very good, in fact."

I felt the telltale warmth of a betraying blush. It seemed all it took for my blood to boil was for Rick Townsend to cock a "come hither" eyebrow at me.

Who was I kidding? All I had to do was think about the roguishly handsome ranger and the shiver-me-timbers night we shared on the *Epiphany*, and I got all sea legs shivery and quivery.

"Well, good for a laugh at least," I said, determined to keep things light and loose with the man who could turn what good sense I had into cannon fodder.

"Isn't that what all women say they want?" The ranger asked. "A guy who makes them laugh?"

I couldn't speak for all women, but what this ranger-type made me feel was no laughing matter.

"I do like a man who loves to laugh," I responded. "At himself as well as others."

"Absolutely," Rick said. "No sense taking oneself too seriously."

I nodded, uncertain of just what Rick Townsend was doing on my doorstep and equally uncertain as to whether I wanted him there or not.

Yeah. I know. I'm an idiot.

"Can I...come in?" Townsend asked.

I hesitated long enough for him to notice.

"Tressa?"

"Sure. Of course, you can come in. Why wouldn't you come in? There's no reason why you shouldn't."

Babble. Babble. Babble.

Damn. Damn. Damn.

I stood to one side to let Townsend in. A potent whiff of his cologne, coupled with his own unique "Ranger Rick" scent, hit me with the force of a "snap out of it" slap to the face. My house suddenly smelled better than the movie theater on free popcorn refill Wednesdays.

I closed the door and followed Townsend into the living room, rubbing my lower back as I limped along behind him.

"What the heck is this for?" Townsend asked, and picked up the bag of frozen peas and the heating pad. "You do know there are easier ways to cook peas than with a heating pad."

"Really? I wondered why it was taking so long," I said, grabbing the frozen veggies out of his hand, longing to put it back where it belonged: on my aching heinie.

I moved toward the sofa, trying my best to cover the distance without looking like an arthritic octogenarian.

Townsend's next words told me I'd failed.

"What's wrong with you?" Rick said. "You move like one of the walking dead."

Kind of the way I felt.

"I'm fine," I said. "In fact, I'm better than fine. I'm fabulous. Better than fabulous. I'm...I'm...stupendous."

Blither. Blither.

"You're in pain, that's what you are," Townsend said, and took my hand and led me to the couch. "Give me that." He reached out and took my peas and dropped them on the sofa cushion. "Sit," he instructed.

I dropped to the sofa.

"Ahhh." I sighed. "That hurts so good."

Townsend took a seat beside me. "What the hell am I going to do with you, Tressa?" he asked, and I frowned, trying to select what had prompted this latest query from a list longer than the list of slights (both real and imagined) my gammy swears have been perpetrated upon her by old foe and new neighbor, Abigail Winegardner.

"What do you mean, do with me?" I hedged.

"Why do you insist on keeping things from me?" Townsend asked.

"Things? What...things?" I evaded.

"The TribRide fiasco for one. Your pedaling partnership with Drew Van Vleet, for another. Team Trekkies, isn't it?"

Small towns had way big ears.

"It all came up rather suddenly," I told him. "And Joe said you were out of town."

"Funny thing about cell phones. You can carry them with you everywhere, so people can call you anytime, anywhere."

"You were working, and I've been—"

"—busy," Townsend finished. He shook his head. "No. What you've been, Tressa, is avoiding me. Admit it. Ever since we got back from the cruise, you've been more elusive than my grandfather when he knows he's got a butt-chewing coming for eating too much bacon or for spying on his neighbors again," Townsend said.

"I've had a lot on my mind."

"Ditto," Townsend came back.

"This ride—"

"Is a smokescreen," Townsend said. "A dangerous smokescreen."

"When you say 'dangerous'—"

"How many times did you wipe out?" Townsend asked.

"I beg your pardon."

"On the tandem. How many times did you fall over? You know. Crash and burn. Bite the dust. Get up close and personal with gravel?"

I frowned. "Who told?"

Rick took hold of my arm and positioned it to reveal my skinned elbow. "This told. Along with your peas and heating pad and painful-to-watch impression of the undead. TribRide? What the hell? You've got to be kidding. It was like pulling teeth for me to get you on a bike on a path, for crying out loud. Now, you're planning to ride across the entire state on a tandem. How do you figure that's going to play out?"

Painfully probably.

"What can I do?" I said, with a lift of my shoulders. "It's my job."

"It's reckless and ridiculous."

"You mean *I'm* reckless and ridiculous." After what happened between the two of us on the cruise, somehow I'd hoped we were beyond the judgments and second-guessing.

That *I* was past feeling insecure and threatened by the slightest criticism.

Okay. So maybe I wasn't above using my—what's that called again—*righteous indignation* as a bit of a smokescreen. Maybe there was more angst than anger in my emotional response. Maybe fear rather than ego was in the driver's seat here. Maybe the fact that Townsend and I *had* put our Hatfield and McCoy history behind us and were moving into uncharted and unfamiliar territory was giving me heart palpitations that screamed, *Defibrillator! STAT!*

But I'm just guessing here.

"Give it a rest, Tressa. You know that's not what I'm saying," Rick said. "I'm simply pointing out that as a biker, you're a novice. Exhibit A here demonstrates that painfully sad, but true, fact. And that fact puts you at risk on an event like TribRide. Accidents happen every year on the ride. Some serious ones." He squeezed her arm. "I'm partial to that bootie of yours. I don't want to see it bruised, broken, battered, or the hide ripped off and left along some county blacktop."

His graphic observation made me a tad bilious.

"I appreciate your concern," I began, but Townsend cut me off with a don't-even-try-it wave.

"No, you don't. You're insulted and pissed off that I would even suggest you aren't up to the task."

Damn. He read me like a *Field and Stream* magazine with a feature on stag-hunting Dallas Cowboys cheerleaders.

He picked up my laptop. Clicked the mouse.

"What's this?" He scanned the web page I'd been browsing. "You planning a journalistic jump to the *Enquirer* or *TMZ*?"

I grabbed the computer.

"It's research," I snapped. "You know. Just in case."

"In case you have an opportunity to interview Keelie Keller and her hangers-on."

I shrugged. "I'm supposed to cover TribRide. And that includes the riders, as well as the events. So I thought I'd better bone up on the celebs. Not that I think I'll actually get close to any of them."

Townsend chuckled. "Somehow I imagine you'll find a way. Have you thought at all about your strategy?" Townsend asked.

"Strategy?"

"Your TribRide strategy."

"I figured I'd just put my best foot forward," I said with a snort. "Get it? Best foot forward."

Townsend lifted an eyebrow. "I'm not talking about the physical strategy," he said. "I'm referring to your psychological strategy."

I frowned. "Psychological...strategy?" Holy spandex. What was I getting myself into?

"There are definite subgroups that participate in TribRide," Townsend told me. "You have to figure out where you fit in best and plan accordingly."

"What do you mean, 'subgroups'?" I asked, my throat getting tighter.

Townsend leaned forward. He rested his elbows on his thighs and rubbed his hands together.

"First of all, you have the early birds."

I already didn't like the sound of that.

"Early birds?"

"The gung-ho, aggressive bikers who get up at the butt crack of dawn or earlier and take off on the next leg of the ride before the ride has officially started. The early risers are the biker athletes. Early birds push themselves. They're the ones who take the longer, alternative routes when available, are obsessed with their times, and performance, and can't wait to get up and do it all over the next day. It's all about the biking experience."

That sounded about as fun as being poked in the eye with a sharp spoke.

"You can cross me off that subgroup membership roster," I said.

Talk about stating the obvious.

Townsend grinned. "For which that particular subset should be eternally grateful."

I stuck my tongue out at him.

"The next sub-group?"

"The drop-ins. These riders join the ride for a day or so, but aren't officially registered. Since they aren't paying for the experience, they tend to try to cram as much as they can into the short time they are riding. Occasionally, some can be a pain in the ass."

Oh, to be a drop-in.

"Then you have the stragglers, aka, the partiers. They get a late start because they've spent the previous night partying. Due to hangovers and lack of sleep, you'll typically find the greatest instances of roadside ralphing with this group. They drink hard and party hard. And it shows."

Riding a tandem in the middle of July in the summer heat with a hangover? Fuggetaboutit.

"Next," I said.

"Then you have the easy riders. This is the largest group by far and consists of people who ride for a lot of different reasons. Some are up for a challenge. Others take their vacation each year to ride and renew acquaintances. Others just want to experience something new and different. These folks are low-key, salt of the earth types. They're men, women, and children. They're families, friends, and coworkers who are low-maintenance and fun loving. They take in the entire experience and in a positive way. They follow the rules and are respectful. They leave on time and arrive on time. They get a kick out of all the attractions, activities, and scenic views along the way. They don't set any speed records, but they probably receive the most pleasure from the experience than their counterparts in other groups."

Ah, slow and steady wins the race. At last I'd found my

niche.

"I can be an easy rider," I told him. "Well, maybe an uneasy easy rider."

"More likely the other riders near you will be the uneasy ones," Townsend suggested.

"Does that include you? You are riding this year, aren't you?" I asked, not sure whether I was hoping for a yay or a nay.

"I registered, but due to firearms certification scheduling, I can't do the whole ride this year. If I'm lucky, I'm looking at day three or day four to hook up."

I winced. By day three or day four, I could be road kill.

"Still in pain, huh?" Rick asked, and reached out to take my hand. "Poor T. What am I going to do with you?"

I grew all flustered and burning hot at the mere possibilities.

"Tressa? What are you thinking?" Rick asked.

"What makes you think I'm thinking anything?" I replied, figuring my pea throne had to be pea soup from the sudden heat radiating from my body.

"You're one of the few women I know who still blushes," Rick explained.

"Oh."

"I've told you before how good you look in red, haven't I?" he asked, putting a hand to my cheek.

"You might have mentioned it a time or two," I rasped, my throat suddenly dry as my gammy's legs at winter's end.

Rick's hand slipped around to the back of my head. "There is one thing you look better in than red," he told me.

"Oh?"

"Bed," he said.

"Oh."

He lowered his lips to mine, sending shivers along the same path that moments earlier had been in risk of overheating. His kiss was soft, searching, seductive. I schooled my response to be tentative, lukewarm. Take it or leave it.

And failed big time.

"I suppose you're too...sore," he said against my lips.

"Sore?" I mumbled into his mouth.

"Bike butt," he elaborated.

"Oh. That."

"Yeah. That."

Rick's lips moved to nuzzle the side of my neck, putting all thoughts of my bruised and battered buttocks clean out of my mind. I felt my earlier vow to proceed with caution where the good ranger was concerned disappear faster than Cadbury eggs and chocolate bunny rabbits from my Easter basket.

Butt? What butt?

He kissed me again. Cupped my face in his hands.

"So?"

"Perhaps if I were to, well, you know, be on top…"

"What did you just say?"

I felt blood pool in my cheeks.

Oh. My. God.

It was happening!

I was turning into my gammy!

I bit my lip.

"Uh, er, I—"

"No backing out now, young lady," Townsend said and pulled me to my feet. "You've reached the point of no return."

Funny. I thought I'd done that on the last night of the cruise.

"I really don't think—"

"Don't think," Rick ordered. "Just feel."

"But I'm in training." I tried to reel my trash talk back in. "You know what they say about, well, you know, abstaining when you're training. It's bad for the legs, you know."

"You planning to go a few rounds with Rocky?" Rick teased, and reached out to switch off the light.

"Wait!"

"I've waited long enough."

"No. Hold on!" I grabbed Rick's arm and pointed at the sliding door to the patio. "There's someone out there!" I whispered.

A hand appeared at the window, followed by a face pressing up against the glass, trying to look in.

I gasped. What the—

"Mom?"

I disengaged my fingers from Townsend's forearm, hurried over to the door and flipped on the outside light.

"What in the world? Mom?"

I unlocked the door and slid it open. I caught a sudden whiff of freshly popped corn.

My mother stood on the back deck. Dressed in light blue cotton pajamas, she held a bag of popcorn in one hand and what looked suspiciously like a jumbo bag of peanut M&Ms in the other.

"I come bearing gifts," she announced, and lifted her hands to show me the goodies.

I frowned.

My CPA mom. On my deck. At ten o'clock at night. In her jammies. Hands filled with junk food.

It's the end of the world, as we know it.

CHAPTER SEVEN

I waved Townsend out the front door and waved my mother over to the sofa.

"Okay. Spill it. What is going on?"

"Can't I drop in on my daughter without something being wrong?" She asked, and dropped to the sofa, making an "eww!" face when she landed on the mushy bag of peas.

I made a "who are you?" face when she picked the pea bag up, looked at it, shrugged, and tossed it on the coffee table without saying a word.

"You've never just dropped in before," I pointed out. Unless, of course, it was to check up on the previous tenant, clean the trailer, check my fridge, or to remind me of a family function, funeral, or church event at which my presence was required. "And you usually come bearing sticky note reminders for that calendar you bought me, not peanuts and popcorn."

"What can I say? I'm a caring person. Sue me."

I blinked. We'd switched from *Twilight Zone* to the Scary Mary show.

"Did Dad...do something?" I asked.

"Your father? Mr. Agreeable?"

"You're mad at him because he agrees with you?"

"Oh, no. He doesn't agree with me. He just pretends to agree with me so he can avoid confrontation."

"And that's...a bad thing?"

"It's ethically deceitful," she said. "And emotionally dishonest."

"So you didn't have an argument?"

"It's hard to argue with someone when they just sit there like a lump and don't say anything."

Ouch. The mother had claws! Who knew?

"So, what was your *non* argument about then?"

"Just...things," she said, and tore open the bag of candy sending colorful ovals of chocolate in every direction. "Damn. I hate when that happens." My mother got down on her hands and knees and started collecting the colorful jots of chocolate.

I watched with growing concern when she blew them off and popped them into her mouth.

"Ten second rule," she snapped, catching my surprised look before taking a seat on the couch again.

"Okay, Mom. What's going on with you and Dad?" I took a seat in the chair across from her.

She shook her head. "Nothing," she said. "Nothing at all." Her voice sounded husky and, for a moment, I thought she might start crying. Instead, she tipped the bag of candy and poured reds, yellows, blues, browns, and oranges into her open mouth.

I could only stare.

"What do you mean...nothing?" I asked.

"Zip. Zilch. Zero. Nada. Nil. None."

Sweat beaded on my upper lip. Oh, God. She couldn't be talking about *that*. Could she? I'd always tried to keep thoughts of my parents...together...*that way*...out of my head. That's what all offspring do, isn't it? Think of their conception as just this side of immaculate?

"Are you saying—? Are we talking about—? Is there a problem in the, uh, er, um...boudoir?" I stammered.

Now it was my mother's turn to stare.

"This is not about sex, Tressa." My mother opened the popcorn bag and dove in. "It's about closeness. A connection. Intimacy."

"I'm not exactly following—"

"We've become torpid. Moribund. Stagnant."

"Oh, God. Is it contagious?"

"We're in a rut, Tressa. Your father and me. He's grown complacent. Disengaged. Apathetic. Unfortunately, he refuses to acknowledge the fact."

"I haven't noticed anything out of the ordinary," I said.

A low-key, middle of the road fellow, not prone to extremes, my pop is a "come through for you" kind of guy who gets the job done without frills or fireworks. I should point out that my dad takes after his father rather than my grandma. Oh. You figured that out already? You're good.

"It's a progressive malady," my mother said.

Huh?

"So what happened tonight to send you on a junk food binge?" I asked.

"Really, Tressa. Popcorn and chocolate do not constitute a binge. You'd have to have alcohol and something like pizza to constitute a binge."

I shook my head. Seriously?

"To answer your question, I made a perfectly reasonable request of your father, and he refused to even consider it."

"Request. What request?"

My mother waved a hand. "That isn't important. It's your father's attitude that is at issue."

Now who was being slippery and evasive?

And who was dying to know just what "perfectly reasonable request" Jean Turner had made?

You get three guesses, and your first two don't count.

"So, what do you plan to do about it?" I asked—not about to take sides in a parental dispute.

"I plan to sleep here, of course."

Not the answer I expected. Or, welcomed.

"Come again."

"I'm sleeping here."

"You're sleeping here?"

"You have a spare bedroom."

"Yes, I know. But, what about Dad? Won't he worry?"

"He'll likely never know I'm gone. Popcorn?" She held the bag out to me. "It's movie theater butter."

I took a handful.

"I'll grab us a diet soda," I said, and got to my feet, still freaked out by my mom's odd behavior.

"Thank you, Tressa."

I limped in the direction of the kitchen. The doorbell rang before I made it to the fridge. I frowned. What was this? Grand Central Station? I turned and headed back in the direction I'd come from.

"Open up. I'm getting eaten alive by 'skeeters!"

I stopped dead in my tracks. I knew that voice.

What I didn't know was what the person who belonged with that voice was doing on my front porch at this time of night.

Bam! Bam!

"Tressa! Open the door before these bloodsuckers get me!"

I bowed to the inevitable and opened the door.

My gammy stood on the porch. She wore a hot pink cotton nightie and baby blue fuzzy slippers. In one hand was a bottle of wine. And the other? I blinked. Was that...sticky rolls? A bright yellow taxi sat idling in my driveway.

"Uh, what's going on, Gram?"

"I'm moving back in. That's what's going on." She patted my hand and walked past me and into the house. "Pay the driver, would you, dear? I'm a little light."

I stared after her, shaking my head to clear it.

I could see the sign now: Tressa's Twilight No Tell Motel: Questionable ambience. So-so cleanliness. But four-star female bonding opportunities.

Bring your own chocolate.

CHAPTER EIGHT

"Consider this your prep talk, Turner."

I sat across the table from my employer in the tiny break room that also served as conference room and client meeting room and decided what I needed was a "pep" talk instead. Or "pep" period. I'd tossed and turned on the sofa the night before stewing over my mom and dad. Then this morning I'd had to convince my gammy that just because Abigail Winegardner gave Joe a plate of sticky rolls for helping hang her "lame" birdhouse, it didn't mean Joe was game for a little extra-marital bird-watching.

"Prep talk?"

"The final briefing before you embark on your mission." He nodded at Shelby Lynn who sat to his right. She gave him an are-you-sure look. Stan nodded. Shelby Lynn shrugged, picked up a sheet of paper in front of her, and cleared her throat.

"TribRide. The open road frontier," she recited. "These are the stories of Team Trekkie. Its seven-day mission. To explore strange new vistas. To seek out news stories and increase circulation. To boldly go where no Calamity has gone before!" Shelby hesitated.

Stan nudged her.

Shelby Lynn cleared her throat again.

"*Duh, duh, duh, duh, duh, duh, duh. Duh, duh, duh, duh, duh, duh, duh. Da duh—*" Shelby performed the TV show theme. Poorly.

I made a slashing motion at my throat.

"All right, you can cut the mood music, Shelby Lynn," I said. "I get the point."

She pointed a long finger at our boss. "He made me do it!"

"Sounds about right," I muttered. "And for the record, Stan, although I'm moved by your touching send-off, all things considered, I'd rather have a bump in my paycheck than a private performance of *Star Trek, the Musical*." Unless, of course, the private performance included trekkie hotties Chris Pine and Zachary Quinto. Hubba hubba.

"You're up to speed on the event itself, right?" Shelby asked.

I winced. Up to speed? Not so much.

"I've done research," I hedged.

"Then you know the schedule, the stops—"

"The rules," Stan inserted.

I licked dry lips.

"Refresh my memory," I said.

Shelby Lynn sighed and shook her head. "You never studied." She shuffled her notes. "Start times are staggered. You know. Like with marathon runners. This is done to avoid traffic congestion resulting in bicycle mishaps."

I frowned. Note to Tressa: Crashing and burning at the starting gate? Not cool.

"There is a designated host city for each mid-day break and lunch and another designated city to host the ride overnight. These overnighter cities provide various food venues and entertainment options along with camping sites and housing options."

"Go on."

"Historically, these overnight host cities try to outdo each other in terms of hospitality and recreational opportunities," Shelby explained. "For example, one year a town actually brought in snow-making machines. Their theme was Christmas in July. They had all kinds of holiday booths and crafts. Another town put on an old-time fair and carnival. This year you'll see things like street dances, sand volleyball tournaments, talent competitions, and donkey softball."

"Donkey softball?" I snorted. "The town can stop looking for a shortstop," I said. "I'm sharing a bicycle with the perfect jackass."

"Would you get serious, Turner?" Stan said.

"I am serious!"

"Can we get back to the pertinent details?" Shelby asked.

I did a mea culpa number and held out my hand, palm up.

"You have the floor, Yeoman."

Shelby shook her head. "The daily ride distance will range anywhere from a minimum of roughly thirty-nine miles to the longest day total of around sixty-six miles."

I felt my throat passage thicken and my breathing passages narrow.

"Wait a minute. Did you say sixty-six miles? Sixty-six miles in one day?"

"I thought you said you'd done your homework," Shelby said.

"I've never been good with numbers." Especially big numbers that translated into enormous pedal revolutions.

"Let's move it along," Stan said, looking at his watch.

"The ride concludes with the traditional dipping of the rear tire in the Mississippi River at the final host city," Shelby concluded. "I understand you already have your cycling shoes."

I nodded. "I'm not altogether satisfied with the color," I began. "You see, they're black and blue. Not feel-good colors considering the circumstances."

Stan ruled on my objection with a barked, "Next!"

"Now, you have gone over the checklist. Right?" Shelby asked.

"Checklist?"

Shelby slid a list across the table.

"It's a pretty generic list. You'll need to individualize it to suit your needs. I've taken the liberty of adding several items that I've learned, via word of mouth, can be helpful."

I scanned the list closer.

"Extra large trash bags, shower cap, baby powder, nose kote, ear plugs?"

"Trash bags are handy to use as a rain poncho. The shower cap goes on your bike seat, not your head, to keep it from getting wet in case of rain. The ear plugs are to help you sleep in a noisy campground."

"And the baby powder?"

"Trust me. You don't want to know, Turner," Stan said.

"Baby powder or talcum powder can be used to prevent...shall we say, diaper rash?" Shelby offered.

I flinched. Diaper rash? What the hell was I letting myself in for?

"You forgot jock itch," Stan chipped in. "But you don't have to worry about that, Turner. Just the rash. And maybe athlete's foot fungus."

Oh, hell, no.

"What kind of bike ride is this?" I asked.

"One where an ounce of prevention is well worth the pound of cure when you're talking diaper rash, Turner," Stan said.

"Baby powder. Gotcha," I said.

"Did you tell her about the underpants thing?" Stan asked Shelby.

I stared at Stan. "What underpants thing?"

"Exactly," Stan said, with a grin that brooked no good for an uneasy rider.

I looked at Shelby. "What underpants thing?"

Shelby took a deep breath. "Well, you do know with bike shorts—I mean, I don't want to be indelicate here, but—"

"But what?"

"You don't wear underpants when you wear bike shorts."

I looked at Stan. "Is this another one of your sick ideas of a joke?"

"Who? Me?" Stan raised his hands, palms out. "Hell, no. I didn't have a clue either. Shelby Lynn told me about it."

I turned back to Shelby. "You're joking, right?"

She shook her head back and forth. "You pretty much negate the benefits of biking shorts if you wear underwear," she said. "Something about aerodynamics and the motion of sliding back and forth on the bike seat."

"Less friction," Stan said with an evil grin.

I winced and looked back down at the list with a sense of dread.

"Toilet paper?"

"Self-explanatory," Stan said.

Could it get any worse?

"Do you have a fanny pack?" Shelby Lynn asked, and I felt my left eye begin to twitch. I have a fanny pack aversion. I had a very bad experience with one at the state fair last year. Since then, I have avoided them religiously.

"Why?"

"Because a fanny pack is essential in the overall biking experience."

"The hell you say?"

"You obviously can't carry a purse on the ride. You can wear a backpack, but it will be bulky and uncomfortable. What's the big deal anyway?"

The big deal was I vowed never to be caught dead in a fanny pack again.

Okay. Given my impending bike trek over hundreds of miles of pavement, perhaps I should amend that last statement.

This cowgirl don't wear no stinkin' fanny pack.

"Everyone will be wearing a fanny pack. Suck it up."

"I'm sure Drew Van Vleet has matching ones made up with the *Star Trek* emblem on them," Stan said. "Won't that be special, Turner?"

I mumbled a few words that wouldn't survive radio or TV's seven-second delay and promised myself a good, old-fashioned fanny pack campfire the last day of TribRide.

"What about food and lodgings?"

"A tent will be provided."

Hell. Stan hadn't been kidding.

"A tent? One tent?"

"One for each of you," Shelby elaborated.

Thank God.

"You do know how to pitch a tent, right, Turner?" Stan asked.

"I've been camping before," I said. Besides, how hard could it be? "Now about meals and necessities—"

Stan rubbed a hand over his eyes. "Oh, God. She's gonna bankrupt me."

"Now, about the waiver—" Shelby said.

"Waiver?"

"We're heading into uncharted territory here, Turner," Stan said. "And we can't be too careful."

I made a face. "What do you mean 'we'? Are you planning to hitch a ride on the handlebars, Stan? Last I knew I was the only one at this table heading into the great unknown on a flimsy, two-wheeled contraption with zero airbags and Khan at the helm."

"Khan?"

"The super villain from *Star Trek*. You need to get out more, Stan. See a movie once in a while. Something other than Dragnet reruns."

"Funny, Turner. Now sign the waiver."

"What exactly am I waiving?"

"It's a generic waiver of liability," Stan mumbled. "Standard stuff. It holds the *Gazette* harmless from liability stemming from any incident—man-made, woman-made, Mother-Nature made, act of God originated, that results in injury, loss of life, property damage, etc. As I said, pretty standard stuff."

I raised an eyebrow. "I see." I looked over at Shelby. "Would you sign it?"

She hesitated. "I probably would, but I don't have your...predisposition for...uh, mishaps to consider."

"Don't worry, Turner. We've got you covered." Stan said. "Literally." He winked. "In exchange for your waiver signature, you will receive a very broad, all-encompassing insurance policy that covers you from now until you dip your tire in the Mississippi. All paid for by your generous sponsors."

Insurance policy? All-encompassing?

Pen in hand, I bit my lip.

"Before I sign..."

"Yeah?" Stan said.

"That thing about the underpants and the baby powder—"

"Yeah?"

"It doesn't leave this room."

Stan nodded.

"Where do I sign?"

TribRide: Where no Calamity has gone without underpants before.

And lived to tell.

CHAPTER NINE

My bags were packed. I was ready to go.

I considered belting into that sappy sixties song I'd hear my gammy warble when she was channeling her inner flower child, but, frankly, I felt like singing about as much as I felt like giving up beer and chocolate.

The no-escape noose was tightening around my neck like a hackamore bit on the nose of a high-strung stud, my final hours of freedom dissolving like a Trekkie crew through a transporter.

TribRide loomed—a gargantuan black hole in the galaxy, ready to suck this novice in like so much space debris.

Danger, Will Robinson. Danger! Danger!

With Shelby Lynn's help, I'd started a competing blog to counter Drew Van Vleet's site. The guy had made a photographic record of every preparation for the ride—and every Tressa Turner pothole moment.

I'd been immortalized down and dirty in the ditch, pitted out and sporting a Bozo frizz below my helmet after my ponytail came loose. I'd been photographed spewing water, wiping sweat, dozing in the grass, and—humiliation of humiliations, pulling a wedgie out of my whazoo. On multiple occasions. From various angles.

I'd finally received the promised 4G phone. From my ultra-exclusive backseat vantage point, there was a decent chance I'd be treated to views of Van Vleet's pale, ugly butt crack from time to time. I planned to post each and every crack shot with the urgency of a breaking news flash. Get it? Flash? As in *flasher*? Oh. You did? You're good.

I'd survived Stan's last briefing—basically a reminder to use the cash card conservatively and to avoid *impugning* the reputation of the *Gazette*. I had to Google that one. It took a while. I kept leaving the g out.

Once final instructions had been given—and my pleas for an alternate pathway to a pay raise summarily rejected, (I'd suggested something more up my alley like an America's Rodeo Sweetheart competition) this *stroker* had been deemed road worthy.

Yeah. Right.

Our elusive sponsors (I had yet to find out just who the sadists were.) had made arrangements for our transportation and gear to be delivered to the ride's starting point. A local bike shop had been commissioned to deal with any mechanical kerfuffles that arose.

We were good to go.

"Good" so being a relative term here.

I finished up the barnyard chores, mucking out the last stall and putting down fresh straw. My mother would be feeding and watering the animals in my absence. It made sense considering one of them belongs to her. Queen of Hearts, a flashy sorrel Quarter mare with a striking white blaze is my mum's horse. I stuck with the male of the species: Blackjack (or "Jack" when he's behaving himself) a half-Quarter-half-Morgan, and Joker, a lovable goofball Appaloosa-Quarter.

I left the stall, put my pitchfork away, and grabbed the curry comb and brush and headed outside to give each of the horses a quick grooming.

"Wait your turn, Jack!" I pushed the dark horse's head away. "I'll get to you!"

Our horses are like pets. They tend to follow you around hoping for a handout and some attention.

I patted Joker's neck. Joker held a special place in my heart. I'd learned to ride on Joker—could do anything on the horse. I'd come close to losing the old boy last year when a psycho's bullet narrowly missed me and struck the Appaloosa instead.

There was hell to pay, I can tell you.

"Blackjack! Stop that!" I swatted the air near my backside. "I said to wait your turn."

A sudden tugging in the center of my waistband hauled me backwards and practically off my feet.

"What the—?"

I looked around.

Rick Townsend, one hand still inside the waist of my jeans, laughed down at me.

"Blackjack's innocent," Townsend said. "I'm the guilty party."

The touch of his fingers inside the waistband of my jeans sent a shiver clean down to my toes.

"I see. So what do you think the punishment should be?" I asked and turned slightly. He reached up to cup my elbow with his other hand.

"I don't know. I've been a very naughty boy." He grinned.

This time I felt the warmth of a blush all the way to my toes.

"I usually give Jack a quick bop on the nose or a tap with the quirt when he's ornery," I said.

"The quirt sounds kinkier," Townsend said with a Groucho Marx lift of his eyebrows.

"It also leaves marks," I informed him.

"Oh? Like a brand?" he asked.

I felt a renewed flush of heat at the idea of Ranger Rick wearing a Tressa Turner brand.

"Isn't that raccoon tat sufficient body art?" I asked, a reference to a cute raccoon tattoo Ranger Rick had gotten on a certain fleshy—and flashy—part of his body, the result of a bet we made and I won.

He grabbed my other arm and turned me around to face him.

"I still think you should get a matching tattoo," he said.

I shook my head. "If I choose to desecrate my flesh, it'll be with a critter I'm more partial to than Ricky Raccoon," I said, wishing I'd known he was going to drop by. When you're up close with a hottie, you'd rather not smell like manure, mighty mutts, and horse. "So, what brings you out this way?"

"I wanted to wish you luck. I hear you're heading west later today."

I nodded. I planned to catch a ride with Taylor and Frankie. No way was I spending an additional two hours in Drew Van Vleet's company. We'd practically be joined at the hip for the next week as it was. No sense extending the torture.

"We're leaving after lunch. That'll give me time to finish here and shower. I'm going to help get the Freeze Mobile set up. I guess traditionally there's a TribRide eve shindig planned."

Beer. Brats. A country band. A good ol' girl's down-home good time.

"I'd hoped to have some time to take you out with the tandem and give you some tips," Townsend said, reaching up and tucking a stray, sweaty curl behind my ear. "But this week's been a bear what with state-wide firearms and CPR recertification. I don't like the idea of you riding without proper preparation."

"That's okay. Van Vleet's been a real pain in the padded bike shorts," I said. "He had us out from dawn to dusk, stopping and starting. Mounting, dismounting. Going up hills and down hills. Turning left. Turning right." I felt my body move side to side and up and down with each verbal cue. Ugh. I'd better add motion sickness pills to the checklist.

"It's good that you'll have Taylor there to keep an—" Townsend left the rest unsaid. Probably because I'd turned from putty in his arms to Play-Doh that's been left out too long.

"Keep an eye on me? Is that what you were going to say?" I asked. "Need I remind you, Mr. Ranger, Sir, that I happen to be the big sister in the Turner pecking order? If anyone should be keeping an eye on someone, it should be I. Er...me."

Son of a...gun.

Like a bad penny, the old insecurity was back. Just when I thought I'd proven I was capable of looking out for myself, someone, by word or by deed, would resurrect those old familiar doubts, and I was right back to Miss Righteous Indignation.

Déjà doubt time all over again.

"That's not what I meant, Tressa," Rick said, alerted to the need for damage control. "I just feel better knowing you have family going along for the ride. That's all. I'd feel that way about any novice rider."

"Novice rider?"

That's what I was to him? A *novice rider*?

Okay. On one level, I realized I was being deliberately difficult. But the stress of the last several weeks—not the least of which was the post-cruise, post-coital second-guessing—had my innards knotted up worse than the macramé hanging planter holders Gram tried to make two years ago.

"Novice *bicycle* rider," Townsend clarified. "But, put you on a horse—or in a cruise ship cabin—and your riding is anything but amateur hour."

I could feel my backbone give slightly. Tell me. What cowgirl wouldn't want to be praised on her…riding ability?

"I was thinking," Townsend said, lowering his mouth to nuzzle my neck. "Maybe we could finish what we started the other night. You know. When your mother came bearing junk food. You mentioned a shower…"

I swallowed way loud. "You might be right," I said. "It's probably not a good thing to leave things…unfinished." My breath now came in fits and starts. "You know. Considering I'll be…unavailable in the short term."

Townsend sighed against my ear and brought his hands up to cup the sides of my face. "I'm hoping to make you unavailable in the long term," he whispered.

What? Wait! What was that? What did he say? My thoughts ricocheted off each other like spastic pinballs. He couldn't mean—

Steady, girl. Steady.

For a long moment, he looked into my eyes, the level of intensity in his gaze apparent from how his irises grew darker and darker.

I couldn't look away.

"What…are…you…saying?" I managed to squeak out.

Blackjack suddenly shoved his nose between Townsend and me.

Whop!
Snort!
Bl…oo…w!

"Ugh!" Strings of mucous and gobs of gunk covered Townsend's face. "Son of a b—! What the hell?"

I shoved Blackjack's head away

"Blackjack! No!"

Jack nudged Townsend's shoulder again, leaving behind a big patch of greenish, white spittle.

"Jack, go away! Go! Move!" I shoved the big horse away.

"Oh, God, Townsend. What a mess! I'm so sorry!"

Townsend shook his head and put a hand up to his face.

"That's all right. I needed a shower," he said. "You know, I don't think your horses like me much."

"Only Jack," I said. "He gets jealous."

Townsend grabbed a handkerchief out of his back pocket and wiped it across his forehead and eyes.

I looked at his uniform. "Ugh. Your shirt. It's gonna need professional cleaning," I told him. "That green is pasture grass."

"Maybe we could go in and put it to soak," Rick suggested with that telltale Townsend gleam in his eye.

"We could do that."

"Besides, I have something to give you."

I felt my toes curl in my boots. "I'll bet you do," I managed. "I'll just put the comb and brush away."

I hurried to the barn and tossed the grooming tools on the bench and shut the barn door behind me, stopping to appreciate the picture Townsend made as he leaned on the barnyard gate, trying to make nice with Blackjack, who, unfortunately, was having none of it.

God, he was a looker. Townsend, that is, not Blackjack. Which is not to say Jack isn't a striking piece of horseflesh. Oh, you know what I meant.

I sighed.

Am I in love, or am I in lust?

I'd asked myself that question before. I was still waiting for the answer.

Townsend's words echoed in my head.

I have something to give you.

Oh, God. Was I ready?

I was about to say, "Yes! Yes! Hell, yes!" when the sound of an engine snared my attention. I started across the barnyard, catching sight of a mammoth-sized vehicle pulling into the driveway.

What in the world?

I blinked once, twice, when I saw the huge lettering on the side of a bus that had to be a city block long.

"Keelie and Company," I read.

"What the hell is that?" Townsend asked when I joined him

at the gate.

I shook my head. "I have no idea."

The bus stopped. Gravel rose in white swirls around it.

"Keelie and Company? As in Keelie Keller?" Townsend asked.

I shrugged. "Search me."

"What would Keelie Keller's bus be doing in your driveway?"

"Search me," I repeated.

The air brakes sounded and the engine stopped.

I reached out and pulled myself over the top of the gate. Townsend copied my move, and we walked toward the bus.

"That's one big ol' bus," Townsend observed.

I nodded.

A big, fancy bus with dark windows and "a celeb sleeps here" written all over it.

The seconds ticked by.

I was just about to bang on the door and demand to know what the hell was going on when the sound of a microphone being pegged over a loudspeaker stopped me in my tracks.

I looked at Townsend and frowned, waiting. A voice came over a loudspeaker on the bus.

"Biker Barbie need a lift? Your chariot awaits."

I stared at the bus, stared at Townsend, who stared at the bus and then stared at me.

"Is that Manny DeMarco?" Townsend said. "What the hell is he doing here, and what the hell is he doing driving that thing?" He pointed to the vehicle filling my driveway.

I winced. Then lifted one shoulder and bit my lip.

Giving Cinder-Tressa her very own pumpkin coach transport to TribRide was my guess.

Who said chivalry was dead?

CHAPTER TEN

"Barbie getting bus sick?" Manny sent a quick glance over at me in the oh-so-comfy co-pilot's seat—having rejected outright my request to take a turn behind the wheel. Surprise. Surprise.

"Why? Do I look sick?"

"Barbie looks…pensive."

I raised an eyebrow. Pensive? Not a word I expected to hear Manny DeMarco utter. I shrugged. "I'm good."

"Barbie like the ride?" Manny asked.

I nodded. "Barbie likes. Barbie likes a lot." In fact, my inspection of Keelie Keller's top of the line custom motor coach left little to criticize other than the fact that it had me hankering for more than a nibble of how the "other half" lived.

Hey, tell me you wouldn't crave a go at the good life.

"So. Manny. You're the bus driver? I said, starting to flip open various overhead compartments to explore the contents, nosing into all the nooks and crannies within arm's reach. Okay. Listen. I'm a journalist. I look into things. It's what I do.

"Manny's no bus driver."

I raised an eyebrow.

"*Oo*kay. Not a bus driver. Got it." Jeesch. People can be so touchy. "So, you're just delivering the vehicle."

Manny shot me a look. "Manny's not a deliveryman."

Hmmm. Maybe I'd have to learn what Manny was by eliminating what he wasn't.

"Okay. Procurer then," I said.

He shook his head.

"Transportation chief? Chauffeur? Event planner?"

Manny grunted. "Facilitator," he finally said.

I made a face. "Facilitator? What does that mean exactly?"

"Barbie's got her dream phone. Barbie can Google it."

A bittersweet feeling of pain tinged with regret hit me. Since I'd first met Manny a year ago, he'd called me "Barbie." In fact, he'd only just started calling me "Tressa" during our recent fateful cruise where I'd realized for the first time that Manny DeMarco-Dishman had more than faux feelings for his make-believe bride-to-be.

Once our pretend betrothal ended, and I'd made up my mind to see where things went with a certain ranger-type, I was back to being "Barbie."

"'Facilitator: Someone who enables a process to happen; an organizer and provider of services for a meeting, seminar, or other event,'" I read from my smartee-pants phone display. "How is that different from an event planner?" I asked, not about to let an opportunity to learn more about Manny the mystery man pass me by.

"Manny doesn't plan. Manny...*anti*-plans," he said.

I wrinkled my nose. "You...*anti*-plan? You mean like contingency planning?"

He stared out the front of the bus for a long time before his eyes met mine once again in the massive mirror.

"Manny prevents the need for contingencies," he said. He handed me a wrapped candy from a container on the dash, apparently signaling that this subject was closed.

I unwrapped the candy.

"Barbie check out the fridge yet?" Manny asked.

Ah. Manny was trying to divert me with food. Maybe I was getting too close for his comfort.

"Not yet." I popped the thin, sweet square into my mouth and sighed. Ahh. Quality chocolate.

"Barbie's off her game," Manny said.

"Oh? Well-stocked, huh?"

Manny gave me a "what part of *luxury* did you miss?" look.

"Beer?"

"The good stuff."

"I'm so there!" I made my way to the kitchen area—moving like an inebriated airline passenger on their way to the john. I opened the fridge. And almost wet my pants. Bottle after bottle featuring Blue Moon's pale blue label greeted this Bud Lite devotee.

I picked up a bottle. "Sweet," I said.

"That's not the good stuff," Manny said.

I raised an eyebrow. "It isn't?"

"Check out Tut."

I frowned. "Tut?" I checked out the fridge again, pulling out a bottle that featured labels with hieroglyphic-like symbols.

"*Tutankhamen Ale*," I read.

"That's the one."

"I've never heard of it."

"Barbie wouldn't," Manny stated.

"What's the big deal with this beer?" I asked.

"Barbie knows the story of King Tut, right?"

"Who doesn't?"

"The recipe comes from Tut's stepmom, Queen Nefertiti's, royal brewing chambers."

"You're kidding."

"Manny doesn't kid. Brewing chambers uncovered in a dig contained remains of the Queen's brew."

"You're kidding." Wow! Apparently the Queen enjoyed tipping a cold one way back, too.

"Scientists analyzed the beer. Came up with the recipe."

Holy tomb raider! This brought a whole new meaning to "handing down the recipe".

"Then this beer has to cost a pretty penny," I surmised.

"Try a lot of pretty pennies," Manny noted.

"Oh? So, how much does a bottle of beer like this run?" I asked.

"Barbie doesn't want to know," Manny said. "Barbie would only make herself miserable."

Ah. The old "ignorance is bliss" bit. The concept was not...unfamiliar.

"How much?"

"Fifty-two dollars a bottle. *If* you can get it."

I almost dropped King Tut.

I gripped Tut with both hands and ever so carefully replaced the ancient of ales and stepped slowly away from the not-so-mini fridge.

"Barbie chicken out?" Manny asked.

More like Barbie could be opening a can of worms if she opened that bottle and developed a taste for the very good stuff.

"Too rich for my expense account," I said. I could see the fireworks now if I submitted a receipt to Stan for a fifty-dollar bottle of beer.

On the other hand, where was the harm in having a bit of fun at Stingy Stan's expense?

I grabbed my phone, hit the camera button, opened the fridge again, and cautiously removed the Valley of the Kings brew. I put it to my lips, held the camera up and hit the little camera icon.

Click.

A few maneuvers later and the picture appeared on my blog where Stan was sure to see it and go ballistic.

I gently set Tut back where I found him.

"Blue Moon's more Barbie's speed," Manny said.

I eyed the Blue Moon bottles lined up on the refrigerator shelf.

"Three bucks each tops," Manny said.

"You're sure it's okay?" I asked.

"Go for it," Manny said.

I grabbed a bottle, sashayed over to the luxurious sectional and sat. I lifted the bottle to my lips.

"Ahh. This is the life," I said, sitting back and surveying the splendor, not one bit guilt-ridden for giving up my seat in Uncle Frank's Suburban in lieu of this sweet ride. I brought the bottle to my lips again and felt the bulge of the small box Rick had given me before we'd said our goodbyes.

I set the bottle in a built-in beverage holder and reached for the small package. I examined it.

It couldn't be a ring.

Could it?

It didn't look like a ring box.

I performed a mental head bump. I was at it again, imagining things—connecting dots that didn't go together—leapfrogging to far-fetched, fairy tale endings that proved to be no more than a children's fable.

An amateur profiler could see a pattern here.

I'd done the same thing on the cruise—with near fatal

results.

Now here I was again. Making assumptions. Reading more into the story. Losing perspective. Tressa Turner's very own production of *Fantasy Island: The Sequel*.

I took another long drink of Blue Moon—an apt ale given my present angst—and unwrapped the package. Tucked inside was a silver chain. I pulled the chain out and held it in front of me. Attached to the chain was a delicate, adorable, infinitely precious raccoon.

Tears stung my eyes, the lovely tell-tale nose drip threatening to drip-drop at any moment. Damn. If I didn't get a grip, I would be literally crying in my beer.

I snuffed up the snot and cradled the raccoon charm in my hand. I turned it over. Inscribed on the back were two words: *For luck*.

I made a grab for the tissues housed in another built-in and mopped at my eyes and nose.

"Biker Barbie okay?" Manny asked, checking me out in the rear-view mirror.

Was I?

Let's recap:

My parents were on the outs.

My sister was playing word games with my psyche.

My Maybe Mr. Right was keeping me guessing.

And me?

I was about to explore a strange, new world: A redshirted, Trekkie stroker spinning across Iowa on a fire engine red bicycle built for two.

Hmm. Was I okay?

I am a Vulcan.

I feel no pain.

CHAPTER ELEVEN

"Isn't this something? Look at all these people! This is insane!"

I took a drink of my draft and made a face. The observation came from a wannabe cowgirl who looked all of twelve.

Hmm.

Insane...

A biking virgin agrees to ride a tandem across Iowa in July?

If it looks like a duck, walks like a duck, quacks likes a duck...

Yup.

Insanity.

And that flirtation with madness currently found me sardined inside a vast, canopied tent-like structure in the middle of a Boy Scout camp that bordered the wide Missouri, drinking beer (so not the good stuff), munching on peanuts, and listening to a so-so country western band twang a totally lame TribRide version of Willie Nelson's oldie, but goodie about being on the road again.

Don't get me wrong. Normally, you give me a beer, some munchies, and a good ol' boy band playing a song you can two-step to, and I'm as happy as my labs when I bring them "lab leftovers" from Uncle Frank's kitchen.

Normally, I wasn't facing the sobering prospect of a statewide tandem bike ride with a journalistic jerk with a grudge.

All right. So I'd made Drew Van Vleet look like the contemporary equivalent of the journalist who'd proclaimed some other dude president when Truman actually won. It was like that song I couldn't get out of my head.

He'd had it comin'.

He only had himself to blame.

And how long could someone hold an unfair, unfounded, and unreasonable grudge anyway?

I thought about my gammy and her nemesis Abigail Winegardner.

To infinity and beyond. That's how long.

Thanks to my man of mystery, I'd ridden in style to the kick-off city. Once Manny dropped me off at the Mini-Freeze location and we got the stand open for business, I'd vamoosed. Uncle Frank had agreed to spring for a hotel room (one room for all four of us, the big spender) for TribRide eve. The remainder of the week, Frankie, Dixie, and Taylor would be pitching a tent like the rest of us, or sacking out in the Suburban.

I'd showered and slipped into denim shorts, a T-shirt featuring a black silhouette of a cowgirl kicking it up that said, "It's all in the boots", and my comfiest pair of slouch boots. I plopped one of my favorite Stetsons—the one that sported a totally cool, black and turquoise band—on my head. I might be consigned to wearing a Trekkie Tee, padded pedal pushers, pedal-friendly footwear, and a dorky-looking bike helmet during the ride, but dang if I was going to hang out in a beer tent wearing tennies and hatless.

After all, this cowgirl had a reputation to uphold.

I looked around and frowned. I stuck out like my gammy on Easter Sunday. Bless her heart, each spring Gram embarks on a search for the perfect Easter bonnet. Last year's creation had a brim so wide we had to leave the seats on either side of her open.

"Hey you! Blondie! Calamity! Calamity Jayne!"

I turned my head in the direction of the call and was rewarded with a click and a camera flash.

"What the—!"

"Thought I'd better commit the pre-TribRide Tressa Turner to photographic memory," Dixie Daggett, also known as The Destructor, said. "You know. To immortalize the moment. Just in case of..." She raised her shoulders. "Well, whatever."

"I thought this get-together was for registered riders only. What are you doing here?" I asked.

"Vendors pay a fee so we're comped," Dixie said. She pointed at my beer. "What's that? Liquid courage?"

"Seriously? Since when do I need a reason to drink beer?" I said.

"Oh. So you're not even the least bit apprehensive about the ride?"

"Apprehensive? Do I look apprehensive?" I followed the query with a hearty gulp of beer. Unfortunately, it dribbled down my chin.

"Oh, no. You don't look the least bit nervous. In fact, you exude confidence and aplomb."

Aplomb?

"Why, you're just...full of it," Dixie went on.

I resisted the urge to accidentally spill my beer on her. Hey, it's beer, after all.

"I'm surprised you could take time off from your law enforcement academy pursuits to cater to cyclists," I observed. "What's up with that?"

"I've finished all the application requirements, and I'm just waiting for Public Safety to make offers," Dixie said. "Besides, I wouldn't miss Tressa Turner's Tandem TribRide for anything."

Great. I'd have Dixie Daggett dogging my tail across the state.

"Speaking of duos, where *is* your fiancé?" I asked. "You are still engaged, right?"

Dixie lifted her brow. Yes, that's right. I said *brow*. You know. As in *unibrow*.

"You know perfectly well we're still together," she said.

"Just checking," I said.

"Right." Dixie grabbed a handful of nuts. "We all were surprised to see you climb down out of that bus yesterday. We were even more surprised to see who had delivered you in said motor carriage. Manny DeMarco? Word on the street has it Manny took you by surprise by showing up on the little honeymoon cruise. Now, he shows up here in a customized bus and, lo and behold, who should step out but Grandville's answer to Baba Wawa, Calamity Jayne Turner."

"Was it a good surprise or a bad surprise?" I asked, not exactly thrilled with the blatant speculation concerning my love life.

"That's what *I'd* like to know," Dixie asked. "What exactly is going on between you and that guy?"

"Which guy?"

"Okay, I'll play. Just what are you doing hanging out with Manny DeMarco?"

"No comment," I said.

"Okay. How are things going with your new step-cousin then?" Dixie said.

I winced. That just sounded...wrong.

"There you are. I see you found her." My cousin, Frankie, walked up and wrapped a long, gangly arm around his fiancée's shoulders. He gave me one of his goofy grins. "Tomorrow's the big day," he said. "So. Tressa. How are you? Are you ready to r...r...rumble?"

"More like tumble," Dixie offered.

Frankie shook his head. "No, really. How *are* you, Tressa?"

I made a face. "How are you, Tressa? Are you ready, Tressa? Do you have a helmet, Tressa? A living will? Life insurance? Jeesh, guys. Give me a break, would you? What part of 'bike ride' are you missing?"

"Maybe the part where this bike ride goes on despite rain, heat, wind, hail, thunder, and, sometimes lightning, if you're really unlucky. Or that this particular ride historically averages sixty to seventy plus miles a day or four hundred seventy-five miles total," Dixie observed. "And, that this bike ride—"

"Thanks for the illuminating information, Ms. Statistician," I cut her off like a jagged toenail.

"You can't blame us for being...skeptical, Tressa," Frankie said. "It's a lofty undertaking."

"Like getting into the peace officer academy?" I suggested. "Hmm. Let's go back in time. Back to a time in the not-so-distant past when you aspired to such *lofty* heights—and where, if memory serves, your beloved and loyal cousin gave you unconditional support—this despite her own sense of er...skepticism."

To this day, just the memory of Frankie's grim performance on the state public safety academy obstacle course made me wince. The photographic evidence I shot that day? Well, it was enough to give you the willies.

"Well, uh, er, since you put it like that," Frankie stammered.

"Oh, please. You had a calendar made from the pictures you took of Frankie on the obstacle course," Dixie pointed out.

"It was meant as a light-hearted gift," I explained. "A funny scrapbook moment to look back on later in life."

"Really? Like Frankie wants to remember flip-flopping around on the ground in the middle of a row of tires like a bluegill out of water," Dixie said.

"It was a private family joke," I told her. "Frankie gets it."

"Oh? And I don't get it because I'm not family," Dixie said.

I lifted one shoulder. "Not yet. At least, not officially. However, rest assured, once you tie the knot, you too will become fair game for my little gag gift proclivities," I assured her.

"'Gag' being the key word here," Dixie said. "Thanks for the warning, Miss Practical Joker. Just bear in mind that no good deed goes unpunished."

"A sentiment worthy of toasting!" I raised my glass. "Here's to good deed doers!" I gave a quick salute before draining the contents. A burp that could have come from a man twice my size resulted.

"Biker Barbie better lay off the beer. Beer and bikes don't make a good combo for the road, if you get Manny's drift."

I turned. Manny DeMarco stood over me, arms crossed, biceps bulging.

"Oh. Hey, Manny. I didn't think you went for the boot scootin' boogie scene," I said. "What's up?"

"Gotta be here, Barbie. Job's here."

I gaped. "Wait! What? Keelie Keller is *here*?" I grabbed one of his arms of steel and hoisted myself to my tippy-toes and peered around the room. "Where? Where?"

"Reel it in, would you, Miss Celeb Stalker?" Dixie said. "You're attracting attention."

From where I stood (in Manny's enormous shadow, that is) it seemed like Manny was the one attracting the most attention. His massive physique and tall, dark, and dangerous good looks bill-boarded "bad boy" and made the guy a chick magnet of epic proportions. His own, uh, er, own epic proportions didn't hurt.

Manny checked his watch. "Runnin' late," he said, with a slight shake of his head. "Typical woman."

I poked him in the chest. Okay. So I *tried* to poke him in the chest. It was like poking plywood.

"There are no typical women, Mr. DeMarco," I responded.

Manny DeMarco smiled down at me. "If you say so...Barbie."

Barbie. The distance one little word created.

"How'd you get such a sweet gig, Manny?" Frankie asked. I saw Dixie's head pivot in Frankie's direction like a heat-seeking missile.

"Sweet gig?" Dixie said. "You think providing security for some big-boobed publicity whore is a sweet gig?"

"And presto!" I said with a wave of my hand in Frankie's direction. "May I present what is known as your typical *male*?"

"I didn't say it was *my* idea of a sweet gig. You know, for *me*," Frankie's sudden fancy footwork put the two-steppers on the dance floor to shame. "I meant it was a sweet gig for a, uh, single guy, you know. Like Manny here."

"Right," Dixie said. "Right."

Manny suddenly put a hand to his right ear.

"Yo. 'k. Got it."

I frowned.

"What are you doing? What's that in your ear?" I asked. "Who are you talking to?"

"Gotta go."

"Is that a headset?" I asked. "You're outfitted with electronic headsets? What is this? Men in Biker Black? Manny DeMarco, Junior G-Man?"

"Standard security equipment," Manny said.

For Sarah Palin maybe. For a reality celeb? Overkill.

"Oh? Is that right?" I said.

Manny shrugged. "Gotta look the part."

I narrowed my gaze.

"You've done this before, haven't you?"

Beyond a slight lifting of gi-normous shoulders, as usual, Manny DeMarco de-man-of-mystery gave nothing away.

"Manny catches on quick," Mr. Evasive said.

"What kind of qualifications did you have to have to get this 'sweet gig', Mr. DeMarco?" I asked. "You know. What kind of résumé?"

I'd Googled and Binged the guy until my fingers were calloused, and so far I hadn't discovered anything about Manny DeMarco/Dishman. It was just plain spooky. And frustrating as a swimsuit diet pledge undertaken just when the unsold Halloween candy went on markdown.

Manny grinned down at me. The bright white of his teeth almost blinded me.

"Like I've said before, Manny knows a guy." He recited his well-used mantra, as if that answered all my questions.

"You know a guy."

"Who knows a guy."

I nod. "I get it. Who knows a guy, who knows a guy, who knows hi-tech stuff."

My head hurt. The chance that I would get a straight answer from Manny DeMarco was the same as me suddenly growing manageable hair.

Manny put his hand to his ear again.

"Duty calls," he said.

"You mean your 'sweet' duty," Dixie hissed, shooting another dark look at Frankie.

Manny smiled. "See you," he said, and walked off, parting the crowd with Red Sea precision.

"What a guy," Frankie said, hero worship evident in the tiny bubble of drooly spit that collected in the corner of his mouth. He followed in Manny's wake like a devoted lap dog.

Dixie shot his retreating back another cold look before focusing her evil eye (yes, "eye"—as in Cyclops) on me.

"Just what is the deal with Manny?" she asked. "He's here. He's there. He comes. He goes. What is his story anyway?"

I blinked. Doth me detecteth an unlikely ally?

"You know. I've wondered the same thing, Dixie," I said. "The guy is all closed up. Tight-lipped. Beyond private."

"It's weird. Just plain weird." Dixie scratched her chin.

"It's what you call an enigma wrapped up in a riddle and tied with a chain and a padlock," I said.

"It's irritating as ass," Dixie stated.

"There is that," I agreed.

"You're supposed to be a reporter. Investigate."

"I've tried. I've dug 'til it hurts. His history reads like a blank page."

"How long have you known Manny anyway?" Dixie asked, and I gave an edited version of how I'd first met Manny at the Thunder Rolls bowling alley when investigating how a stiff found its way into my car's trunk. Actually, it wasn't *my* car. I just drove off in it by accident. But, yeah. Totally another story.

"It was after I bailed him out that we became…friendly," I said.

"You bailed the guy out."

"He paid me back."

"And there was that engagement…"

"*Faux* engagement. What would you have done? I thought his Aunt Mo was on her deathbed. I wanted to make the old girl's last hours on this earth happy ones. How was I to know she'd recover and live to become a wedding planner stowaway stalker?"

Dixie did an eye-roll number.

"Frankie thinks Manny is God's gift to mankind," I ventured.

"Tell me something I don't know."

"Wouldn't it be kind of nice to, er, remove Frankie's rose-colored glasses where Manny is concerned?" I said. "You know. Tarnish that crown Frankie has seen fit to bestow upon Manny just a wee little bit. Make your future spouse see that Manny, like all mortals, is human and, therefore, flawed."

Dixie tilted her head in my direction. "I'm listening."

"Perhaps we could be of…assistance to each other," I posed.

Curious Dixie disappeared. Hell No Dixie took her place.

"Have you forgotten what happened the last time I attempted to be of assistance to you?" she asked. "I barely survived the experience."

"Please. We weren't in any real danger. We were in a morgue. It's probably the safest place you can be."

"I'm talking about the campus psycho with the big, sharp knife." She shook her head. "People who 'assist' you don't usually end up with fond memories."

"I'm not sure that's the case—"

"Joe Townsend. Rick Townsend. Manny DeMarco. Shelby

Lynn Sawyer. Frank. Frankie. *Me*. And that's just in the last twelve months."

"Okay. Fine. Let Frankie continue to idolize a guy whose stock in chic trade is shrouded in mystery and intrigue," I said. "Never mind that exposing the truth behind the action figure could help keep your future husband's feet on the ground and on the straight and narrow, if you get my drift."

Dixie appeared to consider my words. She finally shook her head. "I can't believe I'm saying this, but what do you want me to do?"

"For now all you have to do is keep your *eye* and ears open." Snort. "Maybe chat up anyone affiliated with Keelie's reality show and find out how Manny got the gig in the first place. Anything you learn, pass on to me. Later we'll plan a covert ops or two and get some real dirt."

"Covert ops? You've been playing *Call of Duty* again, haven't you?"

I winced. Busted.

"Come on. It'll be fun," I assured her.

"What'll be fun?"

I turned. Taylor had joined us.

"The bike ride, of course,"

The smug, knowing look Dixie gave me told me she was on to my attempt to keep my sister out of this particular loop. The less Taylor knew, the better.

For me.

"Speaking of the bike ride, have you seen the hunky Trooper Dawkins yet?" I said. "I guess he's probably busy protecting and serving."

Taylor bit her lip. "He'll probably seek you out before me." She hesitated. "You aren't going to say anything to him about…anything. Right?"

"Me? No! Never. Certainly not. I won't say a word. Not a word."

"I'm feeling ill," Taylor said.

"Hey. What am I missing here?" Dixie asked. "I sense…sisterly conflict."

"Taylor's in lust with P.D. Dawkins," I said.

"I thought you weren't going to say anything!" Taylor

protested.

"Well, not to *him*," I said. "We have to play it cool. Keep it light. Keep it loose. Until we go in for the kill, that is."

"Brother. *I'm* gonna be sick now," Dixie said.

"Listen, Tressa. Please, just stay out of it. If something happens, it happens. Don't try to help me out. Okay?" Taylor pleaded.

"Hey. Chill, would you? It's gonna be fine. Your big sis has everything under control."

"Oh, God." Taylor groaned, and Dixie put her arm around her.

"Come on. We could both use a lemon-lime soda to settle our stomachs," Dixie said, and led my sister away.

I smiled.

Mystery. Romance. And a touch of Hollywood glam thrown in for good measure.

Is this the left coast?

Hell, no.

It's Iowa, pilgrim.

CHAPTER TWELVE

While not exactly working the room, I spent the next hour meeting, greeting, and eating—not necessarily in that order. I'd taken Manny's advice and switched to cola—my TribRide bracelet entitled me to free drinks and munchies, and I aimed to take advantage of that perk.

I eat when I'm nervous. Okay. So I also eat when I'm not nervous. However, the looming specter of a fifty-mile bike ride the next day had my mindless bingeing on hyper-drive—not a great idea when restroom facilities could end up being miles down the road.

How do you say "cornfield"?

I belched again, put a hand to my mouth, and looked around to see if anyone heard. I didn't need to worry. Everyone's attention was on a bus pulling into the parking lot next to the tent. Curious spectators crowded around the shiny, mile-long motor coach.

"Somebody's arriving in style," I heard.

"Ugh. Don't tell me it's some politician already out politicking for the caucuses next January," another person said.

"Maybe it's Elvis," another partier weighed in.

I migrated in the direction of the front window and took a seat at a recently vacated table. I looked out in time to see Manny muscle his way to the bus through the cluster of onlookers beginning to gather.

The bus door opened. Keelie Keller stepped out. She paused on the top step and looked down on the assembling crowd as if surveying her royal subjects. The sudden click, click, clicking of digital cameras and the hum of excited onlookers served as the cue for Keelie Keller to begin her slow descent from the bus.

Stocky men with cameras perched on their shoulders aimed

their bright lights at the striking redhead as she made an entrance fit for the Reality TV royalty she appeared to be.

I took a final swallow of cola, wiped a hand across my chin, permitted myself a quiet burp, and watched the princess of prime time greet her gaping, giggling groupies with a smile, a nod, and a wave. Towering head and shoulders (and, oh, what shoulders!) above Keelie, Manny DeMarco made like a human border fence, separating celeb from serfs. Close on Keelie's heels came her reality show cast of characters: feisty, finicky Tiara Fordham, and long-suffering Langley Carlisle.

"Just look at her! Ohmigosh! She's even more beautiful in person than she is on TV!"

I turned. The guy sharing the cheap seats with me stared at the star and her entourage with the same level of intensity my gammy showed when she was spying on Abigail Winegardner. A ginger himself—the short, freckled, and pasty-pale variety—this fan was practically panting at the sight of the glamorous redhead.

"Isn't she amazing?"

I couldn't resist an eye roll, followed by an "Oh, gawd."

"What? You don't think she's amazing?"

Uh-oh. The Ginger's ire was on the rise.

"I don't see what the big deal is. We all pull our britches on one leg at a time," I told him.

"How can you say that? Just look at her! She's…an…an angel."

A rather loud, prolonged raspberry escaped my lips before I could muffle it. "Puhlease."

"You don't know her like I do," the fan insisted.

I looked at him. "Really? You know her?"

He shrugged. "We sort of have a connection."

"Oh? What kind of connection?" I gave him a look of friendly interest, hoping I hadn't inadvertently insulted someone who might have some pull with the reality star that could help me score an interview.

Righto. And maybe I'd finish this bike ride in one piece, win the Pulitzer Prize for journalism, and unravel the snarl that was my tangled love life. (Betcha thought I was gonna say tangled hair, didn't you? Gotcha!)

"It's, uh, well, it's more along the lines of an, uh, psychic connection."

"A *psychic* connection?"

Bye, bye Pulitzer.

"It's hard to explain, but there's something special, something *real* between us, and when I heard she was going on TribRide, I just knew."

I frowned. "Knew? Knew what?"

"Knew that our paths were meant to intersect on TribRide," he explained. "It's providence. Destiny. Fate."

"Ah." I nodded. "I see."

What I *saw* was a star-struck dude several spokes short of a Schwinn.

I turned in my seat, as if looking for somebody—okay, anybody—to help me end the interaction without appearing rude.

"You're doing TribRide?" he asked, bringing his drink over to my table.

I nodded. "Rumor has it." I looked around some more. Where the hell was Dixie the Demon Slayer when you needed her?

"I wouldn't miss it for anything." His gaze still followed the progress of the celebs. "You on a team?" he asked.

"Team Trekkie," I said, thinking it sounded even more lame when you said it out loud.

"Wow. Cool name! I'm a Trekkie, too! Love that show!"

"Congratulations," I said.

"You've got Post-its printed up. Right?"

"Post-its?"

"To post at each host town so people know where to find you."

"Oh, yeah. Uh, no. We don't have any Post-it thingies."

Like I wanted to draw a map so people could find me. The fewer witnesses, the better, I say.

"Maybe we'll see each other on the ride."

"Yeah, maybe."

"You got a phone number?"

"I, uh, it's a new phone, and I don't—"

"Here's mine." He pulled a business card out of his fanny pack.

"Oh. Thanks." I looked at the card. "Kenny's Caricatures?"

"I'm an artist. A cartoonist. I do caricatures." He took out a felt tip pen, turned the business card over, and in a few short strokes, a frizzy-haired cowgirl complete with turned up nose, a bit of an overbite, and sporting a pretty nifty Stetson stared up at me.

"Wow. How do you do that?" I asked, envying his artsy gift. I totally go all green-eyed-monster on folks who draw, paint, or create objects-de-art. The best I can manage are stick figures—and most of the time they look more like freaky looking spiders than humans. Van Gogh, I isn't.

"Name's Kenneth. Kenneth Grey." The artiste held out his hand, and I got one of those handshakes that make you feel like you've taken hold of a large, overcooked noodle. Ugh. I supposed artists, much like pianists, brain surgeons, and hand models, had to protect their hands and digits. "It's Kenny for short, like the card says. And you are?"

Before I could give him Dixie's name, my hat was yanked off my head.

I whirled around. Patrick Dawkins grinned down at me, my hat now sitting on his blonde head.

"Hey! That's my hat! Anyone know where to find a trooper so I can report a theft? Oh, wait. You *are* a trooper!"

Patrick grinned. "Tressa Turner. Am I glad to see you! Someone has been circulating scandalous rumors about you. I'm pleased to see they were unfounded."

"Trooper?" That got Kenny's attention. "You're a trooper?"

"Guilty," Patrick said, with a questioning tilt of his head in Kenny's direction.

"Oh. Sorry. This is Kenny Grey. He's doing TribRide, too." I showed him the business card drawing. "Kenny does drawings."

"Hey. How you doing? Oh. Look at the time. I have to go," Kenny said.

"Have a great ride," I said, staring at Kenny's back when he hurried away.

"New friend?" Dawkins asked.

I shrugged.

"Interesting fellow," he observed.

"You have no idea," I said. "So what was this scandalous rumor you made reference to?"

"You haven't heard about the wagers?"

I frowned. "Wagers? What wagers?"

"The pools at the Dairee Freeze. And the *Gazette*. And Hazel's."

"What *are* you talking about?"

"According to my sources, there are various wagers and pools being set up regarding your...TribRide experience." Patrick explained.

"Pools?"

"You know. Bets on when you'll take your first spill. How many days you'll get through before you quit. Wagers on whether you'll even show up. On how many tubes you'll go through."

"Bike tubes?"

Patrick had the good sense to look embarrassed. "Hemorrhoid cream," he said.

"What! The gall! The nerve!"

The sheer moneymaking genius!

"I see your buddy, Manny, over there. Security detail, huh?" Patrick observed.

"He knows a guy who knows a guy," I explain.

"He's done the security thing before," Patrick said.

I looked at him. "What do you mean?"

Patrick shrugged. "He looks like he knows what he's doing."

"How can you tell?"

"Well, for one thing, his eyes are always moving. He's always looking. And he makes a habit of watching people's hands."

"Hands?"

"It's what pros do. They focus on the movement of a person's hands. That way, they spot a threat sooner."

"And you say professional security personnel use this, er, technique?"

"Security, as well as professional law enforcement."

"Law enforcement?"

"Sure," Patrick said. "It's SOP for EPUs."

"Huh?"

"Standard operation for executive protection units," Dawkins translated.

"Is that right?"

Interesting. *Very* interesting.

"How are things going? You went on that cruise, right? Frankie mentioned something about a high seas mishap."

I nodded. "There was a bit of a storm at sea, but I weathered it."

Patrick laughed. "I don't doubt it for a minute."

"Taylor's around. Have you seen her?" I asked, doing just what my sister had warned me not to. Please. Isn't that what sisters are supposed to do?

"Oh, that's right. She's got Dairee Freeze duty." He looked around the beer tent. "She's here?"

"Dixie took her off somewhere. You should hang around. I'm sure they'll be back soon."

I gotta admit. My setting Taylor up for a change was strangely titillating.

Taylor had almost given my folks dual coronaries when she up and dropped out of college, claiming she wasn't sure what she wanted to do with her life. My folks were used to hearing that from their elder daughter. But Taylor? They were still reeling from the shock.

"Hello, you two. Are we interrupting?" Dixie, Taylor still in tow, appeared at the trooper's elbow.

"Of course not," I said. "We were just talking about you, Taylor. Were your ears burning?"

Maybe not. But the look she gave me was boil-me-in-oil hot.

"Tressa said you were here," Patrick removed my hat from his head, and held out a hand to Taylor. "Good to see you again, Taylor. It's been a while. How have you been?"

"Well, thank you," Taylor responded.

Oh, brother. Talk about your cool customers. If I didn't know better, I'd believe Taylor had no more interest in the handsome lawman than I do in becoming a vegan.

"Where's Frankie, by the way?" Patrick asked Dixie.

"Probably still sniffing after Manny DeMarco, and probably hoping to get a bone thrown to him." she grumbled.

A chorus of cat calls and whistles erupted from the dance floor of the beer garden where Keelie, Tiara, and Langley whooped it up with dance moves that told me none of the trio had ever stepped foot in a country western bar.

And that was probably a good thing.

"Talk about your fish out of water." Dixie echoed my thoughts, and I looked at her.

I made the sign of the cross with my fingers and held them out.

"Get out of my head, Demon Dixie!" I warned. She shook her head.

"Would you get a load of DeMarco?" Dixie continued. "Keelie's trying her best to convince him to join the party, but he's having none of it."

I got up on my tippy-toes to check it out. Dixie was right. Manny was putting off the same vibe I did when my gammy tried to convince me to join her circle of friends for water aerobics at the rec center.

"It's pathetic how low the bar for fame has fallen," Dixie went on. "Just pathetic."

"Uh-oh. Heads up." I chirped, watching the reality trio make their way in our direction. "Snooki wannabes at three o'clock!"

The cosmopolitan clique wound their way through the crowd, stopping on the fringes of our group.

"OMG! Is this state corny or what? Get it? Corny! Corny and like totally Dullsville." Keelie announced. "It's like that song. Corn, corn, corn, corn, corn! Look, a tree! Corn, corn, corn. Council Bluffs."

I wished I'd brought my earplugs to the party with me when Keelie, Tiara, and Langley broke into their version of the "Corn" song.

"Corn, corn, corn, corn, look, there's road kill!"

"Corn, corn, corn, corn, look, there's a cow!"

"Corn, corn, corn, corn, look, there's a pig!"

"Corn, corn, corn, corn, Manny, it's your turn!" Keelie sing-songed.

Manny's lip twitched. People who don't know any better might mistake it for a smile.

"Ah, come on, Manny. Don't be a party pooper," Keelie

said.

She poked Manny in the chest. "Manny here won't dance with me." She turned to our group, spotted a certain trooper. "So, how about you?"

"Uh, sorry. I'm engaged," Dixie intervened before I had a chance to chime in, "but if it doesn't work out, I'm all yours."

I found myself grinning like I did when I got my bank statement and I actually had a respectable balance.

Note to Reality Red: Diss Dixie Daggett's home state at your peril!

"As if," Keelie snorted and her hangers-on howled. "I'm talking to *him*." She pointed at Patrick. "You're cute. Well, for a farm boy. What about it? Wanna boot scoot?" She elbowed Tiara who giggled like crazy.

Patrick's face turned red. I could imagine the ribbing he'd get from his trooper buds if video of him kicking up his heels with Keelie Keller went viral. His superiors probably wouldn't be all that thrilled either.

I opened my mouth to help him out by telling them to take a hike, he was taken, when, once again, someone beat me to the blurt.

"He's with me," Taylor snapped.

It was hard to tell who turned to stare at her quicker—me or the trooper in distress.

"Did you hear that, Tiara? He's with *her*." Keelie crossed her arms and gave Taylor one of those look-you-up-and-down numbers. "Oh? And am I supposed to give a shit?"

I winced. I hoped they bleeped out the naughty words before airing.

"I have no idea whether you're supposed to give one or not," Taylor said. "I guess it depends on how you were raised."

Rrrear!

Cat fight! Cat fight!

Sensing a ratings booster in the making, the cameramen moved in for a closer shot.

"I thought you two were a couple," Keelie said, and motioned at Dixie.

"You thought wrong," Taylor said.

I looked from Keelie to Taylor.

Thirty seconds passed and no one blinked. Not even me. Worth the price of admission? You betcha.

"What's the hold up?" A dwarf of a man—roly-poly and reminding me of Danny DeVito with a bad toupee—stepped between Keelie and Taylor.

"Just pre-ride meet and greet, Vinny," Keelie said, still not taking her eyes off Taylor.

"We've got a schedule to keep, Keelie. Live blogging. Photos. Interviews. Tick-tock. Tick-tock! There'll be time for schmoozing up the local-yokels later."

"Ah, come on, Vinny. What are you? Keelie's manager or her mother?" Tiara whined.

Keelie gave Taylor a final stare down.

"To be continued," she said, and grabbed hold of Tiara's and Langley's arms and pulled her pals off in the direction of the bus. "Let's leave the hicks from the sticks to their red meat and corn pone, shall we?" she said.

I watched Keelie flounce her way up the stairs of her bus. When she reached the top, she stopped, turned around, and stuck both middle fingers up in our direction.

"Tressa?" Taylor put a hand on my shoulder.

"Yeah?"

"This week. On TribRide."

"Yes?"

"Whatever you do. Beat that biatch like a dusty saddle blanket."

I blinked.

What just happened?

My sister just punched my ticket to ride, that's what.

Gulp.

CHAPTER THIRTEEN

"A little help would be nice."

I turned a still-sleepy gaze to where Drew Van Vleet stood fidgeting with our tandem torture devise. I sighed. One of those "my life sucks" sighs the drama queens in all of us like to let loose with on a semi-regular basis.

I was down in the dumps even before I discovered Van Vleet *had* managed to find matching fanny packs with the *Star Trek* emblem.

And now? I'd have to perk up considerably just to reach glum.

My tent, clothing, toiletries, etcetera, were stowed in my Uncle Frank's Suburban—admittedly an upgrade from the big ol' trailers that generally hauled riders' belongings from each day's overnight city to the next.

I'd taken the opportunity our modest sponsorship provided to do a bit of TribRide clothes prep. Come on. Tell me you wouldn't take advantage of an opportunity to shop on someone else's plastic if you had a chance.

My casual attire usually consisted of tanks and T-shirts with cute cowgirl slogans and happy horse sentiments. For my two-wheeled work assignment, however, I'd selected novelty T-shirts with clever biker quips.

Today's tee sported a lone biker followed by zombie stick figures with the caption: "*I ride bikes because zombies can't.*"

It totally worked for me. It's like when people tell you the only time they run is if someone is chasing them with a knife. Yeah. I'm one of those.

I yawned. "What kind of help does *El Capitán* require?" I asked. Besides the obvious, of course. "Every time I try to check out the two-wheeled wonder, you tell me to back off, that I'll screw something up. Besides, I'd rather not be seen with you in that shirt until I have to."

"Which reminds me." A plastic bag smacked me in the head. "Your Inaugural Day Team Trekkie tee. You left it behind."

Which time?

I pulled the red shirt out of the bag. I wrinkled my nose.

Good grief. Along with the words, TEAM TREKKIE on the back, the shirt also included ads from various local merchants. I shook my head. I guess I should be thankful I wasn't sporting tat ads. Hello. Talk about "peddling" flesh.

I flipped the shirt over and saw the now familiar emblem. I let loose with a "the hell you say" when I noticed the word stitched in white above the arch.

Stroker.

"Is this really necessary?" I said.

"You heard the bosses. They think it's a great idea."

"Only after you promoted it like a Hollywood agent promotes his star of the moment," I said thinking of Keelie Keller's rum ball of an agent.

Van Vleet shrugged. "You have to admit, it's brilliant PR. Especially considering this year the ride goes through Riverside."

"Yeah? So?"

"Don't you know anything?" Van Vleet tsked and grabbed his water bottle. It also carried the *Star Trek* insignia. "Riverside is the birthplace of Captain James T. Kirk of the Starship Enterprise."

"Birth place? I hate to break it to you, dude, but *Star Trek* was a fictional television show. None of the characters are real, including your Captain Kirk."

"Okay. So the *fictional* James Tiberius Kirk was born in Riverside, Iowa."

"You actually know what the 'T' stands for?"

Van Vleet shrugged. "Doesn't everyone?"

Oh, Lord. Give. Me. Strength.

"The *Star Trek* connection has actually been a windfall for the city of Riverside. They've hosted a number of Trekkie events, some even with the series' actors," Van Vleet informed me.

I put my fingertips together like Mr. Spock was so fond of doing. "Fascinating," I said, borrowing his oft-used adjective. "Quite fascinating."

"You're hopeless," Van Vleet said with a shake of his head.

"Let me guess!" I snapped my fingers. "Lucy! *Peanuts!*"

"Good grief."

"Charlie Brown!" I yelled.

"Would you stop that?" Van Vleet snapped.

I grinned. It's official. I'm a little stinker.

"So, when do we take the show on the road?" I asked.

Van Vleet shook his head. "Obviously you didn't read the TribRide for Dummies info provided."

"I read it. I'm aware they stagger departure times. After all, they can't have over eight thousand cyclists taking off at the same time. You'd have riders running into the back of each other right and left. Not to mention the traffic nightmare for the motoring public," I parroted Shelby Lynn's lecture.

But seriously, dude. Who knew a person had to bone up for a bike ride?

"You look like hell," Van Vleet observed out of the blue. "Are you even awake enough to ride?"

"I was up late. Taking care of last minute assignments—"

"Drinking beer and line-dancing," Van Vleet finished. "Oh yes. I saw you trying to use your buddy DeMarco to get you an 'in' with Keelie Keller. Didn't look like it worked. In fact, I'd say it was one of those epic fails."

"You'd know one," I responded.

"Just what did your sister say to Keelie that got her all reality raging on social media anyway?" Van Vleet asked.

I frowned. "What are you talking about?"

"Keelie's network feeds. Let me guess. You haven't been keeping up on your social media obligations either."

Wow. Mark this down, folks. I, Tressa Jayne Turner, had just been formally declared *not* a twit. Or is that not a tweeter?

"I've been—"

"Busy. Right."

"So what's this about a raging reality diva, and what's it got to do with my little sis?" I asked.

"I'm pretty sure it was your sister Keelie called a—" Van Vleet suddenly stopped. "What the hell am I doing? Why should I tell you squat? You're the one who supposedly has the nose for news. Sniff it out on your own—*stroker*." Van Vleet snarled.

Might be a good thing I had the backseat, after all. Drew Van Vleet had shown he wasn't above a little back-stabbing in his quest for journalistic glory. No sense giving him an easy target.

Especially one clad in *Star Trek* dispensable red. Gulp.

"Well. If you're going to be that way," I said, pulling out the new Smart phone I was supposed to be utilizing for my social media networking.

I hit my phone's power button. Fortunately, I'd charged the battery the night before. During Shelby Lynn's Technology for Tressa Tutorial, she'd stressed the fact that the phone drained the juice from a battery quicker than a fat baby with a bottle of chocolate milk.

Okay. What Shelby really said was quicker than I suck the filling out of a crème Bismarck, but you get the point.

Shelby had set the phone up to be as easy for me to operate as possible, downloading apps that would get me to the social media outlets with the push of a button. In theory. It took me longer than it should have to get to Keelie Keller's page. But when I did—

"Oh! Hell, no! She didn't! She couldn't!"

"Is there a problem?" This came from Van Vleet.

"A problem? Uh, yeah. For Keelie Keller," I said. "I can't believe she posted that!"

"I know. She really ripped your sister a new one. Ouch!"

"My sister?" I hesitated. "Have you seen the picture she posted?"

"Yeah. Your sister's hot."

"I'm in that picture, too." I pointed out.

"You are?" Van Vleet walked over and checked out the phone over my shoulder. "Oh Jeez. Talk about your blackmail photos." He hesitated. "What exactly are you doing?"

Belching.

But I wasn't about to tell him that.

"What kind of sadistic, sick, twisted psycho puts up pictures like that of complete strangers?"

"Obviously, you've never been to *WhoShopsWallysWorld.com*," Van Vleet said.

I shook my head. "No. Why?"

"It's a freak show of garish outfits, disgusting butt cracks, messed-up mullets, and nasty-ass nose-pickers on parade," he said. "And I gotta tell you. That photo? It would fit right in."

Nice.

"So what happened between your sister and Keelie Keller that prompted the vitriol?"

Vitriol? Who knew I'd need to bring a pocket dictionary along on a bike ride?

"It's personal," I said.

He snickered. "Personal? Not anymore. You're everywhere!"

I winced, took one more look at my belching face, and decided that no way did I intend to be immortalized for the world to see looking like a bullfrog letting loose with a bullhorn-amplified croak.

I got up and walked over to the terrible tandem, put one hand on the rear seat, and held the phone out with the other one. I touched the camera icon and the phone clicked.

I looked at the photo I'd just taken and frowned.

"What's the deal? I so don't want a picture of you."

"If you're trying to take your own mugshot, you have to turn the phone around or press the button to reverse the camera, ditz," Van Vleet informed me.

"Oh." I saw the button he referred to. "Gotcha."

I put the camera out in front of me, assumed my earlier cute cowgirl pose, cocked my head to one side, smiled, and took the picture.

I reviewed the photo. I looked like a movie poster for a *Death Walks Among Us* horror flick. I took another. And other.

Snap. Review. Delete. Snap. Review. Delete. Snap. Review.

"Oh, for crying out loud, enough already. Take a picture, post it, and be done with it already!"

"Sorry for wanting to produce a quality viewing experience for my followers," I said.

"If we wait for a *quality* photo of you, we'll miss the

damned ride," Van Vleet said.

Is that a promise?

I settled for a mediocre picture with a "Gearing up for TribRide: Getting ready to dip my tire in the wide Missouri" cheery caption I so wasn't feeling.

"What time do we shove off?" I asked.

"Nine-fifteen," Van Vleet said.

A forty-five minute reprieve.

I watched group after group of cyclists of varying sizes, sexes, shapes, and ages, dip and take off. In the midst of the organized chaos, a now familiar bus pulled into an adjacent parking lot.

"Speak of the devil woman," I muttered.

Two black SUVs and a white Econo-line van pulled behind the bus and stopped. Manny DeMarco got out of the passenger side of one of the SUVs. A sliding door on the van slid open, and several cameramen exited the vehicle, converging on the bus, cameras at the ready. A crowd flocked to the bus. It wasn't long before the bus door opened and Keelie Keller exited, her cast of cohorts close on her heels.

"Good morning, Ioway!" Keelie waved to the crowd. "TribRide rules!"

"Whoo hoo!" The crowd cheered. I resisted the urge to put my finger in my mouth and gag. Who did she think she was? POTUS stepping off Air Force One?

"I'm super thrilled to be here in Iowa and taking part in the totally radical TribRide! Whoo hoo!"

Well, well, well. Reality Red was singing a different tune this morning.

"If you're done rubber-necking, we better get lined up," Van Vleet advised, pushing the tandem down to where the traditional tire dunking would take place.

I grabbed my helmet and trotted after him, casting a curious eye to where the celeb, joined now by her entourage, clowned around with fellow cyclists. A young girl approached Keelie and handed her a bouquet of wildflowers. She smiled and took them. More flowers and tokens of affection passed from drooling, doting subjects to the reigning reality princess.

Newsflash: This is America. The only monarchs we allow

are orange and black, have wings, and only live for two months tops.

We received the go-ahead signal to dip. Poised to lift the front tire into the water, a sudden scream pierced the excited chatter around us. Stunned, I turned in the direction of the commotion. The bike tilted precariously towards the water.

"What the—!"

I self-corrected. Van Vleet counter-corrected. I could feel the bicycle begin to tip. I looked up in time to see Van Vleet hurdle off the bike, leaving this lowly red shirt to go down, down, down, into the murky depths of the river.

I came up sputtering.

"Now that's what I call a ceremonial 'dip'," Van Vleet said, whipping his camera out of his fanny pack to snap a picture of me in all my water-logged glory.

"I thought the captain was supposed to go down with the ship," I fumed, when I managed to haul myself out of the water.

Van Vleet shrugged. "I'm new at all this."

I attempted to shake the soppy tangle of hair out of my eyes, managing only to distort my vision more.

"Where is she? Where is that psycho sicko?"

What on earth? I frowned and shook my head again. Drops of water shot out left and right.

"Get out of my way! Where is she? Where is the rat killer?"

Rat killer?

"There you are!"

I turned. Keelie Keller advanced on me, a look on her made-up face that told me this was one encounter that wasn't gonna end up on the cutting room floor.

"Where's your sister?" Keelie asked. "Or are you the sick and twisted nutcase who's responsible? Maybe you're both in on it."

I shook my head again, and noticed Manny had taken up a position to Keelie's right.

"What is she talking about?" I asked Manny.

"You talk to *me*, not to him!" Keelie demanded. "And you damned well know what I'm referring to. The perverted little *departing* gift you and your sister left me."

I looked at her, over at Manny, back at Keelie, and raised

my shoulders. I had nothing.

"Why would I give you a gift?" I said.

"Why? Because you're sick. That's why!"

I looked at Manny. "You're gonna have to help me out here," I said. "'Cause, I got nothing."

"I'm talking about *this*!" Keelie grabbed the box Manny held and shoved it at me. "Your furry friend!"

I stared down at the box. Obviously *not* chocolate.

"Open it!" Keelie shrieked. "Go ahead! Open it!"

I shrugged and pulled the lid off and looked inside. I felt my insides do a trap-door number. A dead rat peered up at me.

"Did you see the note?"

It was kind of hard to miss. It was attached to the poor rodent with a pin and was written in bright, red ink.

Happy Bike Trails, Keelie!

I was just about to observe that, indeed it was someone's idea of a cruel, sick joke, but certainly not mine, when I spotted the product lettering on the side of the box.

Chocolate sandwich cookie—generic variety.

A chill that had nothing to do with my recent water ride sent a shiver down to my soggy bike shoes.

I didn't need to see the business name on the box to recognize some sobering truths:

One: Uncle Frank was using the cheap Freezee cookie fillers again.

And two: Someone was out to turn this reality ride into a case of real-time road rage.

How do you say "roadkill"?

CHAPTER FOURTEEN

"Pump! Pump!"

"I'm pumping! I'm pumping!"

Head down, thighs burning, I fantasized various payback scenarios specifically designed for a certain short, balding, grouch of a boss who'd orchestrated this week-long sweat fest. Scenarios featured in my "road rage revenge" ranged from lame pranks featuring fake poop and angry, red insects, (or, alternatively, sneaky, sleepy ones) and over-the-counter aids designed to increase the movement of waste through the colon. Okay. So I wasn't as diabolically creative as *Nine to Fivers* Judy, Violet, and Doralee. I was plotting under pressure here.

Rather than, "Pump, pump!" my mantra became "Payback, payback!"

We all have our own motivational tools, right? And revenge? Gotta be near the top of the list.

I had no clue how long we'd been riding or how many wheel revolutions we'd put between the Mo River and us. It was all I could do to pedal and breathe at the same time.

"Come on! Pick it up a bit."

"Hey! I'm operating on impulse power back here," I yelled. And my impulse reserves were how-low-can-you-go.

"We're falling behind," El Capitán barked.

"So what?" I hollered back. "You don't get brownie points for time."

"No. But the brownies could be gone if we're late for the noon meal."

"Brownies?"

"Obviously, you haven't heard about the TribRide fare."

"Remind me again." I had heard some delectable rumors, but none had yet been confirmed.

"Baked goods galore. Brownies. Bars. Cookies. And pies of every type. Berry. Custard. Chocolate."

"Chocolate?" My formerly dry mouth began to water.

"And that's just dessert. The entrees? They are out of this world."

"Such as?" I could feel my legs pumping faster.

"Well, for lunch you've got your brats, your barbecued chicken and beef, pulled pork. Subs. And dinner—" He paused.

"Yes! Yes!"

"Carbs are king. That's when you get your pastas. Plates piled high with spaghetti, hot, cheesy, lasagna, and buttery, garlic bread."

I pushed myself harder.

"And then you have the church ladies' specials like chicken and noodles, or beef and noodles. And there's pizza, fried chicken, steak."

"Steak?" I stepped into it even more. "Pump! Pump!" Now I was leading the charge.

"Well, would you look at who we have here? The rat-killing rodeo queen. Off any rodents lately?"

I hazarded a quick look to my left. Keelie Keller sat astride a bicycle that would have cost me six months' salary to pay for. Close on her heels…er wheels…biked pals, Tiara and Langley, shadowed by several reality TV crewmen with cameras mounted on their bicycles and helmets.

I'm pretty sure my mouth did one of those "no-friggin'-way" jaw drop numbers here. Keelie Keller looked like she'd just stepped off the pages of a fashion magazine. No sign of armpit perspiration. No blotchy, sweat-smeared mascara. No dirt streaks or sunburned noses. Not one freaking hair out of place.

Keelie Keller does TribRide?

My battered butt. This biker babe was getting the star treatment and—I suspected—frequent shuttle service.

I sent a disgusted look at Manny on her left.

"How's the babysitting gig going?" I inquired. "Any super-dooper security vulnerabilities? You know. Like, broken fingernails. Smudged makeup. Unglossed lips?"

Manny's lips twitched.

"Don't like serial killers get their start killing small

animals?" Keelie asked. "I read that somewhere."

Read *it?* She *read* it? Oh, puhleaze. She picked that little tidbit up from the drop-dead gorgeous profiler Derek Morgan via *Criminal Minds* like the rest of us.

"I did not send you that rat," I responded. "And, for the record, neither did my sister."

One of the cycling cameramen turned his camera in my direction.

"Says you," Keelie fired back.

"Yeah. Says me."

"Miss Keller. Drew Van Vleet. *New Holland News*." Drew turned briefly in Keelie's direction and put a hand to his visor. "I want to assure you I had nothing whatsoever to do with the unfortunate rat incident. My riding partnership here is professional, not personal."

Van Vleet sold me out quicker than my uncle Frank sells out day old coney buns and ice cream cakes nearing their expiration date.

"Is that right?" Keelie said.

"I'd love it if you would let me interview you." Van Vleet gushed. "And I assure you, I wouldn't be the kind of low life who would write a hit piece or anything—unlike a certain competitor I could name."

I resisted the temptation to deliver a sharp jab to his ribs. There was that collateral damage to consider if we took a spill, after all.

I could see the headlines now: Newsflash: Newshounds *On the Trail* of a Story...*Literally.*

"So, you're not...a couple?" Keelie's eyes shifted back to me.

"Gawd, no!" I wasn't sure who screamed the denial first or louder—Van Vleet or me.

"We write for competing small town newspapers in the same county," Van Vleet explained. "The ride was our bosses' collective brainchild."

Collective brainchild? Try collective brain *fart*.

"Isn't that special, Tiara?" Keelie said. "Pedaling *paparazzi*!"

Tiara giggled.

"And look at their cute little Trekkie tees!" Keelie went on. "But, oh no! A red shirt?" She clicked her tongue. "Not a good omen."

If I hadn't been focusing on keeping my feet on the pedals and sucking oxygen into my deprived lungs, I'm sure I could've come up with a snarky comeback. As it was, all I could manage was a gravelly grunt and a disgusted shake of my head.

"Aren't you like, really far behind?" Tiara asked. "You know. The back of the pack. Bringing up the rear? Last place?"

"Losers," Keelie offered. "At the ass end of the line."

"It's her fault. She had to wait until her soggy butt dried out," my teammate whined from the helm. "Consequently, we got a late start."

Traitor.

"Obviously we weren't the only ones late out of the gate," I huffed, irritated that we were being labeled slackers. "That is, presuming you all began at the starting line."

"What is that supposed to mean?" Keelie asked. "Are you suggesting we didn't begin the race where everyone else did?"

I managed a shrug. "All I'm saying is you all look way too...*fresh* to have twenty Iowa-in-July bike miles behind you. That's all."

By now—and this is just a guess since I hadn't actually sniffed an armpit or anything—I imagine I looked and smelled like someone who didn't survive *Survivor*. But, again I'm just guessing.

"Maybe we're just in better shape than Team Trekkie," Keelie said. "Or maybe we don't perspire like Team Trekkie."

"Yeah, and maybe you just got out of your air-conditioned luxury bus and hopped on your bike a mile back," I suggested. "'Cause, unless you're a cyborg or have serious glandular issues, Toots, you're gonna sweat. Buckets."

"I resent your implication," Keelie protested.

"Resent away."

"Now, now, ladies," Langley Carlisle III chided. I raised an eyebrow. Between the neon green bike shorts and matching neon and white tee, the funny little Brit looked like he'd raided Joltin' Joe Townsend's closet. Even his bicycle was a funky green. "Can't we all just be friends? Or at least, friendly? No need for fisticuffs."

I made a face. Fisticuffs? Really? Next Keelie's bosom bud would be suggesting we hold hands, braid each other's hair, and strike up a chorus of *Kum ba Yah*.

"Friends, Langey? Be friends? With someone who has armpit stains that reach her waist?" Keelie stuck her tongue out in an ew-gross face. "I'll pass. Come on, Manny. Let's pick up the pace," she said, and off she went.

Manny pedaled alongside. He put a hand up, the middle finger and ring fingers forming a V—the Vulcan equivalent of the fist bump.

"Live long and pedal Barbie," he said.

I gritted my teeth. Oh, for a phaser set on stun about now.

CHAPTER FIFTEEN

Van Vleet and I pedaled in silence for the remainder of the morning. He sulked. I steamed—in more ways than one. Obviously, I hadn't logged nearly enough pre-TribRide road miles. My rear felt like a flank steak my gammy had taken the tenderizing hammer to after enjoying too many tipples of the cooking sherry.

"We're almost there!" Van Vleet yelled back to me.

"Where?"

"Glenwood. Our noon stop."

I felt a surge of adrenalin. I'd done it. I'd completed the first leg—er, half leg—of TribRide. Hoo-rah!

We pedaled towards the city limits. People lined the street, waving, clapping, yelling, and handing out water to the cyclists.

"How cool is this?" I said, grinning and waving to the crowd. "This is some welcome!"

Several "squirts" with pistol-sized squirt guns aimed modest streams of cooling water at the riders as we rode by.

"Ahhh!" I said, savoring the cool spray on my heated skin. "Go ahead!" I joked to a bunch of kids with pistols. "Make my day!"

"Whatever you say, Miss Ratfink."

I opened my mouth to say something along the lines of "Nooo!" when a torrent of water just this side of a fireman's hose, blasted me full in the face, filling my mouth with a liter of tepid water and knocking my sunglasses askew. Water dripped from my helmet like rain through a faulty gutter during a downpour.

Through a waterlogged haze, I spotted Keelie Keller armed with a Super Soaker that looked as big as a rocket launcher. I pursed my lips and expelled the water from my mouth, hitting

Van Vleet in the back of the head in the process.

"Hey!" Van Vleet protested.

"Hit her again, Keelie!" Tiara shouted. "Hit her again!"

Another blast from Keelie's weapon of choice nailed me—once, twice, three times—dousing me from head to toe.

"Look at that girl, Mommy. She looks funny!"

"Hey, Captain Kirk. Scotty doesn't look so hot."

"Now you see why you'll never get me on a bike."

The comments stung my saturated psyche like tiny light sabers.

Zing. Zing. Zing.

Hello. Hadn't these people ever heard of Iowa *nice*?

We battled our way through a squadron of locals armed, suspiciously enough, with Super Soakers identical to the one a demented diva had unloaded on yours truly. It felt like we were riding through the falls of Niagara. By the time we made it past the assassins, I was soaked to the skivvies.

My only solace? Van Vleet hadn't been spared either.

"Why did you have to go and make an enemy of the biggest celebrity to come on TribRide?" Captain Wet Underpants harangued, as we walked our bike into town.

"Excuse me? I'm the innocent party here. Can I help it if some publicity hungry Hollywood type has me playing Darth Vader to her Leia to boost ratings? There I was, simply minding my own business—"

"Blah, blah, blah, blah, blah," Van Vleet interjected.

"Well, you did say you wanted to get Keelie's attention," I reminded him. "You got your wish."

"Funny."

We walked in silence for the last block.

Squeak. Squish. Squeak.

I thought about Stan's foot fungus warning and winced.

"I'll need to stop by the Mini-Freeze and get some dry clothes out of the Suburban," I told Van Vleet.

"Whatever," Van Vleet said. "What the heck? Wonder what's going on."

I looked up. A crowd of people carrying signs on sticks had formed a circle in front of a vendor. They seemed to be chanting.

"Looks like a protest of some kind, but I can't read the signs from here."

The closer we got, the slower and shorter my footsteps became.

Squish. Squeak.

"Come on! Hurry up! There might be a story here!"

Yeah. *The story of my life.*

"Wait. Frank's Mobile Mini-Freeze? Isn't that your uncle's ice cream stand?" Van Vleet asked.

By now my steps had slowed to a near stop, offering stubborn resistance as Van Vleet applied more pressure to the handlebars.

"Stop dragging your feet!" he ordered.

"Okay! Okay! Can you see the signs?" I asked, preferring to receive the bad news secondhand in the vain hope some of its sting would be lost in translation.

"Let's see. There's 'We Love Keelie.'"

I let out an audible sigh of relief. Thank God. Just groupies, after all.

"Wait. Here we go. Another one reads, 'Dairee Sleaze.' Then there's 'Rat Rights' and 'Fresh Roadkill Served Here Daily.' Should I go on?"

I winced.

"No. I get the gist of it," I said.

"Looks like you got your basic boycott going on," Van Vleet observed. "Democracy in action. It's a beautiful thing."

Easy for him to say. What wouldn't be so red, white, and beautiful for me was when Uncle Frank found out his ice cream windfall was in a total free fall.

"Keelie rules! Mini-Freeze drools!"

I made a face. "Oh, brother. Is that the best they can come up with?" I asked. Even for reality TV writers, it was pretty awful.

"Who?"

"Oh, please. This has Keelie Keller, Reality Princess, written all over it," I said.

"Here." He shoved the bike in my direction. "I'm going to get some pictures. This will make great blog material."

"Hey!" I yelled. "Wait a minute! You can't post that!"

If anyone should be getting mileage out of this drummed up

catfight, it was moi. Who was in the line of fire here anyway? Who was putting it out there? Putting it all on the line? Dripping like a drowned rat? (Ooh. Sorry. Unfortunate word selection there.) Who had been targeted unfairly for something she didn't do?

Me! That's who," I mumbled.

"Well, hello there, *me*. How are you today? Besides soaking wet, that is."

I turned to give the speaker one of my trademark snarky comebacks, but the crazy gorgeous guy looking down at me, eyes hidden behind a pair of dark glasses, va-va-va-voomed the snark right out of me.

"Oh, er, uh, I, um..."

He stuck out a hand and took one of my cold, clammy, pruned ones with nary a shudder or grimace at what had to be akin to grabbing hold of a halibut.

"Jaxson W. Whitver at your service. Jax to my friends, which I'm hoping you'll become, of course."

I blinked. What was happening?

"Rat got your tongue?" he asked. When I opened my mouth to take umbrage, he grinned, and put his hands up in a "don't shoot, I come in peace" move. "Come on, Tressa. You have to admit, it's a little funny."

Tressa? The plot thickened.

I reclaimed my hand.

"I suppose since you missed Tressa Turner Super Soaker target practice you have to be content with taking cheap shots," I said.

"Now, Tressa. I thought we were going to be friends."

Friends? With teenybopper heartthrob, Jax Whitver? Yeah. Right.

"I'm not sure your girlfriend would approve," I said.

"I don't have a girlfriend," he said, and reached up to remove his sunglasses, cocking a hey-baby eyebrow at me. "Or haven't you heard?"

"Oh, that's right. Keelie kicked you to the curb."

His smile faltered.

"We needed a break. To take a step back. Slow things down. We were moving way too fast."

I shivered. Not because his words had any significance for *me*, you understand. Certainly not because *my* own relationship with a certain ranger-type had gone from a first-time sailor guarding her bootie to "batten down the hatches, full speed ahead" at warp drive.

"Sorry. That was mean," I said, and meant it. I'm a real softie at heart, but I try not to let it show too much. It could hurt my rep as a tough-as-nails investigative reporter, don't you know? (Hey, now. Quit yer sniggering.)

Jax shrugged. "Thanks. But I'm cool."

"Oh, my God. The natives are becoming hostile," Van Vleet said, jogging back, checking out images on his camera as he approached. "Looks like your Mini-Freeze is going to have to close down shop due to the angry mob mentality. Damn shame. Your uncle stands to lose tons of profits. Wait! Whoa! Hey, you're Jax Whitver! Drew Van Vleet, *New Holland News*." Van Vleet sent me a dirty look before starting to snap picture after picture of the hunky hottie. "Today's blog is going to be stellar!" he crowed.

I thumped my forehead with the butt of my hand. "Idiot, why didn't you think of that?" Lois Lane would have had my ass.

"What's this about your uncle?" Jax asked.

I gave an abbreviated explanation.

"We can't have that," Jax said. He grabbed my hand again. "Come on."

I shoved the bicycle back at Van Vleet.

"Permission to leave the bridge, Sir!" I queried, barely managing a so-so salute before Jax Whitver dragged me off in the direction of Keelie's "Ratpack."

"Whoa. Your boyfriend was right. The natives *are* restless." Jax observed.

"Boyfriend?" I shook my head so hard that I risked whiplash. "He's not my boyfriend. He's my saddle burr." I stared at the crowd assembled near the Mini-Freeze. And restless? Try rabid.

"We're goin' in." The boy crooner waded into the thick of things, pulling me along.

"Look! Look! It's Jax Whitver! Jax! Jax! Hey, Jax!"

The mood of the masses flipped quicker than my gammy's

disposition does when her fiber supplement finally kicks in.

"Hey. How are you? Hi there! Good to see you! How ya doin'?"

Jax Whitver glad-handed the crowd like a veteran politician, winding his way through the throng as he made his way to the order window.

"I've been hankerin' for a good old-fashioned root beer float," he said. "And a beefburger sounds awesome."

"You're eating *here*?" A protestor asked.

"Hell, yeah," Jax said.

"But...but Keelie!" Another gaping groupie exclaimed.

"She can buy her own burger," Jax said, and gave his order to a jaw-dropping Frankie behind the window. Moments later, I joined Frankie in the OMG realm when Jax Whitver began to sing.

"When you are hungry and your tummy is growling, you can always go, to Frank's Freeze. When you want food that is filling and delicious, you can always go to Frank's Freeze. Frank's Freeze! Get all your favorites now! Frank's Freeze. Don't hesitate now! Frank's Freeze! Where all the cool people eat! Frank's Freeze. Frank's Freeze!"

In the time it takes to spoon loose meat beef on a hamburger bun, Jax Whitver had altered the group dynamic from pitchforks and torches to main street flash mob mentality.

Now I knew what they meant when they said "star power".

Shaking myself, I pulled my phone out of my fanny pack and hit the record button.

Beat this little love fest, Van Vleet, I thought, reveling in the huge coup that had fallen into my lap. Not to mention the mega-advertising exposure Uncle Frank would receive from a video sure to go viral.

By the time Jax had completed a third stanza, people had abandoned their signs and protests and were standing in line for their own Freeze food. If super hot Jax Whitver thought it was super cool to eat at the Mini-Freeze, then so did they.

I hurried to change out of my "wet suit" and into a pair of Levi shorts and a white T-shirt with a black stitched horse and golden sun that proclaimed "Born to Ride".

I caught sight of Jax at a nearby table, signing autographs

and schmoozing with the crowd. I hurried over to join him, but before I could thank him for saving the day for Uncle Frank, Vinny Vincent red-faced and toupee askew, stomped up to Jax.

"Whitver! What the hell do you think you're doing? You've got no business being here. You and Keelie are over. *Finito*. Yesterday's news."

"Well, well, well. If it isn't Vinny Vincent, agent and promoter extraordinaire. Still as much fun as ever, I see," Jax observed.

"Jax Whitver. Still as much of a pain in the ass as ever," Vinny shot back. "And up to no good, as usual. What's this?" He stuck a hand out in my direction. "Some sick 'sleeping with the enemy' gig?"

"Now just a minute!" I objected. "You're wrong. I'm not anyone's enemy."

Vinny shot me a dark look. "Except for rats maybe."

Again with the rats? Who knew people were so concerned with the welfare of a species complicit in a pandemic that wiped out like a gazillion Europeans. (Amazing what you can recall from a high school history report.)

"How many times do I have to say this? It wasn't me."

"Keep saying it enough, and you start to believe it, kid," he said.

"Vinny? Jax! What are *you* doing here?"

Oh, God. Another country heard from.

"It's a free country, Kay-Kay," Jax told his ex.

Keelie set her water bottle, sunglasses, and cell phone on the table with a shaking hand and crossed her arms over her chest. "Yes, it is. And you're free to go to any of forty-nine other states," she pointed out. "So why are you here?"

"Iowa has its manifest attractions," he said, and gave me an audacious wink.

"Keelie, I told you, if he turned up, I'd handle it," Vinny said.

"Yeah. Vinny's good at *handling* things for you," Jax replied.

"That's my job, punk."

"And you do it with such…obsessive compulsive vigor," Jax jabbed.

Now that Keelie had joined the spectacle, the crowd around Jax grew even larger. Taylor and Frankie, along with Drew Van Vleet and Kenny Grey, the groupie I'd met at the bike night party, volleyed for position along with Tiara and Langley.

"Jax! Go home!" Keelie ordered. "Just go home."

"Sorry, Kay-Kay, but I'm just havin' way too much fun," he said."

"You'll regret this, Jax," Keelie said, leveling a dark look at me. "You better believe. You'll regret this."

She stomped off in a huff.

"You really should take her advice, Jax," Keelie's agent said. "You're not wanted here. So, beat it." Vinny stomped after Keelie.

Jax grinned and picked up the cell phone Keelie had forgotten on the table with her sunglasses and water bottle. He fiddled with it and shook his head.

"She never changed her password," he observed. He put his head next to mine, held the camera out, and snapped a picture, Seconds later, our picture appeared on the phone's background.

"I'd rather you didn't do that," I told him. "Keelie already has it in for me."

Jax grinned. "Join the club, Tressa Turner," he said. "Join the club."

Red alert! Red alert! I finally make it on someone's A-list only to find out it's a *hit* list.

CHAPTER SIXTEEN

The heat was on. The sun beat down on us, unforgiving and unapologetically brutal. We trekked on with nary a cloud in the sky to give us a respite from dew point and humidity that duked it out in an atmosphere you could wring water from. Twice, we'd gotten off our bike to push it up hills neither of us had the fortitude to tackle.

"How much further?" I sounded like a spoiled brat on a road trip for the first time.

"About half a mile less than the last time you asked," Van Vleet responded. "We'll get there when we get there."

"But we'll get there, right?"

"If we don't expire first." Even Van Vleet's characteristic smug pettiness had evaporated in the steamy haze of an Iowa summer.

"On your left! On your left! On your friggin' left!" The now familiar alert warning you a cyclist was about to overtake and pass (a polite way of saying, don't turn, look or swerve into my path, or I'll hit you, moron) reached us with an anxiety level I hadn't heard before. We pulled the bike close to the shoulder of the road. I gaped as Keelie and her street team raced past us—Keelie's face the color of my Trekkie shirt.

"Wonder what's up with that." I said, and Van Vleet shrugged.

"Who cares? You ready to ride again?"

"I guess."

I mustered as much enthusiasm as I do for dental visits and big girl exams and mounted. We caught up to Keelie's team parked alongside the road and passed them.

"Weird place to take a break," I commented.

"Just shut up and pedal," Van Vleet snapped.

We rode in silence for several miles.

"On your left! On your left!"

Once more we slowed our bike and hugged the yellow line.

"On. Your. Left!"

"Show offs," I mumbled as Keelie and Company raced by us again.

A mile down the road we passed Keelie's crew taking another roadside break.

"I wonder what they're up to," I said.

"Just pedal," Van Vleet ordered.

We'd chugged up another small hill and were enjoying the reward of a downhill respite when—

The warning, high-pitched, panicky—and not suitable for young ears, pierced the afternoon malaise.

"On your left! On your left! On your frigging, blankety-blank left!"

I watched Keelie pass us, and suddenly slow up and stop at the side of the road again. Before you could say, "Vrroom, Vrroom," she was off her bike and heading for the ditch and the green fields beyond.

"I wonder what's up with that!" I said.

Van Vleet pulled his phone out of his pack.

"My guess? Another unscheduled stop in the cornfield."

"You mean—"

Van Vleet winced. "The big D."

"You mean—"

He nodded.

I gagged.

"In the cornfield?"

"It's better than the alternative," he said and fiddled with his camera.

"You mean—" Holy crap! (Pardon the pun). This gave a whole new meaning to "stop and go" traffic.

Van Vleet nodded again, and held his phone up at the general area of the field Keelie disappeared into.

"Wait! What are you doing? You're not thinking of—. No way. You couldn't! You wouldn't!"

"Hey, Blondie. I'm a journalist. I report news. It's what I

do."

"What's newsworthy about a bodily function run amok?"

"Not a thing if it's *your* bodily function. But Keelie Keller's? Enquiring minds want to know."

"Sick, pathetic, dangerous minds want to know," I said. "Not normal, healthy, sane ones."

"Oh, get over yourself, Red Shirt. Who are you to tell people what's news and what isn't? Great! Here she comes!"

I took one look at the pale, bedraggled creature plodding through the high grass back towards the road and knew, despite our… er…misunderstanding—that I couldn't in all good conscience let Drew Van Vleet humiliate her like this. It was so not the right move.

"Oh, no, you don't!" I covered the camera lens on his phone at the same time a big ol' shadow covered both of us.

"Not a smart choice, pencil neck." Manny the mind reader, appeared out of nowhere, his massive paw encasing Van Vleet's. I sucked in a better-Van Vleet-than-me breath and let it out in a hiss.

"Ow. Hey, man. Ever heard of Freedom of the Press?"

"Pencil dick ever heard discretion is the better part of valor?" Manny asked, giving Van Vleet his don't-eff-with-me look. (I'm familiar with the look although, thankfully, I've never been on the receiving end of it.) I did a double take. Since when did Manny DeMarco use Shakespearean phrases in the course of a conversation?

"You have a point," Van Vleet conceded, withdrawing a hand that now looked like it belonged on a bird of prey, and trying his best to act like it was no big deal. "It's tabloid journalism and, therefore, beneath me and my exacting standards of ethics."

All right. I admit it. I lost it on that one. I laughed so hard I almost wet my pants. I was still laughing when Keelie staggered up, her camera crew circling her in a way that made me wonder how anyone put up with this circus without feeling claustrophobic.

"How dare you! How dare you stand there and laugh! This is all *your* doing!" She stuck a finger in my chest. "*You* are responsible for this!"

I frowned down at the finger violating my *Star Trek* insignia.

"We know what you and your sister did! You put something in Keelie's drink at noon. We all saw you there," Tiara defended her friend. "And we saw you—cozying up to Jax."

"I don't know what you're talking about. I didn't put anything in anyone's drink."

Jeez-a-lou. I'd issued more denials in the last two days than government officials in the latest whatever-gate.

"Liar! You spiked my water with a laxative! You or that stuck-up sister of yours!"

For the briefest of seconds, I let myself appreciate Keelie's characterization of Taylor as "stuck-up." Then it was up with the metaphorical dukes again.

"Listen, I don't know why your *people* chose us to use as props in your ridiculous reality charade, but would you cool it, already? There's enough drama in life without inventing it. Trust me on this one. I know of which I speak."

"You're saying someone on *my* crew is creating and manipulating this situation for ratings?" Keelie responded.

I thought for a moment. Was that what I was saying? I thought some more. Yes, I guess I was. I just didn't realize I was. (Are you following this at all? It's clear as an intergalactic dust storm, right?)

Sigh.

I lifted my shoulders. "You'd know better than I would who on your crew might be sufficiently motivated, and er...devious enough...to stage this kind of theatrical intrigue."

"None of *my* people would dare perpetrate the type of outrageous stunts you're suggesting. You're just trying to divert suspicion from you and your hoity-toity sister. That's what I think."

"Then you'd be wrong. And no closer to finding out who's really behind the mischief."

"I know who's behind it."

"Prove it," I heard myself saying.

"I don't have to prove it, Trekkie. All I have to do is say it. I'll just tell my half a million friends and followers that it was your uncle's concession stand slop that made me so violently ill.

And *adios* to Uncle Frank's Mini-Freeze featuring Frank's infamous belly burner burrito." She crossed her arms. "It's either you or your uncle's eatery. Pick your poison, sweetie."

"You wouldn't," I said. I took a step toward Keelie.

"Oh, wouldn't I?"

"Girls, ladies. Please! This is really very untoward!" Langley Carlisle number three protested. "While it may be tempting at first blush to act out in anger or frustration, no good can come of it in the end. Please. Let's explore other avenues in an effort to remediate the situation before we resort to brawling like hoydens along a public thoroughfare."

I raised an eyebrow. What an extraordinary speech, I thought, giving Langley Carlisle the Third a quizzical look. See? I can do Austin.

"What are you saying, Langley?" Tiara asked.

"Well, unless one of you agrees to withdraw from the event, perhaps a friendly wager might give both parties an incentive to comport themselves with a level of dignity and apply themselves to the physical challenge at hand."

"Huh?" The query came from the trio of girls present.

"A wager. I'm proposing a wager."

"A bet?" I winced. My experience with bets wasn't stellar. Well, except for one adorable raccoon tattoo, that is. Fan me.

"I'm proposing a wager on who goes the farthest on the bike ride, or, alternatively, who finishes the ride first."

I frowned. I had enough to worry about just getting from Point A to Point B each day. The last thing I wanted was to have to compete for time against America's Reality Sweetheart.

"I'll pass," I stated.

"Ah ha! Only a guilty party would decline such a reasonable solution. That, or a coward." Keelie said.

Coward? I could feel the camera zoom in on me, invading my space, documenting my reaction.

"Sticks and stones," Saint Tressa told me, all pious and reasonable. Meanwhile, Sinner Tressa was making a fist and itching to give Reality Red a reality check upside the head.

Bam!

"Maybe we should start with a more modest wager. Something more…immediate." Langley suggested. "Something that, hopefully, will assist you two in finding common ground and, perhaps, even burying the proverbial hatchet."

For some inexplicable reason, both Keelie's and Tiara's eyes grew big and wide before they erupted in peals of laughter.

"Oh, Langley, you are brilliant!" Keelie said, and gave the beanpole Brit, a hug. "Isn't he brilliant, Tiara?"

"Brilliant," she concurred. "Just brilliant."

I felt like the last person to be let in on the joke.

"How would you like to spend the first night of the ride somewhere other than a tent, Miss Turner?" Langley Carlisle III asked.

Okay. Give me some credit. I'm no dummy. I know there's got to be a catch.

"Is that an option?" I kept it vague. Casual.

"Could be. Interested?" Tiara said, and winked at Keelie.

"You can't be asking me to stay on your bus," I said.

"Oh, God. No!" Keelie said, and the best buds started to giggle again.

"We aren't actually staying on the bus tonight," Tiara said when she'd stopped giggling.

A hotel? Even better.

"We're staying in Villisca," Keelie said. The threesome fixed expectant gazes on me.

"*Villisca?*" I frowned. "They don't have a hotel there, do they?"

"No. Not exactly. But they do have certain overnight accommodations that have been…procured for us."

"Accommodations? What sort of accommodations?" One of those "somebody's tromp…tromp…tromping over my grave" feelings hit me with the force of a squadron of super-duper Super Soakers.

"*Supernatural* lodgings," Langley said.

"*Ghostly* ones," Tiara offered.

"Things that go bump in the night accommodations," Keelie added.

"You mean?"

It finally registered.

Villisca.

Home to the Ax Murder House.

A place only Lizzie Borden could love.

I've lost you, right? Let me just say that the town of Villisca is as infamous to Iowans as Amityville is to New York residents. The rural Iowa hamlet has the dubious distinction of being home to what is known simply as, the "Murder House."

That's right. The Murder House. Why, you ask? Because in 1912, eight (Yes, I said eight.) people were murdered in their beds in the modest white two-story by an ax-wielding assailant or assailants unknown. That's why.

The perp or perps were never caught and, over the years, ghostly occurrences had become as synonymous with the Murder House as the Tower of London—the house reaping a notoriety that comes with high-tech paranormal investigations and eyewitness reports of strange and frightening phenomenon.

Tours of the Murder House were available, and, for a pricey rate, overnight stays at the house promised to give the lodgers a night they wouldn't soon forget. That fact was what currently had me breaking out in a cold sweat and my innards knotted up worse than my air-dried hair after a swim in the rec center pool.

"I don't understand." I said, although I was beginning to.

"I think you do," Keelie said, a decidedly evil glint in her blue eyes. "Convinced the location will be a ratings gold mine, my producers have arranged for us to spend the entire night at the Murder House. You want a truce, Ratfink? You spend the night. If you dare. Bwahaha!"

"Oh, hell, no!" I said.

"What's the matter? Is Team Trekkie afraid of ghosts?"

Ax-wielding ones with a history of chopping people up while they slept? Duh.

"Wait a minute! Team Trekkie? Am I…are we…are you asking both of us to spend the night with you in the Ax Murder House?" Van Vleet stammered.

"Of course. The more the merrier, sport." Langley gave Drew a robust slap on the back.

"Awesome!" Drew said, pumping his fist in the air. "Awesome!"

"That invitation is only good if Blondie here is in," Keelie qualified.

"I need just a minute to confer with my team partner," I

said, and grabbed hold of Drew's elbow, herding him away from the eyes—and ears—of the show's crew.

"Listen, Drew. This is not what I signed up for. Uh-uh. No way. Not gonna happen."

"Are you joking? This is my ticket to the big time!"

"*Your* ticket. Hate to break it to you, dude, but it's a twofer. And this half of the twofer ain't interested."

"Why the hell not?"

"What part of *haunted* and *murder* did you miss?"

"I don't believe you're actually considering refusing Keelie's invitation!" Van Vleet ran a hand through his hair. "Unbelievable. And you call yourself a journalist!"

"You're not at all concerned about spending the night in the Ax Murder House?" I asked.

"No. Hell no! Why should I be? It's just a house. But you heard what Keelie said. It's pure gold in terms of the public's fascination with the supernatural," he said. "And with Keelie and her entourage along for a sleepover, big media markets, here we come!"

I frowned. "But...the murders, Drew! The murders!"

He shrugged.

"And the ax."

Nothing.

"The hauntings. The gouge in the ceiling. The ax killer!"

"All the better to pique the public's interest."

"People died, man. They died. You're sick to want to capitalize on that. Sick, I tell you."

"And you are a wimpy little red shirt," Van Vleet said. "And undeserving of that Star Fleet emblem on your chest. Go ahead. Chicken out. Spend the rest of the ride wondering what dirty trick Keelie will come up to torment you with next. And when your boss finds out you passed up an opportunity to spend a night in the Murder House with Keelie Keller and her cast mates? I wouldn't want to be you. But you go ahead. You tell Stan Rodgers your high moral code kept you from capitalizing on the biggest story of the summer. Go ahead—*loser*."

Dirty tricks? Wimp? Chicken? *Loser*?

Okay. Someone, tell me. Is there a sign on my forehead that instructs people on which buttons of mine to push, because Van

Vleet had pushed nearly all of them—in one fell swoop.

The ass.

"Fine. Whatever. I couldn't care less," I heard someone say. It took a second for it to register it was me. "I'm a country girl. Better a farmhouse than pitching a tent, I say. No big deal. Nothing to see here, folks. Just me getting a good night's sleep out of the elements. That's all. Yup. Piece. Of. Cake."

"You're full of crap, Witchiepoo," Van Vleet said. "You're scared shitless, and you know it."

I tapped my chin. "Isn't that like an oxymoron?" I asked. "How is it possible to be full of crap and shitless at the same time? As Mr. Spock would point out, 'most illogical.'"

Van Vleet muttered some words that would never come out of Captain Kirk's mouth and hurried to break the good news that Team Trekkie would gladly accept Keelie Keller's Ax Murder House invite.

A few minutes later Keelie joined me. "So, I hear you're in."

"With a few of my own conditions. You get your peeps. I want mine."

"When you say 'peeps,' who exactly did you have in mind?"

"My sister, Taylor. You know. The one you call 'stuck-up.' My cousin, Frankie, and his…his…his…Dixie."

"What about that handsome trooper?"

I shrugged. "I'm not in charge of the trooper's itinerary."

"I don't know. The producers already had to do some major arm-twisting to get the owners to exceed the customary limit of ten people," she said.

"Those are my stipulations," I said. "Take 'em or leave 'em."

"I don't—" A growl the likes of which I'd never heard erupt from my gammy even after she wolfed down the six pack and a pound from the taco joint, ripped out of the petite redhead like the rumbling of Mt. Vesuvius. "To…be…continued," Keelie managed through clenched teeth, and hightailed it in the direction of the nearest field.

I'll take that as a yes.

The next hurdle? Sealing the deal with my "peeps."

This could be a little dicey. I winced. Considering the history of our first night's lodging, *dicey* probably wasn't the best word choice. Let's go with…*tricky*.

I pondered the magnitude of the challenge before me. It would take pleading, cajoling, overt manipulation, blatant arm-twisting, and, if all else failed, out-and-out blackmail.

Oh, for that Vulcan mind meld about now.

CHAPTER SEVENTEEN

"Lizzie Borden took an ax. Gave her mother forty whacks."

"Tiara, please. Would you please stop reciting that disturbing ditty?" chided Langley Carlisle—and not for the first time. "It's getting on my last nerve."

Personally, I thought the Englishman showed considerable restraint. I was ready to crown her—but not in a Miss America kind of way.

"Come on, Lang. Loosen up. Do you realize how freaky cool this is? We're spending the night in a house where eight people were axed to death! A house that's supposed to be haunted! I'm totally trippin' here."

"I wish I was. Trippin' that is." A disgruntled Dixie Daggett, sitting beside me on a rolled-up sleeping bag muttered. "I still can't believe I let myself get roped into this."

I smiled. It had been nothing short of genius to approach Frankie first with my proposition. Hooking Frankie hadn't been tough at all. The allure of an unsolved murder mystery? Hook. Having the opportunity to spend the night in the Murder House? Line. Sharing the haunted digs with Keelie Keller with Frankie's hero providing security?

Sinker, baby.

And once Frankie was on board? Well, it didn't take a harpoon net to reel Dixie in.

But alas, Dixie Daggett was not your basic happy camper.

"I'll have you know I don't appreciate being manipulated like this."

"Manipulated? How did I manipulate you? I assured you over and over again that in no way should you feel obligated to participate," I pointed out, suddenly finding it hard to keep a straight face.

"Wipe that damned smirk off your face, or I will," Dixie said.

There *is* a downside to being your basic open book, I've discovered. And an inherent risk, especially when it came to Dixie.

"Manipulate is such a harsh—"

"Oh, please." Dixie shook her head. "You knew good and well that there was no way in hell I would let Frankie come here on his own."

"On his own? Helloo! Look around. There's like a dozen other people here. And I'm here. I'd watch out for Frankie."

"I feel so much better."

"And there's Keelie and Tiara..."

"Just...shut up."

I lifted an eyebrow. "Is this about not trusting Frankie with me or not trusting Frankie with *them*?"

"What are you talking about now?"

"They're both single, attractive young women. And Frankie's, er, enamored with the idea of being a protector like Manny. Put those characters in a spooky, haunted murder house for an overnighter? I'm just saying. It's understandable if you are feeling some insecurity here."

"What I'm feeling insecure about is Frankie spending his time with you and your former faux beau, Manny—not those two shallow party girls who wouldn't take a second look at Frankie if he stripped buck-naked and began belting out *New York, New York.*"

Sad...but true.

"I suppose you used Patrick Dawkins as bait to hook Taylor," Dixie accused.

"I resent the characterization. It was Keelie who brought up the possibility of Patrick joining us. Her people agreed. Since he is a certified state peace officer, it made perfect sense to enlist his expertise, and I certainly didn't object."

"Especially when securing his presence was the only way to gain your sister's acquiescence."

"Her what?"

"Her agreement. Her consent. Her compliance. For God's

sake, read a book once in a while, would you?"

"You're not going to be Dixie Downer all night, are you? Because that might not project into a very appealing reality TV persona, if you get my drift. This could be your big break. I can see it now. A reality television experience not to be missed: *Dixie Downer: Ghost Huntress*."

"Funny. But you know what? I don't think you're as ho-hum about this little adventure as you put on."

"What are you saying?"

"The only reason you wanted all of us along is that you were too scared to stay here by yourself."

"What? Me? Scared? Of what? The boogey man? Michael Myers? Freddy Krueger? Puhleaze. I can assure you, I didn't invite you along because I'm afraid of a big, bad house."

"Boo!"

I screamed and made a grab for Dixie when Frankie yelled and dropped to the floor beside her.

"Glad to see you're not afraid," Dixie said. "Now if you would be so kind as to extract your fingernails from my arm."

"God will get you for that, Frankie," I warned. He shrugged.

"Manny and I just did a perimeter check," he said. "He's got this really cool night vision equipment. You gotta try it out. It's amazing."

Dixie patted his arm. "Maybe later," she said, and shot me a see-what-you've-done-now look.

"Why was Manny checking the perimeter? Is he looking for ghosts?" I snorted.

"No, no. Strictly security protocols," Frankie informed me with a Barney Fife nose sniff. "Very hi-tech stuff."

"Is Manny expecting...trouble?" I asked, thinking of the incidents that had targeted his protectee. You know. The incidents everyone seemed to think I had a hand in. *Those* incidents.

"Manny always expects trouble," Frankie said with the glow of admiration in his eyes—which resulted in Dixie sending me yet another glare.

"Did you see Taylor when you were out doing your security sweep?" I asked.

"Yeah. She was there with Patrick. He and Manny were

talking shop."

"What do you mean 'talking shop', Frankie?" Dixie asked.

He shrugged again. "Oh, you know. The usual stuff. Comparing guns and firepower. Discussing loads and ammo. That kind of thing."

"And Manny can converse on these topics with a fairly broad base of knowledge?" I asked.

"Of course. Manny knows all about weapons."

"I see," I nodded at Dixie. She raised an eyebrow in return. "And what did Taylor bring to the table in terms of this discussion?"

Frankie suddenly looked uncomfortable. "I can't recall—"

"Spill it, Frankie."

"She said something about learning how to shoot a gun because a person should never be without personal protection if they plan on spending any time at all with…er…uh…certain relatives," Frankie faltered near the end.

"Oh. Nice. See if I try to set her up with a hunky guy in uniform again."

"Come back to planet Earth, Miss Trekkie," Dixie said. "Taylor's probably had more dates in the last year than all three of us have had our entire lives. You're just in a snit because someone is telling it like it is and you can't handle it."

"I can handle it," I said. "I just don't like people dissing me behind my back."

"You diss me all the time," Dixie pointed out.

"Ah, but I look you in the eye when I do it," I said. "Like that. Right there. Did you notice I said 'look you in the *eye*'? Like you had only one eye rather than two. In this way I do you the courtesy of providing an opportunity for you to take a defensive posture or mount a full-fledged attack in retaliation."

"I feel so honored," Dixie said. "Well, I'll return the compliment in an equally direct fashion. You got out-maneuvered by Keelie Keller and had to accept her invite to spend the night in this little house of horrors. As a result, you bamboozled the rest of us into coming because you were too chicken to do it on your own…*Nancy*."

"Well!" I jumped to my feet, trying to project the bluster of outrage. "If that's the way you feel, you and Frankie are certainly free to vacate the premises!"

Dixie shook her head. "Not your best performance, Turner. You forget. I've seen you act before."

"Oh. That's right. Carson College, wasn't it? As I recall, you were a captive audience. Literally."

Dixie gave me a dark look.

"Everyone! Everyone! Gather round!" Keelie Keller skipped into the tiny parlor, a great-looking accessory on each arm: Manny on the left and Patrick on the right. Taylor trailed behind, her expression hard to gauge.

"It's almost the witching hour!" Keelie announced. "And you know what time that is! It's Ouija time!"

Tiara started clapping.

"Ouija! Ouija!"

"What the hell are they squealing about?" Dixie asked.

Tiara held up a game box.

"Oh, God. Kill me now," came out before I could stop it. I clapped a hand over my mouth and looked up at the ceiling. "That's not meant to be taken as literal or like an invitation or anything." I patted the wall with a hand that wouldn't stop trembling. "Nice house. Nice house."

"Oh, brother." Dixie's snort was unmistakable.

"I don't think that would be a capital idea, Keelie," Langley said.

"I think it just plain sucks," Dixie echoed.

"You're all just a bunch of scaredy cats. Aren't they, Keelie?" Tiara said. "Party poopers and scaredy cats."

Call me what you like, but I've watched enough *Supernatural* to know you don't screw around with the demon world, even if it gets you an introduction to the Winchester bros.

"So, learn anything about windage and elevation?" I inquired of Taylor when she joined us at the far side of the room. (I have no idea what the words actually mean. I got the terms from a John Wayne movie where Duke was trying to teach a prissy woman from the east how to handle a rifle.)

"What are you talking about?"

"Your NRA meeting."

She gave me a "don't start" look.

"This was a bad idea," Taylor said. "Bad. Bad. Bad."

I was ready to concede it wasn't my finest moment.

"Okay, everybody! Gather round. We are going to try to contact the spirit world." Keelie announced. "Come, come! Don't be scared. We have two big, strong, muscle men to protect us."

"What am I? Chopped liver?" Frankie whined.

"Come on, everyone! Form a circle in the center of the room." Tiara instructed.

"Tressa." Keelie skipped over to me and grabbed my hand. "Come on."

I dug in my heels. "I'd rather not. On religious grounds."

"You're doing this!" Keelie insisted. "Taylor." She put a hand out and motioned to Frankie. "Frank. *Debbie*."

"It's *Dixie*." Dixie corrected. "And I'll pass. I find this kind of activity sophomoric, insensitive, and offensive."

"Debbie's scared," I blurted.

Dixie shook her head.

"Well, okay. Whatever. Everyone else. Gather around the board. Manny? Patrick? You'll protect us, right?"

Manny grunted.

"Yes, ma'am. We'll do our best," Patrick said.

Ahhh. You gotta love a guy who calls a girl younger than he is "ma'am."

"Don't forget about me, gentlemen. My body may be in need of guarding, too," Langley reminded the security detail.

"Ooh, Langley! Silly boy! Haven't you heard every man for himself?" Tiara asked.

The reality BFFs hugged each other and giggled.

"It's almost midnight, ladies," Langley chided. "Are we doing this or not?"

"Sorry, Lang. We'll behave. Pinky swear," Keelie said, and wrapped her pinky finger around Tiara's. "Okay. Everyone has to take this like seriously."

Keelie took a deep theatrical breath.

Someone tried to stifle a yawn. Unsuccessfully.

"Now, for our back story," Keelie began her voice low and hushed. "On the night of June 9, 1912, the family of Josiah B. Moore and Sarah Montgomery Moore returned with their children from a Children's Day celebration at church. Two young friends of Katherine had obtained permission from their parents to spend the night with the Moore family.

Early on the morning of June 10th, 1912, a neighbor of the Moore's noticed that the Moore family had not let their chickens out or begun their chores. In fact, the neighbor had seen no sign of the family that morning at all. The neighbor approached the house and tried the door, but found it locked from the inside. She went back home and called Josiah Moore's brother, Ross Moore, who rushed to the home. He looked in the windows and knocked on the door and shouted, attempting to rouse someone within the home, but to no avail. The brother used his house key and entered the parlor—this very room. He opened the door to that room"—she pointed to a small room off the parlor—"and discovered what appeared to be two bloody bodies. Ross left the home and contacted the Town Marshall, who entered the home with the brother. To their horror, they discovered a blood bath. Eight victims—had been butchered in their beds by an ax-wielding assailant. Something had been draped over each of the mirrors in the home. A pan of bacon sat on the stove."

Bacon? I perked up.

"Although there have been many theories regarding the identity of the Villisca ax murderer, no one was ever found guilty of the heinous crime. Now, a hundred years later, the malevolent shadow of a heinous crime hangs over this home and eight victims still cry out for justice."

An eerie silence fell, our collective breathing, in and out, in and out, the only sound in the room.

Throughout Keelie's recitation I'd tried to distance myself from the words, tried to think of anything but the story she told, the story of a tragic and horrific murder that took place in this very home while the innocent victims lay sleeping and oblivious in their beds.

You're surrounded by big, tough men, I reminded myself. Patrick and Manny and two sturdy cameramen were just steps away.

"The owners wouldn't give us permission to use candles so we'll have to make do with these penlights. Manny," Keelie was saying, "lights please."

Manny flipped his badass flashlight off and the room went dark. Well, *darker*. The light from the cameras cast creepy shadows on the walls and around the room.

"Now, everybody put their fingertips on the thingy here. That's right. Nice and easy. Eww. Gross. Who's the nail biter?"

Frankie snatched his hands back. "I think I'll keep Debbie, er, Dixie company," he said.

"Everyone must clear their minds completely," Keelie said.

"That shouldn't take long." That observation came from "Debbie's" corner of the room.

"Clear your mind and let it flow throughout the house, out, out, into the great beyond. We are reaching out to the spirit or spirits in this house. Spirits, are you there?"

"Uh, excuse me." I raised my hand. "Could I have some clarification here? Which spirit or spirits are we reaching out to? Victims of violent murder spirits or...ax-wielding, murderous psycho spirits?" My voice did a quivery vibrato number at the end.

"Does it matter?" Keelie asked.

"Uh. Yeah. What part of ax-wielding, murderous psycho spirit did you miss?"

"Listen, Turner. If you want to wimp out—"

"You smell that?" Langley said.

"Smell what?"

"That smell. It smells like—"

Bacon.

Shhh!" Tiara hushed. "Listen! Did you hear that?"

"Hear what?" Keelie said.

"That."

I strained to listen.

Thump.

"Did you hear that?"

"It came from upstairs."

Thump. Thump.

"There it is again."

"Hey! Who's moving the mouse?"

"Mouse?"

"The pointer! The indicator! It's moving!"

I stared down at our fingertips. The pointer *was* moving.

Thump! Thump!

"Listen! There it was again!"

"Shhh!"
"I don't like this."
"Knock it off! Quit pushing the pointer!"
"I'm not!"
"Are too!"
"Am not!"
Thump. Thump. THUMP!
"What the hell!"
"Oh. My. God!"
"Turn on the lights! Turn on the lights now!"
Camera lights bounced off the walls in a frenzied dance.
"Where's the light switch?"
"Manny?"
"Just a minute. Manny's light won't work."
"You're shitting me."
"Wait! What are you doing? Hold on! Where are you going?"

I jumped to my feet. Others around me did the same, kicking penlights and sending them rolling across the floor, their beams creating creepy, distorted shadows on the walls and curtains.

"I'm outta here."

As someone had aptly pointed out earlier, it was every man/woman for his/herself.

Thump, thump, thump.

The sound came from the top of the staircase, and I did what any sane, young woman would do under the circumstances. I bolted like the scared little Nancy-girl I was. I ran in the direction I figured the front door should be, only to have my way blocked by a tangle of torsos, arms, and legs.

"Could we have a little light here," Langley's voice shook, the calm, British façade cracking under the pressure.

Thump.

Manny's big ol' light suddenly came on.

Thump. Thump.

I watched in terrified slow motion as a bright red ball bounced down the stairs.

Thump. Thump. Thump!
"Aaaaaa!"

I'm pretty sure I screamed bloody murder, but it was hard to know for sure because Langley Carlisle the Third and Drew Van Vleet had a scream fest competition going on to see who could sound more like a female 'fraidy pants than I did.

I pivoted, changing direction. Now that I was better oriented, I saw my opening. I felt my way to the kitchen, just off the parlor, aiming for the back door and escape.

Like those balance-challenged scary movie heroines who can't seem to master the concept of putting one foot in front of the other without falling, my own feet wouldn't seem to cooperate. I felt my knees buckle, and I went down, crumpling to the floor like blonde bimbo serial killer bait.

"Oomph!" I reached a hand out to see what I'd fallen over and gasped. I shoved myself away when I realized it wasn't a "what" but a "who" that had tripped me up.

I swore. One itty-bitty curse word.

This was not good. Not good at all.

I could see the headline now: Villisca Murder House Claims Teen Idol Victim.

Talk about your reality checks.

CHAPTER EIGHTEEN

"Oh, my God! Jax?" Keelie knelt over the latest body I'd stumbled across and cradled her ex's head. "Talk to me! Jax!"

"Aaaaaa!" The "body" in question suddenly let loose with a bone-chilling scream and sat up, grabbing at Keelie. "Gotcha!"

"You son of a bitch!" Keelie jumped to her feet and shoved Jax away. His head smacked the wooden floor.

I winced. Judging from Keelie's reaction, a bump on the head would be the least of Jax Whitver's concerns.

"You scared the shit out of me!" Keelie railed. "What the hell do you think you're doing?"

Looking surprisingly alive and well—at least for the moment—Jax chuckled and sat up, resting a hand on one knee, his pearly white teeth standing out in the darkened house.

"Providing some very entertaining footage for the show, I'd imagine," Langley observed.

"You're sick!" Tiara gave Jax's leg a nudge with the toe of her shoe. "He's sick!" She repeated for the benefit of those of us who were too dense to pick it up the first time.

She'd get no argument from me. I'd be lucky if my hair wasn't white when I got a look at it come daylight.

"What's the big deal? I came in the back door, heard you getting your ghost on with the Ouija fest, and decided it would be fun to lie down and wait for someone to discover me."

"You son of bitch!" Keelie said again. "You scared us to death! That's what the big deal is!"

"Yeah. And what about that ball?" Tiara asked.

"Ball?" Jax shook his head. "What ball? What are you talking about?"

"The ball you bounced down the stairs!" Tiara said.

Jax shook his head. "Down the stairs? What the hell are you talking about? I was never upstairs."

"Sure," Tiara said. "Sure."

"I'm serious. I never went past the kitchen. You would have seen me. And heard me."

To prove his point, Jax got up and walked to the tiny staircase. He mounted several steps. The resulting squeaks and creaks were deafening.

I frowned. No way could he have gotten up that staircase without the rest of us hearing.

"Well, if you didn't—" Langley started.

"And we didn't," Tiara said.

"Then...who?" Keelie asked.

"Or what?" Jax said.

A sound, not unlike someone might make when he or she steps on a hundred-year-old creaky board, made us lift our eyes to the ceiling. We stood, hushed and waiting.

"You know. I could do with a loo break," Lang suddenly said.

"Yeah. Me, too."

"I could go for a break."

"Yeah. Good plan."

The occupants of the Murder House made a collective beeline for the back door that led to the barn, restroom, each battling to keep from being the last person left in the house. We reached the small, but well-lit porch off the barn when a figure stepped out from the side yard. This one, thank God, didn't yell, "Boo!"

"Vinny! What are you doing here?" Keelie asked.

"My job. What the hell is going on?" Vinny Vincent, flashlight in hand, took in the scene, a scowl spreading across his face when his gaze lit on Jax.

"Jax thought it would be funny to drop in and scare the hell out of us," Tiara accused. "He's sick," she parroted again. "Sick!"

Vinny frowned. "I thought we had an understanding, Whitver," he said. "You were going to keep your distance."

"You'd like that, wouldn't you, Vinny?" Jax said. "Well, lucky for me, this is America, and I am free to roam where the *spirit* moves me. Pun intended, by the way."

"And I suppose you're responsible for *her* being here." Vinny cocked his head in my direction. "It just keeps getting better and better."

"Actually, er, uh, sir, Keelie extended the invite…er, challenge," I stammered.

"Keep your friends close? Keep your enemies closer, ay, Duckie?" He winked at Keelie.

"Now listen here—" I objected.

"You listen, Blondie. These pranks are not just petty anymore," Vinny said. "The furry send-off gift. Spiking Keelie's drink. The graffiti. Tampering with her brake cable. That doesn't add up to harmless summer fun, Toots."

"Graffiti? Brake cable?" This time the clueless look on my face was the real thing. "What are you talking about?"

"Someone left 'Keelie, go home!' signs in various places along the bike route. She also had her brakes tampered with," Vinny said. "Lucky for Keelie, Manny here conducts a thorough inspection of all the bikes."

I shot a look at Manny. His chin lifted in silent confirmation.

"That's awful. Really. But I had nothing to do with any of those incidents," I said.

"Incidents? Those are crimes, Blondie. *Chargeable* crimes. Am I right, Officer? Mr. DeMarco?"

Patrick frowned. The corner of Manny's mouth lifted slightly.

"What's a crime, Vinny, is the way you manipulate people to suit your own ends," Jax interjected.

An elbow jabbed me in the ribs. "Sound like anyone we know?" Dixie said.

"Surely you can't mean…*Moi*?"

"Can't I, Miss Piggy? Thanks to you, Frankie and I now have supporting roles in this freak show."

"Well, excuse me for thinking you might actually appreciate some national exposure."

Dixie shook her head. "Why would I need or want the kind of exposure this voyeuristic venue promotes?" she asked. "It's objectifying, demeaning, and contributes to the increasing and pervasive intellectual dumbing-down of the populace."

"Tell us what you really think, Debbie," I responded. "And haven't you ever heard no publicity is bad publicity?"

"Yeah. Usually from the mouths of attention whores who don't give a flip about the impact they're having on young, impressionable minds."

Debbie Daggett does the soapbox. I only hoped the soap box wouldn't buckle under the weight.

"You're one to talk about manipulating people, Whitver," Vinny was saying. "What the hell do you think you've been doing to Keelie with your little prankster friend here?" Vinny asked.

"Hello! Read my lips: I am not responsible for any of the malicious pranks targeting Keelie. Maybe you'd do better to spend your time checking out your own back yard," I suggested.

"What the hell do you mean by that?" Vinny barked.

"You can't deny Keelie's reality TV ratings are getting a shot in the arm from all the drama," I said. "And ratings bumps benefit everyone involved with the show: producers, advertisers, cast members, their agents…"

"I resent your implication!"

"Welcome to the club," I responded.

"Vinny, you're spoiling our séance!" Keelie hooked an arm through Manny's and Frankie's arms. "Nothing's going to happen to me when I have all these big strong men here to protect me."

"I think I'm gonna be sick," Dixie muttered.

"Come on, everybody! Let's finish our potty breaks, make nice, and go back in and see if we can raise a little hell!" Keelie pumped a fist in the air. "Murder House! Murder House! Murder House!"

Tiara joined her pal in the ghoulish chant.

"You will join us as we repair to the haunted Ax Murder House for another go-round at a ghostie, won't you, Vinny, ol' boy?" Langley asked, putting a hand out to the owly agent.

"Hell, no! I'm going to sit out here, have a smoke, and thank God I'm too old and too smart to piss away what time I have left on this earth trying to contact the damned boogeyman."

Langley raised an eyebrow and an "I tried" shoulder.

"As you say, Vinny," he said. "Miss Turner?"

He lifted his elbow, inviting me to take his arm.

I found myself accepting.

What can I say? I'm a sucker for a guy with good manners

and an accent.

Langley tucked my arm into his and patted my hand.

"You mustn't take Vinny too seriously," Langley said. "His bark is worse than his bite."

Somehow I doubted that. Vinny came off like a feisty pit bull with a bone to pick.

With me.

By the time we returned to the parlor, Keelie and Tiara had lost interest in the boogeyman board. Instead, they began to dance around the parlor to a pretty awful rendition of *Monster Mash*.

"Sorry, love," Langley said, and gently let go of my arm. "Sounds like the duet could do with a soprano." He gave me a wave and went to join his BFFs. Soon Tiara had grabbed Frankie and pulled him into the chorus line.

I grabbed my sleeping bag and claimed the wall nearest the front door. You know. Just in case.

"I hope you're happy," Dixie said, dropping to the floor beside me.

"What? Frankie's finally coming out of his shell. That's a good thing."

"Shells exist for a reason. It's called protection," Dixie pointed out.

A second later, Langley threw an arm around Patrick and pulled the reluctant trooper into the sing-along.

"I hope you're happy." Taylor dropped to the floor on my other side.

"What? Patrick's showing he can be a good sport. Gotta love that in a guy."

"Oh? And being a good sport includes being groped by someone you just met?" Taylor asked.

"What do you mean, groped? I can see both of Langley's hands."

"Not Langley, you idiot. Keelie," Taylor hissed.

I blinked. She was right. Keelie was definitely putting the moves on Patrick, who was now the yummy, meaty filling between two slices of bread.

He looked like Mr. Spock did when his human half was showing.

"Are you just going to sit there, or are you going to rescue that lawman from the clutches of Reality Red?" I asked Taylor.

"He hardly looks like he needs rescuing," she said.

"Are you kidding? He looks about as comfy as our mom does when Gram volunteers to read the announcements at church."

"Oh, Lord. That bad?"

I nodded. "Trust me on this one."

Taylor made a face. She turned to the grumble puss next to me. "Dixie?"

"As much as I hate to agree with the Trekkie here, it's pretty evident, that dude is miserable."

Taylor hesitated for a moment.

"Okay. I'm goin' in," she said.

I raised a hand. "May the Force be with you."

Taylor shook her head. "Some Trekkie," she commented and left to rescue her trooper in distress.

"So, who do you really think has it in for the Kardashian wannabe over there?" Dixie asked, nodding at Keelie who was currently giving Taylor the Voodoo eye. "Do you think it's someone with the show?"

"Did I sound credible when I suggested it?" I asked.

Dixie scratched her chin. "Credible? That's not exactly a word I'd associate with you, but you certainly sounded like you believed it."

"Well, if you rule out Taylor and this reluctant Trekkie, it almost has to be an inside job."

Dixie snorted. "Inside job? Ooh. Look at you going all Sherlock Holmesy on me."

"I know. You thought I was just a pretty face, right?" I snorted.

"I suppose you think the guilty party could even be Keelie herself," Dixie said.

I gave Reality Red a long, considering look. "It occurred to me. What better way to gain sympathy and support than by being a victim? She paints a target on her own back and then proceeds to fire away. Splat! Splat! Splat, splat, splat!"

Dixie shook her head. "Speaking of 'splat,' what about the case of Hershey squirts the tabloids have had so much fun with?

You're saying she did that to herself?"

"Well, no one witnessed any actual…anal…leakage," I pointed out.

"Anal…leakage?"

"Montezuma's revenge could have been an elaborate performance."

"Then, judging by what I saw, Keelie Keller is a pretty good actress," Dixie said.

"But you see my point, right? It could all be a series of Keelie Keller hoaxes."

"Still, any number of people stand to benefit from the notoriety," Dixie said.

"Or, it's someone who doesn't like Keelie at all and is using the ride as an opportunity to get back at her."

"I thought you ruled yourself out," Dixie snarked.

"I don't know her well enough to dislike her," I pointed out.

I wrapped my sleeping bag around me and tried to suppress a jumbo-sized yawn. Okay, so I didn't try to suppress it. I let it rip. I felt my eyelids begin to droop. Beat didn't begin to describe how tired I was.

I could hear singing. Boisterous and off-key. We were now being treated to a totally whacked version of Mr. Sandman.

Music to snooze by, as far as I was concerned.

I struggled to keep my eyes open, finally surrendering to that blissful ignorance of sleep in a place with soft mattresses, clean sheets, fluffy pillows, and strong arms to hold me.

I awoke to find my head cocked at an uncomfortable angle and a bladder full enough it wouldn't let me fall back to sleep. Drool dribbled out of the corner of my mouth. I reached up to wipe it before anyone noticed.

Not that I had to worry. Everyone else was camped out on the parlor floor, different sizes of sleeping bag lumps, filling the room with the sounds of sleep.

I checked my cell phone. Three o'clock.

I got to my feet, winced at the stiffness and pain, and rotated my neck and shoulders to get the kinks out. I'd be lucky if I could get on my bike in five hours, let alone pedal the frigging thing.

I made my way to the back door, down the ramp, and to the

sidewalk that led to the barn—the same path we'd used during our en masse exodus earlier. I shuffled along, barely able to keep my eyes open.

All right. All right. I did the zombie walk. I was working on less than three hours of sleep spent camped out on the floor of a haunted murder house. Give me a break.

I slow-moed my way down the sidewalk, each step an accomplishment. My "walker" steps took me down the short sidewalk to the porch of the barn. I frowned at the now dark structure, and sleepily ripped whoever had turned the lights off a new one. I climbed the porch steps and tried to recall where the john was located.

The buzz-buzz of a mosquito tickled my ear, and I slapped it away.

"Bloodsuckers!" I mumbled.

I remembered my cell phone and took it from my pocket, hitting the button to wake it up. I held it out in front of me to light the way.

I took another "walker" step, hesitating at the porch rail when I caught the outline of a figure on the bench to my right.

Busted!

Some 'fraidy cat had crept out of the house to bed down on the bench. I did a forehead bump with the butt of my hand. Why hadn't I thought of that?

I approached the sacked-out sleeper, curious to see who had struck out on their own.

A mosquito dive-bombed me. Then another. And another. Slap! Slap! Slap!

"Damn." I was being eaten alive. I swatted another potential taste-tester away and decided I'd better wake the oblivious sleeper or, come morning, he or she would be a prime candidate for West Nile Virus.

"Hey! You! Not a good place to crash," I said.

No reaction.

"Helloo." I bent over and put a hand on the sleeper's shoulder and shook. "You're so gonna regret this in the morning," I said. "You'll wake up short a pint of whole blood."

I pulled my hand back. It felt wet.

I frowned, and pushed the button on my phone, shining

what wimpy illumination it provided at my fingertips. I stared down at my hand.

It wasn't. It couldn't be. Uh-uh. No way was that dark red, wet, sticky substance blood. No way.

I raised my fingers for a closer look.

It sure looked like blood.

My phone went dark.

I said a few words I promised to ask forgiveness for and fumbled around getting the phone to wake up.

"Hey. You. There." I said.

Finally, the phone's light illuminated the sleeper's profile. I sucked in a ragged breath.

Vinny Vincent, the dark shadow of blood standing out in sharp contrast to the white collar of his shirt, lay sprawled out on the bench.

Holy Hell-Raiser!

I could see the headlines now: Hollywood agent gets the ax!

And one cursed cub reporter?

She gets the shaft.

CHAPTER NINETEEN

I stared at the phone number displayed on my cell and bit my lip.

To answer or not to answer? That was the question.

I opted to punt and hit "ignore."

In the dawn's early light, my vantage point from the second floor/hayloft level of the Murder House barn provided a spectacular view. The small, white two-story at the corner of South Sixth Avenue and East Second Street in Villisca, Iowa, probably hadn't seen this amount of curious gawker foot traffic since the infamous morning of June 10, 1912, when—according to Frankie—a good share of the citizenry tromped through a mass murder crime scene, moving bodies and cleaning up blood, and destroying evidence that might have helped solve the crime.

Back then, however, they didn't have things like live links, satellite trucks, or smart phones to broadcast the unfolding events to a worldwide audience live.

Gotta love twenty-first century technology.

Patrick and Manny, along with local law enforcement, had herded us up to an area staged for tour group talks. A row of old theater seats, along with webbed lawn chairs, provided seating for those who took the tour.

"And you didn't take any pictures? Any at all?" Van Vleet asked again.

"Gee, I'm sorry, Drew. It didn't occur to me to snap pictures of an unconscious and bleeding assault victim before I dialed 9-1-1," I said.

"What about afterwards?" Van Vleet pressed, and I gave him my version of the you-are-pond-scum' stare. Take my word for it. It's intimidating.

"Looks like you could use a cup." Patrick appeared and pressed a cup of coffee into my hand. "And...a bit of a break." He performed a get-lost nod in Van Vleet's direction.

"Coffee does sound good," Van Vleet said, an up-and-down of his Adam's apple showing he received the trooper's message loud and clear.

"So. How is he? Vinny, I mean?" I asked, cupping the warm coffee with both hands.

"He'll live. Actually, his injury isn't all that severe. A slight concussion at worst."

"But all that blood—"

"Head wounds bleed buckets," Patrick said. "And often look much worse than they actually are. Mr. Vincent is being evaluated in a hospital, but it appears the injury isn't serious."

I let out a long, relieved breath.

"Thank goodness. Has he said anything about what happened? How he was injured?"

"He says he was having a smoke on the bench, felt a sharp pain, and it was lights out until he came to with you standing over him."

"Surely he doesn't think I—"

At Patrick's expression, I stopped. Of course, he did. Hadn't he spent the better part of the bike ride accusing me of all kinds of nefarious criminal activity? Why not a blitz attack?

"He was blind-sided. He didn't see or hear a thing," Patrick said, trying to reassure me.

"I'm sure Vinny has his own theory." It didn't taken a ton of smarts to figure out Vinny had given me the finger. I mean fingered me. Oh, you know what I mean.

Patrick shrugged. "At this point, anyone in the house or in the vicinity of the house is a suspect."

"How's Manny handling the fallout?" I asked. When you're supposed to be in charge of security and an assault with injuries occurs right under your nose, it's gotta suck.

"Manny's...highly motivated to discover who's responsible."

I figured "highly motivated" was an understatement. Manny was probably ready to bust a kneecap or two over the incident. But I'm only speculating here.

"He's suggested that Keelie reconsider the bike ride,"

Patrick went on.

"Oh? What does Keelie think?"

"She's refusing to pull out."

"I see." I chewed my bottom lip. Just the reaction you'd expect from the reality star if she knew for certain she wasn't in any real danger. "I bet the show's producers are tickled green—as in advertising bucks green—at Keelie's show-must-go-on attitude," I mused aloud.

Patrick grimaced. "I don't get all the reality show hype and popularity," he said. "Apparently, living vicariously through others appeals to a certain demographic of the populace."

I was with Patrick on this one. I'd never been comfortable cast in the role of a sideline observer.

Oh, I see. You could tell that about me, huh?

"So, what happens now?"

"The locals investigate," Patrick said. "With assistance from the state."

"Couldn't we figure out if anyone left the house at the approximate time of the attack by looking at the cameraman's footage?" I asked.

Patrick shook his head. "I wish. They shut down for the night shortly after the little brouhaha with Jax Whitver."

"Oh? What about your moves on the dance floor? Did your stint on the chorus line end up going viral?"

He reddened.

"God, I hope not or else I'll never live it down. I had a devil of a time getting permission from the brass to participate in the first place. I should have known it wasn't the sort of setting a small town Iowa boy would comfortably fit into."

I put a hand on his shoulder.

"There, there, Mr. State Trooper. Everything will be okay. I promise."

"Am I interrupting?"

I turned. Taylor, looking like a harbinger of death, stood there.

"You're not interrupting a thing," I said. "Why? What's up?"

Taylor held her phone out to me.

"It's for you," she said, tight-lipped and curt. "It's Rick. He says he's been trying to reach you for hours."

My tummy did a flip-flop like it used to when my dad took us out on what he used to call "belly-button hills." You know. Where you're going really fast and your tummy feels like it's in your throat. One of those numbers.

"Oh. Well, er, my phone's like really low on its charge, so I turned it off to save the battery."

"Uh-huh. Well, lucky for you, I have a full charge," she said. "So take all the time you need to catch up."

"Oh, uh, thanks," I said, feeling anything but grateful as I swallowed past the wad in my throat.

"We'll just give you a little privacy, won't we, Patrick?" Taylor said, and spirited the trooper away.

I cleared my throat.

"Uh, hello?"

"Good to see you figured out how a cell phone works," Ranger Rick said. "Well, other than as a flashlight to point out unconscious assault victims at the haunted Murder House, that is."

Okay. I deserved the sarcastic salvo. Avoidance has always been my fatal flaw. Okay. *One* of my fatal flaws. Geez. What is this? Pig-pile on Tressa Turner day?

"Sawree," I said, and meant it. "You know I'm not a phone person."

"I'm well aware of your phone phobia, Tressa," Ranger Rick said, "But I thought even you could manage to hit a button when your phone rings, put it to your ear, and say hello."

I grimaced. Things were not sunny in Jellystone Park.

"You're right," I said, too weary and too weirded out by the previous night's events to adequately defend myself. "Like I said. Sorry."

One of those ass-awkward phone hesitations I referenced earlier followed.

"Wow. Now that I didn't expect," Ranger Rick said, and I frowned into the phone.

"Expect…what?"

"Not only one, but two apologies. Two in less than thirty seconds! That's got to be a record."

It was, but the ranger would receive confirmation of that factoid from me when my gammy stopped playing her fortune cookie numbers in the lottery.

Not. Gonna. Happen.

I rubbed the phone against the buttons of my shirt and held it away from me.

"I can hardly hear you! There's too much static."

This scam rarely worked with the savvy ranger anymore. I'd used it way too often. Still, it generally got my point across.

"I hear you, Tressa. Loud and clear. I've been following the Keelie Keller stuff. What the hell is going on out there?" Rick asked.

Like I had a real clue.

"It's all smoke and mirrors," I assured him. "These reality shows? They're all very carefully choreographed and scripted. Nothing happens by accident."

"Oh? What about the attack on Keelie Keller's agent and you stumbling on him in the dead of night?" Rick asked. "Was that staged, or was it an accident?"

"Well, of course *that* was an accident!" I huffed. "You don't think I stumbled across another bloody body on purpose, do you?"

"That's not what I mean, and you know it, Tressa," Rick said. "I'm just saying, from what I hear of the agent's injury, it would have been impossible for him to inflict it himself."

I frowned.

"Just whom have you been talking to, exactly?" I asked.

"Taylor and I visited before she put you on the phone. She said it was obvious someone attacked the agent from behind. Dumb me. I thought I'd only have to worry about you when you were on your bike. It didn't occur to me that the stopovers would prove more dangerous. What made you agree to a night in the Murder House anyway?"

"Would you believe my *id* made me do it?" I asked.

"It's time you stopped blaming Freud for your destructive impulses, Tressa," Rick said. "We both know there's more than a personality triad run amok going on here. You have a gift, Tressa Turner. A gift for finding trouble."

We were making progress. Used to be Ranger Rick would tell you my gift was "making" trouble. Now, it appeared I was merely an innocent wayfarer skipping blindly into it. So. Yeah.

Progress.

"There's sort of this wager going," I began.

"Wager?"

"You know. A team wager."

"On what exactly?"

"Well, that's not well-defined." I gave a short synopsis of how the contest climate had started and eventually shook out, including an overview of the back and forth with Keelie and Kompany and my hopes for a truce, as well as Stan's behind-my-back bet with Paul Van Vleet of the *New Holland News*. "So, you see, I'm really operating on several fronts. One. I'm trying to win a bet for the big guy, and, two, I'm trying to uphold the honor of my fellow Heartland inhabitants by taking on a bratty, big shot reality star from a Beverly Hills zip code."

"In other words, your compulsion to win is driving you."

"Hey. There's been no backseat driving of Miss Tressa here, Mr. Ranger, sir," I said, trying to divert Rick's attention away from my foibles and back on my amazing accomplishment. "I'll have you know this amateur biker has pedaled each and every mile of this hot, sticky, butt-numbing road show so far." Something, I would bet my poor, abused bottom dollar my famous competitor could not lay claim to.

"About that butt," Ranger Rick said, and my heart went pitter-patter.

"Yes?"

"I like it the way it is so make sure it isn't pounded down to a mere shadow of its former self," Rick said.

A flash of heat hotter than my Uncle Frank's deep fat fryers at high noon produced the sheen of perspiration on my face. I set my coffee down and fanned my cheeks with my free hand.

"Is that an order, Mr. Ranger, sir?" I asked.

"I know better than to give you an order, Calamity," he teased. "Look at it as a heartfelt request."

I fanned faster.

"I guess I'll er...see you when we overnight in Grandville," I stammered.

"Is that an invitation?" Rick asked.

Was it?

"Anything's possible in Team Trekkie's Rootin' Tootin'

Reality Road Race," I hedged. "By the way, will you be joining TribRide when we leave Grandville?" I asked.

A pause.

"Anything's possible in a Ranger Rick to the Rescue Ride Across Iowa," he finally said.

"Thanks for the warning," I said, and hit end.

I could see the T-shirt logo now: Bikers do it in circles.

And cockeyed cowgirls?

They go along for the ride, of course.

Snap! Snap!

Van Vleet flicked his fingers in my face.

"Snap out of it, Red Shirt! Time to hit the road. Move it, Blondie. It's a long, hot ride to Creston. And, as you're so fond of saying, 'we're burning daylight, pilgrim.'"

I made a face. "Uh, quick point of fact here. That Duke Wayne quote—or any Duke Wayne quote, for that matter—should never, ever, ever, be recited by anyone wearing socks with sandals. It's just...wrong." I said, looking down at his feet and shaking my head.

"Funny. But it will be me laughing when your cousin's girlfriend pulls out leaving you to hoof it back to Highway 34, where we pick up the ride," he said.

"She wouldn't dare."

No sooner were those words out of my mouth than I understood how totally removed from reality *I* was.

"Yoo hoo! I'm coming! I'm coming!" I announced via the hayloft door to the masses still assembled in the yard below. "Don't leave without me!"

I hoofed it to the narrow staircase.

I made it to the Suburban and jumped in the back seat and met Dixie's eyes in the rearview mirror.

"I knew you couldn't leave without me," I said.

"Wow, Frankie. You never told me you had a psychic in the family," Dixie said. "And I didn't wait for you. Lucky for you, you still had Taylor's phone, and she wouldn't let me leave without *it*."

I held Taylor's phone out to her, and she snatched it from me like my gammy grabs the last chocolate chip cookie on the plate.

"Your texts were safe with me," I assured her with a big wink. On the other hand, if some of her more interesting selfies happened to find their way onto my phone? I shrugged. Stuff happens.

We'd driven five minutes or so when a ker-thunk, ker-thunk got my attention.

"What *is* that noise?" I asked.

"Oh, please. We're not going to play that 'ghost, ghost come out today' game again, are we?" Dixie said.

"She's right. Listen," Taylor said.

Ker-thunk. Ker-thunk.

"Damn." Dixie pulled the Suburban over to the side of the road. "Sounds like a flat."

We got out of the car and, with collective dismay, surveyed the rear passenger tire.

"Dammit. I hate when Tressa is right. Fortunately, it doesn't happen often enough to be all that taxing," she added.

"I suppose someone should grab the jack," I said.

"Someone?" Dixie said.

"Someone big and strong...and male," I clarified.

"Right."

"Oh, for heaven's sake," Taylor said. "Tressa, help me with the jack."

About that time I heard a sound like an air horn from a semi truck. I looked up in time to see Keelie Keller's bus pull slowly alongside.

"Oh, Turner! Tressa Turner!" Keelie's voice erupted from the loudspeaker. "All's fair in love and war—and wagers! Toodles!"

"Hey! What about our truce?" I yelled.

The luxury coach drove on by, oblivious to the Romulan death stare directed at it.

"Yep. That's right. I'm lookin' at you," I said to the bus's bumper.

"That's it? That's all you've got?" Dixie's mouth flew open. "Here we are: disabled vehicle, a psycho head-basher on the loose, and your newest BFF and your former faux beau drive right on by, and that's your reaction. I'm lookin' at you? Ooh. Scary."

I sniffed.

"That shows what you know," I said. "Even as we speak, this crack mind is spinning various payback scenarios."

"Cracked mind is right," Dixie mumbled.

Okay. I was bluffing. Beyond my Romulan role-playing, I had nothing. Team Trekkie was fresh out of photon torpedoes.

And Tressa Jayne Turner?

For all I knew, this cowgirl could soon be a wanted woman—and not in your "Oh, baby, baby!" kind of way.

Talk about your final frontiers.

CHAPTER TWENTY

Stretched out on the Suburban's tailgate, I waved my fan-on-a-stick, a complimentary handout given to riders as they entered Creston, the host town for night two of TribRide.

Back and forth. Back and forth.

I wanted to bawl like a weary baby but couldn't summon the energy.

Night two? Night friggin' *two*!

Judging by the condition of my carcass, (Yeah, I use that word deliberately.) I could swear I'd ridden to hell and back on a bike with no seat.

I winced. The description even hurt.

To say the day had been tough going would be as much of an understatement as me saying I like bacon. The fact was Day Two of TribRide would go down as Murphy's Law Day. Yep. One of those "everything that could go wrong, did go wrong" days. I know. I know. We've all had them. (Just normally not while riding a bicycle built for two.)

Day Two's ride wrap-up went something like this: Sleepless night. Cold breakfast. Late start. Bitching Van Vleet. Flat tire. Intense heat. No sweet corn left at noon stop. Bitching Stroker. Flat tire. Telltale signs of a hemorrhoid. More intense heat. And a partridge in a pear tree.

That I had been able to make the fifty-mile trip was nothing short of miraculous. Most of those miles were a total blur. The ones that weren't fuzzy consisted of me staring at the advertisements on the back of Van Vleet's Rent-a-Trekkie shirt.

Need brakes? Big Bob's in New Holland can fix you up. Craving a Dutch letter? Stop by the Dusseldorp Bakery. Want the best burger in town? The Windmill Grill is the place to go. Have a toothache? Anderson Family Dentistry will drill your pain away.

Honest to God. I would've gotten off the bike and kissed the "Welcome to Creston" sign when we reached it, but it required energy reserves I didn't possess. My Dilithium Crystals were drained to nubbins.

"I, uh, er, excuse me, but you look like you could use this."

I managed to open one eye. Kenny Grey, cup in hand, stood over me.

"It's lemonade. Ice cold. Freshly-squeezed."

I sat up. It wasn't beer, but it was wet and cold.

"Thanks!"

Kenny nodded.

"How's the picture business going?" I asked.

"Great! Really great. You haven't dropped by the kiosk for a sitting yet."

I shook my head. "That's right. And I won't be any time soon."

"Oh? Why is that?"

I made a face. "What woman in her right mind would sit for an artist's rendering looking like this?" I did an up-and-down wave of my hand. "Gotta be honest. That artist's eye of yours could use prescription lenses, dude."

"So...when you've cleaned up?"

I shook my head. "I wish. Even on days where I have access to soap, water, and hair care tools, my hair does its own special wild and crazy thing, the essence of which would be almost impossible to capture on canvas. Being the caring, compassionate person that I am, I couldn't in all good conscience inflict such a hopeless and daunting challenge on a poor starving artist. You understand. Right?"

"Oh. Sure. I guess so."

"You lure any celebrities to your booth yet?" I asked, feeling sort of sorry for the fledgling artist. "How about that reality star you favor? Has she stopped by yet?"

He shook his head. "Not yet."

"Well, it's early days," I reminded him, seeing his hangdog look. "But you said business was good, right?"

He perked up. "It's fabulous. Everybody wants a picture to remind them of the bike ride. Er, almost everybody."

My cell rang. I pulled it from my fanny pack.

"Hello?"

"Turner? That you?" Stan's growl left me little doubt what kind of mood my boss was in. And why.

"I think you have the wrong number—"

"Give it up. I know that's you, Blondie."

"Oh, hey, Stan. How's it going?" I took my fingertip and scratched back and forth on the microphone. "Sorry. What's that? I can't hear you! You're cutting out!"

"Can you hear me now, Turner?" Stan's voice boomed out of the phone. "You're fired!"

I blinked.

Fired!

I hauled the phone back to my ear. "Now, just a minute! You're telling me I'm fired!"

"I knew that would get you back on the phone," Stan said.

I could imagine the "gotcha!" grin gracing Stan's face.

"I'm having issues with the 4G network," I lied. "I can hear you fine now. How's everything in Grandville? What big news stories am I missing out on?"

"That's a good question, Turner. Maybe you should go to Drew Van Vleet's blog at the *New Holland News* to find out. *Like. I. Did.*"

I winced.

"I can explain," I said.

"You can explain? You can explain how a competitor managed to scoop a news story my own reporter was in the middle of? This I gotta hear."

"Well, you see, I'm not quite used to this phone yet—"

"Cut the crap, Turner. How come I have to read a competitor's blog to find out *my* reporter stumbled onto a big shot assault vic, after participating in a séance, while spending the night in a haunted murder house with the cast of one of the most popular reality TV shows? What do you have anyway? A career death wish?"

"Hey. I'm doing the best I can. Van Vleet has an iPad at his disposal. Built-in web cam. Camera. Nice big keyboard to type on. It takes me an eternity to tap out a blog update on this teeny tiny keyboard."

"Excuses, excuses. Whine. Whine. Whine. Can't you borrow a laptop from someone and post something more substantial than 'Stumbled onto big time agent, Vinny Vincent. Literally! Location Villisca Ax Murder House.' We need pictures! We need details, Turner! Details! You know. The who, what, where, when, why, and how."

"Okay. I'll play. Let's see. *Who* went behind my back and made a wager on whether I'd finish TribRide or not? *What* kind of boss would send a novice biker employee on a tandem bicycle on a risky bike ride? *Where* is the appreciation for the effort this boss's ace employee is making? *When* will said valuable employee be appropriately compensated? And finally, *why* does this outstanding employee have a hint of a hemorrhoid? So, *how* do you like those for details, Mr. Who, what, where, when, why, and how?"

I waited, fully expecting to hear, "You're fired!"—this time for real.

Okay. So maybe I'd stepped over the insubordination line with the boss man. Still, surely there is such a thing as justifiable insubordination. If not, there should be.

"Geez, Turner? Back off on the pedals, would you? I'm not altogether *dis*pleased with your performance. After all, you're still on the ride. Which means I'm still in the game. And you've managed to garner a helluva lot of attention with this Bikezilla war you've got going with Keelie Keller. Now if you could be so good as to actually report what's going on, too—you know—the job I pay you to do, then everything will just be hunky dory."

I made a face. Hunky dory, my half-developed hemorrhoid. Stan wasn't sweaty, gross, and disgusting and running through lawn sprinklers to shower.

"I'll see what I can do," I managed.

"You do that, Turner."

"And you keep your checkbook handy, Boss Man. 'Cause in a week, it's pay-up time!"

"Just keep telling yourself that," Stan said, and ended the call.

"You lead an interesting life," Kenny observed.

I shrugged. "What can I say? I got a gift."

"A gift? A gift for what? Stalking? Knocking old guys over

the head? Having the worst hair ever?"

The scent of a pricey designer fragrance over-powered the pungent odor of my own sweat, and I knew even before I turned, who had invaded my space.

The Captain of Team Reality Red and Kompany.

"Doesn't that 'same tune, different day' stuff ever get old?" I asked. "You know. You accusing. Me denying?"

"I'll quit accusing when you quit doing."

A crowd gathered, Taylor and Dixie among them. Great. Eye witnesses and video evidence.

"Ladies, ladies!" Langley stepped between us like a World Wrestling ref separates wrestlers. Okay. I hear you. Professional wrestling refs rarely wade into the fray. Let's go with boxing refs then. "Keelie. Tressa. I thought we agreed to take our differences and channel them into contests of will, determination, and stamina."

Good grief. Did this guy ever give it a rest?

"No offense intended, but I think you've got this reality ride confused with *The Amazing Race*," I said.

"No. Wait! Just think about the global impact settling your differences through a peaceful—and harmless—series of challenges could have. The example you two set could become a blueprint for diplomacy and communication between nations. You could spark a chain reaction of contest rather than *con*test! Olympians rather than Gladiators! Talk about climate change!"

Talk about a twit of a Brit.

"Listen, Lang. All I want to do is to finish the ride with all of my hide," I explained. "I'm not looking for an ambassadorship or a medal."

"What about personal growth?" Lang asked.

"Overrated," I said.

"So, I guess this means you're conceding the sand volleyball match," Keelie said, lifting her chin and crossing her arms.

"Volleyball match?"

Keelie let out a long-suffering sigh.

"This evening's entertainment spectacle," she said, "which I'm sure qualifies as a hot time in this hellish hamlet. But I suppose it's always hot in hell. Get it? Hot. Hell."

"Oh, Keelie," Tiara giggled. "You're so funny."

"I hate to burst your bubble, Tiara, but generally if someone has to explain why something is funny, it isn't," I pointed out. "And just so you know, this 'hellish hamlet' has a long and colorful past that includes a rich railroad heritage. Even now, Creston is an Amtrak stop-over for the *California Zephyr* continuing that lasting tradition of railroad history." I knew this because I'd eavesdropped on one of the townsfolk on the square while waiting in line at the Open Bible lasagna supper tent.

"What are you? Like a Wiki-Trekkie?" Keelie said.

I caught myself before I laughed outright.

Score one for the Red Queen.

"Very well. I win. You lose," Keelie said. "Game over. Uncle Frank's franchise is toast."

"The hell you say?" Dixie took a pugilist's pose.

I waved her off. "Please. That same old, tired threat? Believe me, my Uncle Frank's food has survived bigger and nastier food critics than you," I said, sticking my own chin out.

"Oh, really? How many friends do those critics have influence with? Do you really want to take a chance that I can't put your uncle out of business?" Keelie asked. "Do you, Trekkie Tressa?"

Did I?

Hell no. I love my Uncle Frank and Aunt Reggie. They're like family to me. I mean, they are family to me.

"You should know I was a volleyball player in high school," I informed the Reality Red Team, you know—in the interest of full disclosure, "and I personally hold the record for breaking the most noses."

Okay. So I didn't add that those noses I referred to belonged to my teammates.

"And that's supposed to...what? Intimidate me? Scare me? Oooh. I'm so scared!" She put her hands on her hips. "Are we playing or not?"

I could see the tweets now: *Trekkie Tressa Turns Tail. Reality Red Rules the Ride. Small-town Grill and Chill Goes Bust.*

"I don't think that would be—"

"Team Trekkie accepts the challenge." Taylor announced. I turned to stare at her.

"What are you doing?" I asked.

"Defending the good name of my state and looking out for the family, of course."

"*The family*? Who are you? Michael Corleone? Well, just so we're clear. Keelie made me an offer I *can* refuse. And need I remind you, you were the one who advised me to back off, be the bigger person, turn the other cheek—"

"Since when have you ever listened to me? You're planning to start now?"

She had a point.

"Seven sharp. And don't be late!" Keelie warned and moved off with her fan club.

I collapsed on the tailgate again.

"We'll have to field a team," Taylor said.

"How many do we need?"

"Well, they have Keelie, Jax, Tiara, and knowing them, they'll stack the course with ringers.

Great. Reporter-to-biker-to-volleyball recruiter. It just kept getting better and better.

"Who do we have so far?" Dixie asked.

"Well, there's you, me, Tressa, Frankie."

Dixie shook her head. "Count Frankie out. The last time we played volleyball, he just stood there with his hands over his head like he was bracing for impact."

"What about Van Vleet?" Taylor asked. "I can't see him passing up the opportunity to play sand volleyball with Keelie and Kompany."

Knowing Van Vleet, he'd throw the match for the other team.

"How about Patrick? Is he available?" Dixie asked.

I felt a pinch on my arm. "Don't say it, Tressa!" Taylor hissed.

"Hey! I'm the innocent party here! I was all set to follow your sage advice and gracefully decline the Red Queen's offer, but oh, no, you two had to go all *Avengers* on me. So, you two can come up with a roster."

"Oh? So, you'd let Frank's business go broke, huh?" Dixie asked. "Think about that for a moment, Miss Be the Bigger Person. No more fun money from pulling a shift here and there.

No more free Freezes and fries. No more belly burners, pulled pork. No more hot fudge brownie sundaes."

I winced. Dixie the Destructor was not above hitting below the belt. So to speak.

"Any fallout will soon blow over," I espoused.

"No more double bacon cheddar burgers with a heaping side of rings." Dixie paused for dramatic effect. "And…no more doggie bags."

I bounded from the tailgate.

"Let me at 'em!" I said.

"I could play."

That softly worded statement came from Kenny Grey. He'd hung around after the entertainer's exodus—surprising given his devotion to Keelie.

"Who are you again?" Dixie asked.

"He's Kenny the cartoonist."

"Caricaturist," Kenny corrected.

"Have you played volleyball before?" Taylor asked.

"Are you good?" Dixie grilled.

He shrugged. "I've played some. I think I'm okay."

"We don't need okay. We need super hero. We need Spiker Man!" I proclaimed. "Oh. And just so everyone knows, I won't be wearing one of those skimpy bikini suits."

"God, I hope not." Dixie grabbed her stomach. "Think of all that vomit on all that sand."

"So? Are we ready to get down and dirty?" I asked.

Dixie sniffed the air around me.

"Looks like you're already there."

I sniffed a pit and made a face.

Point to Dixie.

* * *

As overnight host, Creston had gone all out for the ride, turning the Midwestern city into a beach lover's paradise. Tons of sand had been trucked in. Lounge chairs and beach towels dotted the landscape. Attractive, young men masqueraded as cabana boys and fit females in itty-bitty, teeny-wienie bikinis served fruity drinks with pastel-colored umbrellas. Beach volleyball courts gave bikers a place to play, and sand sculpture competitions provided a creative outlet.

If life were fair, I would be reclining on a lounge chair, ogling a cute little cabana boy offering me a drink with a colorful umbrella.

So. Not. Fair.

"Would you look at that?"

Dixie pulled me out of my beach baby moment.

"I don't believe it."

"Talk about your Benedict Arnolds."

"What does the Pope have to do with this?" I asked.

Dixie shook her head.

"Oh. I get it. Talk about your *traitors*," I said, staring Brutus-like daggers through the volleyball net at a guy I'd bailed out of jail, masqueraded as a faux fiancée for the sake of his ailing Aunt Mo for, and been an all-occasion, all-round, stand-up gal pal to.

"What a piece of work," Dixie said.

"Hello. What does his to-drool-for physique have to do with being a turncoat?" I asked.

"I'm not talking about Manny's muscles. I'm talking about his manhood."

"What!"

"Not *that*!" Dixie growled. "Manhood as in the qualities and characteristics associated with being a man, such as courage, determination, *loyalty*."

"Ah. *Manhood*! Gotcha!" I gave a grim nod. With Manny playing for the Red Queen's team, we were so screwed.

"Who's that other guy? The big one with arms that almost reach his knees?"

"One of the cameramen," I said, with another look of disgust and turned to leave.

"Where do you think you're going?" Dixie asked.

"To get my bike helmet." No way was I gonna be across the net from Mr. Muscles and Gumby the cameraman without proper head protection.

"What about Patrick? Has he called you back?" Taylor asked.

"Ten-seventy-four," I said.

"What?"

"That's negative in police ten-code."

Taylor shook her head.

"So we've got me, you, Taylor, probable saboteur Van Vleet, and Kenny the cartoonist?" Dixie asked.

"Caricaturist. And our roster sounds even worse when you say it," I said.

Someone (okay, me) had insisted on the new Trekkies wearing red shirts. Misery loves company and all that. Van Vleet had somehow managed to come up with gold Enterprise Insignias to pin on each enlistee's shirt.

Our opponents, by contrast, sported hot pink bikinis (the girls not the guys) bare chests, (the guys not the gals) and knee-length gray shorts trimmed in hot pink. Well, with the exception of Manny, who wore shiny black shorts and a rich mahogany six-pack that made Langley Carlisle look like a walking ad for anemia.

We took our places on the sand, a ragtag group of interstellar patriots defending our home planet.

I stood across from Manny and tried for my best (or, rather worst) Badass Barbie look.

"I wish you well with the alliance you've chosen," I said.

"Biker Barbie's displeased?" Manny asked.

"Of course, not. You're free to align yourself with whomever—or whatever—you chose. It's nothing to me. Live your life."

Manny shook his head.

"It's just a job," he said.

I smirked.

"Right. A job. Very well. I just have one small request. You know—from the person who freed you from incarceration and gave your dear aunt something to hold onto at a difficult time in her life."

"What's that, Barbie?"

A whimper escaped me.

"Be gentle."

CHAPTER TWENTY-ONE

If Keelie was the Red Queen, we were *Resident Evil's* Umbrella Corporation Commandos, getting picked off one by one as we attempted to infiltrate the hive.

I hadn't seen so many flailing arms and out-of-control balls since the time I talked my dad into taking me golfing with him. (I was responsible for the whack-a-doodle balls. My dad did all the arm waving.) I dove to the sand so many times, I had sand where sand should never be—and where it would be tricky to remove.

"Match point!"

Positioned across from me, Keelie let us know the blessed end was nigh in a contest that surely must qualify as the shortest (and ugliest) sand volleyball match on record. You listening, *Guinness Book of Records*?

"For crying out loud, get on with it!" I yelled.

"Yeah. Put 'em out of their misery!" Someone in the peanut gallery contributed.

Big flippin' deal. Team Trekkie had become the target of so many catcalls, insults, and heckles—not to mention a downright rude play-by-play—that our collective morale had to be lower than Cubs' fans at play-offs time.

Better luck next time. See you next year.

Manny held the serve.

"Come on, Manny! For the win!" Keelie cheered.

Manny shrugged, tossed the ball in the air, brought his arm up, and smacked the ball. Into the air it went.

"Get it! Get it!" I yelled to Taylor behind me. "Set me up! Set me up!"

And then I saw it. An opening. My opening! The Red

Queen, still magazine-cover pristine, was mere inches away—vulnerable—representing what is referred to as an irresistible target.

One shot. Just one harmless bounce off the bean so we wouldn't be totally humiliated. That's all I asked. *Just. One. Measly. Noggin. Shot.*

Taylor moved into position, palms up, wrists together, textbook set shot posture. She bent her knees.

Whop!

The ball sailed upward in a perfectly executed set-shot, the placement spot on.

I watched the ball reach its apex, tracked the ball's descent, and timed my jump.

I brought my hand up.

Just. About. Now!

With my final reserve of energy, I leaped into the air, stretching ligaments and tendons that screamed, "What the hell are you doing to us, woman?" and thrust my arm up—and elbow out.

Thwack!
Smack!
Crunch!

Next to me, Dixie the Destructor dropped to the sand.

The follow-through instinct kicked in. I snapped my wrist and sent the ball downward over the net.

Bam! Boom!

The Red Queen went down like a basketball guard defending against a power forward's drive down the lane.

Back at ground level, I surveyed the carnage. Across the net, Keelie Keller, flat on her back, her arms outstretched, stared up at the sky, a dazed look on her face.

Next to me, Team Trekkie enlistee, Dixie the Dragon lady, lie curled up in a fetal position. Her hands covered her nose, but not her moans.

I grimaced. Another "red shirt" bites the dust.

I crouched beside her.

"Dixie? You okay?"

"Do I look okay?" she asked, putting a bloody hand up. "I think you broke my dose!"

"Dose? Oh! *Nose*. I'm sure it's not broken. Injuries in the area of the head tend to bleed more," I parroted Patrick's earlier head-wound factoid.

"I feel *so* much better."

"Oh, my God! Dixie! Darling! Are you all right? What happened?" Frankie stood over his down-for-the-count beloved.

"*She* happened," Dixie pointed the bloody finger of blame in my direction. "That...that...psycho spiker caught me with her elbow."

I looked up at Frankie.

"It was an accident! It could happen to anybody! Frankie. Frankie?"

Faster than a fainting goat, and in less time than it took for Dixie to drop, Frankie keeled over.

"Frankie?" I crawled over to my cousin. Eyes closed, deathly pale and eerily still, Frankie looked like he was ready to have final rites said over him and be sucked out the air lock into deep, dark space.

"Don't worry about him. He always dakes a swan dive when dere's blood involved," Dixie said.

I shook my head. An aspiring crime scene analyst who passed out at the sight of blood? *Dexter* would be appalled.

"I thought Frankie only did that when it was *his* blood."

"It depends on the day," Dixie said.

I put a hand on Frankie's cheek. His eyes fluttered open.

"You gonna be okay, cous?" I asked.

He looked up at me.

"What happened?"

"You fainted, dude. Passed out. Hit the deck. Down for the count. Had a case of the vapors. Swooned."

"He gets it!" Dixie snapped.

I helped Frankie to a sitting position.

"Feeling better?" I asked.

He nodded.

"A lot of people can't stand the sight of blood," I said, and patted his hand. "It's no biggie."

"Blood? What are you talking about? I didn't faint because of the blood. No. No. It was the heat. That's it. The heat. I didn't hydrate like I should. Plus, I haven't eaten since noon. You know how I get when I skip meals."

I raised an eyebrow. Methinks thou dost protesteth too mucheth.

I turned back to Dixie. Taylor had an arm around Dixie's shoulders and a wad of tissues against her nose.

"Keelie and Kompany are gonna be out for *your* blood next. You dook out dere Red Queen." Dixie sounded like the wad of tissues was stuck up her nostrils.

I glanced over at the opposing team. Reality Roadshow team members formed a circle around their downed leader.

"I spiked the ball. That's all."

"Oh, doat even. I saw your face. You wanted to make her eat dat ball. 'dmit it."

"I beg to differ. I received a picture-perfect set shot from my sis here, and I executed a textbook spike. That's it. Taylor deserves the lion's share of the credit."

"Don't try to foist the blame for this on me, *sis*. Dixie's right. You wanted to make her eat that ball."

I stood.

"Hey. Wait a minute, missy," I said. "You're the one who wanted me to—what was that you said again? Oh, yes. 'Beat that biatch like a dirty saddle blanket.' And, if memory serves, it was you who insisted we accept this stupid volleyball challenge in the first place. Sounds like you're the one who has a problem with the Red Queen, not me."

Taylor got to her feet. "Well, forgive me for standing up for our home state," Taylor said.

"Home state? Get real, Taylor. This is all about you having the hots for Trooper P.D. Dawkins and wanting Keelie Keller to keep her Tinsel Town talons sheathed."

Taylor's face went from angry red to OMG white. Her gaze slid across the net. Mine followed.

Reality Red's real time cameras had shifted their focus from the wounded warrior queen to the squabbling, finger-pointing siblings across the way.

"Upload it!" That's how long it would take before the cyber world inhabitants discovered Taylor Turner had a thing for State Patrol Officer P. D. Dawkins.

"Oops!" I said.

"Oops? Oops! That's all you've got to say?" Taylor stared at me, her expression a curious blend of horror, embarrassment, anger, and, I discovered with a sudden tightness in my throat, *hurt*. "How could you, Tressa? How could you?"

How could I? How could I *not*? I wasn't equipped for keeping secrets. It wasn't part of my DNA makeup. Was it my fault my particular gene pool was overpopulated with the blabbermouth gene?

"I'm sorry, Taylor. It just…popped out."

"Just popped out? Really, Tressa? Seriously?"

I shook my head.

"How long have you known me? And how long have I suffered from regular bouts of diarrhea of the mouth?" I asked. "Don't act like this occasion is so special, that *you're* so special. I don't discriminate. I'm an equal-opportunity-blurter."

"When are you going to stop blaming biology and start accepting responsibility for your actions, Tressa?" Taylor asked.

"I'm sorry I'm not perfect, like you, Taylor. The perfect baby. The perfect toddler. The perfect student. Perfect health. Perfect skin. Even your hair is perfect. Perfect. Perfect. Perfect. Do you know how annoying your 'practically perfect in every way' gene pool is to the rest of us faulty and flawed specimens? Getting up early on a Sunday morning annoying. That's how annoying."

Taylor took a step back as if I'd hauled off and slapped her one. Creases marred her perfectly smooth forehead.

"You think I'm suffering under any illusions that I'm perfect?"

"See? That's what I'm talking about. Most people would say, 'You think I think I'm perfect?' But oh, no. Taylor Turner can't abide having two 'thinks' in the same sentence so she comes out with, 'You think I'm suffering any *illusions* that I'm perfect?' Who talks like that? Little Miss Perfect, that's who. Or is that *whom*?"

Toe-to-toe, nose-to-nose, eye-to-eye, phasers locked on target and set to stun, the Turner siblings "you blink first" stare-down commenced.

"Uh, if you could save the squabbling sister act for another time, I could use some ice on my *d*ose," Dixie said.

Several more seconds passed before our gazes slid to Dixie. Her Rudolph nose was beginning to swell.

"Is it just me or is she starting to resemble Barbara Streisand?" I asked Taylor.

She squinted at Dixie.

"I was thinking Sarah Jessica Parker," Taylor said.

"She needs ice. *Stat.*" I held a hand out. "Truce while we set up a triage?" I said.

Taylor hesitated and then took my hand.

"*Temporary* truce," she qualified.

We helped Dixie to her feet. Frankie next.

I brushed sand off Frankie and hazarded a look at the opposition. Keelie was on her feet. Other than a bad case of 'sand head,' she looked no worse for the wear. She approached the net. I did the same.

"About that spike—" I started to apologize.

"We win. You lose," Keelie announced.

I frowned. "Hold on. We won control of the serve. So, technically you haven't won yet," I pointed out.

"You're conceding then," she said.

"Team Trekkie hasn't conceded anything."

"Team? What team?"

"Huh?" I turned. Only Kenny Grey seemed to have hung around. He sat in the middle of the court playing in the sand.

"Would you believe they transported back to The Enterprise?" I said. "Something about troubles with Tribbles."

The hint of a smile lifted one corner of her mouth. I figured now was as good a time as any to minimize the fallout from my blurt fest earlier.

"Uh, Keelie, about that video—"

"You mean the video where you betray your sister's confidence and reveal her super secret crush on the super sexy Trooper Dawkins to the entire world?"

I grimaced. "That's the one."

"Sorry. All rights reserved."

"You have a sister, right?" I began.

"I'm an only child, Einstein. Jeesh. Don't reporters research anymore?"

Okay. Rewind and try again.

"If you *had* a sister, wouldn't you want to have a good relationship with her? Wouldn't you want to correct past…mistakes that might have led to bad feelings between you? Wouldn't you do just about anything to repair the damage you caused?"

Okay. I was a little "out there." Truth was, I did feel bad about divulging something my sister told me in confidence.

"How touching," Keelie said. "You know. I'm not totally without sympathy here. Maybe we can come to some arrangement that benefits both of us."

"Like what?"

"Like how about you quit TribRide. Right here. Right now. Walk away. Pack up and go home, and I'll consider hitting the delete button on your sister's true confession."

"You want me to quit?" I asked, feeling suddenly queasy. "And what do you get?"

"Bragging rights, of course," Keelie said. "And the chance to kick back and enjoy the ride."

"From the luxury of your custom motor coach, I presume," I said.

"Of course, you silly goose."

In other words, she'd be the Belle of the Bike Ball, and I'd be relegated to the pages of Loser's Lore. And my raise? It would be sucked out an air lock like so much space debris.

If I even had a job waiting if I bailed.

"Come on, Tressa. Think about your sister. Think about Taylor. Think how grateful she'll be for your sacrifice."

I did think about it. I thought long and hard. Quitting—giving up—didn't come easy for me. I'd never been a quitter, wasn't comfortable being the kind of person to wave the white flag or throw in the towel. To admit defeat.

But I loved my sister. I wanted her to be happy. I wanted us to have a close and lasting relationship based on mutual trust and respect.

And yes. I wanted world peace, too. But I'd settle for making peace with my little sister first.

I felt a crack in my resolve appear—like the teeny-tiny one snaking its way across my car windshield back home. Exhaustion ate away at my willpower. The only grit I had left was in the sand between my toes.

"Come on, Tressa," Keelie cajoled. "Quit TribRide now and the video is yours."

Going. Going—

"Not interested."

I turned. Taylor stood behind my right shoulder.

"Excuse me?" Keelie said.

"We're not taking your deal, Keelie," Taylor said. "Go peddle your snake oil somewhere else."

For a second Keelie acted like she didn't know what to say. She shrugged.

"Have it your way," she said. "And don't forget to check out the YouTube link on my page. I know you'll both 'like' it." Keelie blew us both an air kiss. "Muaw!"

I stared at Taylor.

"You know what this means," I said.

She nodded. "That I'm seeing you in a whole, new light?"

"It means your secret crush isn't gonna be a secret anymore."

Taylor shrugged. "Who believes anything you see on the Internet?" she said.

We started walking across the sand volleyball court.

"How did you know I was considering Keelie's deal?" I asked.

"I could see it in your face."

I sighed. Just once I'd like to pull off a poker face.

"So, we're good?" I asked.

"You still need a muzzle," Taylor pointed out.

"And you could use a chill pill now and then." I looked around. "So, where did everyone hightail it to?"

"By now, Frankie and Dixie are probably sacked out in the Suburban. I have no idea where Van Vleet disappeared to. And your little artist friend? Last I saw, he was up to his knees in sand, creating art. Sand art, that is. He's actually pretty good, too."

I did a forehead bump.

"If only we'd challenged the Red Queen to a sand sculpture contest, we would have won, hands down," Taylor said. "Kenny's sand sculpture of little Miss Reality Star is pretty amazing. I took a picture if you want to check it out."

I shook my head. I'd had enough of Reality Red to last a good long time. What I needed was a shower and a place to crash.

We walked back to the Mini-Freeze in silence. Out of nowhere, Taylor grabbed me and gave me a quick squeeze that just qualified as a hug and hurried into the Mini-Freeze.

I stared after her.

Taylor wasn't touchy-feelie.

Taylor was no hugger.

Taylor certainly didn't squeeze.

Note to Tressa. Check Uncle Frank's saltshakers. We could be dealing with the sodium-addicted, shape-shifting alien from Planet M-113.

Darn it. Where was the tricorder when you needed it?

CHAPTER TWENTY-TWO

Winterset. Birthplace of John Wayne. Epicenter to a collection of historic covered bridges made famous in a bestselling book and hugely popular movie.

The Bridges of Madison County. Synonymous with...romance. Sigh.

I don't remember much about the movie, except it had Clint Eastwood and Meryl Streep in it. I do recall the hoopla. I especially recall a brouhaha erupting in our happy home when my mom and my gammy asked their respective husbands to take them to the movie—and to actually stay and watch it with them.

I was around six at the time. Although a bit hazy, my recollections go something like this:

Grandpa Will: "That's not the kind of movie real men go to. That's one of those chick flicks."

Gammy: "Chick flick? There's no poultry in the movie, Will. It's got Clint Eastwood in it. You like Clint Eastwood. And that actress with the funny name. Merle something."

Grandpa Will: "Does Eastwood have a six-gun strapped to his side? Does he carry a 44 Magnum? Does he call the bad guys 'punk' and let loose with a swear word now and then?"

Mom: "Clint Eastwood plays a photographer in the film, William."

Dad: "Oh? *Field and Stream*?"

Mom: "No. *National Geographic*."

Father and Son Turner: "Chick flick. Count us out."

Literary and film critics aside, every year visitors from around the globe converge on the county, map in hand, to visit the bridges made famous by the book and movie. (An Oprah-on-location extravaganza cinched this slice of Americana's place as the budget-friendly romantic hotspot.)

While I loved the historic bridges dotting the rural landscape around Winterset, for me, the city's attraction has always been John Wayne. I "heart" John Wayne.

Born to Clyde Morrison, a local pharmacist, and his wife, Mary, "Duke" lived in Winterset until he was six, when the family moved to California. The rest, as they say, is movie history. Duke's birthplace, now a museum complete with tours and gift shop, was also a popular local attraction.

Winterset, Iowa. Tourist Mecca? You bet your boots, pilgrim.

In keeping with the western flavor of a town that produced the all-time most famous box office cowboy ever, the host city planned an all-day John Wayne movie marathon and old-fashioned barn dance—entertainment hand-chosen for this good ol' girl. It was a cowgirl's night out. I planned to drink a little, dance a little, watch my movie hero teach the bad guys a lesson- and hit the sack—er, *tent* early.

So far I'd avoided the whole camp-out experience, opting for the front seat of the Suburban rather than face the great unknown. Given the recent publicity surrounding Uncle Frank's Mini-Freeze, for security reasons, Taylor had decided to toss her bedroll on the floor of the food mobile.

At least in the Suburban I didn't have to worry about creepy crawlies finding their way into my bed, but bug-free accommodations came at a cost.

Sleep.

Frankie hadn't altogether broken his childhood teeth-grinding habit. The result? A horrible, high-pitched *whir* magnified ten-fold in the restricted confines of the Suburban. Each time I closed my eyes, I could swear I was in the dental chair listening to someone in the next cubicle undergoing a root canal.

Whireeee!

Between Frankie's grinding and Dixie's snoring, it was all I could do to keep from picking up a jug and blowing my way into the midnight serenade.

Tonight, critters or not, I planned to pitch my tent and sleep the undisturbed slumber of the dead. Er…you know what I mean, right?

The day's ride had been uneventful. Another hot and humid day with little cloud cover to give us a break from the unrelenting sun, neither Van Vleet nor I felt in the mood for chitchat. Thanks to Shelby Lynn, I had a decent selection of songs to listen to on my phone. Currently, George Strait bemoaned the fact that his exes were preventing him from residing in Texas, the only place hotter than my present location.

Our Greenfield nooner had been a quickie. (So not like that sounds!) We grabbed some grub, rehydrated, and took off again. Van Vleet had somehow scored a night's lodging in Winterset and wanted to get to our host city so he could enjoy all the comforts of a home as soon as possible.

Me? I was for whatever got me off the bike sooner rather than later.

I hadn't seen hide nor big hair of Team Hollywood, and that was probably for the best. Whether Stan liked it or not, I intended to keep as far away from the "I've got no talent, but I'm still famous" reality stars. There were stories galore on this ride. Rich and colorful characters.

On our noon stop, I discovered Chester R. Smith. Who is Chester, you ask? Chester's claim to fame is that he's in the movie *Cold Turkey*. What's *Cold Turkey*, you ask? It's a 1971 film starring Dick Van Dyke shot in Greenfield, Iowa, about an entire town that takes a pledge to stop smoking for thirty days. Who does Chester play? He's the guy standing outside the Hotel Greenfield about thirty-seven minutes into the film.

You can quit shaking your head now.

I'd already arranged a time and place to meet Van Vleet the next morning to begin the fourth leg of our trip.

Home. Where, be it ever so humble, my very own bed (and a dishy ranger) awaited me.

I fanned myself thinking of the homecoming possibilities and looked around for a story to appease Stan. I spied Kenny Grey. He had his kiosk set up in an area reserved for vendors. Two girls, sixteen or so, all smiles and giggles, posed cheek-to-cheek for their drawing.

I grinned. Now here was a great down home, goodtime story if I ever saw one.

"May I?" I asked the girls, holding up my camera phone.

"I'm a reporter and I'm blogging about the ride. I'd love to take your picture and post it."

The girls looked at each other and giggled.

"Okay. Sure. Whatever."

I snapped a couple of photos and moved over to stand behind Kenny.

"Do you mind?" I asked over his shoulder.

He shrugged. "I guess not."

I looked at his drawing. It was good. Very good.

"How is it?" one of the models asked.

"It's great," I assure them. "You're gonna love it." I looked at the drawing, then back at the girls. "Are you two sisters?" I asked.

More giggles. "No. We're best friends."

"Ah." I nodded, thinking Kenny's drawing was a little bit off around the eyes. Both sets of eyes seemed…alike—a similarity I couldn't see. Okay. Okay. I hear you. Enough with the art critique, Blondie.

I took some more pictures and a slice of video, watching while Kenny put the finishing touches on the drawing, unveiled his work of art to two very pleased customers, and sent them happily on their way with their purchase and several business cards to pass along.

I sat down in the chair and put up a hand when Kenny slid a clean piece of paper in place.

"Nope. Don't want a drawing. What I'd like is to interview you."

Kenny frowned. "Me? Why?"

"Human interest story. Iowa artist: Have easel. Will travel. Catchy, huh? So, will you do it? Will you answer a few questions? After all, giving you a bit of free advertising is the least I can do after dragging you into that crushing loss on the volleyball court."

He smiled. "I suppose it couldn't hurt."

Good. My reputation had not preceded me. Yet.

"So how long have you had this gig? You know. A traveling caricaturist?"

"I only do it during the summers," Kenny explained. "I'm an art student."

"Cool. Where do you go?"

"I'm actually hoping to be admitted to the Art Institute. It's expensive, so I'm working to save money."

"Good idea. Debt sucks. Seriously. Have you done TribRide before?"

He shook his head. "It's a new experience."

"Is it profitable?" I asked.

"Very."

"How long does it take you to do a caricature?" I asked.

He shrugged. "It depends on the subject. Some take fifteen minutes. Others are more time intensive. Like I said, depends on the subject. How long they want to sit. How much money they want to invest."

"Invest?"

"It's art. Art that comes complete with memories and emotions attached to it. Every time someone looks at one of my drawings, it takes them back to that day, that moment in time, and the people they met and shared that space in time with, people who had a lasting impact on them. So, yeah. It's an investment because the drawings bring with them a windfall of emotions and memories that last a lifetime."

I tapped his words into the memo app on my phone. "That's a cool way of looking at what you do," I said. "You should use that in your promo. Kenny's Caricatures. Memories for a lifetime."

He smiled. "Good thinking."

"A lot of your customers are biking. Obviously they can't take the drawing with them. How does that work?"

"I obtain addresses and mail them before I leave town each day. When they get home, their pictures are waiting for them in pristine condition."

"Sounds like you've got it all figured out."

"Well, look who wants to be immortalized, Frankie! If it isn't Miss Ninja Elbows. Make sure you get her good side, Mr. Artist. Oh, wait. She doesn't have a good side."

I groaned. Just what I needed. Dixie-what-is-that-sucking-sound-Daggett and a guy who gives a whole new meaning to the daily grind.

"I'll have you know I'm not posing, I'm prosing," I said. "I'm featuring Kenny in my blog. His stuff's good. You should sit, Dixie. And beg. And roll over." I snorted. Even with a sore patootie, I still had it.

"Yuck it up, Lois Lame," Dixie said.

"Who's minding the store?" I asked.

"Taylor, who else? Oh. And Patrick offered to give her a hand."

I sat up in my seat. A brown shirt serving up Slurpees? What would the brass think? "Are you playing matchmaker, Dixie?" I asked.

She shrugged. "Taylor told you to butt out, not me."

"So where are you off to?" I asked. "To stock up on ice packs? By the way, your nose, Dixie? Looking good!" I made a thumbs-up. Dixie muttered something not very nice.

"Hey, at least I didn't make a joke about your Roman nose," I said. "You know. Roamin' all over your face. Like that. No. I totally respected your feelings. So, where did you say you were going again?"

"We didn't," Dixie snapped.

"We're taking a bus tour to some of the covered bridges," Frankie said. "Want to join us?"

"No, she does not want to join us," Dixie said. "You heard her. She's busy *prosing*. Besides, it's a couples' thing. You know. *Romance*."

Frankie colored. His Adam's apple did one of those I'm-in-so-much-trouble numbers. "Oh. Yeah. Right."

"Yes, but what trip to Madison County is complete without a visit to at least one of the famous covered bridges?" I asked.

"You wouldn't enjoy it," Dixie said. "Crowded bus. Bumpy roads."

"A bus would be a limo compared to a tandem bike," I pointed out.

"Everyone will be paired off. You wouldn't be comfortable. You'd feel like a third big toe. Isn't that what you call it?" Dixie pressed her advantage.

I winced. That's what my gammy called it.

"A reporter makes sacrifices in order to get the story," I said. "Besides, Kenny here looks like he could use a break. He can be my number two. Besides, what artist could turn down an all-expense paid trip to the bridges of Madison County?"

"The shuttle is free, ditz," Dixie pointed out.

"Even better! What do you say, Mr. Grey? Care to soak up a little local culture?"

"I guess that would work. Business has slowed up for the moment."

"Great! We'll just help you load these up. Right, Frankie?"

Dixie shook her head, and we watched Frankie help Kenny pack up his stuff and move it to the side door of a dirty white, soccer mom minivan.

"Remind me to horn in on your quality time with Rick Townsend," Dixie grumbled.

"Oh, for heaven's sake. I'll make like my dad at a wedding. You won't even know I'm there."

"Right."

Frankie and Kenny rejoined us, neither of their expressions screaming, "I'm excited about this plan!"

We boarded a bus. I claimed the window seat, Kenny, the aisle. "Which bridge are we seeing first?" I asked Dixie, sitting in the aisle seat behind us.

"Roseman," Dixie mumbled, obviously still put out and not afraid to show it.

"Roseman Bridge." I did a quick search on my intelligent phone. "It says here Roseman Bridge is still located at its original location. It was featured in the movie."

"It's the bridge where Francesca leaves the note for Robert Kincaid inviting him to dinner," Kenny provided. "It's also known as the 'haunted bridge,'" he added.

I blinked. "How come?"

"Apparently, two sheriff's possees had an outlaw trapped on the bridge. Legend has it the bad guy rose up, straight through the roof of the bridge, let out a wild, anguished cry, and vanished into thin air."

"Holy Houdini! Did they ever find him?"

"No. He was never seen again."

First haunted ax murder houses. Now haunted bridges. Maybe this wasn't such a hot idea, after all.

"Hey! Look!" Someone yelled. "It's Keelie Keller's bus!"

Definitely not one of my better ideas.

Kenny sat up in his seat, craning his head to see outside the bus.

Oh. That's right. His Keelie connection.

We piled out of the bus. Once outside, the sounds of an argument could be heard. The group quieted, collectively eavesdropping on a not-so-private private moment.

"My best friend? You're hitting on my best friend!" I held my phone up, centering the group of people standing at the entrance to the bridge in my camera frame, and hit the video button. Manny I could make out easily, his bulk taking up considerable lens space.

"Jax Whitver, you are a bastard! Do you hear me? A bastard!"

I zoomed in on the screecher. It was Keelie. She turned slightly in our direction.

"And Tiara. My BFF. You are through! Do you hear me? Your free ride is over!"

"Keelie! Wait!" Jax ran after her. She stopped, whirled—and *wapp*!—nailed him with an open-handed slap.

I winced. That was so gonna leave a mark.

Tour bus spectators, finally reacting to the tabloid bonanza unfolding in front of them, held their phones up to capture the moment.

"Get away from me!" Keelie screamed. "And don't you come near me again, or I'll have you arrested! Do you hear? Just leave me alone!"

Feeling a bit too much like a certain smarmy competitor for my comfort, I turned the camera off and put my phone away. Out of the corner of my eye, I caught Kenny's ashen face. He looked like he was about to charge into the fray and save yon fellow ginger.

I took hold of his arm.

"Better not," I said. "See that big guy? That's her bodyguard. And, no. He's not wearing Kevlar. That's all Manny."

Keelie ran to her bus and boarded. Manny and Tiara, deep in conversation, followed at a slower pace. Jax ran a hand through his hair, shook his head, and walked to a beige Camaro. I watched him get in and speed away, gravel flying from his rear tires.

I looked around. "Hey. Where's your betrothed?" I asked Dixie.

"Over there. With his hero" She enunciated each word like she was spitting nails.

"Oh. I guess now is not a good time to ask if you've learned anything more about our mystery man," I said.

"*Your* mystery man. And, as it happens, I do have a little something. It's something Frankie overheard and let slip."

"Yes! Yes! What did Frankie let slip?" I grabbed her collar. "What? What?"

"Down girl," Dixie said, loosening my grip and straightening her clothing. "It seems Manny DeMarco has siblings."

I stared. "He does?"

She nodded. "A brother and a sister. He and his brother don't get along. Apparently this brother is the black sheep of the family."

I stared. Manny's *brother* was the black sheep?

Oy vey.

The plot thickened.

CHAPTER TWENTY-THREE

"Did you know the word 'hoedown' comes, literally, from the act of putting the 'hoe down'—meaning to cease one's labor for a spell and enjoy the well-earned reward of a night of food, drink, music, and dance?"

"Fascinating, but when I think of a 'ho' down it's in a totally different context," Van Vleet remarked.

Eww! I made a face.

Nursing a major case of the sulks, Van Vleet was drowning his sorrows in beer because he'd missed the ruckus at Roseman Bridge. We were presently bellied up to the make-shift bar in the bogus barn, located in a whimsical, wild west cardboard town.

"Cheer up, Drew. Maybe if you're a very good boy, I'll enlighten you on the origin of the term 'hootenanny.'" I promised. Man, I loved my brilliant phone.

"I still can't believe you didn't upload that video," he said. "Talk about amateur hour. You blew it, stroker. When Stan Rodgers finds out you withheld that video—" He put a finger gun to my forehead. "Bye, bye, Blondie."

I winced. He was probably right. Maybe I was too much of a soft touch. But after viewing the video umpteen times, after hearing the pain and hurt in Keelie Keller's voice, seeing tears—real tears—pour down her cheeks, I just couldn't bring myself to air the clip. It wouldn't be any different from her airing Taylor's trooper true confession

It just felt wrong. And two wrongs didn't make a right. Right?

"I'll leave the tabloid journalism to you, Drew," I said. "I'm looking for something a bit more…extraordinary than that," I said, in my best British accent.

"Sucker," Van Vleet said, and drained his glass of beer. "I

sure hope those scruples of yours keep you fed and clothed and a roof over your head when Stan Rodgers kicks your fanny to the curb. Oh, and don't make me wait in the morning. The earlier we start, the cooler it is."

"I hear and I obey, my liege," I said.

Van Vleet shook his head and moved off.

"Twerp," I said, raising my glass to signal for another beer.

Winterset had certainly gone all out, even building a mock-up of a Wild West town on land donated for the night by a local farmer. Phony storefronts, including a general store and apothecary, blacksmith's shop, a bank, the sheriff's office, and a hotel, added to the old west atmosphere. A massive steel outbuilding had been transformed into the "Ya'll Come Back Saloon" complete with swinging doors, makeshift bar, and a stage for the band. Strands of twinkle lights—indoors and out—added a modern and magical touch to the venue. In one corner of the outbuilding, the requisite mechanical bull sat, surrounded by a mountain of foam mats to cushion the fall.

I grinned, watching as a half-soused, old enough to know better, skinny dude dressed in European Capri pants and a T-shirt with a picture of the Holliwell Bridge on the front, bowlegged it up to the bull and hopped on. Or rather, tried to. The guy kept slipping off and sliding to the ground. And the bull hadn't even been turned on yet.

I shook my head. City slickers.

"Now that, Miss Turner, is a poster child for liquid courage, if I ever saw it," someone remarked, and I turned to find Jax Whitver on the seat next to me. "And I should know." He hiccoughed.

"What are you doing here?"

"Partying," he responded.

"You'd better not let Keelie see you." And her bodyguard, for that matter. "She was pretty clear on wanting you to keep your distance."

"It's a free country. You know. Life, liberty, and the pursuit of happiness," he said, obviously having partaken of liberal libations before arriving at the party.

"Aren't you concerned at all about escalating an already...explosive situation? Or," I finally thought to wonder, "was that dust-up rehearsed, choreographed, and performed flawlessly."

"I wish," Jax said. "Hey, barkeep. Another round for me and my lady outlaw here."

He stared at my chest for an uncomfortably long time.

"*Courage is being scared to death and saddling up anyway*," he read. "Truer words. Truer words. Sometimes I'm scared to death, but hell if I let anyone know it."

I blinked. "Scared? You? Of what?"

The mustachioed bartender set beers on the bar in front of us.

"Of losing myself," he said, and picked up his beer. "Losing sight of what's 'portant. Of who's 'portant."

I winced. The poor guy was drunk and clearly hurting. Separately, I am ill-equipped to deal with either one of these conditions. Together? Fuggetaboutiit.

"I effed up," Jax said. "Bad."

I winced. Drunk, hurting, and potty-mouthed.

"We all make mistakes. That's the easy part."

He turned bleary, red eyes on me. "Whazz the hard part?"

"Learning from them. Trust me. I'm somewhat of an authority on the screw-up/wise-up process."

He grinned. "Yer cute," he slurred.

"Oh? Which one of us?" I teased, figuring the guy had to be close to seeing double.

"You got a sense of humor. Keelie doesn't. She's always angry," he said.

"She's got a lot of responsibility for someone so young," I said. "Lots on the line. Lots to prove. It can't be easy."

"Blah, blah, blah, blah, blah." Jax said, obviously too much in his cups to realize how wise I sounded and how whiney he did. "Enough serious talk. It's time to party!"

"I think you've partied enough," I said, looking around for someone who might assist the singer safely back to wherever he was staying and tuck him in for the night. I so wasn't the girl for the job.

"What the—" I heard Jax say and looked in the direction he seemed fixated on.

I blinked. Keelie Keller sashayed up to the mechanical, got

a leg up from a helpful cowboy, and hopped on the back.

"What's she doing? She's nuts!" Jax said. "Hey, you! Kay-Kay! Yeah. I'm talkin' to you, Red!"

Before I could grab hold of him, Jax vaulted on top of the bar. Keelie stared over the heads of the crowd and found Jax.

"Step down off that bull, missy!" he said, trying to sound like Duke Wayne, but sounding more like Wayne Newton with a bad head cold.

"Go away, Jax Whitver! Go away and leave me alone!"

"You want me to go away? Back off? Fine. Quit this stupid ride, and I'm gone, baby, gone. Like *that*." He tried to snap his fingers, but couldn't get them to cooperate.

"Get off the bar! You're gonna break your neck," I hissed.

"Hear that, Keelie? I could break my neck, she says. Would you even care?"

Oh, God. Talk about gonna regret it in the morning.

"You're drunk, Jax!" Keelie yelled. "And you can't tell me what to do any more. I'm so over you."

"You're gonna regret this, Keelie. I know it."

"Go home, Jax Whitver. Just go home."

I grabbed his pant leg. "I'd suggest a cab."

Jax dropped to his backside, his legs dangling over the edge of the bar.

"I can't leave her," he said. "I can't."

I helped him down off the bar. "Let's call you a cab," I said.

"I'm a cab," he said, and giggled.

I pulled my phone out to Google the cab number and frowned. No bars.

"Dang." A steel building in the middle of nowhere probably wasn't the best place to pick up a cell signal. "You stay right there!" I ordered. "Don't move. I'm going to step outside and call you a cab."

"I won't be able to hear you call me a cab if you go outside," he said.

I shook my head. Why me?

I hurried outside. Still no bars.

I walked about twenty steps, checking for a signal, when everything around me went pitch dark. Lights out. Literally.

Screams and shouts erupted. Cowboys and cowgirls and

everyone in between spilled out of the saloon...er, steel outbuilding, like a herd of stampeding livestock.

"What in God's name?"

I pointed my cell phone at the ground to light my way and started back toward the building.

"What happened? What's going on?" I asked no one in particular.

"Chaos, that's what," a girl near me said. "All of a sudden the lights went out, and it was pitch dark. I heard a bang and a scream, and I just took off for the exit."

"A bang? As in a gun?"

"I don't know. I just got the hell out."

Police cars, top lights going and spotlights shining, rolled up to the scene, illuminating the outside area.

"Calm down, everyone. Take it easy!" An officer shouted and jogged around the side of the building. Moments later, the lights were back on. People continued to stream from the saloon.

I ran back inside in time to see Manny kneeling over a prone figure near the mechanical bull.

Oh, no! Keelie!

I held my breath. Hoping. Praying.

"I'm okay," I heard her say. "Just had the air knocked out of me."

"Don't be a hero. You need to get checked out, kid," Vinny Vincent barked. "We need an ambulance!"

"No. I'm fine. Honest. I just took a spill on the mats. I'm perfectly okay. I was just a little freaked out when the lights went out, but I'm fine now."

Manny helped the petite redhead to her feet and walked her through the crowd to the door. She looked over at me for a moment before Manny ushered her out.

I hurried up to the bar. "Did you see what happened to the guy on the bar?" I asked.

He shook his head. "He disappeared right after you left. One minute he was there, and the next, he was gone. Then, bam! The lights went out."

Despite the warmth of the night I shivered.

Jax's words played in my head. "You're gonna regret this, Keelie," he'd said.

Coincidence or...something more?

I looked at the handmade sign over the saloon doors.

Ya'll Come Back Saloon.

Um, let's don't and say we did.

The party pretty much broke up after that. More than ready to sack out, I hopped a shuttle back to the campgrounds. I stood outside the tent I'd hurriedly erected earlier and ran a dubious eye over the already sagging structure.

"Barbie looks like she's surveying the gateway to hell."

Close. Real close.

"What are you doing here?" I covered my eyes from the glare of Manny's super bright flashlight beam.

"Manny's lookin' for a night's lodging," he said.

All the spit in my mouth dried up. My pulse rate skyrocketed faster than my credit card balance Christmas Eve day.

"A night's...lodging?" I squeaked, breaking out in a cold sweat when I noticed the rolled-up sleeping bag in his hand.

"Bus won't start. No air. Hotter than a blast furnace."

"So, you want to stay *here*?" I wiped perspiration from above my lip.

"Manny wants Red to stay here."

"Red?"

I'll admit it. It took me longer than it should have to get his gist. Totally justified. Tell me your brain wouldn't take a holiday at the idea of sharing a tent with Manny DeMarco, man of mystery.

"Keelie."

"Keelie? Keelie Keller? Wait. You want me to share a tent with Keelie Keller? You've got to be joking." Or on some pretty powerful, mind-altering pharmaceuticals.

"Manny doesn't kid."

I had learned that about him.

"You're serious?"

"Keelie needs a place to sleep. A *safe* place to sleep. Manny's got to see to the bus—and other things."

I swallowed and stared up at him. "By other things, you mean Jax."

He neither confirmed nor denied my statement. Typical.

"Why me of all people? Your 'charge' thinks I'm the one responsible for all sorts of nefarious deeds."

"Manny knows better."

The cockles of my heart warmed. Unconditional trust. What a concept.

"What about Keelie? Does she know better?"

"Did you forget? Keep your friends close, keep your enemies closer." Keelie Keller, big ol' purse in hand, squeezed around Manny's girth.

"Did you forget it's polite to wait for an invitation?" I pointed at the tent behind me. "How do you know I don't have a guy in there?"

"Manny told me. Manny says you're all by your lonesome."

Someone was taking literary license here. I couldn't see Manny using the term "lonesome".

"How accommodating of him," I observed, giving Mr. DeMarco a you-*will*-pay look.

"Yes or no?" Manny, the man of few words, asked.

"You can't find any place else?"

"Whatever. I'll sleep on the bus," Keelie said.

Manny looked at me and lifted a dark eyebrow.

Crap. I was so gonna cave.

"All right. On one condition," I told Manny, figuring I might as well get something out of the deal.

"Manny's listening."

"I ask you five questions. You give me five truthful responses," I said.

"Deal," Manny placed Keelie's sleeping bag in my hands and handed her the flashlight. "Be back at six sharp," he said and was gone.

"They come. They go. They're here. They're there." I said.

"Who?" Keelie asked.

"Men."

She nodded. "Tell me about it."

We entered the tent. I tossed her bedroll on the left side of the tent. "You can bed down there," I said.

Keelie shined the flashlight at the sleeping bag and shook her head. "No. No. Not going to work. I always sleep on the right side of the bed."

I blinked. Was she for real? I know. Dumb question to ask when referring to a reality TV star, right?

"Uh, hello. There is no bed. It's the ground. And, by definition, the ground has no sides. It just keeps going and going and going. Besides, this is my spot. I like to sleep on my right side."

"You said the ground had no sides."

"It doesn't. I do."

Truth was I didn't feel comfortable sleeping with my back to my unexpected roomie, which was what would happen if I slept on the left side of the tent. Yes. There's a method to my madness.

"I sleep on my right side, as well," Keelie said.

"Yes, but it's *my* tent," I pointed out. "And you know the saying, 'beggars can't be choosers.'"

"Yes. I know it. And it's a stupid saying. How often does somebody use the word 'chooser'" anyway?"

She had a point. I shrugged.

"Fine," Keelie said. "Whatever. Take your stupid side."

"You know, it's not really a side. It's a—"

"Oh, just leave it alone!" Keelie put a hand to her head. "Can we just go to sleep? I'm stiff. I'm sore. I have a headache. I just want to sleep."

I'd felt the same way before Red barged in. I'd been looking forward to some undisturbed slumber. But was I getting it? Nooo!

I zipped the tent entrance flap and moved back to my *wall,* dropping onto my bed and pulling the cover over me. I grabbed my own flashlight just in case and settled into the soft warmth of my bedroll, watching Keelie struggle to undo the cord that held her bag together.

"Stupid, stupid bag!" She said, and ripped into the sleeping bag with the same level of frustration I used on my favorite sandwich cookie packages before they switched to the easy open, re-sealable packaging.

"I think you can just slip that elastic cord off one end," I said.

"Oh. Right." She unrolled the sleeping bag and smoothed it out. "Thanks."

"Sure."

She took off the hoodie she wore and collapsed onto the bag.

"Ahhh!"

I knew the feeling.

She shut the flashlight off. I couldn't see my hand in front of my face.

"I think it's supposed to rain," Keelie said, sounding very young.

"Yeah. I heard the rumbling of thunder."

"This tent won't leak. Right?"

I sure as heck hoped not.

"Of course, not."

"What about snakes?"

Damn. She had to remind me.

"The flap's zipped. We should be good."

"Manny says you're not the one playing the pranks," she said.

"He's right."

Silence.

"I wish it was you."

I felt the pull of heartstrings again.

"Yeah. I know."

More silence.

"Night, Keelie," I said, my jumbled thoughts shifting to the five questions I would ask Manny. I'd have to make them count. No telling when I'd get another crack at him.

I yawned, exhaustion creeping over me. Just about to drift off, a hushed whisper reached me.

"Goodnight...*Calamity Jayne*."

Damn! Who told?

CHAPTER TWENTY-FOUR

"Psst! You in the tent! Open up!"

I opened one eye. Still dark. I shut my eyes again.

"Let me in! It's starting to rain!"

I sat up, opened both eyes, and pushed my hair out of my eyes.

"Who is it?"

"What's going on?" A disembodied voice from the darkness called out.

"Someone's at the flap," I said.

"Who?"

"Open up, Turner, or I'll slice a hole in the side of the tent."

"See. Tents do have sides," Keelie said. "Who is it?"

I picked up my flashlight and turned it on, the beam wimpy when compared to Manny's jumbo-sized light.

"That would be Dixie Daggett of Daggett's Cone Connection fame. Where appetites go to die." I crawled to the front of the tent and unzipped the zipper.

"It's about time." She crawled, head first, into the tent. I grabbed her arm and helped reel her all the way in.

"Who were you talking to?" she said, and I shined the flashlight in Keelie's direction.

"Hey!" Keelie stuck a hand up in front of her eyes.

Dixie's lower jaw dropped.

"What's going on?" she asked.

"I'm like wondering the same thing," I said. "What's the deal? What are you doing here? Where's Frankie?"

"Who's Frankie again?" Keelie asked.

"My cousin. You know. The skinny guy at Frank's Mini-Freeze," I said. "Your bodyguard's BFF. Dixie's fiancé."

"I know you," Keelie said. "You were one of Team

Trekkie's volleyball players. The short-stuff who got nailed in the nose."

"I'm so flattered you remembered," Dixie grunted, settling in the center of the tent. She wadded her coat into a pillow, plumped it, put it on the ground, and stretched out.

"You're sleeping here?" I asked.

"No. I just thought I'd haul my cookies out in stormy weather in the middle of the night to say *hey*."

Dixie Daggett: reigning queen of sarcasm.

"What's up with *her*?" Dixie nodded in Keelie's direction.

"What's up with *you*?" Keelie snapped back.

"Keelie's bus is broken. And Manny's got…to see a guy. Now, it's your turn."

"Frankie's minding the bus."

"He's what?"

"He's guarding Keelie's bus. Manny needed someone to keep an eye on it until the mechanic got there."

"And he called Frankie?"

"The cameramen were all drunk. Besides, who else would jump at the chance to guard a broken down bus in the middle of the night?"

"That still doesn't explain why you're here?" Keelie asked.

"Was I talkin' to you, Red? Did you see my face turned in your direction? You'll know when I'm talking to you."

I winced. Dixie was a tad punchy.

"So, Frankie is helping Manny out. Big deal."

Dixie turned back to me. "It is a big deal when your girlfriend is asking for a little quality, alone time and you bail the minute the Hulk calls."

"The Hulk?"

"Am I looking at you, Red Queen?"

"Red Queen? *Red Queen*! Is that what you call me? The Red Queen!"

Dixie and I pointed at each other.

"She started it!"

"So, does Frankie know you're here?" I asked.

"No. Hell, no."

"Won't he wonder where you are when he gets back to the Suburban?"

"*If* he ever gets back."

"But, won't he worry?" Keelie asked. "Won't he be frantic wondering where you are and what happened to you? Won't he search high and low and go to the ends of the earth looking for you?"

Dixie looked over at Keelie, then back at me. "How can someone on a reality show have such a loose grip on reality?"

"If ya'll don't mind, I, at least, have a sixty mile bike ride five hours from now. Can we please just get some sleep?"

"There you go again. Implying that I'm not riding the entire ride," Keelie huffed.

"Are you?" Dixie asked.

"I need my sleep," Keelie said. "I have a very long bike ride tomorrow."

"Make that today," I grumbled, and doused the light. "'Night all."

I'd just put my head down when...

"I have to go."

I sat up.

"Go? Go where?"

"You know. The loo."

"Loo?"

"I have to go to the restroom!" Keelie hissed.

"Now?"

"No. Next week. Of course, now!"

"Well, go then. There's a line of kybos a mile wide just down over yonder hill."

Silence again.

"Kybos? What are kybos?"

Dixie snorted. I shook my head.

"A kybo is a Porta-Potty, a portable toilet."

"Sick," Keelie said. "How do they work?"

Dixie put a hand over her eyes. "Oh, please. Tell me we're not going to get into a discussion of the chemical toilet."

"Chemicals? They use chemicals?"

"Can you latch a door and squat?" Dixie asked.

"Of course."

"Then you're good to go."

Keelie picked up Manny's flashlight, turned it on, grabbed

her hoodie, and shrugged into it.

"You have an umbrella? Here, use mine." Dixie handed her the telescoping version.

"Uh, thanks. So, just down the hill? A line of toilets."

I sighed and threw off my covers. Manny would never forgive me if something happened to Keelie between my tent and the Porta-Potties.

"I'll go with you."

"I don't need a babysitter." Keelie sniffed.

"All your talk about toilets made me have to go," I lied. "You good, Dix?" I asked.

"I went before I left. By the way, who put your tent up?"

"Me. Why?"

"You have set up a tent before."

"Dozens of times."

"I feel so much better," she said.

The wind had picked up and big, fat drops of rain fell sideways, pelting us where the umbrella didn't cover. Lightning lit up the skies and thunder rumbled.

We hoofed it to the row of toilets.

"We'd better hurry. It looks like it's gonna turn into a gulley washer."

"Um, could you, that is, would you, check out the, uh, facility?" Keelie asked. "You know. For rodents. Insects. Reptiles."

Hardly my favorite species.

I sighed. "Let me see the light," I said, and she handed me Manny's light. I entered the Porta-Potty and shined the light around the interior. She squeezed in beside me.

"See?" I said. "Nothing here."

"That's where you sit?" she pointed at the seat with the big, black hole in the middle.

"That's where *you* sit."

Her face looked like I figured mine did when I watched the contestants on a survival show eat pig intestines and wriggling grubs.

"I'll be just outside," I said.

"Promise?"

"I promise." I was just about to make the pinky swear sign

when the kybo door slammed shut.

"The wind must really be picking up," I said. "We better hurry." I tried to open the door. It wouldn't budge. I tried again. No luck.

"What's wrong?" Keelie asked.

I shoved on the door. "I don't know. I think it's jammed." I pushed again. Harder. Nothing.

The ping, ping, ping of raindrops on corrugated plastic played "top this!" with the wind that began to whistle through the cracks of the portable potty.

"Try harder!" Keelie said, helping me push against the door. "The last place I want to be when a cyclone hits is in this smelly death trap."

"Actually, we don't call wind storms 'cyclones' in Iowa. We call them twisters or tornadoes. We do have cyclones, but they're one of our college teams."

"We're stuck in a toilet in the middle of a storm, and you're correcting my word choice?"

"If you knew me better, you'd know that when I get anxious or nervous, or slightly terrified, I'm prone to diarrhea of the mouth."

"I guess it's a good thing we're in a loo then."

I smiled. Wow. She *was* more than a pretty face.

Keelie banged on the door with Manny's flashlight. "Hello! Anyone out there? Help!"

"It's doubtful anyone can hear you over the rain and the wind," I said.

Keelie sent me a dark look and proceeded to ignore me.

"Help! Help! Someone help us! We're trapped in the chemical toilet! Let us out! Let us out!"

I cocked an eyebrow. "Wait a minute. You've said those lines before."

"What are you talking about? What lines?"

"The ones you just said."

"The ones I just said? We're trapped in a chemical toilet? I've said that line before?"

"You didn't actually say the chemical toilet part. I think what you said was more like, 'Help! Help! Someone help us! We're trapped in the root cellar! Let us out! Let us out!' That was from one of your Samantha Sweeney, super sleuth shows. It was the episode where you and Izzy suspected Izzy's creepy neighbor of stealing purebred dogs and keeping them in the root cellar until he could smuggle them out of town and sell them. Turns out, the culprit was his nephew, Basil."

Keelie paused. "I'm flattered you remember." She paused. "You know. That was one of my best performances. Critics raved."

A sudden gust of wind hit the portable loo. I felt the tiny structure shift. The ping, ping, ping of hail smashing against the elimination edifice now sounded more like a barrage of BB gun fire.

Rat-a-tat-a-tat!

I looked at Keelie. She stared back.

"Help! Help! Someone help us! We're trapped in the Porta-Potty! Let us out! Let us out!" We pounded on the door and yelled at the top of our lungs.

Another, much stronger gust of wind, slammed against the outhouse.

"Your friend, Dixie! She'll miss us when we don't come back. She'll come looking for us, right?"

Oh, lord. She was a hopeless innocent when it came to the likes of Dixie the Destructor.

"Anything's possible," I hedged.

"Oh, no!" Keelie gasped. "I've got her umbrella. She won't come! She'll get drenched!"

I patted Keelie's shoulder. "I don't think you need to worry."

The storm outside our refuge unleashed its full fury, the sound of the wind and hail, deafening. I wasn't sure whether we were safer inside or outside. All I knew was I didn't want to be anywhere close if a twister came along and decided to play fifty-two pick up with a row of Porta-Potties.

"I've got an idea!" I yelled, above the roar.

"What!"

"Let's rock it!"

"Rock what!"

"The kybo. It's already been pulled off his base. All we have to do is rock it, and it will probably fall over."

"Then what?"

"We kick the top off or crawl out the bottom."

"I vote for the top," Keelie said.

Me, too.

"Ready? Set. Go!"

Back and forth, back and forth, we rocked the loo. Finally, I heard a crack. And another one.

"It's coming! It's coming! Rock it! Rock it!"

Keelie and I locked arms and gave one final monster shove. At that moment, a powerful tunnel of air swept beneath the tipping toidy. I felt the floor beneath me shift and lift. The top of the kybo started to tip.

"Houston! We've got a launch!" I yelled, and grabbed Keelie and wrapped my arms around her. "Hold on!"

An eardrum-bruising chorus of squeals, groans, and curses, filled the capsule around us—and not all due to the chemical toilet.

"Aaaah!" Our terrified screams were made-for-the-big-screen quality.

"Watch out! Here we go!" I yelled.

"Oh, God! We're falling! We're falling!" Keelie screeched, hugging me so tightly I could hardly breathe.

Boom!

We hit the ground like a lumberjack's latest tree trunk.

It took a second or two for me to gather the courage to open my eyes.

"You okay?" I asked.

"Still in one piece. You?"

"I'll live."

"Phew. That smell!" Keelie coughed. "It reeks."

It did. I didn't have the heart to tell her we probably would too before we got out of this mess. And, no. I don't do poop puns.

"Where's Manny's flashlight? Did it make the trip?" I asked.

"It's down here." Keelie grabbed it and handed it to me.

"Okay. We can do this one of two ways," I said. "Crawl out the bottom. Or kick the top off with our feet and exit that way."

"You already know my feelings," Keelie said.

I did. And I shared them.

"We…just…have…to…get turned around," I said, trying to

maneuver around the capsule-like confines. It took us another five minutes to get in position.

"Oh, God. It stinks like shit at this end," Keelie said.

I had the good sense not to point out the obvious.

"On the count of three, start kicking," I instructed.

"Oh, God. The stench! It absolutely reeks! I'm gonna be sick!"

"You are not puking in this Porta-Potty. Hold your breath and, on three, kick as hard as you can. One. Two. Three!"

"Bam! Bam! Bam! Bam!

On the tenth kick, the top of the kybo flew off. Sheets of rain drenched me. I didn't care. I sucked in the fresh air like a drowning man pulled from a river.

"Oh, thank God. Thank God!" Keelie said. "It's lovely! Just lovely!"

A puddle of water began to seep into the kybo. It quickly became a river.

"We'd better get out of here," I said, grabbing hold of the top of the toilet and pulling myself out. "Be careful!" I said, shining a light on the top. "There are screws sticking out!"

I helped Keelie out of the kybo.

"Oh, my lord! Look at that!" Keelie pointed at the line of Porta-Potties. They looked like a drunk had tried to stack dominoes. Some were upright. Some tipped part way. Some toppled over. "Wow! Look at all that water!"

Where moments before it had been dry, a river of water now crashed its way down the hill. Dislocated tents, swept away by the rushing water, rested against the row of toilets.

I gasped. "If we'd been in the tent when that water came through—"

I stopped.

Oh, no!

"Dixie!"

No sooner had the name passed my lips, than an ungodly howl, the likes of which I'd only heard in werewolf movies and from the occasional drunken cowboy, ripped through the soggy rain-filled air.

"Owwoo!"

I trained my flashlight on the rushing water, certain a

swamped coyote or displaced badger had been flushed out of their beds.

Oh. My. God!

My beam hit the approaching object head on. I gasped, and watched in horror as Dixie rode the waves on my bargain basement tent like a chubby kid on a water ride at the amusement park.

Is it a bird?

Is it a plane?

Nope.

It's the full-speed-ahead USS Dixie Doodle Dandy aiming for an open berth at the Port o' Potties.

I closed my eyes and braced for impact.

How do you say, "braking bad"?

CHAPTER TWENTY-FIVE

"I think it's a good likeness? Do you think it's a good likeness, Tressa?"

I squinted at the drawing my gammy stuck in front of my face.

"It's Joe and me. It was one of them character sketches."

I nodded. "Those are definitely characters," I said, taking my sunglasses off to get a better look.

"Tressa Jayne! Your eyes! You look like one of them vampires with the bloodshot peepers. And look at the dark circles! Joe, come look at Tressa. She looks like a zombie."

My gammy needed to make up her mind. Was I Vampirella or Tressa, Zombie Queen? After all, we're talking two very different classifications of the undead here.

Joe walked up and took his own sunglasses off. He gave me the once-over like my gammy does in the mirror before she leaves the house.

"She looks the same to me," Joe said.

Ho, ho, ho.

I knew I wasn't looking my best. I looked like I'd either spent the night battling the walking dead, or had been recruited by them. And "Gampy" Joe knew it good and well, too.

"Nice of you to say, Joe," I said, in no shape to defend myself in a battle of wits with the clever and cunning senior Townsend. After the previous night's "Toilets and Tents Soiree," and a miserably, rain-soaked ride that morning, the second I'd put the kickstand down on the tandem that afternoon, I hightailed it home, took a long, hot shower, and flopped into bed.

If my gammy and her new hubby hadn't come knock-knock-knocking on my door, I'd still be there, sleeping the sleep of the dead...ish. As it was, I planned on an early night—hopefully in the company of a certain ranger I knew and lusted over.

I hadn't seen Rick since I'd pedaled into town. By design. Come on. Tell me you'd want the guy who set your spurs to jingle-jangle-jingling to see you looking like something that crawled up out of a grave. Even worse, I'd most likely smelled the part.

"So, what do you think about our picture? Kenny gave us a special deal. He said cuz you were friends and all."

"I wouldn't exactly call us friends," I said. "But Kenny was a sport and gave me an interview. He also played for us at the volleyball match."

"You call that a match? More like blood sport," Joe said. "Especially for Dixie Daggett."

I took a deep breath. Nope. I wasn't gonna do it. I wasn't gonna take the bait.

"It looks like us, don't it?" Gram asked.

I took the drawing from her. It did. In a way.

"It's good, isn't it?" Gram pressed.

It was. Sort of.

"Well, what do you think?"

"Yeah. It's great, Gram," I said.

"Show her the other one," Joe said, and I felt the pavement move under my feet.

"The other one?"

"Oh, Joe! You spoiled the surprise! I was gonna give it to her for Christmas!"

The ghost of Christmas gifts past sent a shudder of unease through me.

"I'm not much on surprises, Gram—" Or unexpected presents that put a "trouble for Tressa" twinkle in Joe's eyes.

"You're gonna love this one!" Gram said, and pulled a second drawing out of her canvas bag. "It's an oldie, but a goodie!"

She motioned for Joe to help. He took one side of the paper and they began to unroll it.

I felt a throbbing in my right eye.

It *was* me. The "me" from my terrible, horrible, no good, very bad senior picture.

"Surprise!" Joe said.

Oh. God. In. Heaven. This was worse than the hobo Halloween costume jigsaw puzzle gift I received over and over again from a totally psycho secret Santa.

"Do you like it?" Gram asked. "You like it, don't you? It's you, after all. So what's not to like?"

What's not to like? Well, for starters, my creepy, phony smile that made me look like a serial killer. And there was my choice of eye makeup. Gram wanted me to go with blue to match my eyes resulting in—I learned too late—a fashion faux pas on steroids. And, finally, we had "Mr. Toad's Wild Ride" hair. Given that description, I figure that's all I have to say on that subject. My gammy couldn't have selected a worse picture for Kenny to draw from if she'd tried.

But it's the thought that counts, right?

"Wow! Look at that! It *is* me!" I gushed, regardless of how many times I planned to deny it in the future.

"So. What do you think?" Joe asked. "It's a decent likeness, don't you agree?"

I grunted.

"I didn't know you and I have the same eyes," Gram said.

I frowned. "That's because we don't."

"We must. Both our pictures have the same eyes."

I braved another look at my face and checked Gram's out.

"You're right. They do look the same. That's odd." Odd because our eyes are nothing alike. I got the Blackford eyes. Grandma's baby blues came from her mother's side of the family.

"Maybe them's the only eyes Kenny knows how to draw," Gram suggested.

A one size fits all peeper?

"What kind of artist does that?" I asked.

"A starving one," Joe quipped.

I took a closer look at my "surprise."

"Something else is off, too," I said and bit my lip as I considered the drawing. "I've got it! It's the nose. That is not my nose."

"Whose is it?" Gram asked.

I shook my head. "I don't know. It's just too—"

"Small? Perky? Classical?" Joe asked.

"Conventional," I finished.

"Oh? So, you're an art expert now?" Joe asked.

I shook my head. "I'm an expert on me. And I'm just saying, that is not my nose."

But it *was* an improvement, so who was I to complain?

"You like it, Tressa?" Gram looked up at me, her eyes bright with anticipation.

"Of course. I love it."

Gram smiled. "Good. I've already been to the printers', and I'm having business cards printed for you."

The gift that keeps on giving.

"Wow. Thanks Gram."

"You goin' to the talent show tonight?" Gram asked.

I shrugged.

"I suppose I'll have to. Stan will expect me to write something up about it for the paper and the blog."

Grandville's Got Talent, was the TribRide overnight host committee's version of the popular TV talent search. Not-so-good acts selected specifically for the sole purpose of providing an opportunity for the audience to jeer and heckle were in the lineup along with quality acts from the area. The event, to be held in the brand spanking new community theater and auditorium, included a panel of judges who would provide some fun feedback for the participants.

My plans for the evening? To limit my participation to covering the early acts and then to skedaddle.

"You happen to see this morning's *Capitol City* paper?" Joe asked.

I shook my head. "No."

"How about the *New Holland News* online?"

"Negative."

"That *Star Trek* fanatic's blog? See that?"

"No. I've been on a bike and in bed. Why?"

"Your Porta-Potty predicament. It's headline news."

"What!"

"You're on the front page of the papers and all the tabloids, not to mention the Internet. They got you and that Keelie crawling out the top of the kybo. They're calling it 'Poop Scoop: Number One.'"

"Number One?"

"I know it's said bad publicity is better than no publicity, but I'm not sure that goes for a professional journalist who is filmed crawling out of the top of an up-ended Porta-Potty butt first." Joe shook his head. "Talk about tip you over, pour you out."

"I...she...we...who?" I stopped. Who? Drew Van Vleet, that's who. The weasel must have been staking out my tent. "Was there, uh, any additional footage of the, uh, flooding in the area as a result of the heavy rain?" I asked.

"What you are really asking is if Van Vleet caught Dixie Daggett channeling *Deliverance*? That's 'Poop Scoop: Number Two.'"

Oh, hell. Get my best pair of cowboy boots all shined up, cuz I was fixin' to be a cowgirl angel in Heaven's eternal line dance when Dixie Daggett caught up to me.

"You see Rick yet?" Joe asked.

I shook my head. "I thought he was working." I hoped he was. When he got a look at Poop Scoop: Number One, I could only imagine his reaction.

"He's around," Joe said. "Saw him at Hazel's at breakfast."

Great.

"And what's up with your mother?" Gram asked. "You see her when you washed the stink off?"

I frowned. "Why would I see Mom here?"

"'Cause here's where she's stayin'," Gram said.

"What?"

"Your mom has been sleeping here at your place since Sunday," Gram said. "I think she's having one of them mid-wife crises."

I winced.

"I think you mean mid-life crisis," I said.

"She's a wife, isn't she?" Gram said.

I frowned. Now that I thought about it, my house had been much cleaner than when I left it. I'd just figured my mom had decided to take advantage of my absence to clean. She's done it before.

"I think your folks are having problems," Gram said. "I think someone better talk to them. I think someone needs to straighten them out."

I shook my head.

"We're not getting involved, Gram."

"I didn't mean *us*. I meant a professional. You know. Someone like Dr. Phil. You think your folks would agree to go on his show? You think I should contact Phil's people? Or, maybe now you and that reality star are best buds, you can ask her to use her contacts and get your folks to the front of the line. She's bound to have an 'in' with Dr. Phil."

"What I think is, we need to let Mom and Dad sort out their own issues, if they even have any," I said.

"By then it may be too late. You know how your dad is about communicatin'. When he was a youngun, I thought he'd never learn to talk."

I didn't want to mention the possibility that he probably wouldn't have been able to get a word in edgewise.

"I'm sure things are fine, Gram," I assured her.

"I ain't so sure. I was over to the house the other day and your father was eating beanie weenies and lunch meat, wearing mismatched socks, and beginning to grow a beard."

I blinked. Beanie weenies—and a beard? The situation had certainly deteriorated in the last several days.

"TribRide's done in a few days. If things are still not back to normal, we'll put our heads together and come up with something," I promised.

"By then it might be too late. It's like that movie. You don't deal with things, and they begin to fester. 'Fester, fester, fester. Rot. Rot. Rot.'"

"Okay, Gammy. I get the point. We'll come up with some way to forestall the, er, festering," I promised. "In the meantime, maybe letting them both have a little space wouldn't be such a bad thing."

"Space? Your PawPaw Will and I never got any space. We were practically joined at the hip, like married couples should be."

I shook my head. Talk about rewriting history. 'Gammy Gad About' was on the go night and day. And PawPaw Will? When he wasn't working, he was hunting, fishing, or playing in the garden.

"About Rick," Joe said, as they were taking their leave.

"Avoidance? Not the best way to go. Just ask your pop."

I thanked the duo for my gift and waved goodbye, wondering how bad the situation was between my mom and dad and how on earth couples kept the magic alive.

CHAPTER TWENTY-SIX

"I still don't get why we can't have food in here," my gammy asked. "Where's the harm in a box of Raisinets?"

"It's a new facility, Gram. They want to keep it tidy."

"I don't plan on spilling anything."

Bless her heart. She never did.

I sighed. Gram had insisted on having the aisle seat for the No-Talent Talent Show. I'd ended up beside her. Rick came next, then Joe.

"I've never seen so many lame acts in my life," Gram said.

"They're supposed to be lame, Gram. They're parodies."

"None of these acts would get past Simon."

"Exactly. They're bad on purpose."

"Well, I coulda done that," she said.

"You could, Gram. You really could."

Tap! Tap!

I frowned and shifted in my seat.

Rap! Tap! Tap!

Some jackass was kicking my seat. I turned around.

"If you don't mind—" I began, and then stopped. "Jax? Jax Whitver! What are you doing here?"

"Taking in the show. So far, I'd say Grandville doesn't have much talent."

That one got my gammy turning in her seat.

"Don't you know anything? These acts are pear-a-dees. They're supposed to be crap."

"Mission accomplished," Jax said.

"What happened to you the other night?" I asked.

"I had places to go. Things to do. People to see."

"You were drunk! You could hardly keep your eyes open!"

"Shhh! Please! There's a performance going on!"

I glanced over at the shusher and winced. What were the odds that my former high school principal would be the one to shoosh me?

I thought back to my school days.

Pretty good.

"Who's this?" Rick turned in his seat.

"Jax Whitver, Rick Townsend. Rick Townsend, Jax Whitver." I made the surreal intros.

Rick reached back and shook Jax's hand.

"You're the country pop star," Rick said.

Jax nodded. "Guilty as charged."

"How do you know Tressa?" Rick asked.

"We've shared some, shall we say, ups and downs on TribRide," he said, with a grin. "Our paths seem destined to cross."

"And here you are again," Rick said, turning to give me a "this ought to be good" look.

"I'm not sure it's a good idea for you to be here, Jax," I said. "Especially after last night."

"Last night?" Rick's expression went from "this ought to be good" to "this better be good" quicker than my gammy changes her mind about what she wants to order for lunch.

"Then this will probably be an even worse idea," Jax said. "But damned if I give a shit."

"Ladies and gentlemen." Our community choir director, Jerald Harcourt, took the stage, microphone in hand. "Grandville's Got Talent is honored to announce a special surprise performance from number one country and pop performer, Jax Whitver! Ladies and gentlemen, Jax Whitver!"

Jax moved from the seat behind me to the aisle. Before I knew what was happening, he reached across Gram and grabbed my hand, pulling me into the aisle with him. He dragged me along with him in the direction of the stage.

"What are you doing? Are you insane? Keelie's here! She mentioned a restraining order."

"Not to worry, Tressa, dear. I haven't been served so we're good to go," he said, raising his hand and acknowledging the audience with a wave and a mega-buck grin.

"We?"

"I have to have someone to sing to, don't I?"

"My gammy's been itching to get on stage. Take her!"

"Sorry. I don't go for older women. You know. The image and all."

"But she's spry for her age. The broken bones have mended nicely!"

"Come on. Relax and enjoy the limelight, Tressa. Rest assured, I will deliver you back to your boyfriend with your virtue intact."

"Boyfriend? How do you know he's my boyfriend?" I asked, suddenly flushed.

"From the bulging veins in his neck that popped out when I whisked you off."

"Oh."

Jax yanked me up the stairs and onto the stage to deafening applause. Mr. Harcourt handed Jax a microphone.

"Hello Grandville, Iowa, U…S…A!" Jax yelled.

The audience went wild.

"I'm totally thrilled to help you celebrate your new auditorium and night four of TribRide! What do you say, Grandville? Are you ready to party?" He raised the microphone over his head. "Rock on!"

Jax brought the mic to his mouth and stared into my eyes. I felt like I might pee my pants. I can be such a teenybopper.

Then, he started to sing.

"*You come. You go. You leave. You stay.*"

I stared. Holy Hollywood hype. Jax wrote this song. Keelie starred in the music video. The song's release had fueled speculation that the newest "power couple" was more about a short-term media bump than happily ever after.

Either way, this couldn't be good. For Jax.

Or a certain clueless cowgirl.

"*You scram. You stay.*
Fidelity depends upon the day.
It's a counterfeit courtship.
You laugh. I cry.
'Cause you've got a roving eye.
Counterfeit courtship.

Counterfeit courtship. Where to see, ain't to believe.
Counterfeit courtship. When it gets too real, you leave."
It's a counterfeit courtship."

Okay. So the lyrics probably weren't Grammy quality. But, I'm telling you, once that song got stuck in your head, you required a crowbar to pry it out.

"I paddle. You float.
You just have to rock that boat.
Counterfeit courtship.
Damned if I do. Damned if you will.
Phony as a three-dollar bill.
It's a counterfeit courtship.
Counterfeit courtship: What you see, ain't what you get.
Counterfeit courtship: Hell, you ain't seen nothin' yet.
It's a counterfeit courtship."

Before Jax could begin the next stanza a voice from the audience took over.

"'I'm here. You're there.
That ol' 'check is in the mail.'
It's a counterfeit courtship.'"

I squinted at the darkened audience. When the spotlight found its mark, I couldn't believe my own eyes. Keelie Keller, mic in hand, sat on *my* date's lap.

"You're out. You're in.
The boot-draggin's wearin' thin.
It's a counterfeit courtship."

Quicker than you can say "Sonny and Cher" or "Kenny and Dolly" or "Alvin and the Chipmunks," the power pair blended their voices. I winced when Keelie hit a sour note, but the duet still had me—and the audience—spellbound.

"Counterfeit courtship
Long-term rules do not apply.
Counterfeit courtship.
It's all just one big lie.
It's a counterfeit courtship.
I'm soft. You're hard.
Forever's not in the cards.
It's a counterfeit courtship.
You win. I lose.

*Left to cry the blues.
It's a counterfeit courtship.
Counterfeit courtship
Retreat's your fallback plan.
Counterfeit courtship
It's all a big ol' scam.
Counterfeit courtship
Imitations welcomed here.
Counterfeit courtship
You can't dry a bogus tear.
It's a counterfeit courtship.
It's a counterfeit courtship.
Counterfeit courtship.*

By the time the song neared its conclusion, Keelie stood in the center aisle, alone in the spotlight, staring at Jax. Jax stared back, a pulse beat clearly visible in his neck.

The song ended, joined voices trailing off into silence. The audience, picking up on the significance of the moment, sat hushed and quiet.

And suddenly it was as if the spell was broken.

"I hate you, Jax Whitver. Hate you! Hate you! Hate you!" she screamed. She let the microphone drop and turned and ran toward the doors at the rear of the auditorium.

"Keelie! Wait!"

Jax was just about to leap off the stage and race after her when several uniformed officers, including Patrick Dawkins, converged on the stage.

"Hold that man!" Vinny Vincent, waiting in the wings as they say, pointed a finger at Jax. "Serve him, officers!"

I blinked. Serve him? Serve him what?

A beefy Knox County sheriff's deputy I knew from…an, er, "joint investigation," ambled across the stage and handed Jax an envelope.

"Jax Whitver. You've been served. The No Contact Order contained therein states, in part, that you are restricted from having contact with one Keelie Keller. You may not have contact with her via phone, cellular phone, text messaging, email, or any online Internet or web sites. If you violate the terms of this Order, you may be held in contempt of court and be sentenced to jail time, assessed fines, as well as court costs. Are you willing to sign the receipt of service?"

Jax took the pen and signed, looking like he wasn't quite sure what had just happened.

I know the feeling. Well.

The audience sat in stunned silence as Jax walked off the stage. He stopped in front of Vinny.

"This isn't over, Vinny. Not by a long shot."

"Give it up, Whitver. You sound like a broken record. One that wasn't so hot when it was new."

"This way, Mr. Whitver." A deputy took Jax's elbow, but he jerked it away.

"Get off me! I'm not under arrest, am I?"

The deputy shook his head.

"Good. Stay the hell away from me, or I'll be pursuing harassment charges of my own." Jax stalked out a side door. Two deputies followed at a not-so-discreet distance.

Director Harcourt took the stage again and announced the next hometown act, but for all intents and purposes, the show was over. Audience members who moments before had been hooting and hollering, became quiet and subdued. I headed back to my date.

"How come you got yanked up on stage?" Gram asked. "You can't carry a tune. Every time you sing, Bert and Ernie raise a ruckus to beat the band."

"You mean Butch and Sundance," I said. "And my guess? Jax Whitver was trying to make a point."

"What point?"

"I'm not quite sure. But I know that performance was all for Keelie."

"I don't know," Joe said. "From here, it looked like he was singing to you."

I caught the sudden grim set of Townsend's jaw.

"He's a performer," I said. "And an actor."

"Not a very good one," Joe said. "Did you catch him in that end-of-the-world flick cameo? Talk about your cardboard performances."

"Thanks for your incisive analysis, Mr. Film Critic," I snapped. "Can we go home now? I have to blog—" I put a hand to my mouth. "My blog! The performance! My…ass!"

Townsend shook his head.

"Don't worry. I've got the video right here," he said, holding up his cell phone. "Well, as much of it as I could film around Keelie Keller's breasts."

Breasts?

I looked at Townsend. "You've got video?"

He nodded. "Yes, ma'am."

"From start to finish?"

"Pretty much."

"Are you…can I—?"

"It's yours," Townsend said. One eyebrow rose. "For a price."

I felt the earth move under my feet, but this time it wasn't due to a tipping toilet.

Sold to the cowgirl with the terrified grin.

Pay the man.

CHAPTER TWENTY-SEVEN

I'd soaked, shaved, buffed, loufahed, and moisturized. I'd shampooed, deep-conditioned, and detangled. I'd decalloused, touched up the nails, and lotioned up from head to toe. I'd donned comfy shorts and a tank top with hot pink lettering that read, "Still plays with horses."

I was ready to pay the piper. Er...the videographer. I walked into the living room, my legs doing a jitterbug number. I skipped over to the couch to hide the quivering leg thing. I dropped to the sofa beside Townsend.

"Hey," I said, breathless and hating the fact that he knew why.

"Hey," he said. "Nice...uh, T-shirt. Does Tressa want to come out and play?" He winked.

"Sorry. I only bring out the toys on the second date," I said to hide my nervousness.

"Date? Is that what this is? A date?"

I shook my head. "I thought—well, you know—with the auditorium and all—that this was...yeah, a date."

"You mean our *first* date."

I frowned. I hadn't really stopped to think about it, but yeah, that's exactly what it was. Our first date. Our first friggin' date!

"What's put furrows in that forehead of yours?" Townsend asked and placed his thumb on my forehead to smooth away the wrinkles.

"Furrows? I have furrows?"

He nodded. "What's up? Why are they there?"

Hmm. Why did I have furrows?

Maybe it was because, in spite of knowing Rick Townsend for most of my life, we'd never been on a date. A *real* date. Oh, we'd hung out. He'd saved my cookies a time or two. (Or maybe three, but who's counting?) But we'd never done the dating thing. You know. A night out. Dinner. A movie. We'd never taken in a college game or a concert. We'd never gone to the mall or antiquing. We'd never gone horseback riding or hiking. Heck. We'd never really done the carryout pizza and a Blu-ray thing.

My forehead crinkled even more.

Maybe this was why I had creases in my forehead.

Could it be those creases were there because, despite never having had any of the traditional dating experiences, I'd ended up throwing caution to the wind (along with my skivvies) and shared my bootie—and the swashbuckler's bed—the last night of my gammy's wedding cruise? Did I have creases because this was all more than a little "cart before the horse" for this cowgirl's peace of mind?

Not to mention—dare I say it—a tad bit…slutty?

Gulp.

Sure. Okay. I get that it's a new sexual frontier out there. I understand that lots of people my age view sex as a social and/or physiological activity, rather than an emotional one. I get it. Whatever works, I guess.

But me? I wasn't there yet. Maybe I never would be. I just couldn't see myself engaging in "recreational sex." I still wanted *it* to mean something, to represent something special, something lasting, something more than a few drinks at a bar and off we go for a little mutual gratification.

I'd joked about my chubby Brit counterpart, but one thing was true. I did want something more *extraordinary* than mindless shagging.

"We've never been a couple," I blurted.

Townsend's thumb stopped its soothing motion.

"What?"

"We've never done things as a couple. Not ever."

He seemed taken aback for a second and then grinned.

"I know some things we can do as a couple," he teased.

I reached up and took hold of his hand and held it, unwilling to meet his eyes.

"Tressa?" He took hold of my chin and tilted my head back and looked into my eyes. "Hell. You're serious," he said.

Serious or…deranged? I wasn't quite sure which.

"It's just, how do we know we're even compatible if we don't spend time together, do things together? We don't live back in the days where mates were selected by an offspring's parents or by royal contract," I pointed out, thinking if I took a clinical approach, I might have a shot at convincing myself that I was on the right track here. "Dating is the contemporary method of assessing compatibility. Dating. As in spending time together. Doing things together. Going on dates together. You know. Being a couple."

"We *are* a couple."

I shook my head.

"No. We aren't a couple because we've never *been* a couple."

Townsend got that *look* in his eye. The one that said I'd lost him.

"You're gonna have to help me out here," he said, running a hand through his hair. Another "tell."

I searched for the right words.

"There's been 'Rick,'" I said, putting my left hand out, palm-up. "And there's been 'Tressa.'" I put my right hand out. "But," I brought my hands together, "there's never been a 'Rick and Tressa.' Do you see what I'm saying?"

Rick looked at my hands for an uncomfortable amount of time. He finally sighed.

"You're saying you want the whole enchilada," he said.

Yeah. I guess I was.

"Did that song Jax Whitver sang to you get you thinking about what you've missed out on?" he asked.

I frowned.

"What? No. Of course not!"

Or had it?

"Jax Whitver starts crooning about a courtship, and you realize you never had one. I get it."

That last ranger remark? Pure jealousy talking.

And it set my pulse to pitty-patterin'.

I shook my head. "I don't think that's it. Did you listen to those lyrics? The song might as well have been 'Bang, Bang.'"

No. I was pretty sure it had less to do with "Counterfeit

Courtship" and more to do with not waking up one day to find out you and the guy next to you had never taken the time to make memories to build a life together on.

So why didn't I just say that? Why didn't I just come out and say those words?

Because we hadn't gotten to the point with each other where we felt comfortable saying whatever bloody well popped into our heads.

And why was that again?

Because we hadn't done our homework. We hadn't put the time and effort into our relationship required for you to be comfortable putting it all out there and being totally spontaneous and honest with each other—not screening everything you say through a "what will he/she think?" filter.

We hadn't laid the groundwork necessary to have the confidence that—no matter what—you can share your deepest, darkest, "you" and still be understood, accepted, and loved.

We simply hadn't put in the time.

"What are you thinking, Tressa?"

I was thinking we're not there yet. And I knew we weren't there yet because I couldn't speak up and tell him we weren't there yet.

Does, like, any of this make any sense at all?

"Tressa?" Rick asked.

"I want to do the homework," I blurted.

"Homework?"

"Couples' homework. Do you realize I don't even know what your favorite meal is? Or color. Or TV show. Or author. I have no clue if you're a morning person or a night person. If you are messy or a neatnik or in-between. Whether you like country, jazz, or pop the best. What movie you last saw. What kind of toothpaste you use." I shrugged. "I want to know these things. Couples are supposed to know these things."

"Like I said, you want the courtship."

"I want the relationship."

"You want the dating."

"I want the foundation."

He shook his head. "You know, in a million years I don't think I'll ever understand you," he said, "but, if I want to have that chance, I guess we'd better start now."

He took out his phone. A second later my phone was ringing. I frowned and picked it up.

"Hello?"

"Tressa? It's Rick."

"Oh, hello. How are you?"

"Good. Say, I was wondering. I can get my hands on a couple of tickets to an Iowa Cubs game next week. Would you like to go?"

"Why, that would be lovely, Rick."

"Great! It's a date! I'll be in touch with details. 'Bye, Tressa."

"Goodbye, Rick."

Throughout our little phone chat, we'd moved closer to each other. Now we were inches apart.

I tapped my forehead.

"See? No furrows."

Townsend laughed and brushed my hair back, replacing his fingers with his lips.

"Yep. Smooth as silk," he said, caressing my shoulders and arms and sending shivers down the length of my spanking clean body.

"I also used moisturizer on my cheeks," I said, putting a fingertip on one.

He followed my lead, switching his attention from my forehead to my cheek.

"And there." I pointed to my other cheek.

"Nice," he said and kissed my face. "Very nice."

"And I tried a new perfume. Right there." I exposed the right side of my neck. Soft kisses were my reward.

"How about there?" Rick said, and pulled my tank top down, following his hand with his mouth.

"Yeah. There, too," I managed.

Townsend pushed me back onto the sofa and locked his lips on mine, his hand slipping beneath my top and finding what felt like two very needy nipples.

I arched my back and opened my mouth.

"I suppose we could start our homework later," I gasped.

The doorbell rang.

I froze.

"Damn! Who can that be?"

Townsend didn't say that. I did.

Rick sat up, and I readjusted my clothing on the way to the front door. I opened it.

"Dad?"

"Hi, honey. You busy? I saw Rick's truck out front. I don't want to interrupt you two if you're in the middle of something."

I grabbed his arm and pulled him into the room, thinking he would make a pretty good talisman to have handy to ward off what must be forever classified as Townsend's irresistible charms.

"Don't be silly, Pop," I said. "Come on in. We were just...visiting."

Rick got to his feet. "Evening, Philip. How are things at the phone company?"

"Pretty much the same as always. Except the customer complaints we get now are about Internet service being down, not their phones." He shook his head. "Progress."

"Can I get you anything, Dad? Coffee? Soda? A bottle of water?"

He shook his head. "Oh, no. I was just wondering if your mother was here."

"Mom?" I frowned. "No. She isn't here. Last I knew she planned to help Aunt Reggie man the Mini-Freeze tonight so Frankie, Dixie, and Taylor could have the night off. Why?"

He gave a half shrug.

"I just thought you might've spoken to her this evening."

I frowned.

"You mean she's not home yet?"

My dad shook his head.

"Gram mentioned something about Mom staying here the last couple of nights," I said, chewing my lip. Talking to your parents about their...issues was ass-awkward.

"She did stay here a night or two. Said she needed to clean."

Nice. My mother had stooped to using my untidiness as a front for her to carry on her...her...*midwife* crisis.

"I'm sure she's fine. She probably just got to talking with Aunt Reggie and time got away from her."

"I've spoken to Regina. Your mother left two hours ago."

I looked at my watch. It was close to midnight—way past my mom's bedtime, especially on a weeknight.

"Have you tried her cell?"

"It goes to voice mail."

I patted his hand. "She probably just lost track of time."

"Your mom lose track of time? That isn't like her, Tressa."

No. It wasn't. But that was the other Jean Turner. The one who didn't eat junk food and didn't run around in their p.j.s and didn't take off with an entire bottle of wine.

This new Jean Turner? She was a whole new critter.

I wanted to ask him about Mom's sudden dissatisfaction, the problems, their marriage—but, seeing him standing there, stubble on his chin, shoulders slightly slumped inward, a perplexed, troubled look in his eye, I couldn't find the words.

"It'll be all right, Dad. She'll be all right. Sometimes we just need time alone to 'be.' And you have to admit, it's been a long time since Mom's had the chance to go off by herself and recharge the batteries."

"You think that's what she's doing, Tressa? Recharging batteries?"

"That's my guess," I said, and put my arms around him and laid my head on his shoulder. "You know. It's not just the guys who get to have a midlife crisis. It'll pass."

He smiled and patted my back. "My eternal optimist," he said. "You'll never keep this girl down, Rick."

"Don't I know it?" Rick said.

I felt myself blush.

Lights outside the front window caught my attention.

"Somebody's out front!"

"Maybe it's your mom." My dad hurried to open the door. "Oh. God. No. It's the sheriff."

My breathing stopped. I felt lightheaded. I swayed. Townsend grabbed hold of me before I toppled over.

"No. It's not Mom," I said. "It's not Mom." If I said it enough times, it would be true.

Frenzied balls of light from the patrol car danced in the darkness, lighting up the driveway and front yard. One of the deputies who'd served Jax at the talent show came up to the door.

Manny DeMarco, tall, dark, and definitely not on a social call, stood next to him.

"Evening folks," the deputy said. "Sorry to bother you, but we're looking for a missing person."

I blinked. "You're looking for my mother?"

I know. I know. He couldn't possibly be talking about my mom because no one had reported her missing yet. Give me a break. I was a little rattled here.

"No," the officer said, looking puzzled—and who could blame him? "We're looking for Keelie Keller."

It must be contagious. I was the puzzled one now.

"You're looking for Keelie Keller?" I said.

"Keelie's missing," Manny said. "Has Barbie seen her?"

I shook my head. "Not since the scene in the auditorium. How long has she been missing?"

"She ran out of the auditorium and took off," Manny said. "Hasn't been seen since."

First, my mom. Now Keelie. What was going on?

I felt a chill to the bone. Rick put an arm around me.

"We have reason to believe she might be...drinking," the officer said.

"How do you know that?" Rick asked.

"Beer's missing from the bus," Manny said.

"King Tut?" I asked, and Rick gave me a what-are-you-talking about look. "I mean, how much is missing?"

"Enough to become inebriated," the officer said. "We're thinking the young lady became upset and took some beverages to, uh, console herself."

Ah. Politically correctness was alive and well in law enforcement. In earlier times he'd have just said she wanted to get wasted.

"You're sure she's not on the bus?" I asked.

Manny folded his arms.

"Oh. Right. You're sure. Dumb question."

"Why are you looking for her here?" Rick asked.

I did a mental head bump. Duh. Obvious question.

"The young lady doesn't know anybody here locally except Miss Turner here."

I frowned.

"I don't know her really. We do have a history—" I stopped. "Wait a minute. You don't think I had anything to do with her disappearance, because I'm telling you right now, if you think I—"

"Barbie's in the clear," Manny cut me off like a section of your bangs that just won't lay right. "Manny thought maybe Keelie might find her way here. After the kybo episode, she'd realize you aren't a threat."

I blinked. "What do you mean, kybo episode?"

Manny crossed his arms. "Kybo door was jammed, then duct-taped shut."

"You were trapped in a kybo?" Rick looked over at me. "Eww."

The phone in the house began to ring.

"Maybe that's your mother!" my dad said.

I ran to the phone. Picked it up.

"Tressa?"

"Mom, thank God, it's you! Where are you?"

"Is your father all right? What are the police cars doing there?"

I frowned. "Dad's fine. We're good. They're here looking for Keelie Keller. Are you at home then?"

"I...was." She said.

"Is it your mother?"

I nodded at my dad who'd appeared at my elbow.

"Yes."

"Thank God." His sigh of relief went on for a long time. "Ask her if she knows where the TV remotes are. I can't seem to find any of them."

I stared at him. Five minutes ago he was scared to death something had happened to her. Now that he knew she was all right, he was worried about his TV remotes?

"Is that your father? Is he asking about his remotes?"

I made a throat-slashing motion and shook my head at my dad.

"No. It's not Dad. He's out front speaking to the officers."

"Well, you tell the officers that Keelie is okay. I just dropped her off at the house and she should be making her way to your location shortly. She had quite a fright. Someone almost ran her over. I found her on my way out of town and brought her back home. I picked up on the police scanner that they were looking for her. I saw the lights at your house and the police car—and Rick, of course, and, oh yes, Manny, Keelie's bodyguard she tells me. I figured your place was the safest place for her to be. She should be there any second now."

"Wait a minute. You dropped her off? What do you mean, you dropped her off?"

"Well, I cleaned her up a bit. I had the first aid kit. Nothing serious, really. Some minor scratches and some skinned knees from diving into the roadside ditch. She was a bit tipsy, but I gave her some good strong coffee and got her sobered up before I dropped her off. She didn't want anyone to see her like that. She's really a sweet girl once you get to know her."

Sweet girl? Either my mom was drunk, or she hadn't picked up Keelie Keller.

"Hey! Over there! Look! It's Keelie!"

"Good. She's safe then," my mom said.

I walked to the front door and looked out. A bedraggled, but safe, Keelie stood near the patrol car. Manny draped a blanket over her shoulders.

"Yeah. She's safe, Mom. Good job. Now, about Dad."

"I do have a message for your father, Tressa."

I let out my own sigh of relief.

"Yes? What do you want me to tell him?"

"Tell him to take his remote controls and—"

I held the phone away from my ear and frowned at the display that read "My mum."

The hell it was!

She hung up.

I stepped out on the porch and hurried to the squad car. Keelie stepped away from her bodyguard and pulled the blanket closer around her.

"That was your mom who picked me up?"

I nodded. "That's her."

"She's nice. Cool. Calm. Collected. Compassionate."

"She's good in emergencies," I acknowledged.

"My mom is bossy, always telling me what to do and what not to do."

"I guess that's a mother's deal."

"Your mom got me to do what she wanted, but she didn't yell or call me reckless or stupid or cry to get her way."

"I suppose every mother has a different method of…parenting their offspring," I said.

"Your mom had a message for your father," Keelie said.

I winced. "I think she already relayed that," I said.

"Oh. So she told him she was going on a road trip and would be back in a few days? That's good."

I blinked. Road trip? Not good. Not good at all.

"Tressa?" Keelie leaned in closer and grabbed my arm. "Something awful happened tonight."

I patted her hand. "I know. You were upset. You ran. You drank. You nearly got ran over by a car. I'd say that qualifies as pretty awful."

She shook her head.

"That's not the awful part."

Her fingers dug into my arm.

"It's not? What *is* the awful part?"

"The car that nearly ran me down?"

"Yes?" I held my breath.

"It was Jax's car."

CHAPTER TWENTY-EIGHT

"Uh, Scotty. Any time now."

I gazed toward the ceiling of my home and waited for the transporter beam to lock on me and beam me to the bridge of the Enterprise where I could drool over Kirk and Spock and have some girl time with Uhura, where we would discuss the faults and foibles of the male species.

I tapped a foot. "I'm waiting."

"Who you waitin' for? Everybody and his brother are here already. Your living room looks like one of them mosh pits."

My gammy was right. This house hadn't seen so much foot traffic since the year Gram gave out dollar bills to trick-or-treaters. Okay. I'll cop to it. The sheet-covered ghostie? Me. And the Lone Ranger. Zorro. A kerchiefed bandit. And, my personal favorite, John Wayne. Hey, doesn't everyone have a Duke Wayne mask lying around?

"Did you catch a load of all them poprocksies out on your front lawn? Cameras everywhere. Click. Click. Click. Nearly blinded me when I walked through 'em."

"I saw them."

I'd also observed my gammy's stroll across the yard to the house. She'd stopped and posed for the cameras more times than Oscar nominees on the red carpet before the awards ceremony.

"That Keelie girl must be hot stuff," she said, and pulled her glasses out and put them on to get a better look. "I don't see it. What's the big deal? All that red hair? That don't make her Lucille Ball. Now Lucy? There was a star."

I nodded. She'd get no argument from me. I loved Lucy. And she'd made a very nice living from calamities and chaos, thank you very much.

Meanwhile, my own life was definitely no sit-com.

All the chaos. None of the laughs.

Once I'd convinced Keelie to tell Manny that it was Jax's car that sent her into the roadside ditch, he'd whisked her into the house.

My house.

Somehow the word got out that the reality star was being treated for possible injuries, and the media converged.

Not to mention the entourage.

In addition to EMTs, my house hosted Keelie's cameramen, Keelie's just-released-from-the-hospital manager, Vinny, her co-stars, Langley and Tiara, Manny, Knox County acting sheriff, Doug Samuels, Gram, Joe, my dad, my sister, my, er, date, and two over-stimulated yellow labs that weren't the only ones that were gonna have a hard time settling down for the night.

"What do you think, Manny?" Keelie was saying. "Should I throw in the towel? Go home?"

I chewed my lip, wondering if it was too late for me to place a bet on a certain cowgirl Trekkie biker. Or would that be considered insider betting?

Manny shrugged. "Keelie's call."

"No! It isn't just Keelie's call!" Vinny Vincent's bluster almost made up for his lack of stature. "There are contracts. Sponsors. You quit, you're in breach."

"But surely if her safety is at issue, those corporate sponsors wouldn't expect her to continue," Langley protested.

Vinny shot Langley a dark look.

"You obviously don't know much about the corporate world, junior. She quits and bye-bye future sponsors and advertising. No one's gonna take a chance on a quitter."

Keelie flinched. "I'm not a quitter, Vinny."

"Of course you aren't, kid. That's what I'm trying to tell these meatheads." He took a seat on the couch beside Keelie and nudged Tiara to the side. "Listen. I know it hurts to think someone you cared about has turned on you. I always did warn you about Jax Whitver, didn't I? What'd I always say? It's like the country mouse and the city mouse. Taking a walk in the countryside can be exciting and novel for a time, but eventually you long for the busy streets and sophistication of the big city.

Trust me, kid." Vinny patted her knee. "You're better off with Jax Whitver out of your life."

"But he's still out there somewhere!" Tiara pointed out, apparently either having made up with her BFF, or, I supposed, also having sticky contractual issues.

"Yeah. What about that, officer?" Vinny got to his feet. "What are you doing to find Jax Whitver?"

"We've broadcast his plate information and have a BOLO out for him. The young lady here says she isn't sure she wants to file charges."

"What?" Vinny turned back to Keelie. "What the hell are you thinking? Of course, you're going to file charges! That lunatic tried to run you down!"

She shook her head. "It was getting dark. Maybe he didn't see me."

"Keep telling yourself that, Toots," Vinny said, and shook his head. "I want that guy picked up."

"We've got officers looking for him, Mr. Vincent," my second least favorite deputy said. "Sooner or later, he'll surface. It's not as if he isn't easily recognizable."

"What about you, DeMarco? What are you doing to earn your pay? You've let this thing with Whitver get way out of control."

I saw a muscle pop in Manny's jaw and took a step back. No way did I want to be anywhere near the fallout.

"Manny's got a handle on things."

"You could've fooled me," Vinny grumbled, but seeing the look in Manny's eyes, backed off.

"Keelie," Langley took the seat Vinny vacated. "Girlfriend, I have a bad feeling about this. A really bad feeling. With everything that has been going on, I think it might be best if you pulled up the stakes on this road show."

"Need I remind you, Mr. Carlisle the Third, that you are also under contract? And while your participation is by no means essential to the success of the show, breaking contractual agreements is frowned upon in show business," Vinny pointed out.

"All you care about, Vinny, is the business. What about Keelie?" Tiara said.

The doorbell rang, and I hurried to the door and opened it, blinded momentarily by the camera lights trained on the house.

A trooper stood on my doorstep. *My* trooper.

"Patrick. Come in before you become media fodder," I said, and pulled him into the room. "Any news on Jax?"

All discussion ceased. Everyone stared at the trooper.

"We're waiting, Officer," Vinny snapped.

Patrick looked at Manny and Samuels.

"We've located Jax Whitver's vehicle. It was parked behind some outbuildings south of the county park entrance. The right front tire is flat."

I looked at Keelie. She put a shaking hand to her mouth.

"And...Jax?"

Patrick shook his head. "Sorry, Miss Keller. No sign of the vehicle's owner."

"That's it! You should definitely drop out!" Langley said.

"For sure, Keelie!" Tiara urged. "You can't risk going ahead with Jax on the loose. Lang and I will make it work. We'll finish the ride for you."

Keelie looked up. Her eyes did a sweep of the room's occupants, coming to rest on me.

"What would *you* do?" Keelie asked me.

Vinny turned. "Why the hell are you asking Yeoman Rand over there?" he exploded. "She's not in the business! She's just a hillbilly with a phone and a blog!"

Before you could say "stereotyping" Manny had Vinny by the collar doing the tippy-toed dance.

"Country don't mean hillbilly, Vinny. Apologize to the lady," Manny instructed.

I winced. You obviously didn't talk trash about Manny's turf. Or his...Barbie doll. I hazarded a look at Rick, who looked like he'd like to strangle both Vinny and the black knight defending my honor.

"Sorry," Vinny mumbled, and Manny let loose of him, and he almost fell.

"I'm asking Tressa, Vinny, because she doesn't have a dog in this fight," Keelie said, and I almost found myself grinning. Obviously more than a little of the country mouse's southern speak had rubbed off on the big city mouse. "So, Miz Calamity

Jayne, what would you do?"

I sighed. "Doesn't that nickname give you a hint?" I asked.

She nodded. "It does."

She reached out and gave Butch and Sundance some puppy love.

"I'm not going to let Jax Whitver, or anyone, control my life—or dictate my choices," she said. "As they say in the biz, the show must go on." She stood up. "We ride."

It was late when everyone finally cleared out. I'd relayed my Mom's message to my dad. That she'd taken the RV on her little getaway put more than a few creases in my dad's already furrowed forehead. Like daughter. Like father.

Taylor promised to keep an eye on him until she left the next morning.

I shut the door behind them and sighed.

"Well, no one can say first dates with you are dull," Rick said, preparing to take his own leave. "This night had it all. Stars. Runaway stars. Cameras. Cops. Hollywood agent pricks. Bodyguards."

"You forgot two senior snoops and a couple of hyper hounds," I said, opening the door and letting the dogs in after they'd done their business and run off some of their excited energy.

"How could I forget? Are you okay, T?" he asked.

I shrugged. "I'm okay." So-not-convincing.

"It's your folks, isn't it? Your mom. Your dad. You're worried, aren't you?"

"I guess I am. They've never had problems before."

"That you know of," Rick said.

I looked at him. "Do you know something I don't?"

Now it was his turn to shrug.

"Everyone has problems from time to time, Tressa. Listen, I know I told you I might do the last few days of the ride—"

"Yes? And?"

"Well, you've got your own pace and—"

"I'm too slow."

He grinned. "Tandem bicycles tend to be slower. It's nothing personal."

"Right."

"I was thinking, given your mom is…unavailable, maybe now isn't a good time for both of us to be out of town," he said. "You know. With my granddad and your grandmother."

And now my pop.

"Plus, I thought it wouldn't hurt for me to be around in case your dad needed someone to talk to."

I stared at Rick.

"You'd do that for him?" I said, emotion turning my voice husky.

"I'd do it for his daughter," Rick said.

I ran into his open arms at warp speed.

Stroker to Scotty: Disregard previous transporter request until further notice.

CHAPTER TWENTY-NINE

It was official.

Houston, I have a hemorrhoid.

I caught my breath and gasped as we made straight for a pothole.

Ooh, no! Oh, no! Here it comes!

"Oww!"

Sharp, intense, excruciating pain seared my—well—you know—like a blazing hot poker.

"You're doing that on purpose!" I yelled.

"Doing what?" Van Vleet yelled back.

"You're aiming for every bump and pothole in our path," I said.

"And why would I do that?" Van Vleet asked.

"You know why!" I screamed back.

"Why?"

"Because I have a hemorrhoid!" I yelled.

"Did you hear that, Langley? Calamity Jayne here has a hemorrhoid. You get that shot, guys? That'll make for a great episode teaser."

I looked over and did a double take. Tiara and Langley pedaled next to us on a tandem of their own. Theirs, however, was top-of-the-line. Ours? Top shelf of the local big box store. A fit cameraman pedaled alongside.

"You lose your BFF, Tiara?" I asked. She kept her eyes on the road.

"Keelie and Manny are behind us," Langley yelled over. "Keelie was a wee bit off her biscuits this morning, hence the slower pace."

I'd be more than a "wee bit off" if my former boyfriend had

tried to run me over and *poof!* disappeared into thin air.

Bam!

"Son of a—! Quit setting our course for Planet Pothole!" I yelled.

"Never fear, Miss Turner. The end is in sight," Langley said, and then winced. "Oh, sorry. No pun and all that. Apologies for any offense. But it appears the city limits for our overnight host city is in sight."

Fan-freaking-tastic! And not a moment too soon. I needed a cooling ointment fix, and I needed it yesterday!

"I'm off," I told Van Vleet, signaling I wanted to dismount. He kept pedaling.

"Hey. Doofus. I want to get off!"

He turned a deaf ear.

"Hey! Captain Underpants! Put on the brakes or I start using your back as target practice for lugies."

That broke through the interplanetary interference. The captain slowed the bicycle, and we came to a stop.

"I've just about had it with your dictatorial, unfeeling style of…helmsmanship, Van Vleet!" I said, lifting my leg off the bike in a prudent manner. "Captain Kirk would never have such a blatant disregard for the well-being of his crew. I think it's about time we switched places like we agreed. There are two days left on the ride, and I demand my due!"

"If you think I'm letting you navigate, you've been sniffing too much hemorrhoid cream, Blondie," the weasel wearing Captain Kirk gold that proclaimed *I run this ship.* responded. "I value my hide too much to turn it over to someone who, at best, is a lackluster stroker."

"Lackluster! Lackluster! I'll have you know these thighs have risen to the occasion! These are now road-tested thighs. They've delivered, and they don't take a back seat to anyone."

Van Vleet pulled off his helmet. "Not gonna happen, *stroker*. So, deal!"

He took off, pushing the bike, leaving me no choice but to follow, wincing with each step.

I texted Taylor to find out where the Mobile Freeze was parked and headed in that direction. I rounded a corner, noticing Keelie Keller's bus parked in the lot of a local school. I kept walking. I'd had enough drama to last me for some time.

"Tressa! Over here!" Keelie called out. I kept my head down. "Yoo hoo! Here, Tressa! Over here!"

I sighed and looked up. And spotted my mother relaxing in a lawn chair beneath the bus's canopy, lifting a cold one to her lips.

"Mom?" I walked over to confirm what my eyes were telling me. "Mom?"

"Surprise!" she said, raising her glass.

My world shifted on its axis again.

"Mom, what are you doing here?" I asked.

"I decided to help out with the Mobile Freeze," she said.

I frowned. "That's your idea of a road trip getaway?"

"The object was to get away." She took a long sip of her drink. "Mission accomplished! I ran into Keelie, and we've been visiting. How was your ride, dear?"

"Painful," I said. "Very painful."

"I'm sorry. I can offer you a Navy shower if that helps," she said. "And accommodations much nicer than the front seat of Frank's SUV or the hard ground."

"Thanks, Mom. Have you…did you…does Dad know where you are? I'm sure he's worried."

Her smile faded. "I'm sure he's not." She took another sip. "Maybe I'll text him," she said.

"His phone doesn't receive texts."

"Okay, then you can mention on your blog I'm here. Maybe even take a picture of Keelie and me relaxing and post it."

I frowned. "Does Dad even go online?"

"Mention it to your grandmother. She'll make sure he sees it."

"Why can't you just call him?"

My mother crossed her ankles. "I'm on vacation."

"Keelie! Oh, Keelie! Thank God, you're safe!"

I looked up in time to see a woman with masses of red hair throw herself at Keelie.

"Mom? What are you doing here?" Keelie asked, creating one of those déjà voodoo moments.

"I came as soon as I could." She wrapped her arms around Keelie, nearly toppling the chair over. "I was so worried when I heard about everything going on."

"I thought you were going to that spa in Sedona."

"I was. But when I saw what was happening back here, I was on a flight out of there."

"This isn't like you, Mom," Keelie said.

Must be catching.

"Uh, Mrs. Turner...Jean, this is my mother, Candice. Mom, this is Jean Turner and her daughter—"

"I know who you are!" Keelie's mother pointed at me. "You're the one who's been pranking my baby girl!"

"Excuse me?" my mother said.

"Actually, I might've been mistaken about that, Mom," Keelie admitted.

"You mean that nonsense about Jax?" she shook her head. "Please. Jax wouldn't do anything like that to you, baby. He loves you."

Keelie got to her feet.

"Why are you here, Mom? You've never put yourself out before. Well, unless it was payday and time to take your cut of my earnings, which, thankfully, now that I'm an adult, you can't do."

"That's not true, baby. I've always looked out for you. That's why I'm here. I'm afraid for you. Afraid that something awful is going to happen to you if you insist on finishing this ridiculous ride."

"My, how your tune has changed. Used to be if I'd considered breaking a contract, you'd go ballistic. What's the deal?"

"There is no deal. I told you. I'm worried. And, as it appears, right to be that way. Because here you are, consorting with the enemy."

"Excuse me?" my mother said again, getting to her feet.

Now, my mom? She isn't a big woman, but she's tall. And she's got this strait-laced posture that makes me hurt to look at her sometimes. And when she gets her back up, boy howdy, is she a sight to behold.

"Keelie, dear, it appears your poor mother is wretchedly tired from her trip, and her fatigue is clearly making her react in a manner not in keeping with the dear mother you've spoken so fondly about."

I'm not sure whose eyes got bigger first. Mine, Keelie's, or her mother's.

"Please, excuse us, Mrs. Keller. We'll just be off so you can sit and catch your breath. The Iowa heat can be unbearable this time of year. Thank you for the lemonade, Keelie, dear. Tressa? Are you coming?"

I found myself trailing my mother.

"What was that?" I asked. "What just happened?"

"That was your mother employing restraint," my mom said.

"Restraint? You might as well have come right out and called her a—." I stopped.

"What I wanted to do was grab hold of that big ol' hair of hers and give it a good yank."

"You wanted to pull her hair?" Seriously, what was happening to my cool, calm, CPA mother?

"Don't be ridiculous, Tressa. She's wearing a wig."

"Mom. About you and Dad—"

She picked up her pace and, given my…er, condition, it was all I could do to keep up.

"Come along, dear. I've got a big dishpan in the RV. We'll fill that with a little hot water and Epsom salts, put it in the shower and make a nice little sitz bath."

I looked at her.

"How did you know?"

She shook her head.

"Mothers know. Besides nobody walks like that—unless they're Duke Wayne or suffering from painful inflammation."

Crikey! That smarts!

CHAPTER THIRTY

Ottumwa, The City of Bridges, had decided to go with a Mardi Gras theme. Set along the sparkling waters of the Des Moines River, strings of purple, green, and gold lights provided an air of royal splendor to the street party. Jazz music filled the river walk, and vendors hawked their wares. Cajun favorites such as gumbo, jambalaya, red beans and rice, muffulettas, po-boys, and crawfish got top billing alongside traditional Midwestern favorites like corn on the cob, pork chops, burgers, and turkey legs.

In other words, a food lover's paradise.

Dixie and Frankie had volunteered to work the Mobile Freeze, giving my mother time to spend with her two daughters. My mom and I had shared many hours on horseback. She taught me to ride. Taylor, while not exactly a horsewoman, had preferred to admire the beautiful animals from the safety of a zoom lens. She took amazing pictures of the Queen, Joker, and Jack, as well as Butch and Sundance, garnering ribbons from county and state fairs.

But the three of us? Out on the town? It just hadn't happened. I supposed it was because Taylor and I never really had that much in common. Or maybe it was the fact that whenever we were in the same vicinity, we'd end up in a spat.

Rrearr.

But lately, it seemed we'd been able to peacefully coexist. So. Progress!

"It's so nice to have both of my girls here with me," my mother said. "When's the last time we spent time together?"

"The oral surgeon when we got our wisdom teeth pulled. Tressa was fifteen, and I was twelve," Taylor responded.

I stared at her. "Gee, that's awfully specific. It's like you had the information right there ready to call it up. That's either really impressive or really pathetic."

"Anyone still hungry?"

I looked at my mother.

"Do you know me at all? When am I *not* hungry?"

"Taylor?"

She looked at our mother.

"Do you know me at all? When am I *ever* hungry?"

My mother shook her head.

Ours was a lucky, lucky mother.

I'd already partaken of some (okay, more than some) traditional Cajun cuisine. Hey, how often can you get N'Orleans food in Ioway? Now I was hip to try some authentic Cajun desserts. My highly trained sense of smell led me to a colorful booth. I sucked in the aroma. Heaven!

"What is that?"

I pointed at a jumbo-sized braided pastry, frosted in purple, green, and gold.

"It's king cake," Taylor said. "It dates back to the Middle Ages and Twelfth Night."

"The twelfth night of what?"

"The Twelfth Night after the birth of Christ. You should recall the song, Tressa. You starred in Gram's Twelve Days of Christmas pageant."

How could I forget? I still had flashbacks.

"Back to the cake," I prodded.

"Twelfth Night was a time for celebration and gift-giving. The cake was part of the tradition."

"The young lady is right," the baker said. "King cake is a Mardi Gras tradition now.

"What exactly is in it?" I asked.

"The pastry is laced with cinnamon and filled with things like apple, strawberry, cream cheese, or other fruit fillings."

I felt my mouth watering.

"And, of course, there's the baby."

"Baby?"

"Hidden in each king cake is a plastic baby. Tradition says whoever finds the baby in their slice of cake must host the next party or buy the next king cake."

How quaint!

"One king cake," my mother said.

"I love my mommy!" I said. "Ooh. How about those?" I'd spotted squares covered in a mountain of powdered sugar.

"Beignets. Like a doughnut, but without the hole. They come in threes. Served warm with a glass of chocolate milk or café au lait, they are—" he put his fingers to his mouth and made a kissing sound, "perfection."

I put my head on my mother's shoulder and looked up at her with pound-puppy eyes.

"Please, Mommy!"

She sighed. "Three please."

"When she says three, that really means nine, you know, since they come in threes," I reminded the baker. He shook his head and went to fill our order.

"Look, there's Keelie!" My mom said, and I turned. Cameras trailing in her wake, she looked a far cry from the vivacious redhead I'd first seen five days earlier. Manny trailed a discreet distance behind.

"Is that her mother?" Taylor asked.

I nodded.

"She looks like Jessica Rabbit," Taylor observed.

I stared. "Oh, my God! She does! She really does!"

"Now stop it, girls. Don't you dare make a scene!" our mother warned us.

"Hi, Jean! Hey, Tressa. Uh, Taylor, right? This is my mom, Candice."

"Hello. Nice to meet you," Taylor extended her hand. Candice was too busy fanning herself with a purple, green, and gold Mardi Gras fan to notice Taylor's outstretched hand.

"Are you having a good time with your mother?" my mom asked Keelie.

"I had a tarot card reading," she said, side-stepping the question. "You know. The usual stuff. Be leery of dark, handsome strangers. Unparalleled fame and fortune are within my reach. Beware the masks of Mardi Gras. Danger lurks where you least expect it. Typical mumbo jumbo."

"This whole Creole charade is embarrassing. We can afford

to experience the real thing in New Orleans. Why squander time on this cultural wasteland?" Candice said, and brought her arm up to fan herself again. "And the heat is beastly."

"Well, after all, it *is* the 'Big Easy,'" Taylor said.

"You mean the big sleazie," Candice said. "Talk about your poor excuse for a party. Can we get this lame stroll down by the riverside over with? It smells like fish down here."

"You'd know."

For a second I wasn't sure that I'd heard correctly—or that the softly-worded, but clearly enunciated, remark came from my mother, board member of the state CPA association, food bank volunteer, and deaconess of the Open Bible Church.

"What did you say?"

"Why do people do that?" my mother said.

"Do what?" At least three people responded.

"Ask 'what did you say' when they know perfectly well what the other person said. It seems superfluous to me."

"Superfluous?"

"Unnecessary. Not needed. Redundant."

Okay. That's where Taylor got it.

"What is your problem, lady?" Candice Keller asked.

"I don't have a problem. I'm here with my two daughters enjoying a Midwestern Mardi Gras celebration that a lot of very good people went to a lot of hard work to put together. Which leads me to wonder if your performance is for the camera or if you really are so incredibly miserable and unhappy that you can't keep from spreading it around. Oh, and by the way, Jessica. Where's Roger?"

Candice blinked. "Roger?"

"Mr. Rabbit."

I couldn't believe it. My mother had gone from Debbie Reynolds to Joan Rivers in the blink of an eye.

It took a while before Candice got the gist of the reference. I wondered if, under that wig, there was a blonde itching to break free.

The dumbfounded vendor stared at the show going on, our lovely king cake in his hands, ready to box.

"Oh! Look! A king cake!" Candice exclaimed, stepping up to the booth. "Is it sold?"

The baker's head went up and down. "To the *nice* lady."

"It's not carrot cake, but it'll do," she said, showing she was no pushover in the snark department."

Before I knew what was happening, Candice Keller's mauve nails ripped into the cake like a one-year-old on his first birthday. She pulled out a handful of gooey, crummy cake. She turned.

"*Roger* sends his regrets he couldn't be here," she said and threw the handful of cake in my mother's face.

I stared, stunned by Jessica's surprise attack. When my mother stepped over to the vendor and sunk both hands, into the cake, digging out not one, but two handfuls of king cake, I was mesmerized.

She turned. I held my breath.

"You really must take some cake home for the poor dear," Mom said.

Whoop! Two handfuls of cake pelted Candice Keller.

For the next thirty seconds, all I saw were arms flailing and cake flying. I looked around, waiting for someone to pop out and yell, "You've been pranked!"

So. Didn't. Happen.

When all the available ammo had been exhausted (The vendor had quickly covered his other wares.) and my king cake reduced to crumbs, the battle was over.

Candice fished a hunk of pastry from the gaping crease of her cleavage and my mom pulled frosting from her hair.

Me? I was still trying to wrap my head around what had just transpired. And mourn the loss of my king cake.

"There is a bit of good news!" I said, as Taylor and I helped brush the cake from my mother's shirt and hair. "Jessica got the plastic baby. The next cake's on her."

"Oh, my lord," my mom said. "What is wrong with me? What have I become?" my mother said. "This is awful!"

I patted her on the shoulder.

"Don't worry, Mom. She threw the first piece," I said, trying to console her. "You're not becoming anything. You were provoked."

"Oh, my God!" she shook her head and looked like she'd just eaten an entire king cake. "I'm becoming your grandmother!"

I looked over at Taylor. I had nothing.

"Come on, Mom. Let's get you cleaned up," Taylor the wise said, taking charge, when a sudden commotion upstaged the soulful sounds of a strolling saxophone.

"Oh, my God! Help! Help me please! Someone help!"

We turned. And stared.

Tiara, sobbing uncontrollably and looking like she'd been pulled through a thicket the wrong way, clothes dirty and ripped, hair every which way and loose, ran to Keelie and grabbed her in a bear hug.

"Oh, thank God! Thank God!"

"Tiara?" Keelie said. "What's wrong?"

"Oh, God! Someone attacked me, Keelie! Someone tried to abduct me! Oh, my God. My God!"

Keelie stroked Tiara's hair and looked up, catching my eye.

Beware the masks of Mardi Gras," her tarot cards had said. *Danger lurks where you least expect it.*

I wondered if Keelie was thinking the same thing I was.

Oh, the voodoo that you do.

CHAPTER THIRTY-ONE

Thank God for my mother and Epsom salts. The improvised sitz baths had done wonders for my...er, disposition. And the blessed, cooling relief came at the perfect time—the longest leg of the bike ride—eighty, tortuous miles—and then it was all downhill from there.

Literally.

Iowa City (home to the University of Iowa Hawkeyes) was the final host city. We'd leave tomorrow morning and head south to the Mississippi River and the end of the line.

Hallelujah and pass the inflatable doughnut seat cushion.

The host city has experience with the party scene due to the college town located there. I felt certain the community would pull out all the stops to provide a celebration worthy of their learning institution's past rankings as "most partying school."

In short: the beer would flow.

There would, however, be partying of a very different type in the small town of Riverside. (Yup. Captain James Tiberius Kirk's Riverside.) The tiny town located just south of Iowa City planned its own *Star Trek* fest that would include a carnival featuring out-of-this-world rides (flying saucer, rock-o-plane, space planes, moon-bounce inflatables, etc.) games where you could show off your phaser accuracy, and the big finale, the costumed street dance—the uber-stellar event touted as "your chance to party in the birthplace of the most famous Star Fleet captain." Van Vleet had hailed it as *the* party event of TribRide.

I shook my head.

I could see it now. Everyone dressed as the Trekkie of their choice, jiving to "Space Jam" and attempting to do the moonwalk.

Initially I hadn't been all that gung-ho about the stopover. But since I still hadn't had my turn at the helm, the back seat had little choice but to go where the front one went.

And surely there had to be something blog-worthy at such a spectacle.

We made decent time getting to Riverside. The weather and humidity had inched down from the previous sweltering conditions. Mid-eighties and a slight breeze? Sold!

We dismounted near the town square.

I stared. If I hadn't seen it myself, I wouldn't believe it. Iowa's rural countryside had turned into *Star Trek's* version of Comic-Con.

"Welcome to Riverside, earthlings. Future home of Captain James Tiberius Kirk."

I turned. A rather short, chunky Vulcan and his tall, skinny female counterpart, greeted us.

"Thank you, uh, er, Mr. Vulcan," I said, doing my own Vulcan hand sign right back at him. (I'm lucky. I can do it without having to use my other hand to separate the fingers.)

"I am Sarek. Spock's father. This is Amanda, my wife. Spock's mother."

Oo-kay.

"Hey…there," I said and nodded at them both.

"It is a lovely day here in Riverside. I wish you and your companion enjoyment during your respite here," Spock's *mother* said.

"And I, too," Sarek concurred. "Live long and prosper, earthlings," he said, giving us the 'V' sign again.

I turned to Van Vleet.

"What was that?"

"Role-playing, of course. This is gonna be hilarious. Talk about YouTube fodder."

I looked over at him. "Wait a minute. Is this just another story to you? I thought you said you were a *Star Trek* fan."

He shrugged. "Who doesn't like *Star Trek*?" he said. "And any reporter worth their byline knows it's always about the next story, Blondie. No matter what."

I shook my head. It was the "no matter what" part where my competitor and I parted company. Unlike Drew the Shrew, "anything goes" was not the code of journalistic ethics I wanted to go with.

"Here." He thrust the bike in my direction. "You babysit the beast for a change. And make sure you secure it so it isn't stolen."

I grabbed the handlebars. "I'll keep our transport safe from Romulan raiders, sir!" I clicked my heels. "You can count on me."

Van Vleet muttered a dismissal Star Fleet would throw the book at him for and walked off. Meanwhile, I texted my own earthling mother to find out where she'd parked the shuttlecraft and slowly made my way there, passing the Intergalactic Marketplace that, in addition to various alien species on parade, featured food, beverages, souvenirs, and the assorted wines and spirits. I stared at the replica of the U.S.S. Riverside near the square, making a mental note to get a selfie of me with the spacecraft.

I spotted Kenny Grey's now familiar van and his small, canopied kiosk, but no sign of the artiste at his booth.

"Permission to come aboard!" I called out, pushing the bike up to the RV and propping it near the door. "Helloo! Anybody here?"

The door opened. Keelie Keller stepped out. Her hair pulled tightly back at the crown in a ponytail, Keelie wore the little red mini dress that signified you were either yeoman or communications officer.

"There you are!" She said. "We've been waiting for you!"

"We?"

"Your mum and me."

"Oh?" I frowned. Keelie was hanging out with my mother again?

"Show her, Jean!" Keelie urged.

Jean?

"Show me what?" I asked, feeling the same level of anxiety I'd felt before opening any "gift" from my brother, Craig.

"Ta-da! We give you Yeoman Janice Rand!" my mother announced and stepped out, holding another red *Star Trek* mini dress in one hand and what looked like a Longaberger basket made of blonde hair in the other.

"What—I? Who?"

"The boots are inside!" Keelie said. "Your mum helped with sizes."

My eyes must've done a the-hell-she-did number, because my mother shook her head.

"Said information to be held in the strictest of confidence, right Keelie?"

"Oh, sure. Of course," Keelie said. "It's just between us girls. Come on! Come on! Clean up and get into your costume! This is going to be so much fun!"

I stared at her, confused.

"Where's Tiara? She'll make a much better Yeoman whatever her name is than I will," I protested.

"No, she won't. I can't trust Tiara anymore. First, it was the deal with Jax at the covered bridge. Now the cops think she made up that story about almost being abducted."

I blinked.

"What? Tiara lied about the kidnapping? She made it up?"

Keelie shrugged. "Manny said some things didn't check out, so I don't know what to think."

"Where is Mr. Bodyguard, by the way?" I asked.

Keelie looked a bit sheepish. "He had to take care of something. I was supposed to stay in the bus until he got back, but I kind of sneaked out.

"You and Tiara have been best friends forever," I tried again, because it was true and because I so didn't want to squeeze into a mini dress and woven wig and parade around the square in the role of glorified maidservant. (Although I must admit, the boots intrigued me.)

"I can't deal with Tiara right now," Keelie said, dismissing my protests. "So go on and get dressed, Tressa, and let's paint this town red!"

Hopefully not as in "expendable" red.

I said it before, and I'll say it again, red is so not my color.

Feeling railroaded, I nevertheless grabbed the togs from my mother. As I passed, she whispered that there were clean undies in the bathroom. I only hoped she'd picked up a pair that wouldn't show those unsightly panty lines.

I balked when I spotted the black Spanx. I downright

revolted when I saw the black panty hose sitting nearby.

No way, Mr. Roddenberry wherever you are. No flippin' way.

Panty hose and I share a tattered and torn past. Consequently, I avoid them whenever possible. And on an eighty degree day? That seemed reason enough for going the natural route—well, until I checked out legs that had gone too many days without seeing a razor.

"Nubs Central," I muttered, running a hand down my leg.

"What's that, Tressa?" my mom said.

"Nothing, Mom," I said, drawing a bead on the hosiery. "It's gonna be like this," I said. "You're going to cooperate. You are going to slide all the way up, including the all-important crotch area, and you're gonna stay where you belong, and you're going to do it all without a fight. Do we understand each other?"

"Tressa, who *are* you talking to?" My mother asked.

"I'm on the phone!" I lied. My mom already had enough problems. No sense adding to them with a daughter who threatened control top panty hose.

I took my quickie shower, patted dry, and dressed. Boots in hand, I stepped out of the trailer and took a seat in a nearby lawn chair.

"Hey! Where's your wig?" Keelie asked.

"I really don't think I need it. Yeoman Rand had blonde hair, right? I have blonde hair. So, why do I need a wig?"

"Because, silly goose, the woven beehive hair is Yeoman Rand's trademark. It's what sets her apart. Makes her distinct. Without it, you're just another blonde Yeoman."

I grimaced. "A blonde Yeoman who won't pass out due to heatstroke!"

Keelie grabbed the wig and plopped it on my head. "Sometimes beauty is painful," she said. "Surely you've endured waxes. Besides, you don't have to wear it that long. Just long enough to stroll around Riverside a bit."

I made a "let's get this over with" face and waited while she attempted to hide my mass of hair under the wig.

"Is there a problem?" I asked, wincing when she shoved a handful of hair beneath the wig and my head bent sideways. "Ow! Take it easy!"

"This'll never work!" Keelie said. "You've just got way too much hair."

I turned and looked up at her. "Don't get any ideas, Miss Great Clips," I said.

"I've got it!"

She ran into the folks' RV and was back before I could say, "Okay, Scotty. I'm ready. Beam me up this instant, or you're fired!"

"This'll do the trick!" Keelie pulled a section of panty hose over my head and down over my eyes.

"Hey!" I yelled.

"Oh. Sorry." She readjusted my makeshift hair concealer and stuck the basket weave wig on my head again. "That ought to do it," she said, "if I can just get it on straight." She battled the wig for a few more minutes. "Good! Bobbie pins, please, assistant!"

I gave her assistant a "whose mother are you anyway?" look.

"There! Perfect!" Keelie exclaimed.

I frowned. It felt like I had several, heavy, wrapped towels sitting on my head. I got to my feet, and the wig dipped to one side, its weight sending me leaning in that direction.

"Hey, careful! Don't undo my handiwork, please!" Keelie ordered.

I looked at her costume and back at mine.

"Wait a minute. Why do you get the modern movie version of the little red dress and I get stuck with the not-so-flattering cut of the original design?" I asked.

"Because, Yeoman Rand hasn't been in any of the recent major motion pictures. We want to be as close to the real thing as we can."

"Oh? Then why aren't you wearing a black wig?" I asked. "Uhura has black hair."

"I can't wear wigs. I have a scalp condition," she said.

Right.

"Mom, would you do the honors?" I handed her my phone. If I had to role-play at a *Star Trek* street party, I was going to make it count.

My mom took a dozen pictures before I found one of me

where I didn't resemble a certain leaning tower.

"Ready to role play at Trekkie street dance with the Red Queen! Lights! Camera! Action!" I posted.

"Let's go!" Keelie grabbed my arm.

"Shouldn't we wait for Manny?" I asked. "You know. Your bodyguard."

"I'm done waiting. He was supposed to be here ten minutes ago. He'll catch up to us on the square. We've got the cameraman. We're good to go."

"I'm not sure—"

"Come on, or I'm going without you!"

I looked at my mom and shrugged and let myself be dragged off.

First stop: the sign that announces, "Future Birthplace of Captain James T. Kirk, March 22, 2228."

Next, we strolled the Interplanetary Marketplace, sampling interesting space dishes such as Spock sorbet, Romulan ribs, and Tribblemisu. Keelie hammed it up for the camera, stopping to hug a startled Mr. Spock, moving on to shake her groove thing with a Gorn on the dance floor. A swarthy Romulan attempted to cut in, but you know how testy those Gorns can be.

And Carmen Miranda with her basket on her head? Dance? You're joking, right? It was all I could do to walk upright without toppling over.

I'd just polished off the last of the Romulan ribs followed by a bottle of Blue Moon (an appropriate choice considering the space theme and all) when my cell phone rang. I looked around for something to wipe my barbecue-sauce-coated fingers on, gave up and stuck them in my mouth, before I answered.

"H'lo?"

"Barbie. Manny. You cool?"

"You know me. I'm always cool," I said.

"Manny means are you and Keelie doing okay?"

"Oh." I licked another finger. "Yeah. We're fine. We're pigging out." Rather *I* was pigging out. Keelie had the appetite of a picky three-year-old. "You need to get here and try some Final Frontier fare. The 'gorn' on the cob is the best I've ever had! Where are you anyway?"

"They found Jax," he said.

I took a step back, and my wig sent me back a few more.

"Oh, my gosh! Where? How?"

"Manny's getting answers. Gonna meet with law enforcement and then catch up with you two in a few. And Barbie?"

"Yeah?"

"Hang with Keelie 'til Manny gets there."

"Aye, Aye!"

I put my phone back inside my bra.

"Who was that?" Keelie asked.

"Manny. He said to wait here for him. He'll be here in a few minutes," I hedged.

"What else did he say?" Keelie asked.

"What makes you think he said anything else?"

"The barbecue sauce all over your face and the 'oh, my gosh, where, how?' when you answered the phone," she said.

"Okay. Don't freak out or anything—"

"Oh, my God! It's not...Jax?"

My you-can-read-my-mind face gave me up.

"Oh, my God!" Keelie grabbed my arms, sending Yeoman Rand's wig a wobbling. "Is he okay? Tell me he's okay!"

"I don't know anything more. All Manny told me was that Jax had been located. Manny wanted us to wait here for him. That's it. That's all I know."

Keelie's stricken expression revealed much. It didn't take tarot cards to figure out this city mouse was in love with her country mouse.

"Maybe we should wait at your mom's trailer," Keelie suggested. "I don't feel much like partying."

I nodded. I felt the same way. Besides, the beehive on my head was giving me a heavy-duty headache. And God only knew what the hose cap was doing to my hair.

We started to retrace our earlier steps, me gingerly, Keelie stepping out like she was in Starfleet boot camp when Langley, dressed in a blue Dr. McCoy shirt paired with black Capri pants (Capris with a *Star Trek* shirt? Surely, a cosmic faux pas.) rushed up to us.

"Oh, God! Oh, God! Oh, God!"

I was ready to offer Lang the comfort of a soothing sitz bath when he grabbed my arm, sending my wig weaving to and fro again.

"Where's Manny? Or your trooper friend? Anybody! Hurry! It's an emergency! Tiara's been abducted!"

"What are you doing, Lang?" Keelie said. "Did Tiara put you up to another little stunt? It's pathetic. Beyond pathetic. She needs help. Professional help."

Lang shook his head.

"No! No! I swear to God, Keelie, I'm not lying! This is real! A Klingon just kidnapped Tiara!"

Keelie grabbed the neckline of Langley's *Star Trek* uniform. "So help me, Langley Carlisle the Third, if you're lying to me I will never speak to you again! Do you understand? Never!"

"It's true. I swear it. A Klingon ran off with her! I'm not making this up! Honest! We've got to help her!"

Keelie let go of Langley's shirt.

"Hold on a minute, Lang." I said. "Can you be more specific? Was it a Klingon circa the sixties series, or was it the more contemporary one?" I asked.

The Brit, obviously no *Star Trek* aficionado himself, stared at me.

"Oh, for heaven's sakes! Did he have the funky forehead ridges in the front and a disturbing pageboy thing going on in back?" I asked.

"Yes! Yes! That's the one!" Lang insisted. "That's him!"

"You mean Worf," a rather rotund Kirk nearby inserted.

I turned. "Worf?"

"A main character in *The Next Generation* and *Deep Space Nine*," he said. "Really groundbreaking for the time. A Klingon crewman."

I shook my head and turned back to Lang.

"How big was he? This Klingon? Was he short or tall? Tan or fair?"

Lang shook his head. "It happened so fast. He was on the short side, I think. A few inches taller than Tiara, I think. That's really all I can remember."

A short Klingon warrior. I looked around. Klingon warriors of all sizes, shapes, and colors were everywhere.

I sighed.

Why did it have to be a Klingon? Why couldn't it have been a Romulan? Or a Gorn?

My phone rang. It was Manny.

"Manny, Tiara's missing! A Klingon has her!" I blurted and explained what Langley witnessed. "He's a more recent Klingon. Think Mork on *Star Trek: The Next Generation* or *Deep Space Nine*," I said.

"*Worf*, not Mork," the portly Kirk corrected.

Keelie grabbed at the phone. "Did he find Jax? Is he okay?"

I waved her off, finished listening to Manny, and then handed my phone to Keelie.

"Manny wants to talk to you," I said. Seeing the fear in her face, I nodded. "Go ahead. It's okay. It's good news."

It was. Kind of.

Jax *had* been found. And, mostly, uninjured.

It was how and where he was discovered that wasn't such good news. The country crooner was discovered, bound and gagged, in a Porta-Potty. The kybo door had been duct-taped shut, a "Do Not Use—Out of Order" sign posted on the front.

I made a "eww" face, my own recent Porta-Potty nightmare still fresh in my mind.

Keelie handed me my phone.

"He's okay," she said, breathless with relief. "Thank God, he's okay."

I nodded.

That was the good news.

The bad news?

We'd eliminated our one and only stalker suspect, and our perp looked like a gazillion other alien warriors partying in Riverside.

Talk about lost in space.

CHAPTER THIRTY-TWO

"It's my fault. She was my friend, and I let her down. I didn't believe her, and now she's missing!" Keelie wailed.

No one had heard from Tiara and, so far, the search had turned up zip. Not surprising considering the inflated Klingon population—and a lingering skepticism, despite Langley's assurances to the contrary—that this could be another reality ratings ploy.

"Don't blame yourself. How could you have known, Keelie?" Lang said.

How could she indeed? Unless...

I took a long look at the reality star, wringing her hands and looking frantic and fearful. Could it all be an act? The thought had crossed my mind before. That the whole series of mishaps had been an inside job. And who was more "inside" than the star herself?

I'd had it with the dancing on eggshells bit. It was time for the direct approach.

I grabbed Keelie's arm.

"No more bull pucky, Keelie. Are you or are you not behind all the drama and TribRide turmoil?" I asked. "Is this all just part of Keelie Keller's reality TV ratings bump?"

This time Keelie was the one who looked off balance—and she didn't have the mile-high wig to blame.

"I can't believe you're accusing me—"

I shook my head at her.

"We don't have time for bluster," I pointed out. "Your best friend is missing, and the cops are on the case. A simple 'yes' or 'no' will do. Are you your own stalker, and is Tiara's disappearance part of some sick ratings game you're playing?"

Keelie yanked her arm free and grabbed both my wrists, her eyes locking in on my own.

"No! Hell, no! To both questions!" she hissed. "There! Satisfied? Now, can we please look for my best friend?"

For whatever reasons—the eye contact, the telltale trace of tears, the genuine anxiety I saw in her face, I believed her.

"Sorry." I assumed my best mea culpa face. "I had to ask. And Manny said he wanted you to have an officer escort you back to the bus and stay with you," I told Keelie.

"Well, good thing he works for me and not the other way around, because I'm staying right here to help with the search. If only I'd listened to Manny early on instead of being so sure you were the culprit. You aren't. Right?"

I blinked.

"I had to ask," Keelie said with a right-back-at-you lift of one brow. "Manny assured me all along you weren't the one making mischief."

"Manny told you that?"

She nodded. "He said it wasn't the way you rolled, but Vinny insisted it was you. It's official. I'm an idiot. I've lost Jax. Now it looks like I might lose Tiara."

"There, there." Lang patted Keelie's shoulder. "You're not an idiot. Tiara will be tip-top."

"Show us again how and where the two of you became separated," the police officer in charge said to Langley.

"He grabbed her right about here and took her off this way, through the crowd." Lang demonstrated. "She yelled, 'Help! Help!' but, I guess people thought it was role-playing and just laughed. I screamed for help and tried to chase them, but everyone must have assumed I was part of the act, as well. I ended up losing them."

"You did your best, Lang," Keelie said and hugged him. "You did your best."

A few minutes later, an officer came back carrying a cell phone and a familiar basket-weave wig.

"Was Ms. Fordham wearing this?" the officer asked, and Lang nodded.

"Tiara was Yeoman Rand, too?" I asked.

Tears filled Keelie's eyes.

"We'd planned our outfits together before I told her to take a hike. That she wasn't my BFF anymore."

"We'll find her, Keelie. Honest. It'll be okay." Lang assured her.

The police dismissed us. Worried and despondent, we trekked back to the vendors' village, one eye on the lookout for a short Klingon and the other for Yeoman Rand without her trademark weave.

"I feel so helpless," Keelie said. "Why poor Tiara? Why now?"

I stopped in my tracks—and nearly fell over wig first. I stared at Keelie.

"Oh, my gosh! You're right!" I said. "You're absolutely right! Why Tiara? You were always the target. So, why take *her*? And why *now*?"

Keelie lifted her shoulders. "To get back at me? To hurt me?"

Could be, I supposed. Or...

"Maybe we're looking at this all wrong," I blurted.

"What do mean? What are you thinking?" Keelie asked.

"Okay. Let's take a look at everything that's happened on this ride. The rat. The laxative. The bike tampering. The bus tampering. The bull—the mechanical one. The toilet. The 'Keelie, go home' signs. If these aren't just reality show gimmicks to boost ratings, then someone really did want you to quit the ride. If so. Who and why?"

Keelie shook her head. "I have no idea."

"Who benefits if you quit?"

She shrugged. "I don't know. I'm not sure what they would do if I walked away."

"Would the show go on? *Could* the show go on?" I asked, and recalled the night in my living room when Tiara had offered to go on in Keelie's place.

"I suppose it could—and if I'd quit earlier, Lang and Tiara could have gone ahead and finished."

"So, if the latest snatch wasn't a hoax—"

"It wasn't!" Lang assured me. "I swear it! I love Tiara dearly, but she can't act worth spit. That was no performance!"

"Hmm." I thought for a second. "Then perhaps this hasn't

been about you at all, Keelie," I said, doing my thinking aloud. Yeah. I know. *Dangerous*. "Maybe this has been about Tiara all along."

"I'm not following," Keelie said.

"Ditto," Lang added.

"Who stood to gain if you quit early on? Tiara Fordham. If you quit, Keelie, Tiara would have an opportunity to make a splash in the reality TV world—maybe even get her own gig. For sure she'd get lots of exposure and publicity."

"So you *are* saying Tiara's responsible for the mischief and her kidnapping is a hoax," Keelie said.

I shook my head.

"Well, maybe earlier on. But at this stage of the game?" I shook my head. "It doesn't make sense. It's too late for Tiara to benefit from your quitting now. The ride is almost over."

Langley, the director's son, sighed and shook his head. "Abominable pacing. Too anti-climactic," he said. "Most likely the production company would cut their losses, use the footage they had, pack up, and call it good," he said.

Keelie nodded. "He's right."

"So, maybe someone else decided Tiara deserved her chance in the limelight," I suggested. "You know. To shine like a star! Maybe this isn't about someone *not* liking you, Keelie, but rather about someone liking Tiara *a lot*."

"Like who?" Lang asked.

I shrugged. "I've got no clue. Someone who really has a thing for Tiara. Somebody who really wants her to succeed. To give her the world."

"If you're right, that's good, isn't it? If someone who cares about her, has her? Right?" Keelie asked.

If I wasn't way "out there" with Bowie's Major Tom floating around in an alternate universe.

We stood, a perplexed Trekkie trio, watching, waiting.

Kenny, I saw, was back at his booth. Or rather, Kenny the Klingon Caricaturist. Like most of the vendors, Kenny had gotten into the spirit of the spaced-out party. Too bad, things were at red alert status. I'd rock Kenny's world and ask Keelie to pose for her number one fan.

Kenny the one-eye-fits-all artist.

He raised his hand and waved. I waved back.

I thought about those eyes—the eyes in the drawings he'd done of Gram and me—how they *had* appeared so similar when, in reality, are nothing alike. How despite not resembling Gram's or my eyes, they'd still seemed familiar somehow.

I thought more about those eyes and, remembering something Taylor had said, I pulled my phone out.

"Hello? Taylor? Do you recall a certain sand sculpture—" A few minutes later I stuck my phone back in my bra and approached Kenny the Klingon Caricaturist.

Time for a little Art Analysis 101.

"Hi Kenny. Looks like business is good. May I have a peek?" I asked the giggling coed being immortalized and motioned at the work in progress.

She giggled. "Sure. Go ahead. I hope it doesn't scare you too much."

I grinned. "I doubt that very much. Kenny here does justice to all his subjects, right, Kenny?"

"I try," he said, his eyes on easel.

I took a position behind his left shoulder and observed the drawing.

Holy battle stations! There it was! Right before my very own eyes! Why hadn't I seen it before?

"So? How is it?" the subject asked.

"Very nice," I told the coed. "You're going to be pleased. Especially with the eyes." I saw Kenny's drawing hand jerk as if he'd received a jolt of AC current. "Hey, Keelie! I told you this guy was good. Come and check Kenny's drawing out and see for yourself."

I could see from Keelie's expression she had no idea what the object of this exercise was.

Me? I just wanted a second pair of eyes to confirm I wasn't seeing things that weren't there.

Clear as dirty 3-D glasses, right?

Keelie stepped beside me.

"So, what do you think, Keelie?" I asked. "What do you think of Kenny's drawing?"

She gasped. Her jaw dropped.

That's what we call confirmation.

We continued our "art appreciation" while Kenny finished the drawing, signed it with a shaking hand, gave it to the young woman, and began to gather his supplies.

"Don't you want your money?" his young customer asked. Trembling visibly, Kenny took her money and handed her back the change.

"You've given me back too much," the girl said, and handed him back a ten and left with her picture.

"Everything all right, Kenny?" I asked. "You don't look so good."

"It's the heat. And the costume. It's getting to me."

"That's too bad," I said. "Keelie and I came for a sitting. We'd like our *Star Trek* street dance moment immortalized. Isn't that right, Keelie?"

Still apparently taken aback by the drawing, Keelie nodded. "Love one," she managed.

"Oh. Sorry. Another time? I'm just not feeling up to it, right now."

"That's too bad," I comforted. "Maybe you can show us some of the drawings you've already done," I suggested. "Wait. Where's your van?"

"Parked down the road a piece. Found a quiet spot where I can camp and sketch, so I nabbed it while I could."

"Oh. Well, we'll help you pack this stuff into the van for you since you're not feeling well," I insisted.

"I'm fine. I'll be fine," he said. "I don't want to put you out."

"No trouble at all," I insisted and picked up one of his cases.

"I told you! I can do it myself!" Kenny grabbed the case from my hand. The top flap came loose. Papers spilled out onto the pavement.

Eyes. Sketch after sketch of eyes.

Tiara's eyes.

Tiara's face.

Tiara period.

Picture after picture of Tiara Fordham stared up at me. Tiara in a baseball cap. Tiara in a Stetson. Laughing Tiara. Crying Tiara. Angry, pouting...sleeping?...Tiara. Creepee!

Kenny looked at me. I looked at him.

And before I could say, "Surrender, Klingon!" the amazing

intergalactic race was on.

"Stop! Kenny! Stop! Don't run!"

He kept running.

I took off after him. Two strides and my Yeoman Rand 'do' didn't. I felt a whoosh and a sudden weight disappeared from my head.

"Kenny! Hold on! Stop! We can fix this!" I yelled.

"Stop that Klingon!" I heard Keelie yell from behind me.

For being weighed down with Klingon garb, Kenny could book. It was all I could do not to lose sight of him among the throngs of fellow Klingon warriors.

"Stop!" I yelled. "Hold up!"

"Get a load of baldie there. I wonder what character she is. Yeoman Chrome Dome?" I heard, hoofing it past a group of Romulans.

"Vulcan wannabes," I wheezed.

"Catch that Klingon!" Keelie called out again.

"Fanatics! Some people take this role-playing way too seriously."

Yet another editorial comment. I would've responded, but I needed all my air to stay in the foot race.

We entered the carnival area. To the left was the rock-o-plane. To the right, the flying saucer ride. And straight ahead? A yellow and red enclosure surrounded on all four sides by big blue rocket ships, U.S.A. in big white letters on each rocket. The inflatable rocket bounce!

He wouldn't.

He couldn't.

He did.

With a gargantuan leap, Kenny the Klingon planted both feet on the red and blue air-filled rocket bounce welcome mat, propelling himself through the space and time continuum, and into the out-of-this-world carnival attraction.

I plodded after him, surveying the air-filled launch pad with some misgivings.

Do I?

Or don't I?

Oh, hell, yeah.

I hit the canvas cushion of air off balance and dove towards the opening, face-first, succeeding in executing an ugly belly flop that got me only half way through the entrance. Face down, I bounced half a dozen times before I came to rest and was able to pull the rest of Yeoman Rand inside. It took me several more attempts to push myself to a standing position, my boots sinking into the springy canvas like they did in a muddy barnyard.

Across from me, the Klingon warrior wheezed.

"Kenny. Bud. Listen," I said, doing some heavy breathing of my own. "You gotta give up man."

"Why?"

I blinked.

"What?"

"Why do I have to give up?"

I blinked again.

"Because it's the right thing to do. The only thing to do. You're trapped."

"Am I?" he said and bounced to his left.

Bounce. Bounce.

"What are you doing, Kenny?" I asked and counter-bounced, thinking boots might be made for walking and riding. But bouncing? Not so much.

Bounce. Bounce.

"Bouncing," he said and bounced to his right.

Bounce. Bounce.

"Not a good move," I said, and meeting his bounce and raising it.

Bounce. Bounce. Bounce!

"Maybe this should be my next move then," Kenny said, and pulled out a pencil.

"On the count of three we draw?" I said, confused.

"On the count of three I start poking holes," he said.

"In...me?" Gulp.

"In the inflatable," he said.

Thank the interplanetary gods! I didn't think the pencil could puncture canvas, but I knew it could puncture flesh.

"You don't want to do that, Kenny. Think of all the disappointed little kids who came here to bounce." Think about the damned thing collapsing in on both of us and smothering us to death. "Just put the pencil down and bounce away from it, nice and easy."

"No."

I blinked.

"No?"

"You want it? Come and get it." Kenny said, holding the pencil out.

I moonwalked in his direction. He moonwalked away. Around the sides of the rocket launch we performed our own lunar leaps.

"This is getting us nowhere, Kenny." Literally. "Just tell me where Tiara is. Please."

It was then I started to feel that telltale slippage in the, er, crotchal area.

Oh no! They're going down! They're going down! They're going down!

I put a leg out to leap after Kenny and found my movement restricted by constricting—and confining—control tops at knee level.

Kenny must've sensed his opponent's sudden vulnerability. In one ginormous leap for Klingon-kind, Kenny was out the rocker bounce door, leaving me with my knees together, bouncing up and down as I yanked my panty hose back up.

Holy Moses. It *was* true—all that pride-cometh-before-a-fall-stuff. Pride be damnedth! I should've gone with hairy legs.

I tumbled out of the bounce seconds after Kenny, trampolining to my feet.

Meanwhile, my quarry had widened his lead. We were now outside Riverside proper and heading into areas dotted with food and drink stands and various outdoors activities.

"Stop. That. Klingon!" I managed to get out, finding it as hard to breathe as it was to run in boots I'd thought so cute an hour earlier.

I lost sight of Kenny for a moment, until an accommodating group of folks wearing swimsuit trunks pointed off to their left.

"He went that way! Toward the naked slide!"

The naked *what*?

I shook it off. That was Stan's idea of a sick joke. Stan was a sick, sick man. That's all.

"Kenny! Stop!" I yelled.

"Tressa! I'm coming!" I heard Keelie yell. "I'm coming!"

Through a grove of trees, around a wooden glen, and into a small county park we ran, Kenny the Klingon and Barbie the bald yeoman.

Kenny suddenly stopped dead in his tracks.

I did the same.

And then I saw it.

"It does exist!" I whispered, amazed and...disturbed.

There it was—good old Midwest innovation at its scariest! Constructed from plastic sheeting, tarps, Styrofoam pool noodles, and PVC pipe sat two homemade water slides, side-by-side. Surrounded by trees on two sides—for modesty's sake I supposed—the slide's take-off point was at the top of a long, steep hill, its landing spot near the modest pond at the bottom. The design and construction were impressive. It was the in-your-face execution that had me wanting to gouge my eyes out.

"Eww, what is that?" Gasping for her own next breath, Keelie stood beside me, witnessing vistas so not included in any Iowa travel guide I knew of.

"A TribRide tradition," I said, bending to catch my breath.

"Where's Kenny?"

I pointed at the only other being, humanoid or otherwise, with clothes on.

"What's he doing?" Keelie asked, as we watched Kenny run to the top of the gi-normous water slide, stop, and just stand there, looking down the hill at the twin slides.

"Debating the lesser of two evils, I imagine," I said. I blinked. "What is *he* doing here?"

"Who?"

"My biking partner. Drew Van Vleet. Down there." I pointed to the bottom of the slide where Drew Van Vleet stood, next to a tree, camera in hand.

Keelie gasped. "That...that sicko! He's filming people on the slide! The perv! What a rotten thing to do!"

I winced. Talk about journalism hitting below the belt.

"Wait! Look! Your biking partner is moving out of the tree line to film Kenny!"

I shook my head. Somehow I didn't think Kenny was gonna be one for the limelight.

"What's Kenny doing now?" Keelie asked.

Our *Deep Space Nine* wannabe looked at us and down at the scary-ass (oopsie!) slides in all their gross-me-out splendor.

"I think he's almost decided what the lesser evil is!" I said. "Come on! Let's go!"

We shot off like a blast from a photon torpedo, running up the grassy hill, getting to the top of the slide in time to make a wild grab for Kenny the Klingon as he left the launch pad, headfirst torpedoing down the Naked Slide.

"What do we do now?" I asked.

"We go after him," Keelie said, stripping off her mini dress and down to her skivvies.

"Wait! What? What are you doing?" I asked.

"We'll go faster this way," she said. "Less friction."

About to politely, yet firmly, decline, I finally noticed two other people—one tall, one squatty—near the top of the slide.

I blinked. Blinked again. Rubbed my eyes. Oh, God. They were still there.

"Dixie? Frankie! What are you doing here?"

Which, of course, should have been painfully obvious considering neither one of them had a stitch on.

"Tressa? Is that you?"

They stared. I could only imagine the spectacle I made in my yeoman's uniform, complete with shiny black boots and saggy black hose, a hosiery cap bobby-pinned to my head.

I stared back, hoping I wasn't traumatized for life by the spectacle on display in front of me.

I shook my head, hoping for an Etch-a-Sketch, make-it-disappear moment.

"No time to explain!" I yelled, and reached out and grabbed hold of a wet, sleek, and slim-lined Frankie. I shoved him on the slide, head first, belly down, and flopped onto his back.

Whish! Off we went!

Go greased lightning! Or…whatever.

Water splashed up at me as I leaned into the incline. I heard a high-pitched scream unique to my cousin, Frankie, and decided—what the hell—I might as well enjoy the ride and added my scream to his.

We approached the bottom. I felt Frankie tense for the

impact. Too late, I realized stomach down probably wasn't the optimal position for a naked dude to assume when going down a water slide.

Or a naked anybody for that matter.

I rolled free of Frankie and quickly lost speed. Free of my weight, (Hey now, play nice.) Frankie gained speed, flying off the end of the slide and into the grass like a projectile from a slingshot. He careened into the feet of a fleeing Kenny the Klingon Caricaturist, dropping him to the ground. I entered the grass, hose around my ankles. I crawled over to Kenny the Klingon and collapsed on top of him. Drew Van Vleet, curled up in a fetal position, moaned nearby. Behind us, screams ripped through the air like war cries from James T. Kirk's enemy, Khan.

"Aaaah!"

I looked up in time to see Keelie and Dixie vying for position down the slide. Dixie took the heat by a...er, nose.

Once arms and limbs were untangled, Keelie made her way over to me.

"You got him," she said, breathless.

I shook my head.

"Frankie, the human pin ball, got him."

I shook the Klingon.

"Yeoman First Class Tressa Jayne Turner and Lieutenant Keelie Keller representing the Starfleet Federation," I announced. "Now, about the terms of your surrender."

CHAPTER THIRTY-THREE

The tangle of naked limbs on a grassy hill.
The type of phrase you find in romance novels to describe a poignant and beautiful encounter.
It can also be used to describe the "it's a train wreck but I can't look away" carnage that played out at the bottom of the infamous naked slide. By the time their various owners claimed arms and limbs, two things occurred to me.
One: Some people should never take a ride on the wild side naked.
And, two: This cowgirl should under no circumstances ever wear panty hose—control top or otherwise.
"What happened?"
"What the hell?"
"I think I broke something."
"Oww! You're sitting on my face!"
"Tressa Turner, I will *end* you!"
That last remark came from Dixie, the Denebian Slime Devil.
"I trust you'll don some apparel first," I said, moving aside to let Keelie sit on Kenny a spell.
"Okay maggot. Spill it! Where is she? Where's my best friend?" Keelie planted a hand on each side of Kenny's head and stared down at him.
"She's safe," Kenny said. "From you! You dare to call her your best friend after the way you've treated her."
"Where is she?" Keelie grabbed his collar, looking like she was ready to conduct some Starfleet enhanced interrogation.
"Whoa! Everybody chill out," I said.
"*Chill out?* Is that a naked joke?" Dixie snarled.

I shook my head. "I'm saving those up for later." I turned back to Kenny. "You said Tiara's someplace safe. What did you mean?"

"What do you think I mean? Someone almost abducted her the other night. I couldn't take a chance it would happen again."

I frowned. "What do you mean, someone almost abducted her. That wasn't you?"

He shook his head. "That's why I had to take her. To keep her safe. She's my soul mate."

"Soul mate!" Keelie shrieked, grabbing his shirt again. "She doesn't even know you!"

"That's why I had to do something really big to get her attention. To show her how much I cared."

"So you started stalking *me*?"

"It was never about *you*." Kenny gave Keelie a dismissive look. "It was always about Tiara. About trying to help Tiara."

"Help her how?" I asked, a bit fuzzy on how sending one person a dead rat gift-wrapped could help her best friend.

"I was trying to get *her* to quit." He nodded at the girl sitting on his chest. "Tiara deserves her own show. She's so talented and beautiful and—"

"And you wanted to give Tiara her big break," I finished. "Because you're—"

"Soul mates," he finished. "I thought if I helped her get her own show, she'd realize how much I love her, and we'd be together forever."

Houston. Kenny has a problem.

"Really? And how's that working for you, Kenny?" I asked, thinking a bit of Dr. Phil's get-real strategy couldn't hurt.

"I was just trying to make Keelie quit, is all," Kenny said, "so Tiara would get her shot."

"You send me road kill, lace my water with a laxative, knock my agent over the head, and scare us half to death at a haunted murder house. You turn out the lights when I'm riding a mechanical bull. You lock me in a Porta-Potty—"

"Hey, I was there, too—" I interjected.

"—and you kidnap the man I love and almost run me over with his car, and all because you wanted to give your *dream lover* a shot at the big time! That's sick!" She pointed a finger at his nose. "*You're* sick."

"The things we do for love," I observed.

"You had me terrified, never knowing what would happen next," Keelie continued. "I was scared to death!"

Kenny got a strange look in his eye. Well, strang*er*.

"Maybe you should be," Kenny said.

"Should be what?" Keelie asked.

"Scared to death."

Keelie and I exchanged uneasy looks.

"What do you mean? What are you saying?" I asked.

"Some of those…unfortunate occurrences she just rattled off? The laxative. The kybo. The rat." Kenny shook his head. "That wasn't me."

Keelie gasped.

I stared.

Highly…illogical.

Manny, along with police and EMTs arrived, unfortunately, eliminating any opportunity we had to question our Klingon captive further. Once we'd explained what led up to the intergalactic foot chase across Riverside and Kenny's admission regarding Tiara's kidnapping, he was read his rights and taken into police custody.

Our two innocent, and nude, bystanders were given blankets (Thank goodness!) until clothing could be retrieved. Voyeur—and Team Trekkie Captain—Drew Van Vleet suffered a badly sprained ankle when an out-of-control Klingon careened into him and was transported to the county hospital.

The rest of us had been *invited* to the sheriff's office for interviews and statements.

It was a cluster only the Syfy channel could love.

And, inevitably, led me to wonder, why, oh, why, did this keep happening to me?

* * *

The sheriff's office conference room looked like something from the movie *Space Balls*.

With an ensemble cast that included Jessica Rabbit and a CPA going through a midlife crisis, a ginger Uhura, Yeoman

Rand sporting hairy legs and a Bozo 'fro, a visibly shaken Langley "Bones" Carlisle number Three, a Hollywood agent with a bump on his head the size of a Tribble, and an engaged couple caught with their pants down while exploring their own wild sides, we made a tough act to follow.

"Don't you think it's weird how Kenny admitted to some of the incidents, but not others?" I asked Keelie while we waited for an update.

She shrugged. "He's a freak, what do you expect?"

"Still."

"He's a liar," Keelie said. "What else do you need?"

"Closure," I said.

And to have the mental images of a Free Willie Frankie and his roll-out-the-buck-naked-barrel fiancé deleted from my memory banks.

The door opened. A tear-stained, and very emotional, Tiara Fordham rushed into the room, followed by Patrick Dawkins, Manny, a uniformed deputy, and a woman dressed in nicely coordinated and smartly tailored civvies.

"Tiara!" Keelie jumped to her feet and embraced her BFF. "Thank God you're okay! I was so worried. What happened? Where were you?"

Keelie led her shaking friend to a seat.

"It was awful! Just awful! Out of nowhere this ugly little Klingon grabbed me and took off with me. At first I thought it was a gag. Or a drunk having too much of a good time. Then he takes me to this smelly old van and bounds and gags me. I was so scared. It was so creepy! There were pictures and drawings of me tacked up all over the walls of the van. I thought. Oh, my God! It's *Fatal Attraction* all over again! I was terrified! I thought I was gonna die!"

Keelie put an arm around Tiara.

"I'm so sorry I didn't believe you earlier," she said. "So, so, sorry."

Tiara dabbed at her eyes.

"So, what's the deal, Sheriff?" Vinny approached the uniformed officer. "What's up with the sicko? He cop to the kidnapping?"

The sheriff frowned and looked down at Vinny. "Your

questions will be answered all in good time, sir," He pointed to the woman in the gray slacks and white blouse. "This is State DCI Agent Sandra Marshall. She's assisting with the investigation. We've taken Mr. Grey's statement. Along with Miss Fordham's kidnapping, Grey's admitted to abducting Mr. Whitver, stealing his car, and trying to run you down, Miss Keller."

"Oh, God. And Jax? How is Jax?" Keelie asked.

"You can see for yourself, Miss Keller," Agent Marshall said. "He'll be here shortly."

"Thank God!"

I raised my hand.

"You said, Kenny admitted to several other incidents," I said. "Can you be more specific?"

"And you are?"

"She's my friend, Tressa. Tressa Turner," Keelie said.

I looked at Keelie.

"Gee, thanks!" I said.

"You're friends?" Vinny snapped. "Since when?"

"Since I've started taking back my life," Keelie snapped back.

I raised my hand again.

"Uh, Agent Marshall, in the interest of full disclosure, I should tell you I'm also a journalist," I added.

"I see," the agent said. "Well, as the sheriff here indicated, Mr. Grey has admitted to various incidents connected to what appears to have been a campaign to get Miss Keller to quit the bike ride."

"Sorry to disappoint," Keelie said.

"There are, however, some...discrepancies in Mr. Grey's story we are concerned about."

"Discrepancies? What discrepancies?" Vinny barked. "The kook confessed, you said. It's a wrap!"

"That's right!" Keelie's mother jumped to her feet. "You got your guy. Why drag the rest of us in here? Hasn't my daughter been through enough?" She shoved me aside and put an arm around Keelie.

"There are always loose ends to tie up in any investigation, ma'am," the agent said. "Corroborating evidence to gather. I'm certain you wouldn't want us to cut any corners when it comes to your daughter's safety."

"Is what Kenny told us true, then?" I asked. "Is there still reason for Keelie to be concerned?"

"What did Kenny say?" Not one. Not two. Not three. But *four* people in the room blurted.

I raised a Spock eyebrow. Interesting.

"We've interviewed Kenny extensively. He owns up to certain criminal acts and misdeeds. He's offered to take a polygraph examination, which we're arranging for at this time. However, based on our preliminary investigation, we have reason to believe we may be dealing with more than one perpetrator," the agent said.

Keelie gasped. "What? What do you mean more than one perpetrator?"

"It might be helpful if we started at the beginning," Patrick Dawkins said. "With the rat."

Duke Wayne would have put it, "Let's get to the rat killer."

"Kenny Grey denies any role in sending Keelie the rat," Agent Marshall stated. "He flat out denies it. Which, makes one wonder, considering the serious nature of the crimes he's admitting to, why he won't cop to a dead rat."

"Why? Because he's a whack job," Vinny said.

"Kenny says he got the idea to start pranking Keelie *after* she got that package," Patrick said.

After the rat package?

That meant someone else sent Keelie the rat. Someone with his or her own agenda."

The room grew quiet.

"I didn't do it!" I finally yelled, feeling a lot like Mr. Green from the movie, *Clue*. "I didn't send that parting gift!"

"Of course, you did!" Vinny charged. "You and Keelie had that dust-up at the dance. You wanted to get back at her so you stuffed a dead rat in a damned cookie box and sent it to her. I was right all along. It *was* you."

Each set of eyes in the room turned in my direction.

"Hold on. Wait a minute," I said, rewinding his outburst in my head. "How did you know the rat was in a cookie box? You weren't even there."

And…ba-zing!

There it was. That "oh, crap" moment—that oh-so-telling hesitation that comes when you realize your motor mouth just sealed your fate.

"I, uh, saw the package later," Vinny said. "Manny showed it to me."

Manny crossed his arms and shook his head. "Manny never showed you the box. Manny gave it to the cops."

Vinny swallowed several times in succession. You could tell by the yo-yoing of his Adam's apple.

"No, I'm sure you showed it to me first, DeMarco."

Manny uncrossed his arms. "You callin' Manny a liar?" he said.

Up and down. Up and down went Vinny's Adam's apple.

"Oh, my God, Vinny! What did you do?" Jessica Rabbit…er, Candice Keller yelled.

"Vinny?" Keelie asked. "Was it you?"

Vinny took one look at Manny and back at Keelie.

"Sorry, kid. After you got into it with the cowgirl here, your fans ate it up. I figured, what the hell could it hurt to stir things up a bit? Get a little road rage goin'." He shrugged. "In this business, it's all about publicity, kid."

"But I trusted you, Vinny," Keelie said. "How could you do something like this?"

"You hired me to help your career, make you a star. I was doing my job. No harm. No foul."

Keelie's face turned the color of her hair.

"No harm? No foul? I blamed *her*," she motioned to me. "Not to mention the psycho who took his cue from your little PR stunt and decided to up the ante. Why didn't you say something when things started to happen that you *didn't* do? Like getting knocked cold. And Tiara's attempted abduction. Didn't you even care that people were getting hurt?"

Vinny shrugged. "It isn't the first hard knock I've taken for a client's career," he said. "And the mileage we were getting in terms of publicity? Priceless, kid. Priceless. The ratings were soaring. I told myself, 'Vinny, you might as well see how it plays out.' Like I said, kid. It's my job."

"Not anymore," Keelie said. "You're fired."

"Keelie!" her mother started to protest.

"Be quiet, mother," Keelie said. "This doesn't concern you."

"Well!" Jessica stomped back to her seat.

"Well, that takes care of the rat," the sheriff said. "Let's move on."

"There's more?" Langley Carlisle the Third said.

"There's the little matter of the Porta-Potty incident number one," Agent Marshall said. "Uh, *number one* as in the first kybo incident," she clarified.

Ah. So state agents have a sense of humor, after all. Good to know.

"Porta-Potty incident *number one*?"

Okay, I know what you're thinking. The story has devolved into toilet humor. Be patient. It'll all come out in the end. (Yikes! Didn't mean to go there.)

"We have the first incident involving the kybo at the Winterset location where Miss Keller and Miss Turner were...entrapped," the agent said. "The second incident involves Jax Whitver. Apparently, Kenny Grey saw how well the technique worked in Winterset that he utilized a...er, similar method to hold Jax Whitver captive."

Keelie gasped.

"Oh my God! He really trapped Jax in a portable toilet!" she exclaimed. "We know just how he felt, don't we Tressa? But he was all-alone! No one to share the horror with! Oh, my poor, poor Jax! I say we throw the book at the Klingon warrior!"

"Actually, Kenny wasn't responsible for your...er, entrapment," Patrick said.

"He wasn't?" Keelie and I both said.

"Vinny!" Keelie went for her former agent. "You slime!"

The DCI agent stepped between Keelie and her target.

"Actually, it couldn't have been Mr. Vincent, Miss Keller. If you recall, he was still in the hospital at the time."

I frowned. "If not Kenny or Vinny, then who?" I asked.

"Me," Langley Carlisle Number Three said. "It was I. I did it."

I blinked. Hollywood screenwriters couldn't script a whodunit with more plot twists and turns. I was getting a wee bit carsick just trying to keep up.

"You, Langley? You locked us in that kybo? Why?" Keelie asked. "Why would you do such a thing?"

"Wagers," he said.

"Wagers?" I said. "What wagers?"

"The online wagers on who would finish the ride first, you or Keelie." he said. "You see, I'd wagered heavily against Keelie finishing—sorry, love. So I got a bit desperate when, despite all the kerfuffles, Keelie wouldn't quit."

"So, you thought trapping me in an outdoor toilet was the way to go?" Keelie said.

Way to go? No pun intended, I assumed.

"I hadn't planned to do it at all. I saw you go in, and I propped the door closed as a joke. Then I noticed the big roll of gray tape sitting on the ground, and I thought, why not? No one will suspect me. Maybe this harmless prank will be the proverbial straw that breaks the camel's back, and she'll quit. But you didn't. You surprised me, Keelie. I didn't think you'd hang in there."

"How much money did you bet, Lang?" Keelie asked.

"Too much," he admitted.

"And you bet against me."

He hung his head.

"I feel like a traitor," he said. "Apologies, Keelie."

"Not accepted," she said, and sat down.

"And next we come to Tiara's *attempted* abduction," Agent Marshall said. "Tiara, do you have something to say about that?"

What was this? True confessions of the rich and famous?

Tiara, who sat curled up in a poor-pitiful-me ball sighed—one of those jig-is-up sighs.

"Tiara? What did you do?" Keelie asked.

"I faked it," she mumbled.

"What?" Keelie gasped.

"I faked the attempted abduction. You were getting all the attention, and I was just along for the ride. It wasn't fair."

"Fair? It wasn't fair? It wasn't fair I was getting the attention, not you? That I was being cruelly targeted, not you? You can sit there and say that now after knowing how terrifying it is to be someone's target? What is wrong with you?"

She shook her head.

"I've always played second fiddle to you, Keelie. I just got tired of it."

Keelie sagged in her chair. I felt so very sorry for her. She'd just learned the people closest to her—the people she trusted the most—had conspired behind her back and lied to her in order to further their own ends.

It had to hurt like hell.

The door suddenly burst open. Jax Whitver rushed in.

"Keelie!"

"Jax!"

They ran into each other's arms and—just like you see on the big screen—it was pure magic!

"Are you okay?"

"Thank God, you're all right!"

"If anything had happened to you, Kay-Kay—"

"I know! I know! Me, too!"

They embraced, exchanging a long, passionate kiss that so wasn't "G" rated. It took throat clearing from Agent Marshall to get the two to come up for air. Even then, they held onto each other like they were fused together.

"Oh, God, Jax. I feel so betrayed," Keelie said. "I found out Vinny sent that rat for publicity reasons. Lang locked me in a loo to win a wager. Tiara faked her kidnapping to steal the limelight. And my own mother is all about the money. Oh, Jax, I don't know who to trust anymore."

Jax blinked his eyes several times, looking like he was watching the last minutes of a movie play out and trying desperately to catch up.

"Oh, Keelie. I'm so sorry," he said.

Keelie shook her head. "You have nothing to apologize for, Jax. Nothing at all."

I saw the muscle in his jaw do a popping number. Frowning, he pulled away from Keelie.

"I have my own confession to make, Kay-Kay," he said.

I stared. You have got to be kidding.

"Jax?" Keelie said. "What is it?"

He ran a hand through his hair.

"After you received the rat and all those things started happening, I started to worry. Really worry about you. I know, I know. We'd broken up, and I really didn't have the right to even worry, but I did. And the more things happened, the more I became afraid for you. For your safety."

Keelie took a step back and crossed her arms.

"And?"

"And I looked for a way to get you to withdraw from the ride," he said.

"And?" I blurted, and Jax gave me a WTH look.

"And I spiked your water bottle with laxative," he said. "I figured if anything would get you to quit, that would be it."

"You? *You* spiked my drink! You!"

He nodded. "I'm sorry for what you went through, but I'm not sorry I did it. I wanted you safe, Keelie. I love you," He stopped. Blinked. Shook his head. "I love you," he said again, as if it had just dawned on him.

I watched this scene play out—watched Keelie's mouth fly open. Saw her take a step back.

And, I prayed.

I prayed she'd figure it out. Figure out that, of all the people who betrayed her, Jax Whitver was the only person whose sole motive had been to protect her.

And he'd done it out of love.

Okay, so maybe at the time he hadn't realized it was love. Men can be a bit dense at times.

What mattered to Jax Whitver was Keelie. Her welfare. Her safety.

I only hoped she got it.

Keelie searched Jax's face, her gaze intense. Tick, tick, tick. Seconds ticked off.

"Idiot," Keelie said.

I let my breath out.

Thank the cosmos.

She got it. She totally got it.

Fade to black.

CHAPTER THIRTY-FOUR

It was somehow fitting and proper that this Trekkie's coverage of the breaking news surrounding Tiara Fordham's kidnapping by a caricaturist masquerading as a Klingon happened in the future birthplace of Captain James T. Kirk of the U.S.S. Enterprise.

The even bigger headlines on the blogosphere, however, appeared to be the news that Jax Whitver and Keelie Keller were back together. This time, to stay, according to a confidential source.

It was late—close to eleven—and my mom and I sat in lawn chairs in front of the RV, occasionally swatting at a brave mosquito that now and then ventured into the area protected by a bug zapper and repellent candles.

"Well, I guess this is it," I said. "The end of the line. Van Vleet is out, so my TribRide is finito."

Considering my antipathy towards the ride, and given I was still nursing the remnants of a hemorrhoid, you would think I would be jumping for joy that my TribRide experience was at an end.

All the planets had lined up in my favor.

Stan Rodgers was over the moon with my gripping account of an out-of-this-world obsession gone way off course. He'd particularly enjoyed the detailed description of the catch-me-if-you-can Klingon foot chase and its harrowing climax at the naked slide.

So, why wasn't I content to pop open a brewsky, stretch out, and enjoy the last day of the ride from the comfort of a hammock?

Because unfinished business topped hemorrhoidal concerns.

Because quitting trumped Miller Time.

"I'm surprised. I thought you would be thrilled to have the ride over," my mom said.

"So did I."

"So, what is it?"

"It's me. You know. That whole 'quitter' thing."

My mom sighed. "You never did outgrow that."

And likely never would.

"So, don't quit," my mother said. "You're this close to finishing. You should go for it."

I sat up in my chair.

"I should? But how? I've lost my tandem partner."

"I might know of someone who can help out."

I frowned. "Taylor? We've kind of been getting along better lately. I don't want to rock the boat." Or bike.

"I wasn't thinking about Taylor. Or Frankie. Or Dixie."

Thank the interplanetary gods.

"Then, who?"

"Me, that's who."

"You? You want to ride tandem with me?"

"If you'll have me. It's been a while since I've ridden a tandem, but I used to do quite a bit of it. I even rode some pretty long charity bike rides on a tandem when I was younger."

I stared at her. Who was this woman I called mother?

"Why didn't you say anything?"

She shrugged. "It wasn't relevant then."

"And you'll ride with me?"

"Taylor has already agreed to drive the RV tomorrow."

"What about…you know. Bike shorts?" I asked.

"Keelie has connections. She's dropping off everything I need."

Wow. Just wow. I took a long swig of my beer.

"Keelie assured me it was no trouble since she had to order some for her mother, anyway."

I spewed beer all over.

"Her mother? Why would her mother need bicycle attire?"

"Because she's riding the rest of the ride with Keelie."

I almost fell out of my chair.

"How did that happen?"

My mother sipped her tea.

"I happened to mention to Keelie and her mother that I planned to finish the ride with you. And Keelie somehow got the idea that this might be the perfect time for her and Candice to work on their issues. How did she put it? Oh yes. 'You want a relationship with your daughter, here's your chance to prove it.'"

I stared at my mom.

"Why you little Denebian devil you! You set Jessica up! You knew if you told Keelie you were finishing the race, she would take the bait and run with it."

"I don't have the faintest idea what you're talking about, Tressa."

Right.

And James T. Kirk wasn't a player.

* * *

For the first time since I'd embarked on this ride, I experienced the exhilaration of the wind in my face. (Okay, so I also experienced the occasional bug in my mouth, but let's not spoil the moment.)

At last, I had the helm. I'd received a promotion. No longer a lowly stroker, I was now Captain of Team Trekkie—and I had the gold tee with the Starfleet emblem (and yes, the bug guts on my teeth) to prove it.

My T-shirt, compliments of Keelie, proclaimed, "I don't believe in the no-win scenario."

My mother's Spock-blue shirt boasted a hand with a finger pointing. It read, "I'm with illogical."

That morning, my mother had surprised me with the shirt and the news that I would be taking the helm. A bit apprehensive at first, I soon had control of the vessel. I figured if James Kirk could figure out how to beat the Kobayashi Maru, then I could best a beast of a bike.

We wouldn't set any speed records, but I figure slow and steady wins the race.

Beside us, looking slightly less competent—and confident—Keelie and her mother pedaled.

"Where's your cameramen?" I asked Keelie.

"I gave them a day off. This is strictly mother-daughter time."

I nodded.

"What about your bodyguard?" I said, looking around for Manny.

"He's around."

I raised an eyebrow. Fascinating.

"How's Tiara?" I asked.

"She's swell. Better than swell. She's got offers pouring in from all over. Vinny's agreed to represent her."

"Oh. Wow. Good for her."

"You know what this means, though," Keelie said, with a crinkle in her brow.

"What?"

"I'll be looking for a new reality BFF."

"Hmm. How about Lindsay?" I asked.

"Old news," she said, "and I do mean old."

I laughed.

"I'm thinking you've already got a new BFF lined up, and he goes by the name, Jax," I said.

She smiled. A real smile. Not a fakey phony one.

"You're right. I've got Jax. And, as you can see, my mom and I have agreed to work on our relationship. So, it's all good."

"I'm happy for you," I said, and meant it.

"We're almost to the finish line," Keelie said.

I nodded.

"Who would have thought we'd make it all the way?" I said.

"*You* made it all the way," Keelie said. "You were right. I fudged it. I'm a fakey mcfake fake. That song Jax wrote? I'm the one who was in and out, and here and there, and who wouldn't commit. I'm the fake. I'm the fraud. Me. Not Jax. And you were right about the ride. I haven't ridden. I'd hop on the bike five miles outside town and ride in. That's me. Counterfeit Keelie."

I shrugged. It didn't seem like a big deal anymore.

"That *was* you," I said. "Past tense. And this is an annual ride, so you know, there's always next year," I said.

She grinned.

"Not on your friggin' life! Once is enough!" she said. "I hear they're still betting on who is going to win," she added.

I shrugged again.

"Let them. Not everything is a competition or about winning," I said. "I'm perfectly fine with you and your mother getting to the finish line before us."

"Oh, well. That's good. 'Cuz we're so gonna kick your arses." She put her hand to her forehead and made a lame 'L.' "Losers! Come on, mom! Work for it!"

As they rode by us, Candice's middle finger went up.

"Mother-daughter bonding. Gotta love it," I remarked to my mother. "What do you think? Should we let them win?"

"They already have, Tressa," my mother replied. "They already have."

"Oh." I thought for a second. "I get it. The mother-daughter thing. But I meant the race. Should we let them finish first?"

"Are you out of your friggin' mind? Let that biatch win? Please. Let's give her all she's got, Captain!" she said with a Scottish lilt.

"Switching to warp drive!" I said, and bore down.

Getting to the end of a ride you never thought you could finish? Good.

Getting permission to beat the pants off a pair of Tinseltown celebs on the ride? Better.

Sharing that victory with your mum?

Priceless.

CHAPTER THIRTY-FIVE

"We did it, Mom! We did it!"

I got off the bike and helped my mom do the same.

"I'll be sore for a month," she said, wincing and she stretched. "But it feels great!"

"I wonder where Taylor is," I said, grabbing my fanny pack to pull out my phone.

"Hey. Mom! Tressa! Over here!"

I heard a gasp.

"What in the world is *he* doing here?" my mother said.

I looked up, spotting Taylor. And beside her stood—"

"Dad?"

"Yes. Your father. What on earth is he doing here?"

"Clapping," I said. And he was. He stood there, Cubs cap on his head, clapping for all he was worth.

"What does he think he's doing?" my mother asked. "He must've flipped out while I was gone."

"He's applauding," I told her. "He's applauding us! He's applauding *you*!"

"Oh...my!"

I watched the emotions play on my mom's face. I saw the surprise, the sudden warm glow of happiness. The love.

"Well, go to him, you dope!" I said, giving her a push. "And that's an order, stroker!"

My mother hugged me and took off at a high lope, landing in my pop's open arms.

"Now that's what I call a perfect landing," I heard, and whirled to find Ranger Rick behind me, his arms up, his hands forming a square frame. "Picture perfect."

"What are you doing here?" I asked.

"I brought your dad."

"You brought him? What? He couldn't drive himself?"

"He didn't want to have an extra vehicle."

"I'm not following," I said.

"Your dad took the next two weeks off. He's hitting the road with your mother in the RV. Judging from the look on Jean's face, I'd say he was telling her about now."

I turned.

My mother had her arms around my dad's neck and her legs were doing this really weird Snoopy happy dance.

"What on earth persuaded my dad to surprise her like this?" I said. "It's so spontaneous. So unexpected. So romantic. So...not him!"

Rick shrugged. "I guess he decided to mix things up a bit."

I turned. "This was your idea, wasn't it?" I said. "You convinced my dad to take this leap."

Rick grinned. "I might've had a talk with him."

"Oh? And what might you have said?"

"I might have pointed out that, no matter how long you've been together, sometimes a woman just needs to be courted."

"You said that?"

"Well, since it was your dad I was talking to, I think I put it more like relationships are built on a foundation that, from time to time needs refurbishing."

"Refurbishing?"

He nodded. "That, over time, a foundation can get a little cracked around the edges, and you have to repair it, build it back up."

"Oh? And just how did you suggest he do that?" I asked, finding myself lost in the dark depths of whiskey color eyes.

"By making more memories. Happy ones," he said, and my heart melted to a gooey, runny mess.

I looked over at my folks again. Before, if someone had suggested what Townsend suggested, my pop would have hightailed it the other way.

"You look troubled, Tressa."

"It's like that episode of *Star Trek* with the parallel realities," I said. "I'm just trying to find out which one is real."

He suddenly grabbed me, lifting me clean off the ground,

and kissed me.

"What was that?" I asked when he put me down.

"A dose of reality," he said.

I leaned into him.

"I've been hobnobbing with Tinseltown inhabitants. I may need a few more doses," I said.

A now familiar luxury motor coach pulled up.

"Ah, the chariot awaits, I see," I told Townsend, pointing to Keelie's bus. "I don't think Keelie's here yet. Unless—"

I sighed. She'd taken a short cut after all.

I watched Manny get off the bus and walk over to my folks.

"I wonder what's going on," I said.

Townsend's arm at my waist tightened. "When it comes to Manny DeMarco, God only knows," he said.

Which reminded me. There was still the matter of those five little questions and five truthful answers...If I was gonna crack the mystery that was Manny with only five questions, I would have to be at the top of my game. I had my work cut out for me when I got back home.

Taylor made her way to us, a great, big smile on her face.

"What's all that about?" I asked. "You know. With Dad and Mom and...Manny?"

"Can you believe it? Keelie Keller has offered Mom and Dad the use of her luxury bus for the next two weeks free of charge! She's even throwing in a chauffeur!"

"Manny's chauffeuring our folks in Keelie's bus?"

"No! Manny's not driving. Keelie hired a driver. Seems Mom and Keelie had this all worked out last night."

"Last night?"

"Mom was going to drive home and surprise Dad."

The surface of the planet shifted under my feet again. Townsend steadied me.

"Are you sure those are our parents?" I asked Taylor.

She shook her head.

"I have begun to wonder... Oh. Here." She handed me a phone. "Patrick gave me this to give to you. He initially took it as evidence. It belongs to your teammate, Drew Van Vleet. He thought maybe you could get it back to him."

"*Former* teammate," I said. The sick puppy—filming

unsuspecting nude sliders."

I thought a second. Nude sliders?

"Holy heinies!" I said, and was about to try to access the phone when my own phone rang.

I looked at the display.

Speak of the devil.

"Van Vleet?"

"I hear you have my phone," Van Vleet said.

"As a matter of fact, I do," I said. "I was just about to view some video," I added.

"Sorry. It's security protected," he said.

Rats.

"But if you would care to peruse some of the content, I'll text you the link via my iPad. And don't lose my phone!"

A second later my phone dinged. I opened the link—and stared at a video showing a certain bald Yeoman hitching a ride with a skinny, naked guy down a water slide. Part two featured Reality Red, cast as Uhura, racing a naked Dixie Doodle to the finish line.

"Oh. My. God."

"Tressa? What is it? What's wrong?" Townsend asked.

"Those black hose make my thighs look huge!" I said.

"What?" Taylor said.

"The heat's gotten to her," Rick said. "She needs to lie down."

"That's okay, because it looks like we'll be taking the RV home," Taylor said. "Now that Mom and Dad are going to travel in style."

"What say, you drive my car back to Grandville, and we'll take the RV?" I heard Townsend suggest.

"I guess that could work," Taylor said, with a Mona Lisa smile.

I looked at Townsend.

"We—?"

He put his fingers over my lips.

"Do not attempt to challenge me, Earthling," he said. "Resistance is futile."

I sighed. Seemed my stint as Team Trekkie Captain was at an end. I'd been demoted.

Yeoman Turner to Scotty: Scotty, turns out there *is* intelligent life down here, after all.
You beam me up now—and you're space debris.
Yeoman Turner, over and out.

ABOUT THE AUTHOR

Award-winning author, Kathleen Bacus is a former state trooper and consumer fraud investigator. A Write-Touch Readers Award winner, Golden Heart® Finalist, and Kiss of Death Award of Excellence Daphne® Finalist, Kathleen is hard at work on her next book.

To find out more visit: www.kathybacus.com

Enjoyed this book? Check out these other fun reads available in print now from
Gemma Halliday Publishing:

www.GemmaHalliday.com/Halliday_Publishing

Made in the USA
Middletown, DE
07 October 2014